EXPRESSWAY

The Independ[illegible] for some of t[illegible] others it is the [illegible]

In the pearl-finis[illegible] Walt and Carol Amberton can't talk abo[illegible] the drink that is destroying their lives.

In the black Cadillac, Mr Solo is cruising, searching, waiting to see a fatal accident.

In the Buick Riviera, Dr Brett Hagen is trying to find his teenage daughter and her companion – a middle-aged man.

In the Chrysler Newport, Rod Gould and Nat Renatus start the weekend with murder and bring death along with them.

For these men and women the Expressway leads to something beyond a holiday at the seaside . . .

ELLESTON TREVOR

Expressway

Originally published under the pseudonym
Howard North

FONTANA/Collins

First published in 1973 by William Collins Sons & Co Ltd
under the pseudonym Howard North
First issued in Fontana Books 1975

Made and printed in Great Britain by
William Collins Sons & Co Ltd Glasgow

To Eva Moss

CONTENTS

Book I	Friday, July Third	9
Book II	Saturday, July Fourth	127
Book III	Sunday, July Fifth	225

PROCLAMATION

WHEREAS this season is a time for increased travelling and the visiting of pleasure resorts, historic monuments and other places of interest and beauty, and

WHEREAS it is therefore a time when our streets and highways become hazardous, and too often the joys of the holiday are marred by tragic deaths and injuries caused by improper driving, and

WHEREAS traffic safety officials and police services in the pursuance of their civic responsibilities must engage their highest endeavours to advise, warn, safeguard and in all due ways control the travelling public and thus reduce accidents,

NOW, THEREFORE, I, JOHN G. MORGAN, Governor of the State of New Jersey, do hereby PROCLAIM the period from Thursday, July the Second of this year, through Sunday, July the Fifth of this same year, a time for great vigilance on the part of all, and for the exercise of skill and tolerance upon the roads, and

FURTHER, I ask for the most rigid enforcement of driving regulations by police services, tempered with discretion and due courtesy, and

FURTHER, I ask that these edicts be seen to bear not only upon the special need for our wisdom at this time, but also upon the sanctity, at all times, of human life.

GIVEN under my hand and the Great Seal of the State of New Jersey,

BY THE GOVERNOR

GOVERNOR

Secretary of State

Book I

FRIDAY, JULY THIRD

CHAPTER ONE

Seen from the air, from the height of a bird's flight, there was nothing with identity among the wastes of dark colour below. In this hour before dawn, only the immense arc cutting between the tones of gold and indigo marked the segment of a sphere, of a world. Sometimes, as the last minutes of the night measured its passing, the waves of humidity shifted and left clear patches where points of light gleamed, and were veiled again.

In a while the great arc began glowing, some of its yellow spilling among the night hues as if by chance finding channels where its colour could run; the sky was flooding the ocean and the rivers and forming a pattern, so that the land could now be distinguished from the water, and the earth from the air.

An island lay here, at the edge of a continent, and through the haze that clung to land and water alike the first rays of the sun touched against the shapes of stalagmites that rose in thousands from the island, their silicate columns glinting here and there as the light struck reflections from them. In some places they shone with the purity of quartz crystals growing from baser rock; in others their rectangular facets were darkened, as if long ago the smoke of volcanoes had passed across this region.

With the rising light came shadow, defining the groups in which the columns stood, divided and circumscribed by deep chasms where the night lingered; at intervals a tower was upthrust as if by pressures in the earth's crust, its head taller than the rest and ablaze with the morning. In several places the island was joined to the continent by slender links, black across glittering yellow; and on the water small shapes moved, some bearing plumes of smoke.

Soon there was movement also among the deep chasms as

the light reached there. Shapes, smaller than those on the water, ran swiftly and crossed the intersections, or changed direction and ran straight again for a while, their passage as smooth as that of globules in the arteries of an organism.

A sound had begun, rising softly in the haze: a low thrumming.

Along the waterfront the haze was rose-coloured, the sun's glow striking up from the surface so that the dark boats looked as if they floated through the air. From high over a pier a crane's arm swung and a crate sank soundlessly, spinning on its thread. Higher still an aeroplane, fish-grey and slow, slanted past the tip of a spiked tower.

Here on the earth's surface the thrumming was louder, being trapped by the buildings. It was the sound of engines running, hundreds of them, thousands. Almost everywhere, though the day was only just beginning, painted metal shapes glided and beneath them wheels rolled, softly shod and so smoothly running that they seemed not to be spinning.

The automobiles and long-distance buses swung out of the tunnels and over the bridges to cross the city until they came to other tunnels and bridges, where they vanished or sped between the girders. There appeared to be more of them leaving the city than entering it.

The thrumming sound was now so constant that it seemed it must always have been here.

Across an intersection moved a huge red engine, majestically slow, its decks bearing rolls of whitened canvas and objects of bright brass. Men in helmets attended it, clinging to its rails, so that it could be seen that of all the vehicles criss-crossing the city this must surely be the monarch.

By a tunnel linking the eastern edge of the island with the greater land mass worked two young men, their hands reaching into the opened front of a car that bore no numbers; it stood abandoned-looking, and they seemed to minister to it as if it were something dying.

Through the haze a tanker came away from the island's edge and swung across the water, like a part of the city breaking off and floating toward the ocean in perfect silence.

A man in uniform and with a badge of office walked near the river, seeing the two young men and passing them without speaking. For a moment they stopped work to watch him, wondering what he would do; but he did nothing and they stooped again over the derelict car.

The whole of the sun's disc was now poised above the skyline, its light seeping through the humid air that flowed among the buildings, making them appear to waver.

Officer Nolan reached the call-box and rang the station house, as somewhere not far away a clock chimed the hour. Dawn had come to the island thirty-three minutes ago, according to official reckoning, and this was Nolan's first routine call to be made in daylight; he was on the late tour which had begun at midnight and would end at eight o'clock.

He was sorry the dark hours were over, the lamplit hours; he always felt closer to the city by night, maybe because between twelve and dawn its rhythm slowed and he could hear it beating, and because its streets were empty and he could see how straight they were. Also there was the ever-recurring miracle: he had never quite managed to see how twelve million people could jam-pack the place in daytime so you couldn't hear yourself think, while after midnight you could walk through the heart of the city and hear your own footsteps, as if the whole world had been spirited into space.

'Nolan, Roosevelt at East Thirty-seven.'

'What's new?'

'Lamp blown.' He poked at the grime on the glass with his nightstick. 'Second and East Thirty-six.' He waited while the precinct desk sergeant made a note. One of the radio motor patrols drove past towards the tunnel with its emergency lamp flashing. 'How's Mrs Dimattina?' he asked.

'She's okay.'

'She conscious yet?'

'Oh sure, soon after you left. You plan on seeing her, Nolan?'

'I hadn't thought about it.'

'She'd appreciate it.'

'You think so?'

'She said so.'

'Then I'll go along for a couple minutes when I'm off.'

'Do that.'

It had been soon after one o'clock this morning when he'd

caught movement on the skyline along East Thirty-eighth and gone up the fire-escape to the full eleven storeys and found the kid on the parapet, stiff with terror, couldn't get back up and couldn't climb down.

There was a choice of things to be done and Nolan had to make the right one and it didn't take him long because he was a veteran cop and in thirty years he'd found as many kids this age on parapets as he'd found down drainholes and it didn't mean too much, except of course in a lot of cases he had a life in his hands. This morning if he started hollering for someone to go up there on the roof from inside the building and reach down for the kid they'd sure as hell scream or pass out when they saw him, and the kid's nerves were already near the point where he could pass out himself and fall like a dead sparrow. The same thing could happen if he got someone to call the Fire Department: by the time they'd got a ladder set up there'd be a whole slew of people here to worry the kid out of his wits. So this would have to be just between the two of them.

'Fall, sonny, just fall. Look at these arms I got, they're big as a polar bear's, ain't they? So you just let yourself go and I'll do the rest, see?'

The small white face looking down, the eyes dark with terror; he was too scared to cry, the young mind having to make a real big decision so early in life: would the man catch him or would he miss him and let him go whirling all the way down to where the street lamps looked so tiny?

'Look at these arms, sonny, they could catch a dozen young fellers like you, ain't nothin' to it, I done it hundreds of times, y' know that? Now c'm'on, let yourself fall nice and easy, see, don't jump, just let yourself fall.'

That was the risk. If he jumped. It could carry him out too far.

'I'm right here, an' I'll catch you good, then we'll go see Mom and ask her where she keeps the candy, how'd you like that? C'm'on now, one – two – three –' and it happened so fast he just stood there in surprise with his arms locked round the warm quivering body that a second ago had been way out of his reach.

It would have been okay if Mom hadn't come up through the skylight right at that minute. She must have seen him go over the edge because she'd passed straight out and they found her at the bottom of the sliding ladder inside the building with a bad gash across the temple.

'She was out almost an hour, the Doc said.'

'That so?' The end of his nightstick was tracing a shape on the grime.

'Then she came to and they told her the kid had fallen right in the arms of some bum in uniform who was hanging around the fire-escape and she didn't believe it – who would? Then they brought the kid to show her and she passed out cold again.'

'Kinda tendency.'

It was a right-angle his nightstick had drawn without his thinking, a parapet, with a little blob at the edge. It was going to happen all summer, people leaving their skylights open and letting their kids sleep on the roof.

'Okay, so you got a lamp blown, Second and East Thirty-six, anything else?'

'They've started in picking over the wreck by the tunnel, I leave 'em to it?'

'Give them a hand, it's the only way we'll ever lose it.'

Nolan hung up and got moving again. Exceptionally for this tour he was working a six-block post, but it was a quiet one, the haze across the river seeming to muffle the early sounds of the morning.

The two youngsters already had the hood off the Chevvy near the tunnel and judging by the chain gear they'd brought along they aimed to pull the motor out whole. They stopped work to look at him as he passed and this time he looked right back at them and then away so they wouldn't be left in any doubt. The sergeant was right: it was all you could do. The car had been dragged there without any licence-plates, which meant that nobody would ever claim it; there were thousands of them all over the city, accumulating like barnacles; they were abandoned mostly because autos were cheap to buy these days, with easy payments and all, so when you bust a back axle you simply junked the whole shebang because you'd got tired of that year's styling anyway.

The expense came into it when the city had to haul them off the streets and do something with them, so when funds were low you might as well let people pick them to bits for spares: it was the same as beetles working on a dead coney, the natural way of getting rid of things.

At six o'clock Patrolman Nolan reported again by phone and the desk sergeant told him that Bill Aikins had just got a finger shot off in a cab stick-up but he'd booked the guy good and anyway it was his left hand, that was on Lexington. And Pop Kelly had climbed five floors of a coldwater walk-up to find it wasn't a murder going on like the 911 call said, but just a couple of East Pakistanis trying out some kind of ritual sacrifice on a live goat that had got no appetite for it, so it had busted one of them in his ass and cornered the other one in the john when Pop arrived. They said Pop was okay now, just a few bruises.

'You made up your quota, Nolan?'

'Screw the quota.'

He heard the sergeant give a laugh. The Captain was new to the precinct, a crummy Keystone keen on building up the over-all quota of summonses so he could look good at Division, and he didn't care if you booked every fag and bum and chippie on the post so long as you made up the number. The boys didn't like him, and in this precinct if the boys didn't like the Skipper then he wouldn't be seen around too long: they were mostly seasoned cops in this section, street-wise old-timers who knew their job wasn't to make trouble for people but to help them avoid it. That was a tough enough assignment.

'What's the traffic like along your way, Nolan?'

'Starting to build up, what would you expect?'

'That's what I'd expect.'

He hung up and toured his six blocks while the sun grew warm on him. There were two hours to go but he felt, as he always felt about this time at the end of the late tour, that his real period of duty was over. He was still active all right – last week at this hour he'd pulled a head case out of the East River and got him into a radio car for the psychiatric observation ward in Bellevue – but he'd kind of lost the feel of things, in a way he couldn't explain. Part of him had stayed behind with the night, with the city he'd known in the dark hours that was so different from this one with its bright sky and traffic building up and people on the sidewalk, the day crowding in and getting noisier, getting a nuisance.

He liked the night watch. At night the city was his. He'd been born here fifty-one years ago in a downtown skid-row tenement and he was going to die here if he could arrange not to be someplace else when it happened. The city was in his heart and under his nails and in his hair and he identified with its soot and its stones and the river smell and the roar of it, and the quiet, in a way that expressed itself to him most clearly by night, when he was most nearly alone with it.

The quiet was going now, and the roar beginning. The traffic was coming out of the Queens-Midtown in quite a stream and heading west across Manhattan to the Lincoln Tunnel. Other streams would soon be forming along all the major routes into and out of the city: the Grand Central Parkway and Brooklyn-Queens, the Staten Island Expressway and Henry Hudson, the Shore Parkway and State Thruway, the population shifting and flowing into new patterns that were different from on ordinary days.

Nolan was a little disturbed by this. He liked routine and it was being broken everywhere around him. Today was Friday July Third, yet it wasn't – for practical purposes – a week-day; nor was it a Sunday, yet for practical purposes it seemed like it, with Sunday parking regulations in force and most of the stores and offices closed. Tomorrow the city and the nation were going to celebrate the fact that almost two hundred years ago the representatives of the United States of America had, in general congress, solemnly published and declared that these united colonies were, and of right ought to be, free and independent states, the signatories to which declaration had pledged their lives, their fortunes and their sacred honour.

That was okay. Nolan had no complaints about that. But two hundred years was a long time and people had kind of got over the excitement of being independent, and what they were going to do today and tomorrow and the next day was to get the hell out of town to the seashore, or come storming into the city to watch the parades and the fireworks. And whichever they did, they were going to do it in their hundred thousands, in their millions, and it was up to people like Nolan to try taking care of them all and seeing nobody got hurt too bad.

That was the way he saw it and if he'd seen it any other way he wouldn't have been a cop. Standing not far from the mouth of the Queens-Midtown Tunnel he watched the wheels rolling and listened to the voice of a people in migration.

At 0700 hours a Police Department Aviation Unit helicopter lifted from the US Naval Air Station at Floyd Bennett Field and began its tour of Post No. 1, drifting along the Brooklyn shoreline towards the Narrows. The pilot and observer patrolmen were already in radio contact with Communication Division and transmitting direct to the motoring public over Station WNYC with minute-by-minute and mile-by-mile reports of traffic conditions, observing and analysing the movement and flow patterns at critical zones along the expressways and toll roads and at bridges, tunnels and interchanges.

So far there's no problem along the actual highways and traffic is light to moderate on the Shore and Fort Hamilton Parkways with easy going across the Verrazano Bridge, but it's beginning to build up a little at the west end of the Brooklyn Battery Tunnel. There appears to be a car blocking the downtown lanes at South and Jefferson and we'll be keeping an eye on that situation and reporting any developments. Meantime things are moving well on the Brooklyn-Queens, Williamsburg Bridge and Prospect Expressway.

The Aviation Unit's 'eye-in-the-sky' facility is a permanent factor in New York City's traffic control system and routinely conducts four or five hundred aerial surveys each year, assisting foot and motorized patrols at street level to minimize congestion and delays at workaday peak travel periods; but this morning as N4042-G was lifted through the haze at 0700 by Patrolman Budge Ryan it was in response to a special directive from Police Commissioner Wallace.

One hour before take-off a teletype signal to all commands had activated Operation Safety Chain, an intensive city-wide campaign designed to reduce road accident deaths and injuries to a satisfactory minimum. In an immediate-category press release of late yesterday from the Public Information Division, the Commissioner was quoted as saying that as far as he was concerned the 'satisfactory minimum' was zero.

Safety Chain comprised special patrol and enforcement measures and provided for the assignment of an increased number of police officers to safety duty throughout the city.

Its effectiveness in the past had this year prompted a decision to launch the operation earlier by ten hours; thus it was now running, and simultaneously with the take-off of the Bell Jetranger from Floyd Bennett Field the major radio stations were prefacing their on-the-hour newscasts with special announcements.

Police Commissioner Wallace today urges all motorists and pedestrians to be cautious and alert. In a personal message to the public the Commissioner says: 'My department has mounted a special operation aimed at preventing accidents on the road and their grievous consequences, but our plans can prove of value to you only if you, in your turn, are ready to give us your co-operation. With reluctance I would like to remind you that on the Fourth of July holiday last year the national figures for death on the road reached a new peak at nine hundred and seventeen, while more than thirty-six thousand persons were injured. So let's be determined that for each one of us this year's holiday will be the best, but not the last.'

Implementation of the Commissioner's plans was already under way as specially-briefed platoons left their precincts and radio motor patrols filtered through the early traffic. Coordination throughout the entire complex of Safety Chain was provided by a link system involving the RMP posts and the airborne information relayed by helicopter to Safety-Emergency Division Headquarters and direct to the patrol cars themselves.

To Command and Control Centre: congestion increasing in zone South Street and Jefferson Street caused by an auto breakdown blocking the downtown lanes. Request wrecker. Request wrecker.

On the third floor of Manhattan HQ the availability scene was under continuous checking out by computer and a dispatcher began rerouting the appropriate radio car and alerting the wrecker under contract in the area. Nobody questioned the time lag before the wheels of the truck started rolling, because it was known that no system in the world could operate faster; but the ACDM facility concurrently logging workload statistics for all consoles and Centrex posts would be able to show that ninety per cent of the delay was due to the driver's having to climb into his truck and start up the motor.

It's still light to moderate along FDR Drive but there's quite a backup taking shape on Vernon Boulevard just north of the Jackson intersection because of a trailer truck jack-knifing on one of the outbound lanes. We're moving well across Queensborough and through Queens-Midtown and if you're heading west across Manhattan from this area you'll find Thirty-fourth Street a nice easy trip. Now we'll get back to you in just a few seconds.

Observer Patrolman Bob McAvery flipped the switch to cut out transmission to the public through WNYC and went right on talking as he looked down from two hundred feet at the East River's hazy surface.

There's a junk boat moving downstream at East 38 and it looks like it's going to be pretty close to the northbound freighter around a few minutes from now and I don't see why it shouldn't stay closer to the shore, could be they're trying for a dope switch, you with me, Narcotics?

He shifted the contact.

Well, it's easy all the way down the Franklyn D. as far as South Street and so far the interchanges are keeping up a steady flow on both inbound and outbound with the into-town traffic coming quite a bit faster through Flatbush and over Manhattan. Is anyone interested in the weather? Okay, it's over to you, Phil Thornton.

The wrench had slipped on one of the main holding-down bolts and he'd skinned a knuckle, working now with a rag wrapped round it to stop the blood.

'We could get Abe up here.'

'Hell with Abe, he'd want part-ownership of the darn thing.'

'I don't see how we're going to haul it out, just the two of us.'

The cop went past again but this time they didn't wonder what he'd do. He'd made it plain enough he didn't intend getting on their backs.

'What did we bring the chain gear for?'

'To haul it out, I guess.'

'Right. So will you just quit beefing and let me get this whole thing set up?'

'Okay, okay.' He shaded his eyes and watched the long

dark shape of the freighter sliding upriver, its wake leaving molten gold across the surface. 'Y' know something? If we don't get that motor out inside the next half-hour we're going to be standing knee-deep in our own sweat, y' know that?'

'Christ, will you work up a bit of positive thinking about this thing? We want this motor or don't we?'

'Okay, okay. I just said it's goin' to be a hot day, that's all.'

The thin chopping sound of the helicopter came into the air again but he didn't look up because the glare was too bright now. A shadow sped suddenly across the ground and was gone.

Sunny weather is predicted for most of this holiday weekend, though thundershowers are expected to be widespread in the Northeast and Southeast. Both coasts will remain warm and humid, and temperatures are due to rise progressively from today through noon tomorrow. Last evening a line of heavy storms moved across the Northeast. New York City: warm and humid, with precipitation probability sixty per cent. New Jersey and Connecticut: mostly fair with scattered thundershowers late tonight; day highs nearing ninety; humidity in the lower sixties. Temperature-Humidity Index for both areas seventy-three at noon today. Pollution levels expected to rise markedly due to heavy traffic conditions.

Before 0800 hours specially-assigned teams of police motorcycle patrols deployed at strategic checkpoints throughout the city began making safety inspections of vehicles and drivers, looking for worn tyres, pronounced steering backlash and other observable equipment defects, questioning drivers particularly where a car bore signs of recent damage that might have been caused in a hit-and-run collision.

In accordance with the orders set out in Operation Safety Chain, emphasis was laid on moving violations conducive to accidents and on any suspicion of drunken driving. These checks were being made at key points in all five boroughs, at places where the minimum of delay and the maximum of coverage had been estimated by Traffic Division planners.

In an addendum to these special orders Commissioner Wallace had reminded all patrols that today and over this holiday weekend the public would be in a mood to make the most of the extra-long break from work and was expected to show impatience at the delays caused by safety inspections and general enforcement measures. All officers in personal contact with the travelling public would therefore perform their tasks with customary courtesy and dispatch, endeavouring to foster the holiday spirit by good example.

Mayor McGrath, anticipating a Fourth of July celebration tomorrow on the Mall of Central Park, today pleaded for a sense of national pride befitting Independence Day.

'Not pride,' he said, 'in what we are as a nation, but in what we do as a people. It's easy enough to dedicate ourselves to the honouring of our flag and of our country, but more difficult to pledge ourselves to add, in however small a way, to the contribution this country has already made to the progress of humankind.'

According to a report culled from certain underground newspapers circulating among alienated youth in New York City, the Central Park celebration may be marred by a planned marijuana smoke-in. In the words of one radical youth: 'They can send in hard hats by the busload but finally we're going to freak the rednecks out.'

The sun was getting warm on Officer Nolan's back. There was less than an hour to go but it was the last and therefore the longest.

He'd go see Mrs Dimattina after he'd been home to put on some cool clothes, instead of going straight from the station house. There wasn't any hurry.

'Hey, mister! See that sign?'

'Just for five minutes, d'you mind?'

'Yes I do.'

'I really mean five minutes –'

'Like I really mean I mind.'

'Look, I have to get some keys from my office right in this block and I can't find anywhere I can park around here –'

'Over by the pier.'

'But I'm already late for –'

'I'm askin' you nice, mister, so far.'

'Frankly it's my opinion that the police of this city don't have enough to do, and I'm one of the people who are beginning to wonder what we pay you for.'

'Is that so? Maybe I c'n help you there. One of the things you pay me for is to make sure that when you're riding fast along this street you don't suddenly hit an auto that some stupid jerk's left just where you weren't expecting it. An' if I never did anything else for you that's quite good value because people often get killed that way.'

'Did you say "stupid jerk"?'

'I'm talkin' about his auto, not yours. You wouldn't ever do anythin' stupid, now would you?'

'I'm not sure I shan't take this up with –'

'Okay, how d'you want me to make it out? Just illegal parking or obstructing a police officer in the course –'

'We don't have to lose our sense of –'

'Right. We just lose the auto. As of now. An' don't forget to have a nice day, mister.'

Standing in the stink of the gas he thought that if the rest of the boys in the precinct were taking things this easy today the Captain wouldn't have much of a quota to add up and that was going to make him real mad and that was going to be too bad.

The Ford Pinto was still parked down by the pier when he passed that way again but there wasn't anything he needed to do about it because it stood on a Sunday-parking zone and the two men in it looked okay, hassling over some papers one of them had taken out of his briefcase.

A lot of the haze had gone from the East River now and the boats didn't seem to be floating in the air any more. They left bright arrowheads of ripples that criss-crossed and spread out into what you might call a tapestry from one side right to the other.

'Hi, Officer Nolan!'

'Hello there, Jimmy.'

A bird-bright eye and a bitten apple, a scamper of sneakers along the waterfront.

'Goin' down to the bridge!'

'Take care then, Jimmy. Take care.'

Up to this time it's been nice going most of the way but I don't know how long we can keep on giving out good news because the sun's been waking a lot of people up and there's quite a backup forming on the outbound lanes of both the

Holland and Lincoln Tunnel approaches, so if you're heading for New Jersey from anywhere north of Eighty-sixth Street it could be your best bet is the George Washington and right on to the Turnpike because the Bridge is pretty clear at the moment. And incidentally if you're heading north on the other side I'll remind you there's a detour at Englewood Cliffs because of highway reconstruction, so watch out for the turn-off signs.

Birds flew low across the water, its dappled surface sending light against their wings.

'Did you break it?'

'I guess I did.'

'Well, Christ, we'll have to drill it out. Can't you –'

'Okay, I'll drill it out.'

'It's easy to say. If –'

'Look, I broke it, so I drill it out, that fair?'

He pulled the rag off his hand to wipe at the sweat but the blood had stuck to it and he sucked in his breath.

'Gimme the other wrench, huh?'

'It's right there by your shoe.'

He wondered who'd been the owner of the Chevvy; she wasn't very old, couple of years, maybe three years; it looked like they'd backed across a boulder or a tree stump because the banjo casing was wrecked to hell and the crown wheel smashed.

It was a darn shame the way people just chucked cars all over town, like they were garbage. People didn't seem to appreciate what they had.

'Take this end, huh?'

'Okay.'

They'd spread a square of canvas on the ground and they put the exhaust manifold on to it with the air filter and the other stuff and it was then that they heard the three sharp reports.

'What was that?'

'Uh? Fireworks, I guess. Fourth of July, isn't it?'

'Third.'

'I mean tomorrow is. I mean the kids'll have started.'

'Yeah. Look, we try lifting the whole of the motor with the rad still in place?'

'Sure. If we're tight for space we can –'

A shrilling came into the air and he stopped and looked up and saw the squat shape of a Pinto heeling in a fast U-turn down by the pier and there was something lying on the ground, a coat or something.

A boat was cutting a bow-wave towards the pier and its siren started wailing.

'Joe.'

'Yeah?'

'It wasn't fireworks.'

'No. We better get down there.'

They started running.

Let's give you a brief round-up before handing you back to the studio for the Five minutes to the Hour News. We see the Whitestone Expressway entrance ramp to Throgs Neck Bridge with a progressive backup, Clearview Expressway light to moderate, Grand Central Parkway moderate and moving well, Queens Boulevard in good shape and Northern okay, with the Long Island Expressway beginning to build. But the same good counsel applies wherever you are – if you're driving a vehicle you have lives in your hands: your own, your passengers' and the lives of other road users. Drive wisely, and give them your safekeeping.

The situation at 0800 hours in Communications Division was much the same as on most Fridays except that signals volume was rising above the standard hourly norms, and the team of forty-eight patrolmen operators at the two consoles were having to hurry it up a little today so as to cope with the city-wide 911 and incident code calls coming in.

'But oh God I'm scared he'll do something he –'

'Just a minute, please – is this a family fight?'

'It's my Mom and Dad, but you don't understand – he has the meat-knife and I'm scared he'll –'

'He's threatening you both with it?'

'Just Mom, but she keeps yelling at him and –'

'We'll send someone right away. Try to calm them both down but don't put yourself between them, you understand that? There'll be someone along there in just a few minutes so don't worry.'

A 10-50 call from the Lower East Side.

'There's quite a few ganging up and starting to act kinda wild.'

'How many?'

'Fifteen, twenty. I've tried to break it up but some of 'em look high on pep-ups, y'know.'

'Okay, dispatching an RPM instanter.'

'A what, lady?'

'A cat. In the elevator shaft. It's Mrs Pitowski's cat and it likes getting in there, it got in there last month and we had to call the Fire Department and they sent us a fire truck and –'

'Was it you who called the Fire Department last month?'

'Why, yes.'

'And they got the cat out?'

'Well, not exactly, you see he just walked out before they could do anything, it was really very funny, but –'

'Is Mrs Pitowski home, lady?'

'Oh yes, she's –'

'Is she worried about her cat?'

'Well I don't think she realizes we all have a solemn duty to our dumb animal friends, because –'

'If Mrs Pitowski gets worried, tell her to call us.'

'Oh. Yes, they said that at the Fire Department.'

'Last month?'

'No, just a few minutes ago.'

'Uh-huh. Well, you can relax now. Both departments will be standing by.'

'You mean that? But how exciting!'

'It's just routine to us, lady. Goodbye now.'

From a church, eight chimes floated.

In the street below, wheels rolled. In every street, all over the city, wheels rolled as the cars and buses swung from the tunnel mouths and threaded their way over the bridges and crossed the intersections, their seemingly aimless paths converging and parting again, their constant thrumming an orchestration of the life that had come to the city with the coming of the sun.

The late tour was ended, the midnight to eight, and day was here with its small businesses: a lady in need of a little excitement; a disorderly group on the Lower East Side; somewhere a family fight; and down by the pier a dead cop.

CHAPTER TWO

By 0900 hours the first wave of the outbound weekend and vacation traffic had reached rush-hour volumes and the Port of New York Authority's three highway links with the New Jersey shoreline were handling a computed total of twenty-one thousand vehicles per hour through the Lincoln and Holland Tunnels and across the George Washington Bridge.

Many people had broken away an hour or two earlier last evening to get a headstart on today's out-of-town stampede and make sure of finding a motel room some time before midnight, but this Friday morning saw the big-scale frontal assault on the highway facilities that would log an estimated two hundred million passenger miles during the next twelve hours, and Operation Safety Chain was fully engaged.

The situation was put briefly enough by Deputy Commissioner William K. Joseph of Traffic Division as he watched the monitoring screens relaying printouts of traffic conditions in all areas:

'We've done all we can. Everybody should get home safe. The thing is, they won't. They never do.'

So the general picture on all outbound routes is heavy traffic with increasing congestion at tunnel and bridge approaches but moderate flow conditions once the major toll roads and expressways have been reached. Now here's a reminder from the Police Department which we'll pass on to you right away. 'There are three simple but highly effective life-saving techniques that you won't find in the first aid manuals but which are available to every driver on the road today. They are patience, courtesy and common sense.' And I hope that makes as much common sense to you folks as it does to us here in the studio.

The riverside area at East Thirty-seventh Street was still cordoned off and white-topped prowler cars were nosing around the block, though it was almost certain that the two men they were looking for had cleared the immediate vicinity an hour ago when the first alarm call had triggered priority responses throughout Communications Division.

This call had gone in by radio from a Narcotics launch on the scene, and the IBM 360/40 computer hooked into the Sprint system had made a three-second analysis and thrown an equipment-availability display on to the radio dispatcher's television screen at Manhattan Headquarters, and within the next half-minute the first radio motor patrol had reached the alarm area. A cluster of priority signals had hit the network at the same time, headed by a 10–70 Phase One mobilization order sending in a lieutenant, three sergeants and fifty-six patrolmen in twelve radio cars to blanket the zone as a preliminary.

Since that time, officers of the Homicide Squad, Detective Division, Ballistics Section and Emergency Services had responded to the scene. An ambulance had arrived soon after the first radio car but there had been nothing for it to do; the crew had waited till the last of the photographs were taken, and then had driven at normal speed to the morgue.

The two youngsters who had been removing the motor from the Chevrolet had been questioned by detectives but except for the licence number of the New Jersey registered Ford Pinto there wasn't much for them to tell: of the two men in the car, one was heavier-looking than the other, but as a detective said, that was true of almost every couple of men in New York City.

'We didn't really get to see them, not that close. We heard what we thought was fireworks, then a bit later –'

'How much later?'

'Maybe five or ten seconds –'

'There's a hundred per cent difference in five and ten, can you make it more precise than that?'

'Well, gee. I'd be guessing, I mean we weren't paying too much attention because we didn't know what was –'

'That's a damn shame, sure.'

'Okay, Sam, I'll handle this.'

The first one turned away, his face bitter, not saying anything more. They all looked kind of mean, the youngsters thought; they were quiet but you could feel their anger.

'What was the Pinto doing when you first noticed it?'

'She was in a quick U-turn away from the pier, nearly hit the fire hydrant down there.'

'There wasn't anything else you noticed about it, apart from what you've already told us?'

'I guess not. It happened so quick –'

'Okay, I want your names and addresses.'

'Well, gee, we didn't have anything to –'

'You've been a big help and we could need you again. What's your name, kid?'

The number on the licence-plate had been radioed direct from one of the RMP's to the Vehicle Identification File at Communications Centre. The computer-oriented VIF system took the standard two seconds to register a hit but in this case the information wasn't much use: the Pinto had been reported stolen from outside a bar in Hillside, near Newark, some time during the night. The New Jersey State Police had been alerted by NYC Detective Division as soon as this was known, but they'd confirmed a genuine theft and the owner's unbreakable alibi for the hours of seven to nine this morning.

The field investigators weren't surprised: in their mood they weren't getting their hopes up for some good luck. When two men set out to do something that can end with a slain patrolman they don't often use their own car.

The station house had a deserted air. The reserve patrols who hadn't already been assigned to Operation Safety Chain duties were down by the East River.

'I just called the chaplain. He's on his way to see her right now.'

'Who?'

'Mrs Nolan.'

'Oh. Yeah.'

'That guy has a lousy job, you know that? He doesn't just preach all the time. I only just realized.'

The air was like molasses; you could smell the resin in the floorboards. The air-conditioner had broken down. Today, everything was going to happen.

'How'd it start, Sarge?'

'Christ, where were you?'

'The dentist.'

The desk sergeant sat with his arms folded across the Summons Record Book, looking through the glass doors to the street and not seeing it.

'Air Division tipped off Narcotics about a dope switch on the East River. It looks like it was a feint – they were prising every plank off a clinker-built junk when another boat went heading past the pier. They took their launch in fast but it was too late.'

'There was another car, as well as the Pinto?'

'Right. It got away sooner, nobody saw it. They found the boat empty.'

'What exactly did Nolan do?'

'Tried to stop the Pinto.'

For a minute they didn't talk. The sergeant looked through the glass doors. He and John Nolan had come out of the Police Academy the same week and they'd shared this particular precinct for almost eleven years.

The rookie looked at his shoes. He was very young and this thing had shaken him up a little, and he wanted to express something of what he felt; but it wasn't easy, partly because he thought the sergeant expected him to say something, and he ought to be careful and find the right words. In the end he said something melodramatic, using a cliché because the real words wouldn't come to his mind.

'He was a cop.'

The sergeant looked up.

'So what?'

Turning awkwardly the rookie said: 'I mean – he was one of us.'

'Big deal.' The older man's tone was tight, sounding as if he wanted to yell at the patrolman but he knew that he mustn't, that he must say it quietly. 'He was a husband and a father and a citizen and a taxpayer and a damn fine human being. It isn't enough to be a cop.'

The backup on West Thirty-first was reaching as far as one of the Safety Chain checkpoints and it made things easy for the patrols.

'You have a strap loose on your roof grid.'

The surfboards had shifted, one of them sticking out beyond the overhead profile of the Dart.

'Okay, I've fixed it, but check on these buckles now and then. I'd like to see your licence.'

Motors were idling everywhere and the air was acrid, without a breath of wind to freshen it.

'Okay. You heading for the shore?'

'Long Branch.'

'They say there's some nice waves running, have a good time down there.'

Farther along the street some people had climbed out of their cars to see what was happening near the Buick with the gold-coloured bumpers.

'Two highballs, when was that?'

'Aroun' an hour back. You think a couple o' bloody highballs're goin'a get me stoned?'

'Okay, just blow a good breath into this, please.'

'The hell I will! You smartass bastards think you c'n run this goddam city like you were –'

'Will you get out of your car, please?'

'You betcha life! You'n me look about the same weight, know what I mean?'

Outside the car he got his balance and made an attempt at a fist blow and the patrolman countered it and put a lock on the man's arm.

'Hey Joe! Call 'em up, we got a towaway. Where'd the wagon go?'

'Right across the street. You want any help?'

'No.' He said quietly to the driver: 'We're going across to the other side. Shall we walk there like two grown men or do you want to show all these people –'

The man swung a blow and it grazed the patrolman's face but he recovered his stance and got both arms in a lock and began frogmarching him between the stationary cars. Someone from the wagon had seen what was happening and came and took over.

As the motorcycle cop walked back to his post a voice came from close by.

'I'd call that a pretty good example of police brutality.'

The patrolman turned and looked down at the driver of the station wagon.

'How's that again?'

'I think you were handling that driver too severely.'

'I'm sorry you think so.' He dabbed at his face with his handkerchief. 'It's always a little difficult, handling drunks.' He could see two women in the station wagon, both looking away, upset by the scene or by the man's protest, he couldn't tell which.

'He didn't look drunk to me.'

'He may not be, sir, but I think he is, and if I'm wrong he can sue the Police Department and I'll be heading for big trouble, believe me. But if I'm right, your journey is going to be safer today.' He stood away and touched his helmet. 'Please don't thank me – it's just part of the service.'

Nearer the entrance to the Lincoln Tunnel the line was still stationary and some drivers had switched off their motors, getting out to walk around and show their frustration or trying to shrug it off by reading the news. Sandwiched between a revamped hearse and a muscle-car was a new Chevrolet Mirabelle convertible with the top down. In the back was a girl in a green jumpsuit. She had put the centre armrest up so that she could lie with her legs along the whole width of the seat and her arms open wide, one on the rear squab and the other resting along the top edge of the door.

Her head was tilted back and with closed eyes she faced the sky, her mouth gentle with the half-smile that can only be shown by those whose joy is so private that they have forgotten that other people exist. Contradictorily, her wide open arms seemed as if they were trying to encompass something, perhaps the whole world.

The longest tie-up we have right now is coming down to the Brooklyn-Queens Expressway and you're going to find bumper to bumper delays in the area of the Queens Boulevard intersection all the way down the BQE into Brooklyn and toward the Navy Yard. So if you're on this route it's going to be absolutely miserable for the next half-hour and there's nothing to be done about it that the police aren't already doing just as hard as they can.

Stacked above the city, air pilots looked down on the widening trails of smog that had begun drawing out from the urban areas as the traffic gathered slowly toward the highways. The sun's heat, producing reactions between unburned hydrocarbons and oxides of nitrogen, was mixing a brew of peroxyacetyl nitrate and ozone, the basic ingredients of photochemical haze. It would develop, as the pilots knew from experience, until noon twilight covered the city.

At street level the haze was less discernible because most of the sun's light was still getting through, but its heat was becoming oppressive, so that whenever drivers found a clear patch in the traffic they put their foot down just to make a draught through the windows, slamming their brakes on when they caught up with the crush at the next set of lights. Often this led to glancing collisions as they changed lanes too suddenly, trying to find a slot.

'But let us pray that with these great and abiding truths in our minds and in our hearts we shall yet prevail, despite the awesome problems that we face today. For some, it might seem that things have gone beyond the point where any return to reason and sanity can be vouchsafed us, so beleaguered do we seem by modern life. Do you remember how Nahum the Prophet imagined Judgement Day, thousands of years ago? He said that "the chariots shall rage in the streets, and shall jostle one another in the broad ways, seeming like torches, and running like the lightnings." But it would be more dangerous even than in the streets out there, that we, here in the House of God, should lend our spirits to easy despair because of the confusion we see daily around us.'

Somebody shot a red and a whistle blew and the green ticket was made out.

On West Thirty-first the jam was solid. They said there was a breakdown in the Tunnel.

'Can I see your licence, please?'

'What for?'

'We're just checking.'

The man was alone in the Buick Riviera, the sleeves of his tan seersucker coat showing an inch of white poplin and heavy black links that matched his tie clip, his hands tapping at the wheel as the patrolman took his time.

Orders had come through soon after 0900: *Check all male occupants of cars especially travelling in pairs or alone, especially heading for New Jersey. Refer to description of wanted persons.*

'Going on vacation, Dr Hagen?'

'Yes I am, Officer.'

The patrolman nodded, his eyes cutting from the photograph to the face and back while the man reached for his cigarettes and took one and touched it to his lips and pressed it into the ashtray, breaking it, dropping the pack on to the seat beside him.

'Trying to give it up, Doctor?'

'Who isn't?'

'That's right. Where are you headed?'

'Wildwood.'

'Meeting your family down there?'

The blue compact in front had started moving off and Dr Hagen opened his hand to take the licence but the patrolman didn't respond. The cars in the lane alongside started going forward and the driver behind the Buick Riviera tapped his horn; the patrolman swung his head slowly in that direction and back again.

'I asked if you're meeting your family down at Wildwood.'

'Not exactly.'

There was sweat on his upper lip and his eyes were restless. The officer might have described this face as strong, well-moulded, the face of a responsible person; but the expression was so uptight that appearances could be unreliable. He didn't look like a man going on vacation.

'Dr Hagen, if you'll answer my questions right off the bat we can get this over with. Otherwise you'll waste your own time and I can see you're in a hurry.'

Across the street was an unmarked car from Detective Division standing by, its plain-clothes crew ready to take interrogation further if a patrolman didn't feel satisfied.

'My daughter is missing.' The decision to answer was made with a lack of hesitation that was maybe typical. 'More precisely, I believe she's spending the weekend with a man I don't approve of. My daughter *is* seventeen.'

'It happens, Doc.'

With a flash of anger Hagen said: 'So I just sit back and do nothing?'

'Nope.' He handed the licence through the window. 'You go right on down to Wildwood.'

The Riviera dipped its tailgate and made the lights before they changed, catching up with the platoon that was halted at the mouth of the outbound tube of the Lincoln Tunnel.

Am I speaking to Dr Brett K. Hagen? I think you should know that Tracy is going to the New Jersey shore this weekend with Earl Fallon. Have you heard of him?

He couldn't tell if it were a boy or girl on the phone because the voice had sounded muffled, but it was someone young, maybe someone he knew, one of Tracy's friends. But he didn't know many of them, and had never heard her mention Earl Fallon by name.

He's almost fifty years of age, but he likes them young.

The voice sickened him suddenly and he went to hang up but decided not to because this could be serious, not just a boy who'd lost out to Fallon for Tracy's company this weekend, not just a girl working off some kind of jealousy. Or it could be either of those things and still serious – for Tracy. There was no point asking who was calling: the voice was obviously disguised.

Where had they gone?

Try the Surf Club at Wildwood. He's a member there.

They just hung up and there wasn't a thing he could do: if he wanted any more information he'd have to get it for himself.

The warbler of an emergency vehicle raised its strangely primitive cry among the buildings on Ninth Avenue and the traffic near the Port Authority Bus Terminal began speeding up as police overmastered the lights at the intersection and made a clearway with their whistles shrilling. Heavy black smoke hung on the humid air.

On Thirty-first the Chevrolet convertible had moved a couple of blocks but the girl in the green jumpsuit hadn't shifted her position; her legs were along the seat and her arms were wide open as if to embrace the whole world, or maybe, less ambitiously, just New York City; the only difference was that she had opened her eyes a little and was gazing upwards, the half-smile still on her lips and understandably, since today she was in love with so many people and so many things, with the two people sitting in the car with her and with the car itself and its newness and its showroom smell and bewilderingly lovely name, Mirabelle, a name that leapt and ran in rivulets, Chevrolet Mirabelle, creature of the dream she was dreaming here among the slanting glass trees of the city-forest, their columns tilting at the copper-coloured sky, supporting it.

'Aren't you too warm, honey?'

'No,' she said, 'I'm not too anything.'

When the lights changed the forest began moving above her, the tall glass trees curving and leaning away, and she watched them until her eyes closed and she was no longer awake nor yet asleep, but floating.

A hundred feet below the waters of the Hudson River the closed circuit nine-camera television system of the Lincoln Tunnel was monitoring the traffic flow for the operators in the Weehawken Administration Building and the police officers stationed in their catwalk booths deep in the Tunnel itself. Triggered by the eighteen photo-electric vehicle detectors buried in the westbound tube, amber flow alarm lights had begun flashing on the appropriate surveillance consoles for this zone; but there was no possible action to be taken on this alert because it meant that traffic was flowing below the arbitrary minimum speed of five miles per hour. Administrative and police staffs of the Lincoln Tunnel knew from experience that if anyone could keep moving at five miles per hour through the north tube on the morning of any given July Third they were making out pretty well.

Just before ten o'clock a series of red lamps began showing on the surveillance consoles, a visual signal that was confirmed aurally by a continuous chime indicating that somewhere along the eight-thousand-foot conduit an abnormal gap had established itself in the traffic flow and was increasing. The scene was already coming up on the split-image TV screens and police patrols were heading towards it in their radio-equipped catwalk cars and five seconds after the alert was given a call went out to Big Yellow.

When the double line came to a stop at the New York portal,

the two-tone Chrysler stood half in the shade and half in the sun.

The driver sat stiffly at the wheel, neat in a mod pinstripe suit, watching the line of cars reaching into the tunnel-mouth. He was a thin man, his face narrow and cut with lines. Perhaps, being physically slight, he had psychologically felt the need to put a greater effort into doing things that were easier for other men; so that it had become a habit to squeeze his face against adversity, as against wind or rain, leaving these lines on it.

He jerked the cigarette away and lit another; all his movements were sudden like that, as if his smallest decisions, once made, had to be carried out quickly before anything could stop him.

'I told you,' the man beside him said. 'We should've stayed.'

He was a heavier man than the driver, with a blunt face on big shoulders, his body slack, a wide hand resting on his knee, the other tucked into his coat. He watched the double line of cars with a dullness in his eyes, and when he turned his head the movement was slow. He and his companion were opposite in many ways, as is often the case with close friends.

'We should've stayed,' he said again.

'It's just a breakdown, some kind of breakdown, some punk's blowing steam that's all. We got this far, we can go the whole way.'

The heavy head moved back, facing the windshield.

'We had some luck. The auto on fire.'

'So we had some luck.'

'I'd feel safer in the city.'

'Get out, why don't you? Open the door an' get out.'

The shapeless man said nothing more. He sat with a hand on his knee, a hand tucked into his coat, the blood on his shirtcuff darkening now.

They saw the emergency truck swing out from its bay and go heading into the tunnel.

Big Yellow is an International C-O Transtar special-operations rig that was custom built for the Port Authority to handle in-tunnel emergencies. With a road width of less than twenty-two feet and operating headroom of thirteen, haulage work in the three tubes demands peculiar facilities, and these are built into Big Yellow, a narrow, stubby rig designed for fast turn-around in limited environs devoid of shoulders or turn-outs. Its five-speed direct transmission, its seven and a half ton hoist-and-tow capacity, rear-mounted wrecker lash-up with winch-fitted booms, and its front-mounted six thousand pound electrical hoist combine to give the C-O Transtar a unique ability in unique conditions.

Any officer of the Lincoln Tunnel staff can say the same thing more simply: 'Whatever gets in there, Big Yellow can go drag it out.'

The mean annual figure for breakdowns is in the region of three thousand cases, with flats, vapour locks, overheating and empty gas tanks the predominating causes. When the C-O Transtar headed into the north tube for the fifth time this morning it found a sedan slewed around with its bumpers hooked to a sub-compact and both drivers busy hassling.

Kids had climbed out of quite a few of the cars held up by the blockage and were watching the operation, delighted with their luck. If they could have arranged it, there would have been an emergency of some kind at every mile of the route they were taking, and it looked as if someone was pitching for them right now.

Their parents stayed in their cars, frustrated.

FDR Drive is still okay into midtown with no tie-ups down the West Side Highway, but there'll be minor delays into the Battery Tunnel. The news is good for westbound travellers out of Manhattan because the auto fire has now been dealt with on Eighth Avenue at Thirtieth and we can see that big yellow wrecker bringing some business out of the Lincoln north tube, with the double file already on the move again. Now here's a memorandum from our guardian angels of the Police Department which you may like to think about while you're waiting to whip up your speed along those express-ways, and it goes like this: ask anyone you know who has survived an auto accident a simple question, and if he's honest he'll say 'No, I never really believed it could happen to me.'

Almost everybody had their radio on in the car, whether they listened to it or not. Trapped in the streets of the city that they could suddenly afford to hate, they found comfort in pressing a button to command the only facility that was left to them.

A City Council ruling in Long Beach has decreed that many of the hundreds of thousands of people flocking to the beaches in the metropolitan area seeking sunshine and sea air will be disappointed this year. This city's four-mile municipal beach is now restricted to residents. The decision, taken for fear of overcrowding, is seen also as a measure of keeping out 'undesirables'. In New Jersey, Asbury Park remains free to all, but Avon, which formerly allowed visitors at normal rates, has this year raised its nonresident prices for the use of the beach.

'Anybody here headed for Avon New Jersey?'

'Not this year!'

No abortions will be performed today in most city hospitals because elective surgery has been postponed until Monday. This will permit surgeons and other members of hospital staffs to observe the Independence Day holiday.

'Anybody here feelin' a pain in the middle?'

'It just has to be indigestion!'

From the overseas broadcast newsroom we have a report today from Vietnam that states that the recent bombing –

They tuned the voice out.

Sometimes they thought they should listen to every newscast there was, but they didn't know where he was stationed, so they couldn't tell if it was about him or not; and sometimes they felt disloyal, indifferent, switching off the radio or the television like this, but they knew it was only because they didn't want to hear of casualties. There were his letters, which they read a dozen times over, often aloud to each other to make sure they didn't miss the smallest meaning. That was the only news they wanted.

Coming out of the Lincoln Tunnel two cars accelerated side by side, going as fast as they could to try making up for the time they'd lost. Swinging for the Turnpike they almost touched, and one driver corrected suddenly, seeing the danger but over-steering and keeping to his lane only with difficulty.

Behind them in the black Cadillac sedan the man with the pale neat face and the smoked glasses had seen the potential accident situation arise and resolve itself. At first he had been alerted, braking gently so as to avoid running into the possible smash and so as to be able to pull up at once and get to the scene in case there were people injured. Then he saw that the situation was dealt with, and relaxed. At this comparatively low speed the accident would not have been very serious, even if the drivers and their passengers weren't wearing seat-belts.

He felt glad his time hadn't been wasted in being forced to a halt by a trivial collision. Later, on the Turnpike and the Garden State Parkway, the speeds would rise and he might have the luck to see a really high-impact smash, involving more than just two autos.

He drove steadily, a small man sitting almost unnaturally upright at the wheel, his black tie neatly knotted, the black fabric restraint harness crossing his chest diagonally like a sash. The scene ahead of him flowed against the dark glasses in reflection, hiding his eyes.

His name was Solo.

Mr Solo.

'Look, if we keep on going till Cheesequake we can stop off at the Howard Johnson's.'

'If we're not starving by that time.'

'Well, okay, if we're starving we'll get off the Parkway and find a diner, but I'd like to keep right on moving and try beating the stuff that's piling up back of us.'

'You're the driver, honey, and we'll – oh *look*, there's *Erica*!'

'Who?'

'Erica Sigrist!'

She called through the window but the powder-blue Mustang fastback was swinging left for the Turnpike and all they could see was a scarf in the wind.

'She never told me she was leaving town today!'

'Does she tell you everything?'

'Well, no. I only mean – well, yes, she does, mostly – after all we were at high school together. I think she would have told me. I wonder why she didn't?'

It isn't important.

It'd be a mistake to think that.

It's important to me and I suppose to him but there's nobody else involved, no kids to be hurt, so there's nothing really important happening, just beginning to happen, there isn't an earthquake, the world isn't caving in or anything.

Her scarf blew in the slipstream, the tail of it tugging; but she didn't want to close the windows because of the heat, which seemed to have been switched on all around her, bouncing off the hood and through the windshield, coming up from the roadway to be trapped under the roof. It was a powder-blue scarf to match the paintwork: she liked things in her life to relate, to compose some kind of meaning, a significance that wouldn't have existed if the parts had remained disparate. The yin and the yang. Craig and Erica.

Or I thought I did. I thought I liked the things in my life to relate and create significance. But I must have been wrong about that or I wouldn't have blown the whole thing apart.

Craig: I'm putting this through the mail because I'd hate to leave it in a drawer where I know you'll go, like a booby-trap. It's short because this is the essence of all the much longer ones I've been writing for the past weeks. They were full of self-indulgence and grand verbal gestures, and the fact that I recognized this, when I read them, shows that at least the writing of them helped me to think this whole thing through.

Why don't people like me ever have the guts to say these things face to face, why leave notes, as if we're daubing something dirty on a wall and running away? What are we so afraid of – hurting? Being hurt?

I have to go now. I'm sorry I stayed too long, but you're young enough to start again with somebody else; and we can at least say we didn't let it go grinding on over the bumps until we actually hated each other. At this stage we can make a nice calculated break, and prove how very well-organized we are.

Because we always prided ourselves on that. While most of our friends were spilling things and breaking things and helping each other to wipe up the mess and pick up the pieces and somehow make everything work again and in a better way, we were tiptoeing hand in hand with our heads held a little aloof from the scenes of confusion, never unsympathetic, of course, but too lovingly engaged by the disciplines of the perfect partnership to have time for anyone else. It was just a matter of being intelligent, and of being – as nobody in all the world had ever been before, so deeply as we – in love.

Goodbye, Craig.

A scarf in the wind.

Priority signals had been hitting the Communications Division network since the first alert had come in from the Narcotics launch on the East River, and one of them – attention all precincts – had gone on the air soon after 0900 hours. It was to the effect that RMP cars would distribute walkie-talkies to foot patrolmen, and immediately.

Forty-one minutes later a flash came through the boosted repeater system on the division frequency and a fleet of unmarked cars from Homicide, Detective and Narcotics converged on Dover Street, under the Manhattan end of Brooklyn Bridge. A sharp patrolman, on his way past the graveyard of junked automobiles, had seen a New Jersey-registered Ford Pinto abandoned there.

A mobile laboratory staffed by field investigation personnel from Scientific Research responded to the scene to begin analytic procedures while photo technicians and the Latent Fingerprint Unit set to work. Detectives from the Ballistics Section looked for the bullet that had been fired from Patrolman Nolan's revolver but they couldn't find it lodged anywhere in the bodywork; nor could they find any evidence that it had struck and ricocheted; and this tied in with the still-drying bloodspots on the plastic flooring and the more liquid traces in the ribbing of the front passenger seat.

Major radio stations agreed to broadcast a reminder to all hospitals, clinics, ambulance units and private physicians that under the crime concealment laws their duty was to inform the Police Department if anyone sought medical attention for the extraction of a bullet or the dressing of a bullet wound. The announcement added that the 911 emergency number should be used to make such a report. The message was clear enough: *do it fast.*

A similar broadcast had gone out earlier from WNYC to the general public.

If you can't see your car from where you are, would you care to check? If it's not where you left it, just call us. The sooner you do, the sooner you'll get it back. The number is nine-one-one.

In the trunk of the Ford Pinto there was found substantial evidence that its presence in the riverside area at East Thirty-seventh Street was linked with the suspected dope switch first reported by Observer Patrolman Bob McAvery of the Aviation Unit: a one-kilo reinforced linen bag whose split seam had spilled a brown powder across the floor panel, to be identified by the narcotics men as crude morphine base for processing into heroin.

This, and the mass of more subtle evidence now being analysed by the laboratory, would be vital once it could be superimposed on information from other sources; but so far there was nothing to indicate where the suspects were, or where they might sooner or later be found.

No call had yet come in reporting a stolen car. If the two wanted men had repeated their behaviour pattern and seized another private automobile, it had not been notified. Microscopic examination of the trunk floor had shown that an estimated sixty one-kilo linen bags had been stowed there very recently; and it was assumed that this amount of morphine base had been hastily transferred to another car. Worth upwards of a hundred thousand dollars before processing, it would provide one half million one-tenth-gramme shots of heroin, sufficient to render five thousand junkies irreversibly addicted and commit them to certain death.

At every bridge and tunnel giving egress from Manhattan Island, police were recording the licence numbers of all private vehicles leaving the city. At the Holland and Lincoln Tunnels and the George Washington Bridge the check was duplicated, since the stolen Pinto carried New Jersey plates and the two men might be heading back that way.

The watch on these exits was based on a classic principle: a felon who has taken life will do one of two things. He will go to ground, or will run as far and as fast as he can from the scene of his crime.

The bag of apples rested on the parapet of the bridge; one of them was close by, the bitten part of it white-looking against the grimy girder. It was minutes since the boy had put it there: there just wasn't the time to do both things now the cars kept coming so fast.

Their paintwork went gliding past him like bits of a broken rainbow joined together again with the colours all anyhow; and as he wrote down their numbers he breathed the sharp sweet smell of exhaust gas and warm rubber and melting tar, for him more heady than the perfumes of all Araby.

On the highway, courtesy is another word for safety. When joining parkway traffic, reduce your speed on the approach to the acceleration lanes. Signal, and when the chance presents itself, merge gradually and adjust your speed to that of your fellow motorists. Courtesy counts.

'You feeling okay?'

'I guess.'

Rod Gould didn't move. Except when he moved he didn't feel anything. The shot had caught him somewhere near the stomach as he'd slammed the door of the Pinto and the punch behind it had knocked him against Nat as he was hitting the gears in. But the bleeding had dried up so it could be okay and they didn't have to do anything for a while about finding the kind of medic who wouldn't yap.

Nat Renatus switched on the radio again and this time came right up with the lead newscast from WOR.

– but enquiries have so far failed to turn up any clue as –

'Cut it,' Gould said.

'We gotta know what happened –'

'We know what happened.'

'We gotta know how much they found out, for Chrisake.'

– concerned in the crime, though nobody saw the other car. Certain discoveries made by the continuing laboratory analysis of articles taken from the abandoned auto – described as 'significant' – are being kept secret. Meanwhile the nationwide hunt for the two men is already underway. From Police Headquarters comes the news that John Patrick Nolan, the slain patrolman, who was already a holder of two Commendations and three Meritorious citations, will receive posthumously the Exceptional Merit award for his courageous action just two hours ago. In the words of Police Commis-

sioner Wallace, 'Men of Nolan's calibre are rare, even among the ranks of the Finest. His death brings a loss not only to the Police Department but to the people of New York City.' It is reported that John Nolan will be given an inspector's funeral.

Nat Renatus cut the radio.

'You found out,' Gould asked him, 'what you wanna know?'

'Sure.' He jerked another smoke from the pack and lit it. 'They're ballsed up. An' we got a trunkful of sugar worth a hundred grand.'

Rod Gould swung his head. 'It could've been like that.' His tone was vicious and Nat jerked a look at him. 'But it wasn't enough to do the switch and load the stuff. You had to kill a cop.'

Courtesy on the road saves lives. On highways, always keep at least one car length between you and the auto ahead for each ten miles of speed, to give yourself room to pull up in an emergency. Then you won't bump him – or worse. Courtesy pays.

By ten o'clock most of the city's six thousand miles of streets had become clogged with sluggish traffic despite the efforts of the police to speed up the flow in all areas. Along a given length of roadway a given number of vehicles could move, and no more. It was as simple as that: and as frustrating for police and public alike.

Early readings from the traffic analysis computers showed that private automobiles were at this time carrying thirteen hundred people per lane per hour along city streets, and more than three thousand per lane per hour on urban motorways. Traffic leaving Manhattan Island by the Port Authority's bridges and tunnels had, in the past sixty minutes, doubled.

So it's bumper-to-bumper right along almost every major route with a solid jam at the tunnel and bridge approaches, and at the height we're flying now we can see the build-up taking shape down the east flank of New Jersey, so don't get your hopes up that your troubles are going to be over once you've left the city, folks. I don't like to be negative about this but it's my job to give you the facts and that's what you're getting. Solid on Riverside, Henry Hudson, Major Degan and across the George Washington, with an accident snarl-up at the Weehawken end of the Lincoln Tunnel. And here's a technical tip: impatience isn't a fuel additive so it can't make your car go any faster; all it can do is spoil this fine sunny morning. Now we're handing you back to Bob Whitman at the studio for local news reports.

By noon the thrumming of the streets had died almost away, leaving those isolated sounds that are heard when a concourse has dispersed. The people of this city, hitherto content to shelter here, had today in desperation fled from it, their faces turned in eagerness toward some promised land.

CHAPTER THREE

A man, finding himself upon land where no man has been before, and wishing to cross it, must make a path. Even with his first step a path is begun, and already has direction; if his first step is southwards, that is where the path will lead: to the south.

In this there is a certain magic. A path cannot move, yet it can never be still, as long as men will use it. For it will always lead them, running ahead quicker than they, even though they move with the speed of the wind.

Men have always made paths. If a man's way is special to him, because he chooses to drink where others find the water brackish or because his pilgrimage is to a private god, the path will never broaden, though it will serve this one man well. But if he seeks to reach a place that promises sweet water or a god whose gifts are for all men, then others will follow him. In so doing, their feet will mark the earth, so that the hundredth of them, beginning his journey, will already see the way ahead.

And if some of these, in returning, bring news of such a

place and of its untold bounty, then others will follow the way unto their many millions; and the path will become a road.

Reaching a hundred and seventy-three miles from the north border of New Jersey to the Atlantic Ocean at Cape May, the Garden State Parkway provides the main arterial facility carrying traffic from the metropolitan area and New York City to the beaches and shore resorts.

A twin-road superhighway built on the toll barrier system and with eighty-two interchanges and eleven mainline plazas, it was conceived by men whose courage in excavating seven million tons of earth and replacing it with bituminous concrete pavement derived from their belief that in striking a path through virgin land one can yet preserve its beauty. More than a transport facility, the Parkway is a moving panorama for city-dwelling travellers whose eyes have forgotten the look of dew across grassland, the interplay of light on leaves.

Since the road was opened, three thousand million people have passed this way.

On this summertime Friday the dotted southbound line on the Hourly Travel and Delay Charts had hit the morning high of four thousand vehicles an hour at eight o'clock, with stop-and-go traffic up to thirty m.p.h. and one-hour delays at congestion points and interchanges. Dipping slowly to the three thousand five hundred mark by noon with fifty m.p.h. traffic and only minor delays, the southbound line showed an abrupt drop soon afterwards.

The vanguard shockwave of the five hundred thousand people who would use the Parkway today was now hitting the food and fuel service areas as drivers grew hungry and their gas tanks ran low. Along the twin north and south roadways the traffic volume lightened and the flow speeds climbed into the fifty-five m.p.h. no-delay sector on the charts as the parking bays filled up.

In the Cheesequake area south of Raritan Plaza the staff of the Howard Johnson's Restaurant was at battle stations and every seat in the cafeteria operation was taken before one o'clock, with people standing three deep at the counters. They were not here only to eat or slake their thirst: they needed a rest-room or a telephone or a roll of film or some cigarettes or a map, but most of all they needed to go somewhere cool where the air was fresh and there was no more glare and they could stop trying to figure out if that guy in the Olds hard-top was drunk or only crazy, the way he kept trying to pass the beach buggy when there plain wasn't enough room.

Outside on the highway it was a humid seventy-nine.

'Gimme a Big Jo Jumbo.'

'Yes sir.'

'I'll have a pot of Boston Baked.'

'You want brown bread?'

'I don't have much time, miss, what've you got that's hot an' fast?'

'We have Fried Chicken Croquettes, coming right up.'

'Two butter Pecans and a Chocolate.'

'Yes, ma'am – Chocolate or Chocolate Chip?'

'Do you have something light, please? I'm on a diet.'

'Why don't you try our special diet plate, right here?'

'You free tonight, baby?'

'Cool it, I'm kinda busy.'

'Open Steak, honey, for Number 4. Tuna for 17. Can you see Mr Casazza from where you are? Tell him the man in the Hawaiian shirt's just taken a spoon, okay?'

'The Apple Pie's just great.'

'I'm glad you like it.'

'What's the "A la Mode" bit? Says here, "A la Mode."'

'I guess it sort of means it's in fashion.'

'Uh-huh. When's Apple Pie been outa fashion in the USA?'

'Sunny and Sanka for 23. And tell Mr Casazza the machine's broken again, will you?'

'Oh not again! How're we ever going to cope?'

'By telling Mr Casazza.'

'You doing okay, Betsy?'

''Cept my feet are twice the size. I'd buy shoes twice the size, 'cept on Sundays I'd rattle around like Minnie Mouse. The ashtray's gone from 23, did you know?'

'I'll tell Mr Casazza.'

He was a neat, cool-looking man in a tropical suit and his name was on the door of the little office by the lobby but he didn't anticipate he'd be going in there before Monday morning because the action was out here and that was where he had to be.

This lady has lost her little boy, Mr Casazza.

It would be nice to go into his office near the lobby just for a few minutes' breather but of course he didn't have the opportunity.

Oh, Mr Casazza, the soda machine on B counter has broken down again.

Once in his office he could loosen his necktie, maybe put his feet up on the desk. That would be nice.

Hey, are you the manager? My car's been stolen!

Put his feet up and shut his eyes for a while, take the phone off the hook, just for a couple of minutes. That would be great.

You see that gentleman in the Hawaiian shirt, Mr Casazza? Maggie says he took a spoon.

Take it easy for a brief spell, everyone did it, renew the batteries. They say Abraham Lincoln used to do it, and Winston Churchill, even though they were busy people.

Mr Casazza, there's a man getting fresh with Sally and she can't take it any more, you know how she is.

It would be real nice to go into his office near the lobby and loosen his necktie and put his feet up or pray or kick and scream or get stoned or hysterical and smash things or pour cognac all over himself and strike a match and put it on the menu, *Casazza Flambé,* or just stand and wait till they came for him with a strait-jacket because this was the third time the soda machine had broken down and the fourth time a little boy had been found in the crush at the counters bumming strangers for Hot Fudge Sundaes and so far this morning they'd missed a dozen spoons and by Monday it'd reach the average sixty and thirty or forty knives and forks because they were less popular and a hundred glasses smashed or two hundred, what was the difference and who cared?

Mr Casazza cared.

In this business you learned that people were human. It was a great lesson. You could call it the revelation of a universal truth.

People with bungalows on the shore needed spoons for the coffee tray, that was natural, spoons and knives and forks and ashtrays and table numbers and sugar bowls and floor mats and other little things that make a home. And people who left their car in the southbound parking lot and had lunch and went out the wrong door and looked for their car in the northbound parking lot would want you to call the police, you couldn't blame them, it was a nasty shock. And people who didn't want the pups their dog was clearly about to produce would decide on a clean break and leave it here to litter, knowing they'd all find a good home where the food was free. It was so very understandable. And you could keep your head just by reminding yourself of the universal truth that had been revealed to you. That people – oh, boy – were human.

'Why, hello there, Mr Casazza!'

'How are you, Mr Anderson – and you, ma'am? I hope you've time for lunch here?'

'Where else would we go?'

The Andersons called in every Friday, weekend commuting to their place in Long Branch; and sometimes they brought a trinket for Mrs Casazza, something they'd found during the week – they bought and sold antique jewellery – or a small box of candies for Mary Jane. Last winter their car had broken down right outside here in the parking lot and Mr Casazza had run them to the railroad station in the rain, that was all; but they just wouldn't let him forget how much they appreciated it.

They made up for the other people; yet when he took time off to think about it he realized that most of his customers were like the Andersons, appreciative of the little things he did for them whether it was part of the service or not. The one per cent minority of trouble-makers were conspicuous only because they made trouble.

It was too easy, Mr Casazza thought as he stood in the lobby with his hands neatly behind him, to exaggerate your difficulties under pressure of work. Provided you didn't let yourself get uptight about anything, there was nothing to this kind of job. The problems were all imaginary.

'Mr Casazza, we have a fainting case in the cafeteria, could you hurry please?'

A compact-looking man in a tan seersucker suit was bending over the old lady when Mr Casazza arrived.

'I'm a doctor. It's nothing serious.'

Some of the Johnson Girls were keeping the crowd back and the doctor and Mr Casazza carried the lady to his office. A cameo brooch had fallen on to the floor and someone gave it to him; they had loosened the neckband of her Victorian dress, which was worn tight at the throat.

'It was just the heat out there.'

'Oh, sure.'

It happened a lot in the summer months. They didn't faint on the Parkway where it could be inconvenient; they did it here where there was air-conditioning and immediate help available: instinctively they seemed to hold out till they reached an oasis where they could flop.

'She'll be all right now. Get her a drink, something with mint in it, but not off the ice.'

Dr Hagen went back to pay his check at the cafeteria desk and then made his way through the crowded lobby to stand in line at the phone booths.

The two young Harvards near him were turning their heads.

'Man, just *look* at that girl . . .'

She had come through the doors and was crossing to the rest-rooms and all Brett Hagen could see were a slender back and a powder-blue scarf. Someone left the booth and he moved up a pace.

It wasn't until he'd pulled in off the Parkway that he'd considered the logic or otherwise of what he was doing. His wife, taking his call yesterday at the Euphoria Health Spa where she supervised rhythmic therapy, had been typically relaxed about the situation.

'What does it matter, Brett, as long as Tracy likes him?'

'I think it matters that he's almost fifty.' The next part wasn't easy to say, but he wanted to make her see that they ought to take some kind of action. 'Apparently he has a reputation for being keen on young girls.'

'What man of almost fifty isn't keen on them, whether he admits it or not? I don't see what's got into you, darling – we've always agreed that Tracy should be free to develop as a person in her own right, not just as the daughter of her parents.'

Patiently he said: 'I think this is a case for rethinking, Linda.'

'I know you do. I just don't see why.'

'It's the first time she's spent the weekend with a middle-aged man.'

'Would we know? You mean it's the first time anyone's told us.'

He couldn't argue with that; and he knew by her balanced replies that she wasn't persuadable, so he'd hung up, knowing she didn't like interruptions to her classes any more than he liked distractions when he was in theatre. The last thing she'd told him was: 'Don't worry, darling, this is part of what it's like, growing up. I mean as parents.'

Caught in a traffic jam this morning near Newark Airport and watching a Transcontinental lowering through the pollution haze he had questioned the ease with which an unknown voice on the telephone had badgered him into leaving New York and driving a hundred and fifty miles through holiday weekend traffic in the bare hope of finding Tracy. It wasn't more than that. 'Try the Surf Club in Wildwood' was rather vague.

Now as he waited for a telephone he still questioned the logic or otherwise of his journey. The farther he'd come from New York the harder his conscience had nudged him about his patient at the Clinic: the adrenalectomy. His performance had been correct and in his capacity as surgeon his responsibility was over, and nobody had queried his decision to leave town for the weekend. His wife was supervising extracurricular training sessions and thus wouldn't miss him; and the senior resident at the Clinic – Hugh Mattox, a friend of long standing – had urged him to 'take a break and hang loose somewhere till Monday, you've good and earned it.'

The Gardella girl was now in first-class postoperative care: the quality of the equipment and facilities at the Hausner Clinic at White Plains had attracted a resident staff from the finest hospitals in the state. And Hugh Mattox had promised to supervise the Gardella case personally.

But when Brett had called them last night they'd reported the onset of hypertension and allied symptoms of postoperative shock and it had started him worrying about the possibility of adrenal failure. It wasn't his responsibility, but Ellen Gardella was a nice young girl and had shown a lot of courage and it was natural he should feel uneasy on her behalf; there was nothing, after all, in the Hippocratic Oath to say you didn't have the right to be human or to worry over your patients after they'd left your hands. *I will follow that system of regimen which, according to my ability and judgement, I consider for the benefit of my patients.* This, in his opinion, included worrying.

So it was even more disturbing that something in him had responded immediately to that insinuating voice on the telephone, and that he was already a long way from the Hausner Clinic at a time when his patient's condition could worsen critically.

'Long distance, please.'

A cigar butt was still smouldering in the ashtray and he stubbed it out while he was waiting for the connection.

The senior resident was in theatre just now but he spoke to the ward sister. Miss Gardella's condition was unchanged.

'There are no signs of improvement?'

'No, Doctor Hagen. Unchanged.'

She sounded faintly surprised and he realized his question had been emotional, not cerebal: if she said the condition was unchanged, how could there be signs of improvement?

'Are you still giving supplementary steroids?'

'We are, sir. Fifty milligrams of cortisone acetate, intramuscular, six-hourly.'

'Will you please give me the blood levels?'

'Just a moment, Doctor Hagen.' The smell of the cigar was stale and he inched open the door of the booth. 'Here are the levels, sir. Sodium chloride 161, potassium 5.9, urea 93 per cent, glucose 173.'

'Blood pressure?'

'Blood pressure is 89/50.'

'Is there any skin pigmentation?'

'No, Doctor.'

He paused for a moment and decided not to ask about stomach pains, respiration and general symptoms. She knew he had checked by phone last night and if the condition was the same then he was going to get the same answers.

'All right, Sister. Miss Gardella couldn't possibly be in better hands, but I just thought I'd check.'

'Thank you, Doctor Hagen.'

Coming out of the booth, he realized that he'd just made what amounted to an apology to the ward sister; and he was bothered because he didn't know why. An apology hadn't been necessary: by virtue of his status at the Hausner Clinic he could call up and demand whatever information he pleased. Also he was troubled by the need to make a decision, here and now; and while he spent most of his life making immediate decisions that were important to his patients he was sometimes influenced by doubts when a decision had an importance in his own personal affairs.

In a couple of miles along the Parkway he would come to Exit 120, and logically he should take it and go back on his tracks to White Plains and tell his wife she was perfectly right, and be on hand if Ellen Gardella's condition took a downturn. Tracy might well have spent weekends with older men and it had been agreed that she ought to grow up without any second-hand inhibitions passed on to her by an earlier generation, so there wasn't anything he had to do in Wildwood. And if he wanted to be on hand if Ellen Gardella was going into adrenal failure then he had a right to do things that way, so he had no business out here on the Garden State Parkway.

He made his decision. When he reached Exit 120 he'd keep right on going.

The blue scarf was lying folded over her pocketbook, and she wondered if there were anything symbolic in her having taken it off.

'I'd just like a Coke.'

'Sure, honey.'

People didn't often call her that. Did she look lonesome or something? She didn't feel lonesome. The scarf was the last thing Craig had given her. It wasn't new any more; in fact there was a tear in it, a narrow break in the weave near the hem; but she had always treasured the things he gave her, even keeping the card he sometimes wrote: *To Erica.* Perhaps because his gifts had been infrequent. That was a nice tight-lipped way of saying so much. His gifts had been infrequent. Cool. So perhaps there'd been something symbolic in her taking it off and shaking her hair free, her soul free.

'There y'are, honey.'

A motherly face, plump capable arms, the sort of arms you'd run to if you ever needed help.

'Thank you.'

She said it crisply. She didn't need any help. She didn't want to be mothered. She wanted to sit here looking as chic as hell in her Alex Colman panelled print with a cool Coke in her hand and a cool look in her eyes so that people understood from here on that if anyone tried to touch Erica Sigrist they were going to get frostbite.

The harsh warbling of an emergency vehicle cut across the sounds in the cafeteria and the Johnson Girl at the soda-fountain glanced up through the windows.

'Somebody had to be first.'

The two young college boys were still leaning at the counter and Erica wished they'd stop watching her. She didn't want to be watched, or touched, or loved, ever again.

It was trying to seem big, coming at her like a sort of day-time nightmare, filling the whole place with importance. But it wasn't anything big. *At this stage we can make a nice calculated break, and prove how very well-organized we are.* It was new, that was all. And not even, statistically, very new. One out of every four marriages in America ended up in divorce, Cornelius had told her. So what was new about this?

Cornelius was her lawyer.

'Pardon me, but is that your white Eldorado outside?'

They'd come into the counter section, the two of them, soon after she had. It would be absurd to think they'd followed her in; they were just kids.

'No.'

It took a lot of the sunshine out of his smile but it couldn't legitimately rate as frostbite.

'I'm sorry, I thought I saw you leave it. We came in right alongside and there isn't much room now for opening a door that big.'

He had a good clean-looking smile, the more attractive for the touch of ruefulness he was managing to get into it, breaking his heart inside because she wasn't the girl with the Eldorado so he couldn't go out with her and gallantly make room. There was something so old-fashioned about the whole thing and that was attractive too because good manners were pretty rare.

'I see.'

She finished her Coke, her hand deft with the glass, putting it down on the counter with studied exactitude, Reel 1, Take 29, Miss Sigrist cuts the College Boy dead.

'Are you driving down to the shore?'

'Yes.'

She took her pocketbook, bunching the powder-blue scarf, not putting it on.

'We're heading for Wildwood.'

'Have fun there.'

She walked away.

When you're thirty-two years old are you still so young that you don't have to feel grateful, or at least just gratified, when an eighteen-year-old Harvard boy makes a play for you? And when you're divorced, or as good as, morally divorced, liberated by the letter in the mails, *Goodbye Craig,* are you still so habituated to the proprieties of being a married woman that you can't just let him talk to you for a while, and practise his gallantry?

There'd be quite a few questions like that, for a while. When you've totally recreated your own image you have to get acquainted with the New You, and learn how to handle it. Some of those questions would be hard: easy to answer but hard to take. Why, for instance, did the new image have to be that of a glacial goddess determined to hate people and if possible hurt them?

Because Craig would celebrate. After a token show of regret, he would celebrate.

And because if you could put a man like Craig Sigrist out

of your life you'd find it easy to pass up a college boy. Or anyone.

'Nancy, do you know where Mr Casazza is?'

'He just ducked into his office.'

'Okay, I'll get him on the phone.'

The two-tone Chrysler Newport eased into the southbound parking lot and Nat Renatus cut the motor.

'You stay with the car, huh, while I call Toni?'

'I ain't moving,' Rod Gould said.

Queasily Nat asked: 'Does it hurt?'

He didn't know how the man could do it. He couldn't have done it himself. If ever he got anything in his eye or had a splinter in his hand he just had to get it out fast, before he did anything else. He hated things like that. A bullet, like Rod had in him, Christ, it could be doing some kind of damage all the time, just by being there.

Rod didn't say anything.

'I tell Toni what happened? I mean about the cop?'

'He knows already. He was wise to the set-up.'

Nat buttoned his mod pinstripe coat and got out and shut the driver's door and took a pace and saw the man in the tan suit climbing into the Buick outside the restaurant entrance. He went back.

'Rod.'

'Huh?'

'That guy's a medic.'

'What guy?'

'In the Buick.'

Rod Gould turned his heavy head to look at the car.

'What makes you think so?'

'The MD on the windshield.' Nat flicked the butt away and lit the next from the pack, his thin hands not quite steady. 'You want I should go get him?'

Gould watched the Buick.

'It's too public.'

'I could operate okay here.'

The rod in the spine, all right Doc, don't try anything fancy, and bring that bag along.

'We'd have to turn him off,' Gould said slowly, 'later.'

And lose the Buick. They'd last been seen in New York City. They'd have to do it whether the man got the slug out or not. He'd know too much.

'So we'd have to turn him off,' Nat said and blew out smoke.

The Buick rocked slightly to the torque of the motor as the man started it up.

'He doesn't have to be a medic,' Gould said. 'He could just be driving a medic's car.'

The Buick began backing up and Renatus junked the newly-lit cigarette and turned and started walking and Gould said:

'No.'

Renatus stopped.

'Are you crazy?'

Gould watched him through the side window, wanting to be sure. Nat stood with his thin arms held close as if he was in a cold wind here under the burning sun, his face squeezed into shadowed cuts and his eyes flickering. Gould was sure.

'Go call Toni,' he said.

'Listen. *That medic could fix you up.*'

'Call Toni.'

Renatus turned with a jerk and walked across to the restaurant while the Buick held back for him to pass and Rod Gould looked away and knew he'd been right. A cop was enough. There didn't have to be any more trouble, and the way Nat was feeling right now they could hit trouble just by letting him make decisions; Nat had done it before but never to a city cop and his nerve had gone.

The hiss of the Buick's tyres died and gas hung on the air.

'This is Renatus.'

He could smell sweat and he didn't like that; as soon as they got to Cape May he'd take a shower and go buy a shirt. He liked to be clean.

'How's things?' asked Toni.

'We need a boat.'

'What for?'

'We're moving. An' we got some sugar.'

'Where did you find it, Renatus?'

His voice was lazy, and had a smile in it. It was like the man, lazy and smiling.

Nat waited, squinting in the smoke that was filling the booth. He said nothing, because if he said where they'd found the sugar Toni Lago would know more than that, and if he didn't say where they'd found it he'd know anyway because he'd connect things up. He knew they'd been running with the Istanbul-Naples chain, and he had a radio.

'How wide's the rake, Renatus?'

'Around fifty grand.'

'How's that again?'

'Fifty.'

'Says here in the paper the stuff was worth a hundred, city prices.' Toni Lago laughed lazily.

'Listen,' Renatus said, 'do we get a boat?'

'I only got half a boat.' He laughed again.

Nat's hand was slippery on the phone and he shut his eyes and pulled the smoke into his lungs and waited till everything straightened up, the shot and the screaming tyres and the long drag out of the city, *meanwhile the nationwide hunt for the two men is already underway*, and Rod out there with a slug in him. He didn't want Rod to die.

'Where does the boat,' Toni Lago asked him smiling, 'have to go?'

'Haiti.'

'That's a long way, Renatus.'

'How much?'

A man outside the booth was making signs to him, he had an urgent call, something like that. Renatus turned his back and got the taste of the filter and doused it and felt for the pack and waited to hear what Toni Lago would say, thoug[h] he knew what he'd say.

'Half,' said Toni Lago.

'Okay.' He couldn't believe his luck.

'Half for you. And half for Gould.'

Everything was trying to black out again a[...] bright-ness of the flame hurt his eyes as he lit up.

'Toni,' he said.

The booth was closing in on him, i[...]ning till he stood in an upright coffin listening to [...]nful breath-ing and thinking for an instant th[...]apped animal somewhere, hitting out and bruising his hand on the edge of the coinbox, steadying with the sudden pain, getting a grip again.

Rod wouldn't agree. He'd rather be taken than have a man like Lago sell him out. And that could finish them both.

'Toni. Don't put us on the spot.'

'I didn't.'

'You want cream?'

'Pardon me?'

'On the Jell-O.'

'Oh. No. Yes. I don't really mind.'

'Okay, you got cream.'

He took the two dishes across to the table.

'Oh Floyd, how did you know I wanted cream?'

'Did you? Darn it, I should've remembered.'

He started back to the counter.

'Floyd.'

'Yes?'

'I already have some. They put it on. Look.'

'So they did.'

He sat down, taking comfort, as he always did, in her shimmering smile. But he musn't rely on it because she would smile like this if the world ended, and it would be the last thing they would all see, shining.

'I don't know that you should have cream, Sue.'

'I'm perfectly all right.'

She leaned towards him at the table, a wing of her black hair touching his shoulder. 'Please don't worry.'

'You didn't seem perfectly all right just now.'

'Ely was kicking, that's all.'

fit to fly.' His face was brooding. 'You have to be absolutely

'But e a trip like –'

She m, Floyd. I really am.'

than oned her Jell-O. She thought he looked handsomer

always hen he brooded; he ought to be a movie star,

Six w ooding rôles, he'd be terrific.

brooded at the Unitarian Church of All Souls he'd

over agai ently and she'd fallen in love with him all

on her wed was an appropriate thing to have happen

'Eat it slowly, Sue. The doctor said.'

'Then that's what I'll do.'

Floyd's mother and father had tried to be understanding but had made it plain they couldn't attend the ceremony with Sue in 'that condition' and even Mom had suggested that since they'd 'left things so late' they might as well wait a little longer till 'after the event' so as to 'avoid making an exhibition.'

Floyd had brooded beautifully about it but she'd finally lost her patience and at the intimate tea-party where both families had gathered to persuade her to their way of thinking she'd torn a hole right through the fabric: 'Look Floyd and I made love because we loved each other and now we're going to be married because we still love each other so I don't see why our first-born shouldn't come along too even though he's not quite ready – it's an important day for him too, isn't it? And I'm not going to let anyone sit in for him while we get married so if you want us to wait until after he's born, okay, but he's still coming along even if it has to be in a baby carriage. It'll look kind of cute in the photographs, don't you think?'

A lot of tea had been left to get cold in cups but finally she'd chosen the dress and had it let out and they'd all been there in the Unitarian Church of All Souls on Lexington and the minister had conducted the service with such a show of really monumental solemnity that she'd felt like Elizabeth marrying Philip in Westminster Abbey; and afterwards he'd given her a brand-new silver dollar on a coloured ribbon and said with a totally secular wink: 'This is for our long-awaited young friend. Meanwhile, Mrs Powers, I should like you to think of it as a presentation to yourself – the Unitarian Medal of Honour for courage under fire.'

Floyd saw her put her hand over her middle and was at once concerned. 'I shouldn't have agreed to –'

'I'm just feeling him. I like feeling him.' She took his hand and placed it there instead of her own. 'You see?'

He looked alarmed.

'He shouldn't do that, Sue!'

'Okay, then you just tell him.'

'You have to be absolutely fit to cope with a trip like –'

'Oh, Floyd, please don't make me sound like an out-of-condition football team. After the city I just needed a fresh ocean breeze, and you were wonderful to agree we should all three of us make the trip.'

'But if anything happened to you –'

'It won't, Floyd, so please –'

'But if anything did –'

'The worst that could possibly happen would be that he arrived three weeks early, and we'd simply need an ambulance to –'

'Oh my God!'

Floyd's spoonful of Jell-O flopped on to the table. He'd spent most of the time thinking of ambulances since he'd checked the *Home Doctor's Dictionary* under 'Miscarriage'.

'It's not really so alarming, Floyd. Babies have been born in elevators and aeroplanes and taxis and –'

'They're not the best places, Sue, and I've got my mind set on a hospital – a lot of them get born there too.'

Her smile still shone for him but he didn't see it because he was looking through the windows, sitting perfectly still. The warbling noise grew louder and then he saw the big red cross on the ambulance as it lurched through the string of traffic. Then he looked down and put his spoon in the dish and just sat there.

'I'm not really sure how I'm going to handle this weekend.'

She tried to straighten her face a little.

'It's well known that we can all achieve superhuman deeds when a crisis actually comes, so –'

'Oh my God.'

The telephone buzzed and he picked it up.

'Manager.'

'This is the Cafeteria desk, Mr Casazza. I hate troubling you but I have a traveller's cheque here and I just noticed the signatures don't match.'

'Is the customer still there?'

'No, he left about ten minutes ago. I feel pretty bad over this, Mr Casazza.'

'Think of it as nothing. But call the State Police.'

'Yes, sir.'

'I'll be right along.'

The man in the white linen ducks was standing right outside in the lobby when he left his office.

‘Are you the manager?’

‘That’s right, can I help you?’

The man hesitated, and Mr Casazza had a couple of seconds to size up the white deck-shoes and the magenta shirt with the Thai silk scarf tucked into it, the crisp grey haircut and the yachtsman’s tan, the faraway eyes that said that despite the image of seasoned confidence this man, somewhere along the line, had gotten lost. Mr Casazza had seen them before and would see them again: Madison Avenue in weekend plumage.

‘D’you keep any kind of liquor in your office? Scotch or cognac – I mean for restorative purposes?’

‘No,’ Mr Casazza said, ‘I don’t.’

‘My wife is a little upset.’ The heavy signet ring flashed as his hand gestured towards the entrance. ‘I left her outside in the car. We just had a near-accident, a very close thing.’ The hand fell to his side again.

‘The lady isn’t hurt?’

‘Oh no, just – it was just a shock, you know.’ His manner switched suddenly and became less anxious, more demanding. ‘Surely you keep something in your office for – for this kind of crisis.’ He was reaching inside his white linen coat, his manner changing again, persuasive. ‘Naturally I’ll be glad to pay whatever it –’

‘There’s a liquor store,’ Mr Casazza said carefully, ‘not far off the Parkway.’

In the man’s bright stare he saw desperation.

‘That would take time. Don’t you understand? My wife’s in quite a bad way.’

‘We have rest-rooms here, and one of my girls has had nurse’s training. Let’s bring your wife in and –’

‘You don’t keep any liquor.’

It was a flat statement; the pretence had gone. There was only one thing on his mind and the manager either didn’t keep any or refused to let him have it.

‘No.’

The man stared at him for another second, then drew a sudden breath and turned away with a jerk.

‘Thank you.’

‘You’re welcome.’

He crossed to the entrance doors with the awkward walk of someone who knows he is being watched, and hates it.

When he'd gone Mr Casazza went on standing there for a minute or two, feeling mean, almost, to be free of so much torment. But even if he'd kept anything in his office to offer the man, he wouldn't have done it; if a report came in about a drunk-driver crash he wouldn't want any part of it.

From behind the windshield of the pearl-finish Cougar in the southbound lot she watched him coming. He looked, she thought, handsome; and he knew how to dress.

'They didn't have any?'

'No.'

He climbed in and started the motor. She asked in surprise:

'Howard Johnson's don't carry film?'

'They do, but I need something special, a slow-speed low-grain to use with filters.' He swung the Cougar out of the parking bay, accelerating more than necessary and having to brake for the approach section. 'The man said there's a shop just off the Parkway.'

She tightened her seat-belt a fraction, looking down and away from his set face.

'I'm sure we can find one at Beach Haven.'

Her tone was dull, lacking conviction.

'We don't get there till this evening. I want to take some pix before then.'

The sun flashed obliquely across someone's rear window and she closed her eyes for a moment.

'But we can't stop,' she said, 'on the Parkway.'

He sped up, passing a VW and edging across its bows into the slow lane ready for turning off.

'We might want to leave it for a while, and come back to it. You know I like taking pix weekends.'

As the exit sign came up she said briefly and too late:

'Let's find a shop at Beach Haven, Walt.'

He began slowing and the turn-signal indicator started ticking on the dash panel.

'I'm in the exit lane now. It won't take long.'

Mr Solo was standing in the lobby looking at the big wall plan of the Parkway when the warbling sound began from outside the restaurant.

A short neat man, he stood noticeably upright, just as he

sat noticeably upright at the wheel of the black Cadillac sedan that was in the southbound parking lot. The restraint harness had rubbed at the left shoulder of his clerical-grey summer-weight suit, leaving a shine on the cloth; and the slipstream past the driver's window had disturbed his black brilliantined hair, so that a spike of it was sticking out above his left ear, like a sharp horn.

When he heard the warbling of the emergency vehicle he moved his eyes, only his eyes, behind the smoked glasses; and although motionless before, he now seemed to have been stilled by the sound, his attitude totally attentive. Then suddenly he crossed to the entrance doors and looked out, seeing the ambulance pressing its way through the traffic. The red cross on its white background passed for an instant over his glasses, reflected.

He knew that forty-five minutes ago there had been an accident on one of the Turnpike access ramps at Interchange 11, and he had been delayed by the ensuing snarl-up. He had not been near enough to visit the scene, but had asked about it from the toll collector at Raritan Plaza.

Now there had been another one, and he had seen nothing of it. It might of course be somebody taken sick, or a cardiac, in that ambulance; but he sensed there had been a crash somewhere. He was intuitive that way.

He stood listening until the harsh warbling sound had faded.

'Will you please sign this, Mr Casazza?'

'Surely.'

The lobby was crowded and they had to stand against the wall while he found his pen and signed.

'Thank you.'

'Feet hurt?'

'I guess.' She gave a quick smile.

'Take a break whenever you can, even if it's only for a couple of minutes. That's official.' He saw the Andersons coming through from the dining alcove and went across to them. 'How was the Chicken Shortcake?'

'Just beautiful!'

They always had Chicken Shortcake. Weekends he always made sure it was on the menu.

Anderson drew his wife close as a group of kids came

pressing by. He said to Mr Casazza: 'I'm darned if I know how you can handle a clientèle this big and keep your cool!'

'If I didn't keep cool I couldn't handle it. It's kind of self-compensating.' He shook hands with them both. 'Nice of you to call in, and I hope you have a great weekend on the shore.'

One of his girls was trying to catch his attention from the doorway of the main restaurant.

'Oh Mr Casazza!'

The dish machine. Or the soda machine. Or the air-conditioning or a stolen spoon or a litter of pups or a false cheque or just plain capital T for Trouble, any kind.

'I'm coming!'

CHAPTER FOUR

The Garden State Parkway is more than a traffic artery: it is a transport facility, an artery with its own nervous system, a complex series of toll plazas and police posts in constant radio and telephone communication with each other and directed from the nerve centre at Woodbridge, Middlesex County. The overall task of construction, maintenance and operation is the responsibility of the New Jersey Highway Authority. The task of controlling the actual traffic and public movement is assigned to Troop E of the New Jersey State Police.

The day and night patrol carried out by the field officers and troopers of this greater than hundred-strong force is non-stop and the annual distance covered on normal duty is in the region of four million miles. The term 'transport facility' means what it says: the moment a vehicle accelerates from an approach ramp to merge with Parkway traffic it comes under the protection of a system designed to ensure that its journey is safeguarded and that if any kind of difficulty arises, help is immediately available.

The difficulties arising this Friday were typical of any summer weekend and as the police motor patrols worked their way among the heavy traffic the station aid sheets were slowly filling up, with the eighth column – headed 'Type Service' – reflecting the usual pattern: *Gas. Fanbelt. Mech. Fanbelt. Fanbelt. Gas. Flat. Tow. Flat. Gas.*

Between Milepost 127 at Perth Amboy in the north and Milepost 80 at Toms River to the south the traffic flow was registering characteristic July figures as vehicles began filtering from the main artery to head for the Atlantic shoreline at Red Bank, Long Branch, Asbury Park, Point Pleasant and the smaller coastal resorts.

With the mean volume in this section dropping progressively from the peak 4000 vehicles-per-hour level to the 2,500 mark southwards of Milepost 100, speeds began nudging the 60 m.p.h. legal limit in places where it was possible to move into the high-speed left lane and stay there. Earlier there had been stop-and-go snarl-ups and major delays in the northern sectors due to the brute onslaught of traffic from the metropolitan areas, but by midday the southbound flow was already below saturation level and the movement was getting into its stride.

Estimates compiled from long experience gave an anticipated fifty thousand vehicles for the southbound run over the twelve-hour period 8 a.m. to 8 p.m. with an average of three persons per vehicle. Since this amounted to a day's march on the Parkway by one hundred and fifty armoured battalions, it was appropriate that three days ago the orders from Woodbridge had conveyed the sense of a military operation.

PARKWAY TO ALL TROOP E STATIONS
ATTENTION STATION COMMANDERS

1. Attention is directed to the coming Fourth of July holiday period. An all-out effort will be exerted by Troop E personnel to keep to a minimum the fatalities, injuries and destruction of property caused by motor accidents.
2. Station commanders will do their utmost to ensure a well-regulated traffic flow during this critical period. Marked cars will be used constantly to signal the presence of the State Police among the motoring public. Men taking dismounted posts will retain a military bearing at all times.
3. Patrols will be alert to hazardous violations such as following too close, unsafe lane changing and careless driving, also to shoulder riding and failure to keep to the right.
4. Special attention will be given to the high safety threat offered by the drinking driver. Station commanders will schedule appropriate checks, and all toll plaza personnel have been instructed to report suspected cases. Plazas will close down automatic lanes after midnight so that all

drivers will make contact with a collector, enabling him to assess the drivers' condition. Priority alert will be given in cases of teenage drinking drivers, with patrols giving extra attention to those interchanges in the vicinity of resort areas normally attracting teenage and college students. Breath testing operators will be available during this entire period.

5. Disabled vehicles will receive immediate attention for the safety and convenience of the motoring public, and the yellow emergency ticket will be attached to all vehicles for which aid has been called. Patrols will keep close check on such vehicles until mechanic or wrecker help arrives in response to radio calls, and offer all possible assistance to the driver and passengers, especially ensuring that children remain inside the vehicle and safe from passing traffic. Abandoned cars will be removed from the Parkway in compliance with Operations Order Number 260.
6. The Helicopter Patrol will carry out observation and emergency assistance duties, with emphasis on aiding highway patrols to maintain a smooth and orderly flow.
7. Motor patrols will apply defensive driving techniques at all times except when it is judged that delay in reaching the scene of an accident might endanger life. Otherwise, impeccable driving will set a good example to the motoring public.
8. Special attention is given to the campaign mounted experimentally during this weekend. Many aspects of Operation Homesafe will overlay standing orders, and Captain J. B. S. Darrow of the Federal Council on Traffic Safety will be accorded every assistance by all ranks.

N. T. Westover, Captain
Commanding Troop E

Cruising at traffic-flow speed five hundred feet above the Parkway a Hughes 300 sent its shadow flitting across the meadowland at Milepost 76. Drawn from the fleet operated by Ronson Helicopters Inc. of Trenton and flying under contract to the New Jersey State Police, it was piloted by Jeff Sanmer, a much-decorated Army veteran with four thousand flying hours in his logbook. Sitting beside him was a police observer, his eyes scanning the twin roadways below.

Aware from experience that near the end of a three-hour airborne patrol an observer's efficiency is normally reduced by as much as ten per cent, Trooper MacKenna was compensating by double-checking the slightest irregularity in the flow of coloured vehicles snaking through the heat-haze of the early afternoon. Code-numbered 66, the Hughes three-seater had been on the air for most of the day and mainly with 13's and less frequent 11's. A Signal 13 was coded for breakdowns and Signal 11 for accidents.

66 to Holmdel – 13.
Go ahead 66.
13 on left shoulder at 114 southbound. Seems to be a flat on a 70 Ford.

66 to Ocean Point – I have a 13.
Hear you, 66.
13 on right shoulder at 79, a Dodge sedan with the hood raised, looks like overheating.

66 to Bass River – here's an 11.
Bass River to 66, give it to me.
11 at 52, Entrance Five-Two, approach-ramp and mainline collision, with one of the – hold it and cancel, cancel. There's a groundhog beaten me to it, I can see your Car 78 just arriving at the scene.

At ground level there was a continuous flux of radio and telephone signals passing through the whole length of the Parkway's communication system, many of them simultaneous and most of them now concentrated in the sections parallel to the shoreline below Milepost 110.

State Police Holmdel, Sergeant Croft. Yes. A what? All right, we'll send someone along.
Car 74 – Car 74. Trooper Levy, I have a call from the Howard Johnson's about a false traveller's cheque. Get along there, okay?

Barnegat Plaza to Ocean Point.

Go ahead, Barnegat. Trooper Schultz.

Hi, Harry – this is Mike. Listen, there's a guy just gone through northbound in a '71 Galaxie, licence number RK-84349, you got that? I'd say he's either been drinking or the heat's getting him down, the way he took off.

What colour, Mike?

Huh? Kind of off-white. Ivory.

Okay. Be in touch.

Car 75 – 75.

75 to Base, receiving you.

Ivory-white '71 Ford Galaxie number RK-84349 just left Barnegat Plaza northbound, erratic driving noticed. Roger?

Roger.

On the right shoulder at Milepost 20 near the Shoemaker Holly in Cape May County a '67 Georgia-registered Cadillac stood parked with the hood open. The time was twelve minutes past two p.m.

'Is it somethin' serious?'

'Ah dunno, Mary Lou. There's nuthin' Ah c'n see, but y' know me, if th' whole motor fell clean out Ah reckon Ah wouldn' notice much diff'rence. Y'all got th' map there, have yuh?'

'Ah don' see how th' map's goin' t' git us no place, Abner, if th' whole darn motor's fell clean out.'

'You jes' git th' map, an' fold it so folks c'n read th' bit on th' back where it says SEND HELP. You jes' put it in th' window so folks c'n see.'

'This is Cape May Plaza, right?'

'Right.'

'Then I missed the sign. I'm heading for Avalon.'

'No, you're okay. Turn off in four miles at Exit 13 and it's a straight run to the shore, be there in a few minutes.'

'Oh really? Thank you. Say, there's an old Caddy on the shoulder, couple miles back, you know about that? Needs help.'

Cape May Plaza to Avalon.

Go ahead, Plaza. Trooper Kearney.

I'm told there's an old model Cadillac needs assistance around Milepost 20 southbound.

Car 76 – Car 76.
76 to Base, can hear you.
We have a disabled auto on the shoulder by Milepost 20 southbound, an old model Cadillac.
I'm on my way.

'I guess you let your oil run low.'

'What oil's that, young feller?'

'You have to keep it to this level marked right here on the dipstick.'

'Y' do? Ah ain't put no oil in this here automobile in five years.'

'Then your garage man has. But this time he's missed out, and you only have to do it once. Wait till I call up a wrecker.'

State Police to 250 – calling Two-Five-Oh.
250 – Dunes Garage.
We need a tow. Cadillac sedan, Milepost 20, southbound, Car 76 standing by. Trooper Mills.
Okay, five minutes, 250 out.

STATION: Avalon. AID SHEET NO.: 3. TROOPER: Mills. CAR NO. 76. TIME REPORTED: 2.16 P. MILEPOST: 20. CAR MAKE: Cadillac. STATE: Georgia. REGISTRATION NUMBER: AG-46738. TYPE SERVICE: Tow. GARAGE CALLED: Dunes. WRECKER RADIO NO.: 250. TIME CALLED: 2.21 P. TIME SERVICE ARRIVED: 2.26 P.

So Cape May Plaza had been told about the disabled car at sixteen minutes past two o'clock and by twenty-nine minutes past the Cadillac was hooked behind the wrecker and Car 76 was following up with its hazard lamp flashing. The short delay of thirteen minutes wasn't a record, but nobody got bawled out for being slow.

Since Entrance 90 on the southbound stretch the hardtop Charger 500 had been storming the high-speed lane with its crimson paintwork flashing in the sun and the triple-note Turino horns clearing a gangway as drivers on the sixty m.p.h.

limit moved over, because if you wanted to feel safe with a car like that on the road with you the best thing was to tuck in and let it go right on past and to hell with it.

The black-and-yellow cruiser had made a U-turn near Milepost 86 and was coming up fast and by MP 85 they were nose to tail and the patrol officer used his PA loudspeaker mounted out front.

Police – pull over.

His voice, electronically magnified, sounded from nowhere, from everywhere, from the sky.

Reduce your speed gradually . . . check your driving-mirror carefully . . . Pull over and stop on the shoulder.

The Charger's speed had been hitting the seventies through medium traffic and it needed almost a mile before the lane-changing manoeuvre was completed and the two cars were standing together at the roadside.

Lieutenant Frank Ingram climbed out of Car 73 and took his time as he walked over to the hardtop, checking it for paintwork damage, worn tyres, projecting accessories. Then he stood looking down at the boy at the wheel, his light blue eyes expressionless.

'Get out of your car. Bring your licences, both of you.'

They stood on the shoulder of the road where grass and summer flowers edged the concrete. They were a couple of college boys, one of them folding his arms and staring out across the meadowland as if they'd stopped here to look at the view, the other leaning on the crimson bodywork and lighting a cigarette, his movements indifferent but his hands not quite steady. The lieutenant hadn't been looking at them, but at their licences. Now his head came up.

'Put out that cigarette.'

He stood with his legs braced evenly, his shoulders perfectly squared to the boy who was smoking.

'Is it illegal to smoke?' the boy asked pointedly.

'No.'

'Then it's okay.'

The boy drew smoke in and blew it out in a stream, watching the lieutenant.

'No. I'm not telling you as a police officer; I'm telling you as a man. Forget the uniform. Put it out.'

The boy leaned away from the car, nettled.

'Why should I?'

'Because I'm going to hurt your pride. I mean really. So if you're anything of a man yourself you won't stand there sucking on that little paper dummy to show me how big you are. Because it won't make you look so very big. Will it?'

The other boy had stopped watching the view. He was watching the lieutenant.

'Listen,' the driver said, 'we don't have too much time.' Instinctively he had dropped the cigarette and was sliding his shoe over it before he realized: his foot stopped but it was too late and he jerked his head up angrily. 'I was speeding and you caught me and now I get a ticket, it's as simple as that, so let's just get it over with.'

Lieutenant Ingram half-turned his head as the radio in Car 73 began squawking; then he turned back. It had been squawking non-stop all day and it was going to be that way till the end of the weekend. He gave them their driving licences: Thomas B. Jackson and Mortimer Pyle, both seventeen, the same age as his own boy.

'No,' he said, 'you don't get a ticket.'

'Okay, so I don't get a ticket.' It was a fair attempt to treat the whole thing indifferently but he couldn't quite keep it up because he was too surprised. 'Why not?'

'It wouldn't stop you speeding again. It never does. And it certainly wouldn't buy you the maturity you lack: can a kid buy manhood for ten bucks?'

'If I'm considered old enough to drive a –'

'You're not old enough, at seventeen. Some kids are but you're not. Anyone who drives a powerful car along a highway at seventy-eight miles an hour through holiday traffic with the horns blaring to push other people out of his way has the emotions of an infant so young that it hasn't yet learned how to keep from wetting its pants. You've heard kids that age yelling for attention and you're no better, screaming down the road in your red tin toy so people can see you're the most important mother's darling in the whole wide world. What's your next trick on the programme, you going to wet your pants?'

The boy was standing squared up to him now; his pride was being hurt all right and it was worse because his buddy was listening to it happen. Ingram waited to see if he'd have any kind of an answer but he was probably too mad at him to speak.

'At your age I wouldn't find that image very flattering. It'd needle me into doing something about it. What are you going to do about it, Mr Jackson?'

The 'Mr' was well timed. The boy's pride couldn't be pushed any lower and now Ingram was picking it up for him and helping to dust it off.

The crimson hardtop rocked on its springs as the traffic sped past, its slipstream buffeting.

'Drive slow, I guess.'

'Is that all? That won't be enough.'

'Well, gee, what else do I have to do?'

'Start growing up. What are you studying to be?'

'A lawyer.'

'That's a pretty responsible career. It's time you wondered how you could possibly defend yourself on a charge of endangering people's lives for the sake of a cheap thrill. And if you think driving slow is going to solve anything, you need to ask yourself how you're ever going to do it without blowing your stack. It can't be done that way; you have to drive slow because you feel like it, not just because it's the law. So you need to begin by siphoning off your natural male aggression without hurting anybody. Skiing, high-diving, surfing, there's plenty of choice. Go at it hard, give it the gun, set yourself up to tear hell out of the competition, head for the championships, do it for real. You'll feel great and you won't hurt anybody and – just incidentally – you'll enable yourself to drive on the highway with all the mature intelligence I'm confident you'll soon be capable of showing.'

73's radio was still squawking and he patted the Charger's hood. 'Where are you boys heading?'

'Wildwood.'

'Have a good time there.'

Going up the shoulder on foot, he began slowing the nearside lane and finally brought it to a halt, receiving a wave from the Charger as it started up and turned on to the pavement. It didn't accelerate with the burst of power normally shown by fast red sports cars and Lieutenant Ingram appreciated the gesture, letting himself think momentarily that he might have done some good. One thing he knew for sure and from experience: if he'd given a ticket that boy would have driven away with the motor screaming in low gear just to show his defiance, and all he would have learned would be to keep a sharper eye on the mirror.

Walking steadily back to his car he unclipped the mike.

'Car 73 – Seven Three – receiving.'

'Gillespie, sir. Message from HQ.'

'Go ahead, Sergeant.'

'Captain Darrow is now on his way to Ocean Point. He hopes it's convenient for you to assemble all ranks so he can talk to them for a few minutes.'

Frank Ingram pushed his cap back a couple of inches to let the sweat dry on his brow, his eyes on the traffic stream by habit. Just in these few seconds he could see dangerous driving techniques being used: a Plymouth sedan riding the fast lane and a powder-blue Mustang straddling the centre with the right lane empty and available and a Chevvy shaping to pass on the wrong side. That kind of thing was going on throughout the Parkway and if Troop E had a thousand men they still wouldn't be able to police it as Captain Westover would like it to be done: with full coverage of every situation.

'Lieutenant?' Gillespie's bullfrog voice came on the air.

'Hold it a minute.'

'Yes, sir.'

There was nothing in the sergeant's tone to show he knew why Ingram was having to think before deciding. If the message had come from Captain Westover at HQ it would have amounted to a simple order, courteously phrased, and there wouldn't have been any hesitation. But Captain Darrow held no more than honorary rank in the New Jersey State Police and the situation over this weekend was unusual.

'Do what you can,' the Officer Commanding Troop E had told Ingram yesterday, 'to observe the niceties. We have to fit Captain Darrow's operation into our routine and we have to do it smoothly.'

Westover hadn't voiced the obvious: that there could arise occasions where observation of the 'niceties' might have to yield precedence to more urgent considerations, and that it was up to station commanders to use their discretion.

The black and yellow 73 rocked gently as the windrush of the right-lane traffic hit the bodywork. In the fast lane a tiny Honda was tucked in behind a station wagon, following too close, and Frank Ingram drew a slow breath and held it a couple of seconds, a device he used when impatience threatened to disturb his judgement.

'Sarn't Gillespie.'

'Sir?'

'Call the men in.'

Ocean Point Barracks was located approximately halfway along the Parkway and though Ingram commanded the unit there he also carried out a roving commission that could sometimes take him as far as the New York State Thruway in the north and Cape May City southward, hence his rank as lieutenant, which would normally be too elevated for the commander of twelve troopers. In his absence Sergeant Gillespie assumed control.

Swinging 73 into the parking bay at Ocean Point ten minutes later, he found most of the patrols already in, their cars ranged along the trimmed grass verge and the men gathered in the shade of the big sycamore outside the building. They looked a little disorientated and he felt a touch of impatience again: for several hours at a stretch they'd been shepherding traffic in the fast 2,000 VPH sector, overhauling violators and pulling them down, checking stationary vehicles, constantly watching for careless driving as they co-ordinated the flows and prevented congestion at the critical capacity points. Suddenly they found themselves standing here idle.

'We on vacation, sir?'

'That's strictly for the rest of the world this weekend.'

Pushing open the door at the top of the steps he passed into the air-conditioned cool of the operations room and found Sergeant Gillespie there with Trooper Schultz.

'Captain Darrow not here yet?'

'No, sir.' Gillespie moved his big frame across to the other desk and picked up the station record book without a word from his lieutenant. If Ingram had been absent for more than a couple of hours he always wanted to know the score when he checked in. 'We got three aid sheets filled up so far an' Cooper's down at Milepost 66 putting a fire out right now.' He handed the sheets to Ingram. 'Aside from which we booked a guy doin' a U-turn, three drivers without licences, two drunks, a prostitute hitch-hiking at Oyster Creek and a bunch of speed-freaks in a beat-up hearse – two of them are rapping in the box here now and Doc Medler's on his way –'

'You found hypodermics?'

'Yes, sir, needles, phials, tins of the stuff.' He took the aid sheets back and shut the record book. 'Mrs Ingram called us up around three o'clock to say she's taken over Number 2 Ambulance at the shore station, case you should want to make contact.'

Ingram nodded and took a pace to the window, his eyes narrowed against the glare that struck up through the aluminium slats of the blind. Sam Gillespie folded his big arms and leaned below the noticeboard, watching his lieutenant. Gillespie's face, in profile against the light from the window, had the aspect of a granite rock chipped desperately by an amateur sculptor intent on showing that he was trying to portray a human visage: every feature was bigger than life-size, the jaw enormous so that it could accommodate the length of the mouth, the nose immense with its great bridge keeping the eyes so far apart that they were damn nearly – as Trooper Mack had once said – in his ears. His voice – also according to Mack – was like a bullfrog's recorded at forty-five and played back on full volume at thirty-eight, 'and I mean when he's whispering.'

Watching the lieutenant, Gillespie was half-listening to the base radio and keeping one ear for the sound of a car arriving.

74 to Parkway, NCIC.

Captain Darrow hadn't given him any exact time when he'd be here: he'd just said he was on his way. He wondered how long Ingram would be willing to leave the Ocean Point sector unpoliced with holiday traffic rolling.

74 – go ahead.

NCIC New Jersey registration BLZ-26278. 86 southbound, Levy.

BLZ-26278. Okay.

The lieutenant turned his head.

'Didn't you call Levy in?'

'He was at 102 when I signalled, sir.'

'What's he picked up?'

'He was talkin' about a '71 Montego a while back.'

Ingram faced the window again.

The three men in the room were now consciously listening to the voices that made an almost constant background on the radio. Normally an NCIC call didn't excite interest at the station unless a hit was made, but since early this morning the

NCIC calls had been piling up in the log, with every man in Troop E hoping to pick up the two bastards who'd killed that New York cop.

Trooper Levy, at this moment somewhere south of Milepost 86 and homing in to the station, was tailing the 1971 Mercury Montego numbered BLZ-26278, alerted by something in its aspect or something in the way it was being driven, maybe very fast, maybe with two men on board. He didn't have to pull it down to find out if this car were on file at the National Crime Identification Centre: he could do it quicker by radio and going through the NCIC computer. A 30-second delay was considered pretty slow.

Parkway to 74.

Go ahead.

Negative on your BLZ-26278.

Okay. Thanks.

Gazing through the slats of the blind, Lieutenant Ingram weighed things up. A negative from the NCIC didn't have to mean the Montego was clean. It could have been stolen recently: it often happened that a patrol picked someone up just by intuition, and in a few minutes the station was calling up the owner: 'Excuse me, but do you know your car's been stolen?' Whatever had caught Trooper Levy's attention to the Montego, he ought to follow it through.

'Sarn't Gillespie.'

'Sir?'

'Tell Levy to stay with it.'

Trooper Schultz glanced up, then went on with his work.

From the driveway came a flash of light from a turning auto, and Ingram moved from the window.

Gillespie was at the console.

Base to 74.

74, go ahead.

Cancel your previous order and stay with the suspect.

Okay, Sarge.

As Ingram went down the steps he saw the last of the unmarked cars coming in with Cooper at the wheel, its paintwork splashed with fire foam. Closer, a short briskly-moving officer with captain's insignia was coming across from an unmarked Galaxie 6, looking around him at the line of patrol cars before inspecting the building with a quick sweep of his eyes.

'Captain Darrow?'

'Lieutenant Ingram?'

They exchanged salutes as the men in the shade of the sycamore came to attention.

'We'll assemble inside.'

'I think,' Ingram said, 'it might be a little crowded in there, with so many of us.'

Captain Darrow suddenly focused his attention on the officer commanding Ocean Point, scrutinizing the weathered face and the light blue eyes that looked him back, steady and uncommunicative.

'You've been fully briefed on the purpose of my visiting with Troop E this weekend?'

'Yes I have, Captain.'

'Then you'll understand that I have to talk to your men and since they need to be able to hear me it's more practical that we go inside where there's no traffic noise. I'd be glad if you'd issue the necessary orders, Lieutenant.'

He went quickly up the steps and through the door. His voice had carried quite clearly to the men but none of them moved until Lieutenant Ingram spoke.

'Right, parade in the operations room.'

Darrow had spun a chair around and stood with one foot on the seat waiting for the last of them to come in. As an operations room it was spacious considering it accommodated two desks, a range of filing cabinets, the Telex booth and the radio unit; but as a parade ground it wasn't so adequate and Sergeant Gillespie stood squeezed between two of the cabinets like a bear in a barrel.

'Is this your full complement, Lieutenant?'

Darrow had very quick eyes and they'd been flicking sharply around the room while the men had been coming in.

'No, Captain.'

'Didn't you get my message?'

'Yes, I did.'

The troopers had become absolutely quiet and Sam Gillespie began studying the ceiling with great concentration.

'I asked that all ranks at Ocean Point should be assembled.'

His tone was almost conversational, but not quite. His smooth youthful-executive's face had a permanently interested expression and it didn't change now.

Ingram looked towards the filing cabinets.

'Sergeant Gillespie, what was the message you received from Captain Darrow?'

'The Captain hoped it'd be convenient for you to assemble all ranks so he could talk to them for a few minutes, sir.'

Ingram looked back at the Captain.

'Was that the correct message?'

'Perfectly correct.'

'It just wasn't convenient.'

'I see.' The interested expression didn't change. 'Why not, Lieutenant?'

'I have one trooper still on the Parkway, tailing a suspect car.'

As if Ingram had not spoken, Darrow swung his head suddenly to take in the closely-packed men, his arm resting on his raised knee and his hand dangling, a casual attitude that could have been meant to put them at their ease.

'You have all read about Operation Homesafe in your special orders. I intend to go over the salient details with you so that there's no doubt left about the way we're going to mount this campaign. It's already operating at Holmdel, and –'

74 to Base.

The background of radio calls had been on almost zero volume until this minute, but now Trooper Schultz had to raise it because it concerned Ocean Point. Quietly he said:

Go ahead, 74.

I've checked out the Montego and it's clean. Now at 75 southbound.

Lieutenant Ingram moved his head slightly.

'Bring him in.'

Okay, 74. You're called in, hear me?

Hear you, called in.

Schultz spun the volume down and sat with his head close to the console again.

Nobody looked at Captain Darrow. He hadn't moved, except to lower his head for a moment while he waited for the chance to go on speaking. Now he lifted it.

'Before I take you through the details of this campaign I'll tell you why we have to run it. Statistics give us a clear picture of the problem we're going to lick. Total deaths by accident in the past ten years were close to one million. Deaths by road accident were close to half a million. Last year the figure was more than fifty-six thousand. More than a thousand every week. More than one hundred and fifty every day. Every nine minutes someone gets killed on the road.' He looked at his watch. 'I arrived here just nine minutes ago. Let him rest in peace, whoever he was.'

He took his foot from the chair and stood back from it. 'But figures aren't dramatic enough to make people care. And they'll have to start caring soon or they'll be turned into figures themselves and then it'll be too late for them to do anything about the simple fact they've just learned: that the figures in accident statistics were once people. Now they don't exist any more. Fifty-six thousand of them, every year. You take fifty-six thousand *people* and drive them to the Arizona Desert and drop a nuclear bomb on them – kids, clerks, senators, housewives, bellboys, doctors, *people with lives to live.* That would make news. Then do it next year, and the year after that, go on doing it *every* year. All right, a year's a long time, a lot can happen in a year, so let's bring it down to a period short enough to mean something, make it a couple of weeks. Every two weeks send a ship the size of the *Queen Elizabeth* down the Hudson with a full passenger-list and sink it without survivors: do it today and do it again on July 18th and do it again on August 1st. That would make news too. The whole nation would go into permanent mourning for its dead. We'd be appalled that certain doom was waiting for so many of us, so regularly, that every fortnight more than two thousand of us were fated inevitably to die.'

The passing traffic on the southbound lanes made a rushing sound against the windows, and Trooper Mack felt impressed by what the Captain was telling them: he made it sound that all those automobiles out there were racing to their doom without anyone being able to stop them.

'Death on the highway is every bit as certain. But it's too diverse for people to realize it. Someone gets killed every nine minutes but if it happens in Trenton it's too far away for us to hear the crash, and the next one could be in Los Angeles and the next in Seattle or Denver City or New Orleans and where are those places? On a map. It can't happen here. And it can't happen to us. And that is the attitude that's right at the core of –'

Repeat, Barnegat Plaza to Ocean Point.

Trooper Schultz had put the volume so low that he'd almost missed the call. He turned it to medium.

Hear you, Barnegat.

Captain Darrow folded his arms.

'Lieutenant, I'd be glad if you'd have the radio switched off until I've finished.'

'I can't do that, Captain, I'm sorry.'

Nobody except Schultz was listening to the plaza call any more.

'Why not?' His tone was no more than interested but his youthful face had become suddenly hard and he didn't look away from Ingram.

'I'm prepared to leave fifty miles of the Parkway unpoliced while we go into the theory of highway safety but I can't close down communications. Ocean Point has a fair record for fast post-accident response and although we're proud of that, it's not the main issue; the faster you can reach the scene of an accident, the more chance you have of saving lives. That seems to tie in pretty closely with what you've been telling us, Captain, so I'm confident you'll appreciate my point of view.'

He turned his head to look at the radio console, where Schultz was lowering the volume.

'What does Barnegat want?'

'There's a bunch of students at Milepost 70 northbound, sir, trying to stop the traffic. One car had to go on to the shoulder and nearly –'

'Cooper and Mills, get moving and hurry.'

They were the two nearest the door and they didn't stop to shut it after them. Lieutenant Ingram faced Darrow again.

'You were saying, Captain, that people's optimistic attitude is right at the core of the problem.'

They could hear the bang of the starters in the parking bay as 71 and 76 were got moving. Reflected sunlight sparked through the slats at the window. On the other side of the room a trooper shut the door quietly.

'It's now been made clear,' said Darrow evenly, 'that I shall have to leave out a lot of the essentials. That's a pity because the attitude of the driver is a key factor in the highway accident scene. But you'll all need to listen, and listen very carefully, to the actual mechanics of Operation Homesafe. Its name is self-explanatory: our aim is to see that the motoring public gets home safely at the end of this Fourth of July weekend. There's one enemy – only one – facing us in this campaign to protect the motorist from harm. That enemy is the man at the wheel himself.'

Trooper Schultz moved the knob as an exchange of signals began between the Hughes 300 'copter and Bass River State Police. Captain Darrow waited and then took up again more slowly.

'Now I'm going to give you just one more statistic. Accidents are caused by faults in the design of vehicles and weaknesses in their components: blindspot features, tyres, brakelines; and great pressure is rightly being made to increase the safety standards at the manufacturing level. The highway itself is another cause of accidents: bad street lighting, worn road surfaces, inadequate signposting. The weather is a hazard, with rain, fog, ice, crosswinds and sunglare contributing to the figures. But one final statistic I want to give you is this: of the fifteen million five hundred thousand road accidents occurring last year, the *driver* was responsible for ninety-two per cent. I'd like you to consider that figure in terms of actual –'

Toms River Plaza to Ocean Point.

Go ahead.

Listen, there's a drinking driver just took off on the southbound in a Chevvy Impala station wagon, colour dark green, and if he can stay on the road he'll be going right past your base in a couple of minutes.

'Get him,' Ingram said and the trooper nearest the door dragged it open.

Taking action now.

Okay, Ocean Point. Say, where have you boys gone to anyway? I don't see you around any more, you on vacation or somethin'?

Ocean Point out.

Sam Gillespie looked hard at the ceiling again. The air-conditioning was going okay but just the same he was beginning to sweat. He liked the peaceful life and it was becoming reasonably plain that those days were over for a while.

Captain Darrow had his gaze fixed on the radio console, as if he expected another OP call to come through before he could pick up the thread. He waited ten seconds and said with emphasis:

'Since the driver causes almost all road accidents it's the driver we have to hit. And now I'm talking about the actual methods we're going to use in running Operation Homesafe this weekend. We're going to hit the driver where it hurts and we're going to keep on hitting him till he gets the message and the message is that if he chooses to menace public safety by selfish and careless and flagrant disregard for the lives of others on the highway then he's going to be stopped in his tracks by the only power capable of doing it: the power of the law.'

Lieutenant Ingram hadn't been attending too closely up to now because he routinely studied, as part of his job, the statistics that Darrow had been presenting. There wasn't anyone in Troop E who didn't know that drivers were mostly to blame for accidents, though the man from the Federal Council on Traffic Safety had pointed it up quite graphically. Ingram was watching him now because he'd started to talk business.

'You all know that policing a highway is, in the final analysis, a personal matter. However specific the regulations may be, their interpretation has to be made by human beings. And it's accepted practice that the trooper dealing with a case should make due allowances for any aspects of the situation that might count in the citizen's favour: an anxious mother, speeding so that she can reach the school in time to fetch her children before they wander off somewhere, is different from a youngster speeding in his muscle-car so that his girl-friend will think he's a he-man.'

His glance moved sharply across their faces. 'To be brief, the policy of my campaign is to treat *all* cases the same, and *every* case as serious. If a mother is late getting to school it just means she didn't allow enough time, and does that mean she has the right to risk other people's lives as well as her own? I don't have to give you further illustrations.' Unfolding his arms he began hitting a fist into the palm of his hand with a slow rhythm. 'The rest of today, and all of tomorrow and Sunday, we're going to pull a driver down for the slightest breach of the regulations, we're going to impress on him the fact that even the slightest breach of the regulations is a serious matter since they were drawn up with the intention of protecting human life itself and we're going to force him to recognize the gravity of his responsibilities when he takes the wheel of his automobile. You men have the power of the law in your hands. This weekend I want you to use it.'

Outside the building as the remaining patrol cars heeled on their springs in a tight turn and headed for the roadway one after the other, Captain Darrow stood for a moment by his personal transport and looked at Ingram steadily, his eyes bright in the shadow of his cap.

'I arrived here at a busy time, Lieutenant, and I can see that my visit created problems for you. Just the same I think you should be told that I consider your general attitude obstructive to an extent constituting a defiance of authority and that I shall be making an appropriate report to Captain Westover of Troop E Headquarters, subject to which I shall expect disciplinary action to be taken.'

He turned and climbed into his car.

CHAPTER FIVE

In the heat of the long summer afternoon a mistake was made and there wasn't time to correct it because human reaction was too slow and the next second the situation became irreversible as a wheel spun and glass smashed and paint flaked away and someone screamed.

All cars – all cars. This is a Signal 11.

Sixty miles per hour doesn't seem to be a high speed when everything is normal: you can lean back and use one hand and light a cigarette and talk and when you get bored you can switch on the radio and try all the stations.

. . . soft, shining, and with a lustre that streams from your brush in a starry cascade . . . Spun Gold . . . Spun Gold Shampoo . . . created for you . . .

Only when something goes wrong are you brought to realize how fast you are moving at a mile per minute but there's no time to think about what you are learning too quickly and too late, because there's a rocking motion and the scene dips as the brakes bite and then the world goes wild and great forces rise to hurl you bodily through tumult and you know that this is not you any longer, the you to whom nothing could happen, nothing terrible, nothing so unimaginably terrible as this.

Barnegat puts it at somewhere below Interchange 74 southbound – the driver's report was pretty vague but there doesn't seem any doubt there's been an accident. Is there anyone near?

A lock of gold hair on the ground, its curled tip losing its sheen as from somewhere oil drips from the dark broken sky.

Is there anyone near?

Tailing a speeder in the fast lane northbound Cooper pulled the left-hand mike from its clip and spoke into it.

71 to Base. Yes, I'm at Milepost 73 northbound and I can make a U-turn and get down south into the area you're talking about.

Do that and keep in touch.

Cooper clipped the mike back and checked the tachometer again at a steady sixty-seven and decided not to disturb the situation. If he used his siren or the PA speaker the driver ahead of him would start slowing and he'd have to slow with him.

71 to Base.

Go ahead, 71.

I have a speeder in my sights but I don't want to waste time pulling him down right now. Light-blue Cadillac sedan New York registered AZC-3298 at present heading north from Milepost 73. Okay?

Okay, we'll pick him up.

Cooper operated his left-hand turn indicators and began slowing for the special police and maintenance track, one of the many that connected the twin roadways across the medial strip. Halfway along it he got his siren going and as soon as he reached the southbound road he knew the report of an accident was probably true because the traffic was already building up in both lanes and he had to prise open a gangway to reach the opposite shoulder and ride it southwards. In a mile and a half he was cruising past stationary traffic and could now see what looked like an overturned house trailer and two other vehicles blocking both lanes.

This is 71. It looks like we need a wrecker.

The Chevrolet Mirabelle convertible was in the right lane

and still rolling. The girl in the green jumpsuit was sitting more upright now in the middle of the rear seat, the slip-stream sometimes moving her corn-coloured hair. Her hands were stretched out on each side of her to hold the door grips, as if she were going at a hundred miles an hour, or a thousand, as these silently-flying horses bore green Mirabelle, Goddess of Chariots, to far Delphi where she would ask by whose grace she had been granted this much overwhelming joy.

It was, as of course she knew, mostly Daddy's grace, and a little of Mr Marcellino's because he was the dealer who'd delivered this long low silver-grey miracle to their home, going away smiling with his polished shoes and his parting in the middle and the down-payment cheque. She hadn't believed it when she'd seen it standing there where the old beat-up model had stood for as long, almost, as she could remember.

Now she was riding in it through the coppery haze and the green rushing of trees, Mirabelle the Mirabulous in her silvered coach, serene as a swan upon water. In those rare moments when she instinctively judged that any increased excitement would not occasion actual fever, she reminded herself that in fact she wasn't going to anywhere as dull as Delphi, but to the City of Atlantis, known by the mortals as Atlantic City. She had never ever been there, because up till six months ago it had been much too far from Cincinnati; but now they lived in New York this dream had become possible, and today, on this day now, it was coming true. Of all the coloured postcards she had seen of Atlantic City, the one she had framed and put on her wall revealed it as being entirely composed of alabaster castles piled at the edge of ivory sands, so it was her secret and very reasonable conviction that one day a great wave had rolled from the deeps and washed the fabled city of Atlantis on to the New Jersey Shore.

As she sat picturing those many-windowed towers she was aware that her escort of chariots had begun slowing all around her, and she opened her eyes. And as if it were not enough that she was today journeying in a miraculous automobile to a miraculous place, the star under which she was born chose this moment to throw off another spark. Just possibly there were additional factors involved, since it has been established that in a healthy young girl of fifteen the various glands, hormones and related systems reach a state of quite inspired chemistry, upsetting the delicate balance of heart and soul to a psychedelic degree.

But chance alone occasioned that as the girl in the green jumpsuit opened her eyes at this instant the first thing she saw was the mustard-yellow sports car nearby, and inside it the boy in the straw fedora.

Brett Hagen had got out of his Riviera and was standing on the front bumper, but he couldn't see anything more than vague shapes. The two lines of automobiles reached far into the distance, their colours shimmering through the heat-haze.

He was walking around to keep his impatience down when he saw the back of the girl's head, the one in the muscle-car. Her hair was dressed in a pony-tail that shook as she turned her head quickly, talking to the driver, and that was exactly how Tracy looked from behind.

He couldn't believe his luck but was in no mood to appreciate it; the thing was how to talk to her now he'd located her. She was a minor, of course, but he and Linda had never abused their legal authority: it was part of the whole idea that Tracy should be allowed to develop according to her natural instincts. Whatever he said, it wouldn't have to take long because it sounded like a police siren and the road could be cleared any time.

Could we talk a little? Would your friend mind pulling on to the shoulder a minute? I'd like to say something to you alone.

The muscle-car was three ahead in the other lane and as he crossed to it he reflected that it was exactly the type of automobile a fifty-year-old roué would choose as a means of enticing impressionable girls. From side-view he looked younger to Brett than he'd imagined but it was difficult to see because of the glare bouncing from the paintwork. The passenger's window was down and he looked in at her.

'Tracy.'

She swung the pony-tail and looked up at him with surprised eyes and Tracy vanished.

'I beg your pardon,' he said, 'I thought you were someone I knew.'

On his way back to the Buick his embarrassment increased the resentment, as if it were Tracy's fault that she wasn't the girl in the muscle-car. But so many other things were her fault – or he was consciously prepared to believe they were, because he'd been driving for hours through the heat and the glare and the carbon monoxide and now he was caught in a jam more than halfway to Wildwood and too far from the Hausner Clinic in White Plains to be of any help if his patient finally went into irreversible adrenal failure.

Listening to the siren approaching from the north, he decided there were two ways of creating a worthless citizen and one of them was to discipline your child and make darn sure it grew up to be the shining paragon you'd always dreamed of, even if it finished up too scared to make a move or speak a word without your say-so; and the other was to smother your child with love and attention so that it quit home just to breathe some healthy fresh air in a world where it could get a kick out of making decisions.

Trick or Treat. Make it tough for them or make it soft. But he and Linda had believed they were among the few people who'd worked this whole thing out and found the middle way: the way to create a happy human being as well as a worthy citizen. You had to show your child that she had all the love and affection she could ever want and that she could tap it for herself just when she felt in need of it; and you had to show her there were no strings, that she didn't have to grow up in your own image, but in her own.

There was one additional requirement without which such a relationship couldn't work: and that was mutual trust.

The siren was coming close and he reached inside the Riviera for his bag, making his way between the other cars to the roadside.

He believed that Tracy had let them both down by breaking their mutual trust. Normally she told them where she was going for the weekend, and with whom. This time she hadn't, because she'd known they'd feel concern. And he couldn't see it was anyone's fault but her own.

He walked on to shoulder and stood in the middle with the bag held up, watching the black-and-yellow patrol car slowing, the note of its siren dying away. Then he stepped aside and waited till it drew abreast of him.

'You a physician?' the trooper asked.

'That's right. You might need me down there.'

'Sure might. Jump in. Did you lock your car?'

'There's nothing of any value.'

The trooper got the siren going again as he increased speed along the shoulder.

71 to Base.

Hear you, 71.

I have a doctor on board.

At 3.15 p.m. the traffic flow between Mileposts 70 and 80 had been running in the 3,000 vehicles-per-hour sector and within ten minutes of the accident on southbound there were something in the region of five hundred automobiles, buses, station-wagons and boat-trailers standing immobilized in the humid heat of mid-afternoon. Each minute a further fifty vehicles became piled against the ends of the two stationary lines, building up towards the Forked River Fuel and Food area at Milepost 76.

By 3.27 p.m. the traffic on the southbound exit ramp at Interchange 74 was blocked by a wall of vehicles and the toll station went out of action.

71 reporting to Base.

Go ahead, 71.

We have a collision accident at Milepost 73.2 southbound involving two autos and a house-trailer. One auto and the trailer are lying on their sides blocking both lanes and the shoulder. The second auto has ploughed across the median without much damage. Hear me?

Hear you.

I have a doctor working here but we need a Rescue Squad unit and we need that wrecker, soonest.

Wrecker 150 is on his way. Condition of the injured?

Three persons, two with shock and abrasions and we're checking for broken limbs. The third's pretty bad. Get to me fast, Harry.

250 to State Police Ocean Point. I'm being blocked by northbound congestion, making maybe thirty miles per hour up towards Milepost 72.5. Can you fix me an escort?

73 to Base: this is Lieutenant Ingram. Did you call a First Aid Squad ambulance?

Affirmative, sir. Ocean Point Number Two is already on the Parkway.

Very good. I'm now standing by at the U-turn waiting to escort the wrecker southbound. Order 75 to proceed to the accident location and 76 to patrol the build-up towards the Service Area and warn approaching traffic.

Walt Amberton stood neatly framed in the centre of the tinted windshield, his back to her.

Carol had chosen to stay in the car and now she watched him and thought how instinctively he conveyed his image, and how handsome he was. He was handsome in whatever he wore, because he dressed with the care of a man whose job it is to sell things by creating an aura around them, and the image he felt was suitable to Walt Amberton's particular features was perfectly conveyed by the white linen ducks and deck-shoes, the magenta shirt with the Thai silk scarf tucked casually at the throat, the gold-link bracelet with his name and blood-group engraved on it to denote the man of action whose life he occasionally elected to risk on the track or in his private aeroplane, the even tan deriving from weekends on board his ten-metre international-class yacht on the Sound, the pensive stance hinting at the thinker behind the sportsman.

Talent, training, instinct or just mere habit had produced this image of Walt Amberton, not vanity. He had long ago stopped caring what people thought of him, Carol knew, because it could never be worse than what he thought of himself.

PUBELLA – for his eyes only . . .

He tapped a Stuyvesant on his gold case and flicked the tooled electronic lighter, his fingers shaking enough for him to notice, and to be afraid. The loss of nervous control didn't tally with the image, and that was his final refuge.

'It's an all-timer,' Roy had said. At the vice-presidential level they were still resisting but Roy had quietly made the copyright registration in Washington, telling nobody but Walt. It was Calvin who'd come out to head the hard-core opposition and yesterday Walt had got burned up.

'Listen Calvin, while the rest of Madison's using the sex image as if it were a new breakthrough in human dynamics and pushing it clean across every barrier the Puritans built with their own living bodies, will you tell me why we have to advertise underwear for women as if it were something they tuck under a bustle?'

In the brand name suggested, Calvin told him, the illusion was a fraction too direct. In his opinion.

Walt had noted this down as one of Calvin's classic contradictions in terms. There was nothing anyway that broke new ground in the Pubella copy: he'd used the sex image for every single concept since he'd joined Breen and Logan and already this year they were making a hit in the prelims with the first automobile created as a female, the Venus 1000 – *lithe, compliant, trembling under your touch* – a direct appeal to men's need to dominate. Was it so far out to use the sex image for panties?

'It's just,' Calvin had said, 'that I don't believe we should go so far as to introduce the male element into the traditional female scene. I'm not sure how the Women's Lib would see it.'

'For God's sake, Women's Lib went out with Hot Pants. And we did the same thing in reverse with the Venus 1000, introducing the female element into a traditionally male scene – and it's breaking high.'

Calvin had wanted the message spelled out a little more to minimize the risk of ambiguity and Walt had gone halfway with him on that, keeping the copy short. *Let's not deny a natural truth: hygiene is only one function of underwear, or why would we make it so pretty? Pubella – for his eyes only . . .*

Walt drew the smoke in, shivering in the hot sun. There'd been a time when he'd had enough confidence to persist with an image until they saw what it had, but now he had too many doubts and too often: at a kick-around session on Venus one of the younger account-execs had come right out and said it was 'too damn corny even for kids', and Walt had been shaken for a time. He'd have to get this whole thing off his mind at least for the weekend: it had been crowding him too long, trapping him.

But the only other thing he could think about was the beast on his back; there didn't seem room any more for thoughts of ordinary things. He was already involved, just by switching off the Pubella problem, and could see the manager's indifferent eyes again, the lady isn't hurt? His indifferent eyes and the way he stood with his hands behind his back, a little bored, a little affronted, there's a liquor store not far off the Parkway, able to say it, to handle effortlessly the concept of a liquor store with the rows of coloured glass and decorative labels and the bubble gliding as the bottle was laid on the tissue paper, able to say it and then forget it the next instant because for him a liquor store didn't mean the descent from Calvary.

It hadn't been planned. He'd suddenly found himself asking the bastard, whining in front of him with no more pride than a skid-row bum and being watched as he walked away, denied. There'd been no stratagem beforehand: he'd deliberately left the flask at the office because this was a good chance to start pulling out – it would be difficult anyway to use the flask on the drive down to the shore with Carol right next to him in the car. He hadn't meant to stop off at the restaurant.

But suddenly the whole scene had kind of slipped and while they'd been sitting in a traffic jam at Interchange 11 he couldn't think of anything else but unscrewing the top and tilting it so he had to get somewhere private, and he said he needed film and then he was in the men's room in a cubicle hitting his pockets with the flat of his hands and starting to laugh in an odd way because it seemed just too ridiculous to forget he'd left the flask in the office.

I swear there wasn't any kind of stratagem, only about the film and that isn't important. A lot of them have to use subterfuge but I'm not like them, not that bad, I can pull out, I swear to Christ I can.

He was sweating and shivering at the same time and the sun was beginning to pulse and he shut his eyes and listened to the shouting in his head demanding a drink and the quieter and less effective prayer that of this minute he should never want a drink again, ever again.

A siren sounded and he turned, flicking the ash from his cigarette and lifting a hand to see that the scarf was correctly tucked in. A series of emergency lights were moving from the north above the roofs of the stationary cars and soon a highway patrol came past leading a breakdown rig and an ambulance. Near him a woman pressed her hands to her ears as the siren passed close.

'Must be pretty bad down there,' somebody said.

Carol had taken a Virginia Slim and lit it when she'd seen Walt open the gold case. It didn't have anything to do with togetherness at a distance; it was a conditioned reflex. The togetherness they'd once had was just something faded in an album.

He looked so confident standing out there, just in the way he lit the cigarette, just in the way he stood. Walt was a professional image-maker and his own was perfect. That ought to have been a good advertisement for himself but it wasn't.

'Almost everyone is negative on Pubella,' Roy had told her, 'and he needs support from somewhere. That's why I've made a copyright registration in Washington. If they throw this one out I want him to feel it was a majority vote, not a unanimous rejection. He's sort of –' Roy had looked at her with the decision leaping suddenly into his mind, the decision to put things right smack on the line, and she could remember steeling herself. 'He needs help, Carol. And he needs it soon. Do you know what I'm talking about?'

'Yes. I do.'

'Okay then. I'll do what I can at the office. You don't have to feel alone. It's Walt that feels alone, you know that? Have you –' he hesitated again – 'seen anyone about this?'

'The essential preliminary,' Dr Pabst had told her, 'is to persuade him to admit it. Once you can do that, we can start bringing the situation into the open, and that will make it possible to propose treatment. And of course you are the most suitable person, Mrs Amberton, to approach him.'

'I don't think you understand how withdrawn he's become, Doctor, how terribly isolated. I can't –'

'Oh yes, I understand. There's a big field for study in this country, with six million known cases. Your husband is passing through the characteristic phase of guilt and self-revilement that automatically cuts him off from the contact of his family, friends and associates. He can't bring himself to face them, you see. But that's an obstacle you'll need to deal with just as soon as you can find the courage, because until he can be brought to admit his difficulty we can do nothing to help him. Absolutely nothing.'

A siren sounded and Walt turned and she closed her eyes

in case he thought she was watching him deliberately. He hated that.

Why are you watching me?

I wasn't, darling.

You were, damn it to hell!

I was just – just thinking how handsome you look in your –

Don't give me that.

And always he would go away, slamming his book shut and finding another room, or throwing it down and going out to the car while she waited nerveless and cold for the sound of the motor starting up. It had happened so often that it was as if they'd agreed to play the scene over, for their private amusement. And all she could see on the dark ceiling above her bed, when she knew he wouldn't be home till morning, was his face with its hunted eyes darting everywhere to avoid hers. She had come to learn something that others would have been quicker to see: that his greatest fear was that she would find out about him. And if he saw that this had happened, he would go and never come back.

She was the most suitable person to approach him, and the only one who didn't dare.

The weight of the house-trailer had pulled the convertible side-on to the roadway and there was oil pooling below the buckled fender as one of the wreckers prised at the bent hitch and snapped the ball-joint apart while the other manoeuvred the emergency truck to bring the crane into position halfway along the chassis where the grab could find a purchase and the load was approximately balanced.

Lieutenant Ingram to Base.

Hear you, sir.

The wrecker is now on the scene and working. I estimate a maximum of five minutes' further delay for the left-hand traffic lane and ten for the right-hand lane. Advise toll stations on the entrance ramps at Interchange 74 and order all patrols to reassure motorists whenever the opportunity arises.

The late-model sedan was turning slowly across the median strip with clumps of turf falling away from the tyres. On the north side of the overturned vehicle Patrolman Cooper was protecting the scene as people from the waiting traffic lines formed a group and tried to crowd in. It was to help the patrolman deal with this situation that Ingram had ordered Car 75 to proceed to the accident location a few minutes ago.

'I think that's all I can do right now.'

Brett Hagen started putting the anaesthetic kit into his bag, dodging aside as someone called out and the crane-hook swung past him. One of the ambulance co-drivers helped to gather his instruments, a patch of blood drying on her neat white coveralls.

'Are there any specific orders, Doctor?'

'Will you be riding with the patient?'

'Yes.'

'Keep him in this position during transportation and use the Trilene inhaler again if necessary. Do you have nursing qualifications?'

'I'm a Red Cross trained paramedic.'

'You did very well just now.'

Diesel gas clouded up as the wrecker manoeuvred closer under the load and the cable quivered taut. Lieutenant Ingram was coming across from Car 73.

'Are you blocked in, Debby?'

She nodded, squatting at the ambulance doorway. 'How long will it be?'

'Less than a minute.'

The house-trailer began dragging its metal panelling across the pavement as the breakdown vehicle crept forward.

'Frank, which is it best to do, go north to 74 and meet traffic snarls or south to Exit 69? It's longer but there's a completely clear road.'

'Go south and through Waretown.'

'Okay.' She squinted up at him against the glare. 'Are you all right, Frank?'

'Something blew up at the station.'

'Name of Darrow?'

'Is it on the grapevine already?'

'I called Sam with a message for you.'

'What did he say?'

She turned her head to check the patient for a moment, then looked back at Frank. 'You know Sam. The less he says, the more you know there's trouble.' She was still squatting easily at the tailboard, small and athletic-looking in her coveralls, but Frank saw that the brightness hadn't gone from her eyes. In three years with the Ocean Point First Aid Squad she'd never quite got over her queasiness at the sight of blood, though it didn't stop her from handling the worst cases with perfect efficiency.

'What was the message, Debby?'

'Huh? Oh, just that Vince was an angel and fetched the groceries and your shoes and the laundry so you can come straight on home tonight. What time will it be?'

'It depends how people drive.'

'They're driving like lunatics so you just come right on home anyhow.'

Metal screamed on concrete and the diesel was gunning up as the trailer swung in a half-circle round the six-ton hoist. A man with a fire-extinguisher ducked under the boom to the other side. Frank heard Trooper Hunt arriving in Car 75 and went across to the doctor, who was snapping his bag shut.

'How far's your car, Doc?'

'About a mile.'

'We'll take you there.' They walked through light debris to 75. 'Where did the other two patients go?'

'Back to their car – they were in the Plymouth. All they need is a drugstore now.'

Frank spoke to Hunt through the window.

'Take this gentleman back up the road and check his car's still okay, and give me the PA mike.'

'Right here, sir.'

The left lane will be clear in less than one minute so will you please go back to your cars and be ready to continue your journey. The right-hand lane will be open to traffic soon afterwards. Thank you – and please drive carefully.

He gave the mike back to Hunt. 'As soon as you've finished your mission get right down here and assist Cooper to re-establish the flow with no shunting.'

He crossed over to the gap where the wrecker team had cleared the shattered safety glass from the roadway. The rig had now dragged the trailer free of the tow-car and there was enough room for the left-hand lane to go through.

'You're on your way, Debby. Take care.'

He swung the doors shut and the ambulance heeled softly in a close turn and gathered speed. For a half-minute he stood blocking the gap, his back to the piled traffic. The scene in front of him was rare even in winter: a lone vehicle speeding down the deserted perspective of the Parkway where on this Fourth of July weekend the two-lane flow was normally hitting three thousand per hour at this time in the afternoon.

The white Cadillac with the red cross grew small, and when he judged it had gained sufficient head-start to reach Exit 69 before the traffic could catch up he turned and gave Cooper the signal.

'I don't think it's an accident.'

Nat Renatus said it to himself though he said it aloud. His face was squeezed into fine lines as he stared through the windshield of the two-tone Newport at the split file of traffic extending down the Parkway. He jerked his half-used cigarette out of the window and lit the next; he didn't often finish a smoke because his fingers gripped them too tight and it cut off the air and he couldn't stop holding them like that because it was a nervous reaction.

'Sure it's an accident,' Rod Gould said.

'It's a police check.' The smoke fluttered out on his breath. He could hear another siren and his guts contracted and sweat came and it sickened him because he liked to be clean. 'Oh Christ, the bastards. Oh Christ.' He whispered it but Rod Gould heard.

'We'll call Toni from the next restaurant,' he said slowly. 'This time I'll talk. I'll fix it so he gets us the boat and then we're in the clear.' The knife went stabbing into him again and he blocked his breath and made no sound because if Nat heard he'd start in rapping about finding a medic and they didn't have time for that, they had to reach Cape May. When the knife came out again he said: 'But he only gets half the sugar.'

Renatus watched the people getting out of their cars and trying to see what was going on down there ahead and he wanted to get out too but he didn't know what he could do if he saw it was a police check. They were blocked in and they couldn't turn without hitting against the other cars and going across the grass strip and some bastard would go down there and tip off the cops and that'd be curtains.

'Toni wants it all. He said.'

'Sure. Only he don't get it. See the diff'rence?'

The knife cut again and he made a sound and Nat jerked a look at him and opened his mouth and couldn't think of any words because suddenly all he could think of was Rod dying and he didn't want Rod to die. He was a kind of father.

'Are you – does it hurt bad? Rod? Rod?'

'It's okay.' Between his teeth.

'We should'a' got that medic! We should'a' –'

'Lay off.' He got his breath and swung his heavy head with his eyes focusing on Nat: 'For Christ sake get a grip, will you?'

'Okay. Okay.'

Rod's anger steadied him and he pushed the door open.

'Where you going?'

'Wash.'

Nat leaned in to press the button and then held his hands against the windshield jets as they started spurting. He pressed the button three times and then wiped his hands on the duster in the glove-pocket, smelling his fingers to smell how clean they were while Rod Gould watched him and knew he'd always be this way from here on, trying to wash the smell of Nolan off.

Because Nat had a conscience. He wasn't a cop-hater like some of them and he hadn't shot that cop because he hated him, but because he'd been trying to block their run and Nat had panicked. Rod had told the Istanbul-Naples outfit they oughtn't to let him in but they said he could be useful and they'd been wrong because Nat had come close to blowing the whole fix. He'd never been born for the big-time and now he was in it nation-wide and it was going to kill him like it had killed others. Because if you had a conscience you made mistakes.

'I'm goin' to ask somebody,' Nat said and bunched the damp rag back into the glove-compartment, 'if it's an accident.'

'Get back in this car. I told you: this trip we don't talk to anybody.'

You made mistakes.

'Sue, are you too hot?'

'Of course I'm too hot.'

She sat with her hands over her stomach and he wished she wouldn't. He knew she was waiting to feel something again. *Hoping* to feel it.

'Well, listen, we better try and back up and make it to the shoulder and go on driving to create a draught, or you'll –'

'Most everybody's too hot, Floyd.' Her smile shimmered at him but it didn't have any effect; he went on darkly brooding. She didn't mind; it made him look handsomer than ever. 'It's the heat.'

He drooped his young and hairy and very handsome hands over the wheel and she admired him doing it.

'I sure wish you wouldn't keep trying to feel him like that, Sue.' He couldn't any longer watch her.

'But it gives me a thrill.'

'It scares the pants off me, honest.'

'I know.' She laid her head of glossy black hair against his shoulder. 'You must try to be brave.'

'It's *you* I'm thinking of, Sue! I mean he shouldn't be – be kicking as hard as that three whole weeks before it – before you – oh God, I mean suppose there's something technical we don't know about like a cellular tissue defect or something and he *kicks right through* –'

'Floyd,' she said crisply against his shoulder, 'I am a perfectly healthy clinically-tested Western Hemispherian female of the species and I have categorically *no* cellular tissue defects. I'd like you to feel reassured on that point at least.'

It came again and she quickly took his hand and put it on her middle but he snatched it away in alarm.

'Did he kick you, Floyd? Oh Curly, how can you act so unsociable! Three weeks from now I'm going to ask you to apologize, with your very first breath.'

'I don't see how you can *joke* about it, Sue.'

'It's just a desperate attempt to stave off the onset of stark terror.' She said something more but Floyd couldn't hear because three emergency vehicles were riding past them down the shoulder of the road, the first of them with its siren going. Last in the line went an ambulance and Floyd felt a measure of relief because all the time they were far distant from a hospital an ambulance was the sole chance for them if anything happened. He'd trained himself to look for the red cross whenever they were on the highway and by now he reckoned he could spot one instinctively if it were anywhere within range.

'At least the emergency services on the Parkway are really on the ball,' he said with relief.

'I doubt Curly and I will need a wrecking truck.'

'I meant the ambulance.'

'Oh I see.'

Many people were still standing on the bumpers of their cars, while others had climbed to sit on the roofs with a folded newspaper to protect them from the heat of the metal. Nobody talked very much, except now and then to complain about the hold-up.

'Is this the best they can do? We have to be in Cape May before five o'clock.'

'Can't they let us go through in single file?'

'Say, this heat's a killer, ain't it?'

They leaned forward, craning their necks, their motionless bodies inclined towards the south as if their headlong pace of a few minutes ago still lingered in them, so that it seemed that they were being denied something even more desirable than the fresh sea breeze and the liberating sands that were their acknowledged goal. Motion itself had been halted; celebrating together the ritual of speed for the sake of speed their worship had been interrupted, and they felt a sense of loss.

Those of them who had stayed in their cars had switched on the radio, wanting to know what was happening in the real world, where life had not stopped.

. . . the WOR weather centre forecast. The heat continues, with temperatures ranging in the high nineties almost everywhere except in certain shore areas. Since last night a high-pressure system has become virtually motionless along the coast and far across New Jersey, causing high air-pollution levels . . .

. . . statement by the Commissioner reveals that for the moment there's been no new development in the hunt for the slayers of Officer John Nolan, although the police-laboratory

processing of evidential traces is reported as 'fruitful' so far. 'With the degree of intensive effort now being made by every member of the Department,' he told reporters an hour ago, 'the outcome is certain. Wherever those men are now, we will find them. This I promise you.'

. . . and our phone-number's still the same – Plaza nine, one thousand, and we're here until four o'clock this afternoon. I'd just like to tell you that Al Woodsby makes the David Cross scene the entertaining place to be tonight at eight-thirty. Get with Channel 5 for television like you like it. And the number is Plaza . . .

'Hey Barney!'

'Huh?'

'They're moving, down there. Look.'

'Think so?'

'The left lane.'

'You're right, they're rolling.'

'Better get back in the car.'

Frank took the mike from the facia board of Car 73.

73 to Base.

Hear you, sir.

We're rolling.

Both lanes?

Both lanes.

Yes, sir, I'll inform plazas.

73 out.

He stood behind the patrol car watching the left-hand file getting into its stride and the right lane still picking up speed, shunting a little as some of the drivers slowed to look at the wreckage.

Somebody hadn't checked his driving-mirror.

Things smashed inside the house-trailer as the rig hauled it back past the point of disbalance and it settled on its wheels, rocking to stillness.

The consistent declaration by the witnesses Frank had questioned was that the Plymouth had been at fault. A composite statement would read: *The Plymouth pulled out to pass the house-trailer just when the white sedan was itself shaping up to overtake. So the Plymouth hit the trailer as it tried to pull back into the right-hand lane.*

Wheels rolled. Faces turned to watch the breakdown rig as the traffic flowed past. Frank stood waving them on: it wasn't uncommon for rear-end collisions to occur soon after an accident, as people slowed to rubber-neck.

If the driver, then, of the Plymouth had just looked in his mirror before pulling out to pass, he would have seen the white sedan and given it precedence.

He should survive, with intensive care. The doc had obviously been a top man in his profession, the way he'd gone to work. *But I don't think he'll walk again.*

Wheels rolled and the thousand-vehicle block drew out gradually to reach a 50-60 m.p.h. flow along the Milepost 70 to Milepost 80 sector and the breakdown rig moved steadily down the shoulder. The residue of the glass fragments glinted on the road-surface where the careening metal had gouged dark lines, and the soft green turf of the median carried heavy scoring.

Frank got back into his car and started up, for a moment watching the right-hand traffic flow as it assumed normal speed.

Drive carefully. And use your mirrors. We're not asking much.

CHAPTER SIX

At a few minutes before four o'clock a black Cadillac sedan approached Milepost 73.2 southbound and began slowing.

Mr Solo checked his mirror, pulled over to the right-hand lane and ran on to the shoulder, braking to a halt. Hitting the release-button of his restraint harness he got out and walked back along the roadside until he came to the marks he had seen.

This had been something quite serious: the bituminized concrete was heavily scored for thirty or forty yards and the sand patches meant there had been oil spilled, indicating that one or more cars had turned over. On the other side of the twin lanes he could see the grass and earth gouged from the medial strip where a vehicle had gone in.

He stood perfectly still, a short upright figure with hands behind and feet neatly together. Then his head began moving from left to right as he reconstructed the scene from the marks left as evidence. Judging from the degree to which the sand had been displaced by the traffic, and from the speed of its flow (there would have been a jam reaching towards Forked River, with an accident this important), he thought the emergency services would have cleared the site perhaps twenty minutes ago.

People in the cars going past saw Mr Solo standing there in the heat of the afternoon, though they didn't know his name: they just saw a small man with smoked glasses and a black tie standing by the roadway some distance from his car, doing nothing. Certain of them may have felt this to be odd of him, because it was unlawful to park on the shoulder unless there were something wrong with the motor or you were out of gas, things like that. There should be a reason.

Dust flew against the dark lenses and Mr Solo's clerical-grey coat flapped as some of the cars passed near. They distressed him a little, the cars, their colour and their noise distracting him. He wanted to be alone with the marks of what had happened here, right here where he stood.

He had never in his life arrived first at the scene of a smash. There were always the police and rescue squads and rubber-necks in the way, spoiling everything. Someday he must arrive there first. Once there had been a collision between two autos up on Route 9 near Peekskill and he'd been there before anybody else, but the drivers and their passengers had all climbed out with only a few bruises, and that wasn't the same thing. Nobody had been killed.

Today he had missed the one at Interchange 11, and the one later to which the ambulance had been – the ambulance he'd seen from the Howard Johnson's; now he had missed this one by maybe twenty minutes. It made him despair of ever being there, of ever being there first. These were not thoughts, exactly, in his head; they were feelings, shadows.

He turned and walked back to his Cadillac.

At Barnegat Toll Plaza some of the cars slowed through the correct change lanes, their drivers throwing quarters in, while others pulled up alongside the collectors.

'Can you break this?'

Mike Kehoe looked down from his booth.

'Surely.' It was a five-spot.

'When did the accident happen?'

'Hold on a while.' Mike was busy counting the change twice. Couple of weeks back he'd made a blooper, given a guy too much. You had to make up deficits out of your own pay. 'Four. And seventy-five.'

'Thank you. When did it happen?'

'Huh?'

'The accident, up the road.'

'Oh. Maybe forty-five minutes ago, a bit more.'

'Was it bad?'

'Huh?' Mike looked down at the black glass stare. 'I dunno, exactly. Had to call the rescue squad in. I guess it was bad.'

'Was there anybody killed?'

Mike tried to judge from the man's face what could be making him ask things like that. You couldn't ever tell what people were thinking when they were hid behind their sunglasses. And besides he'd already said he didn't know much about it so how would he know if anyone got killed?

'You want to know, particular?'

The guy could be some kind of official, with a polished black Caddy and all.

'No. I just wondered.'

'Uh-huh.' There was another car coming into the lane. 'Have a good day.' It was what you said to them when they seemed to want to hang around and there was others in the queue.

'Is it straight on for Ocean Point Police Barracks?'

'Nope. You overshot. Go right along down to Exit 63A and head to Manahawkin an' go left up through Barnegat to Forked River, north all the time. Then you get back on to the Parkway at Entrance 80 an' pick up the signs, okay?'

'Thank you. I missed it by quite a bit.'

'That's right.'

The lawn smelt of cut grass.

Debby eased the big Number 2 ambulance through the gates and turned, leaving it to face the road.

'Did you mow the lawn, Vince?'

He nodded from the open window of his den.

She walked close to the trimmed edge on her way in, to let him know she appreciated it. 'Looks great.' He didn't often do it without being asked. And he'd fetched the groceries and everything too, Frank's shoes and the laundry.

'Was it a mess?' Vince asked.

He frowned at his mother against the up-glare from the driveway. She'd been called out six times already today, though four were just cardiacs: it was 98 degrees on the barometer-thermometer in the back yard.

'Not so bad.'

She tugged the zip of her white coveralls as she went into the house. She always said 'not so bad' and they both knew that. She'd said it last year when there'd been a seven-car pile-up at Milepost 60 with three dead and all Ocean Point's ambulances shuttling between the accident scene and the hospital.

When she'd showered she put on a pair of tennis shorts and a tee-shirt because if there were another call she could slip the coveralls over them and stay cool, or at least below actual melting point. By the time she was in the kitchen putting the groceries away she felt okay again, about the way he'd bled.

'Vince?'

'Yeah?'

'Who're the cookies for?'

He came into the kitchen and leaned at the door with his hands in his pockets.

'Anybody who likes them, I guess.'

Debby looked long-suffering at him. 'And I guess that's mostly you.' She took Frank's shoes from the bottom of the bag, seeing at once they weren't actually his: the repairer had made a mistake. She decided not to say anything or Vince would go shooting off to the shops again: for some reason it seemed to be his day for being Boy Scout.

Watching his mother, Vince thought – as sometimes he did – that he was lucky to have such young parents. Danny used to ask him who the chick was in his car when he and Mom rode down to the store together Saturdays, till Danny got to recognize her. It must be real crummy to have a pair of hag-toothed Methuselahs around the place, though maybe at seventeen that would be exceptional anyway.

'They're the only thing that can keep a guy sane,' he said reasonably, 'with all that other krud everywhere.'

'What are?' She was checking the laundry bill.

'Cookies.'

'What other krud?' They'd charged for delivery 'by mistake' again.

'Well, hell, all that polyunsaturated sunflower oil and sugarless banana extract and corngerm and the rest of the whim-wham crowding the fridge out.'

'It's banana essence and wheatgerm and they both helped to make you a big strong handsome young man, so you don't have to –'

'I'd consider sometimes being an anaemic dwarf if it meant I could lash out at a Knickerbocker Glory now and then.' He looked out the window again. 'Is Dad coming home tonight?'

'If he can. And if he can't then I think I'll just go fetch him.' She put the bill with the others and remembered and pulled it out again because she'd have to point out the 'error'.

'Is he overworking?'

'Doesn't he always?' She put a stack of towels on to his arms. 'Where's Danny?'

'I'm watching for him to come by. He wants to show me the new Venus.'

'Well, don't let him talk you into driving it, Vince, and keep off the Parkway anyhow – it's murder this weekend.'

'Yeah. These for the top cupboard?'

'All except the big one: that's for the bathroom. Thanks, sweetheart.'

'Anything for you, lady.'

She watched him cross to the stairs, smiling because he'd picked that up from Frank, calling her 'lady' sometimes and for no reason except to show affection. Vince had picked a lot of things up from Frank, which was perfectly natural; and she didn't have to be kidding when she called him big and strong and handsome, because he was all those things, almost as tall as Frank but not yet so handsome or so rugged-looking in that understated Steve McQueen way.

'Are you eating home tonight, Vince?'

'It depends what Danny's doing, is that okay?'

'Sure, and anyhow it won't be anything hot.'

'And anyhow,' he turned and grinned lopsidedly above the

stack of towels, 'there's always the cookies if I get desperate.'

Heading southbound towards the Forked River Food and Fuel Service Area the blue fastback Mustang was moving in the fifty to fifty-five m.p.h. sector along the left-hand lane when Sergeant Sam Gillespie in the unmarked Car 70 came up on its tail and kept pace for a half-mile before he took the mike and used the public address system out front.

Police. Pull over.

Sam was ready with his brakes: they always slowed at once when they heard their doom announced and you had to be sure not to run into their tailgate. Both cars rolled to a halt on the shoulder and Sam got out and walked towards the fastback, noting its number as he went.

He'd been sweating all day from every pore in his two-hundred-and-ten-pound frame and the holiday weekend drivers were doing everything except actually looping the loop and he was currently needled by the thought that unless he could keep Lieutenant Ingram and Captain Darrow apart like you'd keep two mad dogs apart his peaceful life was going to turn into an all-channels four-colour mirage, but just the same he resisted the very attractive idea of pulling his Colt and drilling both rear tyres and the gas tank just to introduce himself.

Because the least they could do was read.

'Did you see that sign back there?'

'Which one?'

Sam and Trooper Hunt had passed a quiet hour during the February 1969 snowstorm when business was slow on the Parkway playing a game you had to win by getting one of three answers correct. It had already been established by Troop E statisticians that there were only three classic answers ever given by the motoring public when it was asked if it had seen that sign back there: (1) What sign? (2) Which one? (3) Back where?

She was a which-oner.

And also quite a beaut, right out of the social register.

'It said Keep Right,' Sam told her. 'Keep Right and Pass Left. You'll see a lot of them wherever you go, on the Parkway.'

'I'm sorry, Officer. I didn't notice any.'

She didn't smile. Most of her mind was on something else

though she was trying not to show it. She was trying to look attentive.

'Aside from the fact it's against the law to stay in the left-hand lane when there's room on your right, it makes a lot of sense. We get a good many accidents, some of them pretty nasty, just that way.' He looked down at her smooth honey-tanned amethyst-eyed face and knew this was what they called at Ocean Point a lost cause. Every once in a while you'd pull someone in and find there was absolutely nothing you could do as of then on: they hadn't been flagrantly breaking a law and they weren't smart-assing back at you so you couldn't give them a ticket and you couldn't get sore because they were doing their best to listen even though they obviously had something a darn sight more important on their minds than road-signs they hadn't ever seen. So you just kept on talking in the bare hope something would get through and stick. 'The normal rule of the road is to keep right, so if you hug that left lane it's going to make other drivers pass on the wrong side – breaking a good habit – and that means you've got an accident situation nice and set up. Another thing is if you want to stop for any urgent reason, say your motor heats up or you run out of gas, you have to get across to the shoulder just as fast as you can, so if you're already riding the right-hand lane you can do it without endangering yourself or anyone else. Makes sense?'

She nodded up at him, the glare of the sky in her eyes contracting the pupils and enlarging the irises, accentuating her quiet-tiger look.

'I should have worked it out for myself.'

She still didn't smile. Or couldn't. He'd have thought she was maybe on tranquillizers except she looked the kind of woman who'd have a healthy respect for her central nervous system.

'Everyone should,' Sam said. 'But sometimes there's other things on our minds. Thing is, we won't any of us beat our problems by unsafe driving techniques. So do me a favour and read the signs, okay? For your own sake. And have a nice weekend.'

Going back to board 70, he figured the problem about designing and enforcing civil laws was that people were human and it was no good thinking they were robots. Too, you had to teach them that if they respected the laws it'd be to their advantage, and that wasn't too easy to do. Put up a sign reading *Keep Right to Collect $100 at Next Toll Plaza* and you'd have to employ extra staff to cut down the weeds on the left-hand lane.

Watching the powder-blue Mustang heading towards the Citgo station in the Food and Fuel Service Area he wondered what sign would mean most to Tiger Eyes. *Come on Home and We'll Make it Up?* He thought it was something like that.

But it was a shame they wouldn't read the kind of signs that could keep them out of trouble, even save their lives. The signs on the Parkway cost on the average a hundred and fifty bucks each, around five bucks a square foot to make and install, and the Parkway Authority picked up the check. And a whole lot of thinking went into them – sizes, colours, shapes, wording, positioning and the rest. They were designed to the standards of the Manual on Uniform Traffic Control Devices for Streets and Highways issued by the US Bureau of Public Roads and they were posted in laboriously-selected clear-view areas and were spaced apart as much as possible so drivers didn't get the impression they had to read through the whole of the Bible before they could sort out the Commandments. But for all the notice people took of them you wondered how much difference it'd make if you turned them back to front.

So how could you treat these drivers? It seemed nobody'd found out, as yet. Starting the motor of 70, he tried to remember exactly what Captain Darrow had told them at the base earlier today. It'd been something about forcing the motoring public – Sam recalled that word 'forcing' very clearly – to recognize the gravity of their responsibilities, and about the police using the full power of the law, by which terms Sam figured he should have given the girl in that Mustang a citation that would have sent her to court. And if that was what Captain Darrow had meant, Sam thought the best thing would be for Captain Darrow to go screw himself.

He wanted to run.

She was still staring at him through the driver's window of the Mustang with that cold-eyed who-the-hell-are-you kind of look and for a minute it had him almost scared because he didn't understand it.

He stood there in his blue jeans and sweat-shirt with his thumb still hooked in the air and his mouth open a little, wanting to run but holding his ground because she couldn't force him to get into her car if he didn't want. Everything had suddenly flipped: he'd stood here quite a while already, just clear of the Citgo station exit where the gas-pump jockeys hadn't any right to make him go away, and nobody'd taken him on board because they didn't have room or thought he might have a knife or they were leery of lone students, and there'd been no kids here filling up because they couldn't afford gas, leastways if they were like him they couldn't. And suddenly he was standing here rooted and staring right into this phantasmagorically beautiful face with its ice-blue eyes casting a spell on him so he couldn't move.

'Where are you heading for?'

He didn't answer. You can't talk when you've just been turned into glass. The motor of her car was slow-running and he listened to it consciously, comforted by the idea of valves and bearings and dirty old oil splashing around: it made the whole situation seem nearer the ground.

'You can get in.'

She snapped the door open and it felt like being sucked into a gigantic vortex because the more he tried to turn and run the more he found himself pitching into the car. Without actually meaning to do it he shut the door after him and sat back and thought: Jesus, you'll have to help me now.

The blue fastback merged with the Parkway traffic in a controlled burst of acceleration that reminded him instantly of the time when he was five years old and had climbed on to his very first roller-coaster and hit the long roaring stomach-dropping plunge with a yell you'd have heard in Denver. He believed he must be yelling right now; it was just that he couldn't hear himself because he'd gone deaf with fright.

'Where are you heading?'

'Who me? Heading? Well, I, gee, I, you mean where am I atchally heading?'

He was clean out of breath already and he'd not even said. It was the king-size zillion-horsepower kick of actually *talking* to her, *communicating* with her, that had dragged out of him what he was ready to believe was his last breath.

'Are you all right?'

She turned her head and he would've jelled into instant glass again if it hadn't been she was looking at him differently now. She only seemed like a merely phantasmagorically beautiful woman instead of some kind of psychedelic witch. And it occurred to him, as effortlessly as if he possessed untapped sources of wisdom, that she'd stared at him like that before because she'd been scared of him, or scared of what she'd suddenly decided to do, give a lift to a weekending student who could have a knife on him or a home-made bomb or a pants-pocketful of pot.

'Sure I'm all right.'

'What's your name?'

'Russ Carnaby. What's yours?'

She didn't answer. She was shifting into high and checking the mirror, easing across into the fast left lane, and he leaned his bright straw head back against the padded rest and took a long sideways look at her. He'd never been shut in a car with a girl so gorgeous and now she'd stopped turning him into glass he wanted to sit here and watch her till the gas ran out and the great thing about that was that she'd only just filled up at the Citgo station. Actually she wasn't a girl, she was a woman, but what the heck did that mean? If they looked like this, what did it matter how old they were?

'I want to forget it,' she said.

'Huh?'

'My name.'

'Forget it?' He leaned away from the headrest.

He thought she was purposely trying to confuse him or make him ask more questions but that was okay, it gave him the excuse to go on looking at her while they talked.

'Where are you heading, Russ?'

'Wildwood.'

She nodded.

Her blue scarf was tugged sometimes by the slipstream but it didn't seem to bother her any. He watched her slim honey-gold hands quiet on the wheel, the angle of her legs as her feet rested on the pedal and the floorboard, soft blue casual shoes, moccasins, kind of, exactly matching her dress, her brown legs slim like her hands and her bare arms, so he wished he could see her walk some time, her skirt swinging, her soft shoes neatly and rhythmically placed, as he felt he knew they would be. He wished he could know more about her.

'What makes you want,' he asked, 'to forget your name?'

71 to Base.

Go 'head 71.

You got my NCIC still cooking?

Cooper watched the Mercury while he waited. There were two men in it. They weren't moving fast and they were in the right-hand lane and if everybody drove like this guy was driving it'd be a great weekend for everybody, the men of Troop E included. But they were still looking for the bastards who'd rubbed out that New York cop and according to the latest reports from HQ there was a chance they were riding the Parkway south.

I just got a negative on your NCIC. Negative.

Okay and thanks for nothing.

Cooper clipped the mike back and played around with the idea of pulling them in anyway and checking the ownership but there was absolutely nothing suspicious about them and he was coming up on an auto parked on the shoulder near Milepost 65.7 and he'd have to give it a routine check so he began slowing and let the Mercury go.

The auto at the roadside was a dark green E-type Jaguar with the top down, New York registered, a couple inside sitting hitched around in their seats to face each other. On his way across from 71 Cooper thought they were two kids but when he got closer he saw the man's hair was light grey, not blond as it had looked from the distance. As the patrolman came alongside the girl swung her head to glance up at him, her pony-tail flying out and her brown eyes for an instant scared-looking. Cooper was taking in details automatically: the man wasn't looking scared, just annoyed, though he was trying not to show it; though he must be nudging fifty his face still had a lot of tautness in it and he looked like a guy with a private gym and a competent masseur and a diet-sheet that'd keep him going till the girls stopped tiring first – then he'd be good and shot.

This one could be his daughter but she wasn't. The man's hand was still resting against the top of her spine and the tail of chestnut hair had swung to lie across his wrist.

'You folks aimin' to stay long?'

'We're just talking.' The man squinted up at him against the sunshine.

'Guess you'll have to move off.' Cooper talked to the man but watched the girl: which one was she scared of, the State Trooper or the aging Lothario? Hard to tell. 'Okay if you feel tired an' need some rest, but not just to talk. There's a Picnic Area a few miles along, at Stafford Forge.'

The girl was looking down now and Cooper couldn't see her eyes any more but her fingers were nervous and she sat with a lot of tension in her attitude. He didn't think she was scared of him, of his sudden appearance; for girls this age there were normally two kinds of State Trooper, the kind they looked over and made a play for and the kind they looked over and didn't.

'All right, Officer.'

The man didn't move, or reach for the starter. That was okay with Cooper – the guy wasn't expected to jump to it like he was in the army. It was the girl he was still concerned about: if they'd been just a couple of kids hassling he'd have left them to it providing they did it someplace else, but this guy was more than twice her age and she'd looked scared over something and was still sitting tense. Cases like this weren't ever easy for a patrolman to decide on – and you couldn't win, either way. The public was going to say the damn cops were always poking their noses into private affairs, or if the girl was found in those bushes over there raped and strangled the public was going to say why couldn't the damn cops have done something about it.

'Everything okay with you, miss?'

He'd said it quietly and she looked up with her brown eyes very wide. Still not easy to tell: was she on the point of opening up and asking for help, or just surprised he should have asked her such a question?

'Yes.' She gave a little nod and he almost missed what she said, her voice was so small. 'Everything's perfectly okay.'

When the patrolman had gone she went on sitting absolutely still, her head down and her fingers laced and pressed together so tightly that there were white patches.

'Is it really?'

She swung her head as he spoke.

'What was that?'

She'd been thinking of something a long way off.

'Is everything perfectly okay?'

'I don't know, Earl.'

He lifted one eyebrow, quizzing her in silence. Watching him she knew it was nothing to do with him that had given her this feeling of sudden fright, this special kind of fright that small kids felt in a crowded supermarket when just for a minute they couldn't see their mother anywhere, the one long agonizing minute when every face was strange and the whole world was suddenly unfamiliar. The feeling of being lost. It had come over her during the past half-hour as the road unrolled in front of her: the feeling she was going too far, too fast. But it was more than that, and there were questions too horrible to think about without losing touch completely: *Too far from where? Too far from what?* Because there has to be some kind of base you can start out from. Some kind of home.

'Why don't you leave it to me, Tracy?'

She nodded quickly. 'Yes.'

He stroked the nape of her neck for a moment, the warmth of her chestnut pony-tail lying across his wrist as he watched her with his slightly-hooded eyes, her profile in repose now, almost, her young mouth tender and the down glowing on her child's-smooth cheek as the sunlight struck through the windshield, refracting.

She felt its heat, and the different warmth of his fingers at her nape, their movement making her drowsy as if he knew that she should sleep now she was sure that everything was perfectly okay. Earl was like that, giving her confidence just when she felt suddenly lost; it was almost the first thing she'd ever heard him say, three weeks ago at the party when some crazy speed-freaks had tried to make her use a needle. 'Leave it to me.' And a few days after, when she got to feeling so low she'd almost called Hotline because there wasn't anybody else she could think of, she'd had the idea of dialling the number Earl had given her, not expecting to find him home but finding him there, as if from over the distances he'd known she needed him and had flown there by the power of magic.

'Earl?'

'Yes, Tracy.'

To know her voice like that, just from saying his name . . .

to know she needed him . . . there hadn't been anyone like this before.

And twice since then, taking him her problems. 'Why don't you leave it to me? I'll think things through.' His strong fingers caressing her neck, the way they were now, till she felt it wouldn't ever matter if he didn't think things through because the problems had melted away, and all that mattered was that Earl was here, and she was safe.

He moved and she opened her eyes and saw his other hand go to the wheel-rim, the strong hairs on it bleached by the sun, the dark veins showing underneath. The motor began throbbing and he used the gear-shift, giving her his faint crinkly kind of smile to mean hello, and don't worry, leave everything to me. Then they were rolling on to the mainline of the Parkway and he looked back to where the patrolman was waving him on, keeping the right lane free till they got up speed.

'It was nice of you to stop.'

All she'd said was that she was feeling kind of lost again, and he'd pulled right over so they could talk without the wind rushing past. How many men would do that; on the fingers of a thousand hands, how many?

He wasn't this way with the other girls, she knew. Some of her friends had even told her. *A weekend with Earl Fallon? Oh God, you want to get eaten alive?* Judy had just given a strange kind of laugh: *You know what you're doing, sweetheart – or do you?* Lorraine hadn't laughed; she'd been positively shocked, not saying a word till she'd thought it out slowly to get it right: *Tracy, I want to tell you something. If you spend just one night with Earl I won't ever speak to you again.*

Coming south from New York every mile had begun sort of drawing something out of her, leaving her wide open to the feeling, the old feeling she hated so much and sometimes so desperately, of being lost; and she'd heard their voices again, watching his strong hands on the wheel – *you want to get eaten alive?* – and not wanting to think of all the other girls they'd touched, caressed and maybe even hurt – *just one night* – until she'd known she must call Hotline at the next service area, because Daddy would be busy at the Clinic in White Plains and Mother didn't like being called weekdays at the Health Spa and anyway what could they do? She needed the people at Hotline to help her. Or Earl.

Earl himself. Will you please tell me, do you like hurting when you make love, I mean really hurting? Because I don't. I want to trust you to be gentle with me, Earl, but people have said things about you, and only you can put me right.

Then it had happened again, like maybe she'd known it would. She'd only had to tell him she needed him, that she was feeling lost, and he'd pulled off the road where they could talk, where he could move his steady fingers at her neck, making her sleepy; and the stupid panicky questions had melted away before she could bring herself to ask them.

The officious young patrolman had startled her, appearing from nowhere like that and showing her how jumpy her nerves had been getting.

'Okay, Tracy?'

He spoke into the rushing wind but she heard and turned to see him looking down at her with his faint and rather watchful smile.

'Okay, Earl.'

She didn't feel lost any more.

She laid her head against his shoulder and closed her eyes. The others had been stupid, not knowing how to trust him enough, how to trust him with everything. To live in the haven that was Earl Fallon you had to have the courage to give yourself into his hands, wholly; and this she was prepared to do.

The pearl-finish Lincoln-Mercury Cougar was keeping to the fast lane along the medial strip and sometimes when it used its horn it antagonized other drivers, and a mile back a mustard-yellow sports car had put on speed instead of moving over and the Cougar had gone on blaring with its horn until it gave way, the driver shouting something as the bigger car had gone past at seventy miles per hour.

Carol had closed her eyes then.

Could you slow down please, Walt?

She didn't actually say it aloud: there'd be no point. It was like a prayer in her mind, repeated. If she asked him aloud he wouldn't slow; she would only heighten the tension in him, and the danger to them both.

With the seat-belt tight against her body she fretted with a broken fingernail. She didn't remember when or where it had broken; she'd been quietly tearing at it since Walt had moved into the fast lane and begun forcing the other drivers to pull over.

Walt, could you slow, please?

But she knew that he could not, mentally or physically, slow down, however hard she prayed, because somewhere in their precarious and clouded future together there was a bar counter they had never seen but would see very soon and upon it there would be a liquid-yellowed shot glass and when Walt saw it he would lower his head for a moment and shut his eyes, holding the edge of the bar with his knuckles white as for this little time he made the gesture, as a sop to his own soul, of refusing to acknowledge the dominion of the yellowed glass over what was left of him as a man. Then his will would break and he would take the glass and toss the liquor back and push the glass away and draw a long shivering breath that meant that something in him had come alive again, the beast that would one day kill them both.

Carol wouldn't actually be there. She'd be waiting in the car for him, parked out of sight of the bar. He'd be buying some film. Or a paper. Or gas for his lighter. But she would see the bar in her mind's eye, as she had seen the one in their own home a month ago when the dining-hatch had been open and he hadn't heard her in the kitchen. It had been then, seeing his haste and the small driven gestures that had conveyed the sense of ritual, of his submission to an impersonal master, that she had known what had become of Walt Amberton; and only luck had decreed that he shouldn't turn and see her there, staring through the open hatchway, unable to move. She had tried to move, but had been unable. It was a kind of momentary paralysis.

The blue-green grass of the median rushed alongside and she watched it, her eyes half-closed. He passed close to the cars that moved out of his way and some of them swerved, thinking they'd touch. She knew that this was acting-out behaviour: after two crashes in the past year he refused to wear a seat-belt even when he was driving like this.

It wasn't of course at all certain that there would be the bar, somewhere in their unpredictable future, with the yellow glass on it. At this speed and with this self-challenging style of driving, life wasn't guaranteed to go on. But even if nothing happened, other things surely would. He needs help, Roy had told her, I'll do what I can at the office. But Roy couldn't stop him being fired when Calvin's patience finally broke. Everyone was 'negative' on the Pubella copy and it only needed someone to realize why the legendary Walt Amberton was losing his flair for him to be thrown on the heap. On Madison they'd had plenty enough practice recognizing the symptoms.

At home they were recognized even more easily because he could let the façade slip, easing the strain. The children had known before she had: kids were more sensitive, more attuned to reality. They'd started telephoning Fridays from college, saying they couldn't get home this weekend because of their studies, I kind of feel this exam's going to beat me if I don't apply myself, can you understand that, Mom? Of course, honey, but you have to relax sometimes, so how about next weekend?

They always called Fridays, out of kindness, pretending there'd been a chance all week of getting home and maybe bringing friends.

The Ford pulled over but didn't slow and both cars kept side by side for what seemed a long time and the needle showed seventy-two and it was obvious the Ford was having some fun, racing them, seeing how fast Walt was prepared to go if he were challenged. It wasn't a very high speed, though it was over the legal limit; but with Walt driving it was dangerous. Their system is never free of it, Dr Pabst had said with his studied clinical smile, so even when they don't appear to be under its influence their judgement is often critically impaired. You should persuade him to drive at a sensible speed, Mrs Amberton. And of course, even more important, in fact most important of all, you must persuade him to admit his situation. Then we can really start work.

So what're you staring at?

I wasn't, Walt, I was just –

Is there something strange about my face, for Christ's sake, I got smut on my nose or something? I've had a hell of a day, okay? And I need a drink, okay?

Do it this weekend. Today. Don't miss this grand opportunity. Away from home, from familiar surroundings, just the two of us, where we can say what we like to each other. Be brave, Mrs Amberton, yes Dr Pabst, I'll tell Walt I know about him, I'll stand there and tell him and watch him bring his head down slowly like he does in front of the yellow glass, bring his once-fine head low while I stand there as the representative of all the humiliation any man can be asked to withstand. Because I have to be the last person, Dr Pabst, the very last person in the world to find out about him. The rest don't count. He doesn't love them. He loves me.

Overflying Milepost 40 the Pan-Am plane altered course and settled into its approach path for Philadelphia and from the open mustard-yellow sports car the boy in the straw fedora watched it for a time and then looked into the vanity-mirror again and saw the Chevrolet was still there in the right-hand lane about six cars back. The mirror was on the sun-visor and he'd swung the visor down a few minutes ago, thinking of the mirror, and of the silver-grey Chevrolet convertible. His father had looked across to see why he'd put the visor down, because the sun was well over to the right, but hadn't said anything, maybe knowing kids liked to monkey with everything in reach till they were old enough to get that wheel in their hands.

The boy began whistling again, watching the mirror, whistling silently, taking time off to contemplate life in general and the way those big planes came in so low you wanted to take a photograph every time and the way she'd looked, the girl in the Chevrolet Mirabelle.

She'd looked okay. Nothing kind of sensational, you wouldn't sort of ever walk smack into a tree or anything because you were looking back.

'We turn off soon, Dad, couple of miles on.'

'Sure, I caught the sign.'

Plenty of girls around with that kind of hair, bright sort of blonde but natural, but there'd been something different about hers. The way it sort of framed her face, and blew in the wind. There was maybe something in common with people who liked open cars, kind of affinity, blow your mind better in a convertible.

Anyway there she was and there she'd go. He and Dad were turning off at 38A so what the hell. There'd be plenty others on the shore. Not with that kind of way she wore her hair but hair didn't add up to everything. Blew in the wind.

'D'you need that thing down?'

'How's that again, Dad?'

The wind was noisy.

'You want that visor down like that?'

'Huh? Not really. But there's kind of a glare. You want I should put it –'

'It's okay like it is.'

The way she sat, with her bare arms and the green jump-suit, her bare arms spread out like she was kind of sailing along on wings, her hair blowing. Not even pretty.

Not even pretty, not really.

Dodge. The Polara Brougham four-door hardtop, quite a nice line and she'd be hard to catch. Philly registration. There wasn't too much change this year, they'd switched the grille horizontally and put wide centre bars and she had ventless side-window treatment, but nice, be okay if Dad ever got a hang-up on one of those buggies. The way the tailgate sort of spanned the wheels, the wide look, blowing in the wind, though not pretty, still there, five or six cars behind.

'You take Exit 38A, Dad, didja know?'

'Sure, I got the sign.'

Kids really liked navigating, telling you what you had to do. As if you never managed before they were born.

Ford XL, a thin-pillared four-door, they're okay too.

Dad had his turn indicator going. He was always too early with it. People thought you'd forgotten to cancel it.

They slowed and began turning and he swung the visor up and tipped his straw fedora over his eyes, fare thee well my fairy fey, in your Mirabelle Chevrolet.

'D'you think Mom'll be there already?'

'Should be. Aunt Phyllis too.'

Oh holy cow. He'd forgotten Aunt Phyllis was going to be there, with her pince-nez and fan teeth and indigestion tablets. It'd mean keeping *Playboy* under the mattress like last time. Holy cow.

Someone had braked too hard for the exit turn off the Parkway and he tipped his straw fedora back and looked over the tail but there wasn't an accident, it was just the noise of the tyres.

'Well, gee!'

'What happened?'

'Huh? Nothing. They missed.'

But gee, it was curving down the exit ramp, the Mirabelle,

turning off just like they had. Heading for Atlantic City. Her light soft hair blowing, you'd have to be a real dumb jerk not to make a note of that number.

You must never have everything you want. It would be bad for you. Miracles are especially indigestible and should not be taken one on top of another, though of course if they just come your way there's nothing you can do except start right in licking the cream off the top first.

Today she had been granted two wishes: that she should ride under the summer sky with the whole world in her arms to love and to be in love with, and that she should be thus carried, Mirabelle, Goddess of Chariots, to the City of Atlantis, washed from the ocean's deep to the New Jersey shore. That was quite enough. It would be perfectly acceptable if the mustard-yellow sports car went straight on past the exit and she never saw it again. It would be good for her, in fact, and help build her character, not to have three miracles in the same day.

She shut her eyes, because forcing herself to watch the sports car disappear forever would be too much, and she didn't want the strain of an overbuilt character. Yet when she opened them, very soon, and not meaning to, really, she saw that the little yellow car was turning off and heading for Atlantic City, despite all her strenuous wishes to the contrary.

She felt the feverishness coming, and decided that if she weren't to faint she must view the matter coldly and logically, and admit categorically that today it had been granted her that she should ride in a miraculous automobile to a fabled citadel whose castles were alabaster, her knightly escort the one mortal she had chosen among all others: the boy in the straw fedora.

71 to Base. I need an Olds towed. Can I call up 250?

Sam Gillespie was alone in the office, sitting by the radio console and watching the sun go down towards Lakeside.

75 to Base. Barnegat wants your okay on the lane-closing as of midnight. Will you refer to orders?

The sun was dipping against the black-silhouetted treetops, and Sam wondered, as sometimes he did, why the darn thing didn't catch the whole of the earth on fire, it looked so big and so close.

74 to Base. I'm tailing a drunk, Milepost 77 northbound.

Sam watched the trees turn into flames that spread across half the horizon while he okay'd the wrecker call to 250 and confirmed Clause 4 of the RE-25285 All Stations Order from HQ and told 74 to grab that drunk before he had time to do any damage.

For a couple of minutes there was radio silence and Sam leaned his bulk back in the console chair and watched the last of the day going as the blaze along the horizon spread and began dying, streaking the sky with yellow and gold before the twilight came down. Somewhere among the beeches a blackbird sang, piping clearly above the background roar of the traffic just beyond.

So what did we do today?

Sam looked at the drift of papers that had been steadily snowing-up the desk since dawn: the documented histories of flats, gas-outs, fanbelts and steamers; animal incidents and stolen property; vehicle accidents, toll violations, drinking drivers and arrests – the statistical summaries and patrol activity sheets that made up the evidence that today Troop E had been riding the Garden State Parkway and helped a lot of people and booked a lot of others and tried to keep the two-way flows of massed vacation traffic moving below saturation point and above everything else to keep people from being hurt and getting killed.

The boys were still out there doing it and when they came in the night crews would take over and headlights would go sweeping past the knoll of dark beeches along the southbound road. And by morning the pile of reports on the desk would be thicker.

The phone rang and Sam took it.

'Ocean Point, Sergeant Gillespie.'

'This is Captain Westover. Is Lieutenant Ingram there?'

'Not right now, sir. He went off home an hour ago at six-thirty-five to eat and said he'll be back by eight o'clock to check in before he drives south to supervise patrols.'

'Ask him to call me.'

'Yes, sir.'

Sam cradled the phone with his great forehead puckered.

He wouldn't be here when the Lieutenant took over the reports and that was okay by him because it sounded like HQ aimed to give Frankie a bawling out and he didn't want to be here and watch his face go set the way it sometimes did when he was deciding when the most effective time would be for him to blow his stack. And when he did it, Sam didn't want to be here either.

Car 74 slid past the windows and Trooper Levy came in with a stumpy guy in a Hawaiian shirt who hit the corner of the desk with his leg as he came in and stood cursing while Levy stayed close in case he looked like busting the place up.

Sam opened a drawer and got the breathalyzer.

'How was he driving, Levy?'

'Erratically, Sergeant. I tailed him about a mile before I pulled him in.'

'What other indications?'

'Slurred speech, odour on the breath, uncertain movements.'

'Uh-huh. What reactions?'

Before the trooper could answer him the man raised his head and hollered at them. 'Will you two guys quit talkin' about me like I was dead or sumpin'?' He stood with his feet braced apart and his short thick arms folded to show he could stand up without anything to hang on to. 'You think just because a guy's had a few drinks he ain't in any fit state to communi – communicate wi' the rest o' the goddam world?' He pushed his round red face forward and glowered at Sam. 'What'n th' hell's that thing you got there, buster?'

'It's a breath-test balloon. All you have to do is –'

The man threw his head back in a cackling laugh. 'Listen, baby, this is a summer weekend, right? The time when all good men an' true get th' hell outa their daily round o' dull routine, so I fix up with a buddy o' mine for a fishin' trip an' this mornin' my wife's mother gets taken sick an' believe me she's never kiddin' 'cause that ole fatso's got an appetite bigger'n a pregnant pig's, so what happened to my fishin' trip? Go on, ask me what happened!'

Patiently Sam said: 'What happened?'

'Don't rush me, I'm tryin' to tell you. It bites the dust an' I've spent the rest o' the day washin' last night's dishes single-handed an' cleanin' out th' parrot cage an' amusin' the kids on my hands an' knees with my ass in the air 'cause today it's bustin' broncos an' I finally finish up with you two guys tellin' me to blow in a goddam balloon! You call this Independence Day?'

Sam came round the console. 'It won't take a minute. All you do is –'

'Quit crowdin' me, will ya?' He mopped at sweat and leaned back against a filing cabinet. 'You think I'm nuts or sumpin'? I give one breath into that goddam thing an' it goes right up in flames an' I get a two-year suspen – suspended licence an' a five-hundred-buck fine an' what's th' sense in that?'

Sam went back and put the balloon away and got out the yellow form. 'You refuse to submit to the breath alcohol determination test?'

'Why sure I do!' He leaned away from the filing cabinet and looked around the office. 'Hey, you guys got any strong black coffee to help a fallen wayfarer back on his feet?'

As Trooper Levy went over to the machine Sam came round the console and stood in front of the man, reading aloud from the form:

'I have reason to believe that you have operated a motor vehicle in violation of section 39: 4-50 of the New Jersey statutes and I have placed you under arrest for violation of this drinking-driving law. I request you submit to the taking of samples of your breath for the purpose of making chemical tests to determine the content of alcohol in your blood. A record of this test will –'

'What say we skip all that crap, huh?'

'Levy,' Sam said without looking up from the yellow form, 'he don't get his coffee till I'm through with this, okay?' His bullfrog tones kept up the recital. 'A record of this test will be made and a copy given to you when the test is completed. In addition, you may have a person or physician of your own choosing take samples of your breath, blood or urine. No test will be taken from you forcibly or against physical –'

'An' you better not try it, baby –'

'Physical resistance. If you refuse to submit to the test, a report will be forwarded to the Director of Motor Vehicles which may result in loss of your driving privileges for a period of six months. Now – will you submit to the breath test?'

'Are you kiddin'? Which would you rather have, a six-month suspension or two years an' a heavy fine?'

'Answer "yes" or "no".'

'No! You want me to spell it?' He took the cup from Levy. 'Is this good an' strong? I got to pick up the wife at –'.

'You better start now,' Sam said, 'if it's a long walk.'

'How's that again?'

'You won't be driving your car for a few hours yet.'

'Who's goin' to stop me, buster?'

'I am.'

'Uh-huh.' The man took a long swig at his coffee and looked again at the massive Gillespie. 'You mind if I call my wife?'

Ten minutes after Levy had gone back on patrol with orders to drop the man off at a bus stop Car 71 slowed past the windows and Cooper came into the office, throwing his cap on a chair and fixing himself a cup of iced water and gulping it down.

'They're nuts out there. They're loco.' He wiped sweat away from his face and got more water from the machine. 'If they're not nuts or loco they're drunk or they can't drive, and if they can drive they don't want to. What made me join this outfit? What made *you* join it, Sarge?'

'My sweet old mother. She said it was this or the Foreign Legion.'

Cooper slid into a chair and loosened his necktie and Sam threw him a cigarette. Cooper was one of his top patrolmen.

'Where's Ambrose?'

'Checked in a while ago. You're off the hook.'

'An' no complaints.' Cooper lit up.

'They ain't professionals, Coop. They ain't specialists. They don't spend their whole lives thinking how to keep the highway safe for human locomotion.'

'Sometimes I kind of wish I didn't.'

The chair creaked under Sam's mass but he went on tilting it back till he was looking along his great jutting nose at the jaded trooper.

'What are you beefin' about? You're just makin' life tough for yourself. Listen, baby, people who drive automobiles ain't omnipotent or omniscient or totally rational or they wouldn't drive automobiles anyway, they'd get the hell out and go hole up on a pollution-free Pacific island. You should play this whole situation the way I do, Coop. I don't expect *any* son of a gun out there to act like they had any sense, so when someone drives with their brain I get a real pleasant surprise. Okay, it don't happen too often, but what d'you expect? They been sweating their guts out in the city and they're hittin' those wide open spaces like they ain't seen a blade of grass in years. Or they just quit their job or they're overweight or their girl's run out on them or they're just plain bushed an' the only kick they got is to send that Chevvy down our Parkway till she damn near takes off. An' you expect them to behave like a bunch of brainwashed robots, so if anyone's nuts it's you.'

Wheels sounded again and he swung the chair so he could look out of the east window but it was twilight out there and he couldn't see which car it was. It must have rolled into one of the bays lower down. He swung back to look at the trooper, whose eyes were now shut and whose expression told Sam two things: that he was good and listening but that right now he was in no mood to hear anything in defence of the driving habits of Joe Public on a Fourth of July weekend.

Sam's bullfrog voice started vibrating again in the quiet office. 'You wanna get wised up. Treat 'em rough when they're stoned or mean or they smart-ass around but when you can see they're just actin' human, give 'em the break they need. Be their father and their friend and lead them gently by their trembling hand, rock 'em on your all-forgivin' lap an' croon them to sleep. That way they'll co-operate with you. Play it that way and one day you'll be a sooper-doopa trooper, Trooper Cooper.'

He got out of the chair because he'd heard a car door slam and nobody had come across to the office. Schultz was about due in but he would've parked farther up, near the gasoline pump. Sam liked to know what people were doing.

'It ain't how Captain Darrow sees it,' Cooper said.

'It ain't? Gee, that's a real darn shame.'

Sam went out and stood on the steps and automatically checked the traffic situation as the flow streamed southwards beyond the knoll of beeches. There were the gaps to be expected at this hour: since five this evening the travel and delay chart had brought the line dipping into the two thousand v.p.h. sector, sixty m.p.h. and no delays.

There'd been two cars in the parking lot – his own and Cooper's – and now he noticed a third: a black private Cadillac.

Facing straight out from the steps he didn't see the short grey-suited figure till it was almost beside him.

'Good evening.'

Sam swung his head.

'My name is Solo.'

'It's what?'

'Mr Solo.'

Soon after nine o'clock the first headlamps came on, turning the twilight abruptly into night. Others followed, until there was a constant flickering among the trees.

Later still, the moon, in its third quarter, began floating in the coppery haze; and towards midnight the string of lamps threading along the highway grew thin as people turned in that direction, where the moon was. They were the late-comers, the last of the multitude who today had made their migration, instinctively seeking the cool of the ocean where their life, aeons before, had begun.

As the procession moved from the highway, and the town-ships along the coast became thronged, it seemed as if a host of lanterns had been carried from the hinterland to blaze at the sea's edge.

Book *II*

SATURDAY, JULY FOURTH

CHAPTER SEVEN

It was noon when Frank Ingram swung Car 73 past the gates on Marina Drive and backed up past the lawn to park alongside the ambulance in the shade of the tamarisk.

And by this evening we expect shore temperatures to hit ninety-eight degrees, highest on a Fourth of July since 1966. Humidity is already better than seventy-five and is forecast to –

Frank cut the switch and climbed out, throwing his cap on to the driver's seat.

'You look cute up there.'

Debby was in tennis shorts perched on top of the huge white special-series Cadillac, a wash-leather in her hand. Where the water had puddled on the concrete there were her bare footprints, and Frank felt touched, seeing them. They were a child's, small and with the toes clearly defined, reminding him of what Debby had always remained: a highly intelligent and sometimes unpredictable child who in twenty years had driven him beyond patience less often than she had delighted him, enchanted him and on two occasions led him from desolation, her small hand firm in his.

'I'm kind of stuck.'

He caught her as she dropped. Kissing her hello, he felt the tension in her body.

'Tough one?'

'M'mm.'

It was only to Vince that she always said 'Not so bad'. She and Frank were in much the same business.

'Tell me.'

It would make her feel better. He'd been off the air for the past hour, inspecting a proposed sign-cluster site below New Gretna, so he'd missed this one.

'Just a kid fell out of a car.' She squeezed the wash-leather and hung it inside the garage. 'She'll be okay in a couple months, but Frank –' she spread her hands in sudden appeal – 'will you tell me why people who are incapable of keeping their own child safely inside a car are allowed to drive a car at all, allowed to *possess* one? Just what would be their IQ, to the nearest zero?'

He knew there'd been blood at the scene; a kid didn't hit the roadway from a moving car without tearing a whole lot of skin off anyway. The Rescue Squad superintendent had once told Debby, in Frank's hearing, 'If you're hypersensitive to the sight of blood I don't quite understand why you're so keen to stay with this unit, Mrs Ingram, or indeed why you ever joined it.' There'd been a seven-car pile-up at Milepost 60 with three dead, and when the last of the Ocean Point ambulances had reached the hospital Debby had needed to spend a couple of minutes with her head between her knees. 'I'm perfectly all right now, and I should like you to know that I joined this unit because I wanted to do something useful in life and I'm keen to stay in it because I'm the best damn driver-paramedic in the whole team and you know it so let's just talk about something else. If I ever cave in while the action's on you won't have to fire me – I'll quit.'

'Accidents can happen,' said Frank.

He put his arm round her, leading her towards the porch.

'You say they're always caused.'

'I mean where there's kids. You can't always control them – right?'

She knew what he meant. When Vince had been fourteen, only three years back, he'd ridden his brand-new bike right down to Cape May on Thanksgiving Day, not telling them he was going because he'd known they wouldn't have let him. He'd been missing two days and they'd been certain he was dead, with the bike gone from the garage and everything, and the strain of waiting for news.

'Frank, this kid was actually in his parents' car, where they could have controlled him. There are door locks and safety harness, aren't there?'

'Sure. And there are weekends when it's so darn hot and there's so much traffic that you get kind of human – and careless.'

'Shop,' she said, 'my fault.'

They'd long ago made a pact never to 'talk shop' when they

could avoid it, during pressure periods. They didn't often manage.

'Who cut the grass?'

'Vince, yesterday.'

Frank had been too tired, last night, to notice.

'And he fetched the groceries too?'

She smiled up at him. 'You think he's got low in gas?'

'Or something. Did he have his generator checked?'

'He hasn't said.'

'I told him to ask Mr McTigue.'

'Then that's what he probably did.' The door pulsed shut behind them against the air-conditioning seals. 'Can you handle a seafood salad?'

She perched on the high stool in the kitchen while he ate in the breakfast booth. She wasn't hungry: the emergency call had come in less than an hour ago. Watching him for a minute, she thought he'd never looked so beat, and when he'd finished eating she was going to nag him good and hard because he thought he could stay on his feet twenty-four hours a day and he couldn't, not even Frank. And he thought it was his duty to try, and it wasn't.

'How's Mike holding up,' he asked her as he forked his salad, 'did you get to hear?'

'He's fine. I called him.'

Mike Kehoe was one of the collectors at Barnegat Toll Plaza, a senior citizen part-timer not long out of hospital after a prostate operation. He'd been the driver of the cab, twenty years ago, that had taken them both from St Anne's in Ocean Point to their wedding breakfast.

'How long a break do you have, Frank?'

'A half-hour.'

'You'll need extra time. I'm going to nag the daylights out of you before you leave, so enjoy that lovingly-prepared salad while you can.'

She left him, not wanting to see him eat so fast.

When he came out of the kitchen she was standing in the backyard, listening to a siren. It sounded to come from the Parkway.

'What gives?' she asked him. Troop E never used sirens except in emergency, and she knew that all three rescue squad rigs were stationary, or she would have received a general alert call.

'Darrow. I'd say.'

'What's he using the siren for?'

'He's trying to scare hell out of every driver on the Parkway in a misguided attempt to make them behave.'

Going across to 73, he reflected that one of the things Darrow hadn't learned about patrolling a highway was that a police siren could make a nervous driver swerve at the wrong moment and initiate an accident. In an emergency you had to risk that but it was already known in Troop E that Darrow was using his siren whenever he pulled someone down.

Lieutenant Ingram to Base.

Go ahead, sir.

Is there an alert situation in progress?

Negative, sir.

Thank you.

Coming back through the shade of the tamarisk, he heard the siren's note dying away.

'Any action?' Debby was shielding her eyes and watching the distant conveyor-belt movement of the northbound traffic.

'No. It was Darrow.'

'Good for him.'

'Think so?'

She turned quickly to look at him. There'd been a lot of quiet anger in those two words.

'What did I say, Frank?'

'Shop.'

'Okay, so it's shop. What'd I say?'

'You agreed with Darrow. He's had no practical experience of highway law enforcement procedures: he's a fast-talking theorist with a head full of statistics. You're not. You spend most of your time on the highway and in the worst conditions so you should know better than Darrow and it doesn't sound like you do.'

Debby sat on the grass and looked up at him.

'Are you such a big stiff you can't bend your knees?' When he was squatting beside her she said: 'I don't know how many people I've pulled out of wrecks, Frank, dead or alive or due for a wheelchair the rest of their days, but every time it happens I get just as angry as you are now, and wish someone in the State Police would one day find the guts to come out fighting and tell the public that if they go too fast or follow too close or hug the left lane they're going to lose their licence. There's no question of *skill* involved – if the sign says Keep Right you simply keep right and even a certified moron can do it, so we're not asking people to be brilliant drivers. And if that's Captain Darrow's case I'm in full support.'

Frank was watching the line of vehicles threading along the horizon, a gap sometimes appearing as a driver made a passing manoeuvre, the gap closing. The sun flashed on paintwork and chrome, and from this quiet garden their sound could just be heard, a constant murmur.

'They're people in those cars,' he told her, 'not puppets. They drive by instinct, not by the rules. It's less effort to hug the left lane, because it saves having to pull out every time you want to pass. And you're impatient to get where you're going – what's the fun in sitting in an auto when you could be sitting on the beach? – so you go as fast as you can. And if there's a guy in front of you it's instinctive to crowd him so he'll either speed up or pull over. They don't *look* at those signs. They don't *see* them.'

'Take their licence away for a year and they'll see those signs all right when they get back on the Parkway.'

'There's no specific overall solution, Debby, and if there were it wouldn't be that one. When a baby chokes over its food you don't take the food away, you train it to eat correctly.'

'Who's going to train that many people?'

'I am, for one. And I can't do it sitting on my duff.' He got to his feet, checking his watch.

'Isn't Darrow, for another? It sounds like he's trying.'

Some of his anger came back and he looked again at the distant line of vehicles. Take a cross-section of automobile drivers and you'd have a cross-section of the whole nation, a nation where for every two people there was one car. Stop that line of traffic over there and take any dozen drivers and you'd find a dozen people with problems. There were more hospital beds used for mental patients than for people with all the physical diseases combined, and some of the finest brains in medicine said that most of those diseases were psychosomatic anyway, induced by stress. The pressure of modern life came from all sides and you could see the result in the rates for crime, divorce, drug-addiction, alcoholism, child delinquency – and highway accidents. Because it was inside an automobile that people could rid themselves of their tensions and aggressions. How did a man in a temper drive? Carefully?

If cars hadn't been invented as a means of transport, psychiatrists would have invented them as a therapeutic apparatus for static use in their clinics: just climb on board this machine and press these levers and you'll find all your problems are eased within minutes. The road streaming past on a screen, the sense of space annihilated, distance devoured, the machine itself dominated, subdued by your masterful hands . . . a simulated 'audience' cheering you onwards, witnessing your skill, your importance, your power over others as you swing out to pass them and leave them far behind . . .

'Sure,' he said, 'Darrow's trying. He's trying to alter basic human nature and he's going to lose out. People drive as they are and as they feel, and if they feel sore or frustrated or aggressive, is it going to do any good blowing a siren at them and telling them it's illegal to be that way?' He looked down from the horizon. 'He can use your support. He won't find too much in Troop E.'

He turned through the shade towards the car and Debby went on sitting there for a couple of seconds kicking herself hard because in the rare half-hour break that Frank had snatched she'd provoked him into talking shop and put his mind right back on the job when he could have been lying here on the cool grass with his face to the sky, letting it all go by.

'Frank.'

She scrambled up and followed him. He was getting his cap from the driver's seat and putting it on. She knew he was still slow-burning: his face was tensed and his eyes flicked alertly from one item of data to the next as he snapped the door open and checked the facia panel and clicked the radio on and started the motor, consciously concentrating because his anger was disturbing smooth habit.

'Take care,' he said, and looked up at her through the open window.

'Frank, can you spare a minute?'

'For what?'

'Just to tear me in bits and feed me to the sharks.'

'What the hell are you talking about?'

With surprise she saw he really didn't know. All his anger

was for something else and it could only be Darrow.

'What did he do, Frank?'

'Who?'

'Don't hold out on me any more. And I'm serious.'

He sat listening for a moment to the squawking of the radio, an overheating incident at Milepost 81.3, sounded like Schultz; then he decided to tell her because she wouldn't otherwise give him any peace and anyway it wasn't anything important.

'He wanted me to shut down the Base while he lectured the men and I wouldn't let him so he reported me to Captain Westover for defiance of authority and asked for disciplinary action to be taken. Any questions?'

Debby was just staring at him like she'd never seen him before. He said:

'I have to go.'

'*Frank.* When did it happen?'

'Yesterday.'

'You never told me.'

'I've told you now.'

'So *that's* Darrow!'

'Look,' he said, because her eyes were bright with anger, 'it's no big deal. Just don't ask the wrong kind of questions in future.' He smiled reassuringly and it made no difference at all. Her tone was cutting:

'And was there disciplinary action taken?'

'Kind of reprimand. Westover had me call him, then he bawled me out.'

'There couldn't be something wrong with my hearing, could there?' Frank had worked on the Parkway seventeen years, climbing from the ranks. Westover had been a sergeant and they'd built the policing structure together.

'I guess Darrow was right there in the office at HQ. It's difficult for Westover because it was his idea to invite Darrow to mount his safety campaign, so he can't easily kick him back to Washington without looking a damn fool.'

Worriedly she said: 'Sam told me Darrow's going to be on the Parkway the whole of this weekend, till Monday. Today's only Saturday, so how are you going to keep from blowing up?'

'Stay out of his way.'

The police siren was sounding again and she turned her

head, listening. 'It won't be too easy.'

'Don't worry, things'll work out.' He moved the shift into drive.

'Tell you something? That slob's just lost his only supporter.'

'Lady, you've made my day.'

All Vince could see of Danny at first were his loafers, which were lying together outside the front of McTigue's showroom. For a while he couldn't see Danny at all. Chuck McTigue ran a real smart garage cornering Marina Drive and Shore Avenue a couple of minutes from the Ingram home, and it was natural that the smartest part of it was the showroom.

The Venus had been there for three days but nobody had asked to see it because, as Mr McTigue had told Vince, you don't hit the shore on the Fourth of July to buy a new automobile, all you have in mind is to cool off in the ocean.

'Danny around, Mr McTigue?'

'He was here ten minutes ago, Vince. Tried the workshop?'

'Yes.'

'Best give a yell, then, I guess.'

McTigue was under the hydraulic hoist, his white coveralls immaculate and his baseball cap worn back to front so the peak didn't get in the way as he examined the Chrysler's muffler. He was a thin quiet man, never saying much, or more than he meant; the Ingrams hadn't known him long because he'd only recently taken over the garage. The most important thing they knew about him was that his wife had died a couple of years ago, and Vince wondered if he'd been as quiet as this always, or only since then. Danny never mentioned his mother, and Vince didn't want to ask him about her. 'They were close,' Mr McTigue had told him once.

'Hey, Danny!'

The heat struck from between great piles of cumulus that had begun sailing inshore from the ocean: the fishermen had said there'd be an electric storm tonight. Vince could feel the static in the air, and the pre-storm stillness that was a kind of pressure against the ears.

'Danny?'

If he were in the house he'd hear; they'd said they'd meet around three this afternoon, go watch the traffic on the Parkway at Interchange 83, hope to see some of the new models in action.

Waiting for an answer, Vince turned and stood looking into the showroom through the opened glass doors. The Venus 1000 was set dead in the centre of the brilliantly-polished floor, its paintwork rippling in the light with an opalescent quality that reminded him of an outsize jewel in a showcase. From this angle, oblique head-on, the Lorenzo design was shown to the best advantage, accentuating the sharknose front end with the hood-scoop and the pencil-narrow windshield pillars, and the stubby upturned fastback treatment of the rear. Danny was wild about this car, in his quiet way, and they'd both spent almost an hour looking it over yesterday when Mr McTigue had rolled it into the showroom after its final polishing. As Vince looked at it now there seemed to be something remote about it, ethereal, untouchable, as it stood there in silence beyond the glass doors; and it gave him an odd feeling when the headlamps suddenly came on and went out again.

Then it connected: Danny had left his loafers outside so as not to mark the floor, and he'd been sitting in the Venus when Vince had called him, invisible behind the reflections on the raked windshield.

Vince tugged his shoes off too and padded across to the fastback, looking in.

'Hi. Didn't you hear me yell?'

'Sure.' Danny was only half-attending to him. 'That's why I flashed you.'

'I yelled twice.' Vince leaned at the driver's door, smelling the new-car smell and watching the high-cheekboned, rather hungry-looking face of Danny McTigue with its pale and deep-set eyes that gave him the same withdrawn expression as his father. Unless they looked directly at you it was hard to see what they were thinking, though Vince knew what Danny was thinking right now. 'Boy, are you hung up over this baby . . .'

Danny laughed quietly, pleased. It was like when you told a friend of yours he'd gone wild about a new girl: it kind of pleased him. He'd only looked up at Vince once, and now he just went on sitting there with his fingers stroking the wheel-rim, his pale eyes flitting across the facia and the control console that was angled upwards from the gearshift base, its bright chrome switches mounted on matt black trim like silver on black velvet. If this car had anything, Vince acknowledged, it had looks.

'Just think about it, Vince. Zero to sixty in less than five and a half seconds.' His tone had a vibrant undercurrent and he seemed to be talking mostly to himself, not looking up. 'You imagine how she'd feel, doing that?' His pale thin fingers caressed the wheel. 'Top speed a hundred and fifty-seven. Just think about that.'

Vince nodded, looking over the lines of the Lorenzo design and experiencing another slightly odd feeling: that he shouldn't have come here, disturbing Danny. He'd known him six months, maybe a bit more, and they'd become friends right off because they were both a little obsessed by automobiles and Danny had a kind of enthusiasm for them that Vince found infectious – the kid had entirely papered his den with pages from catalogues instead of from stag mags and there were five steering-wheels he'd pulled out of wrecks and cleaned up to hang on the walls. You knew when Danny called you on the phone what he'd be going to talk about, and if you had the same interests, Vince thought, then that was kind of nice, kind of reliable. Danny was a hundred-percenter and maybe that was what he liked about the kid. But just the same he felt slightly odd right now, leaning at the window of the Venus while Danny sat inside half-dreaming.

It felt like something Vince would've been keen to share, if he'd known how: this degree of involvement, this extra dimension to just being wild about a new model. It must be a good feeling, something like being in love.

'We going up to the Interchange?'

'Sure,' Danny said, but didn't move.

'We don't have to.' It'd be hot as hell up there and the showroom was cool, and why did they want to watch a bunch of second-stringers going past when they could use the rest of the afternoon looking over the Venus 1000? It was quite something to be able to do: this auto was the hush-hush mid-season breath-taker fresh off the assembly-lines in Detroit and there couldn't be many people in the whole country who'd even seen one yet.

'I asked Dad if we could take a short trip,' Danny said,

reaching up to feel the thickness of the padded visor. 'He said maybe.'

Vince laughed at the thought. 'I don't know I'd want that much responsibility.'

'He let you try out the Mustang.'

'It didn't pack this kind of kick.' He pulled at the recessed handle and swung open the door. 'Move over, huh? I want to feel how she fits.'

'Long distance.'

Brett Hagen could barely hear the operator's voice: this must be the noisiest hotel in Wildwood and it was jam-packed and he wouldn't have got a room except there'd been a cancellation. He took a cigarette and lit up and remembered and stubbed it out in the glazed seashell ashtray; the way to give it up was not to light the damned things at all, not to keep a pack on him, but maybe there was an excuse this weekend because his nerves were about shot.

'They're ringing busy.'

'Keep trying.'

He looked out of the window across the sea of auto roofs to the flags hanging limp on the Marine Pier and wondered how people in their right minds could stampede into these shore resorts and somehow survive for a whole weekend, let alone have a good time. Maybe it was because they weren't here to look for their daughter.

By now – a quarter after three in the afternoon – he'd covered thirty-one hotels, starting with the plushiest of them at eight o'clock this morning. Anyone who could reserve a room at the Surf Club could afford the best. The receptionist there had been new to his job and uncertain how much he was meant to say about the members. Brett had gone there as soon as he'd arrived last evening but 'Mr Fallon had checked out.' He and Mrs Fallon had reserved a room Friday but it seemed they weren't aiming to use it: they'd left about ten minutes after getting here. The lady with him was Mrs Fallon? Well, yes, she'd be his wife. She often came to the Surf Club? Was she a young lady?

The receptionist had started giving vague and noncommittal answers and Brett was stymied because the more he tried to find out the more suspicious he sounded. The only real information he'd managed to get was that sometimes Mr Fallon stayed at one of the hotels, coming into the Club just for a drink or a meal.

A friend of mine is meeting me here, name of Fallon. Yes, he said he'd be staying here.

Through thirty-one hotels.

He no longer questioned how easy it had been for that young disguised voice on the telephone to send him all this way from New York. For one thing he was too worried now, over Tracy and over his patient at the Clinic, both of them claiming his attention almost as if they'd decided between them to pull him apart. Also he knew now that it was just that one repugnant phrase that had alerted him to the point of using the whole weekend, if necessary, to locate Tracy.

He likes them young.

That phrase mightn't have been chosen deliberately to frighten him, but the effect was the same: it conjured the image of a vampire, a monster, rather than just a middle-aged lecher. His efforts to rid his mind of those words and the image associated with them had inevitably impressed them on him the more surely, and since noon today, when he'd come wearily away from the fifteenth or sixteenth hotel, he'd had the feeling that time was running out, that he must hurry to find Tracy before it was too late.

In the heat of midsummer weekends the human animal behaved differently. Conventions were relaxed; the steadying influence of familiar surroundings was no longer available for people away from their homes; heat was life and the sunshine was a stimulus to its reproduction; and in shore resorts the sight of young girls in swimsuits was an aphrodisiac to men already nearing the bounds imposed by their society. In the long summer months, sex crimes reached their high.

'Hausner Clinic.'

What did Earl Fallon have that could entice teenagers to spend weekends with him, winning their attention from boys their own age? Some brand of animal magnetism, and of a high order. A quality of Svengali.

'This is Dr Hagen.'

Twice during the conversation he had to ask the nurse to speak louder, partly because of the kids yelling in the games room right alongside and partly because he was watching everyone who passed the window on the crowded sidewalk out there; because he could visit every hotel in Wildwood without finding her, and yet might chance to see her at any next second.

More than once already he'd crossed the street or the boardwalk, thinking he'd seen her.

He lit another cigarette and this time went on smoking it, watching the window and sometimes failing to answer, so that the ward sister had to ask him again if he were still on the line.

'Yes. There's a lot of noise here. You're still giving her supplementary steroids?'

'Every five hours, Dr Hagen.'

She began giving him the blood levels and associated values and he listened more closely, concentrating less on the window where people walked in their bright summer clothes.

'Again, please?'

'Blood pressure is now 75/43.'

'Right, I have that.' He pulled out his Parker, writing on the back of the directory.

Sodium chloride value nearing 200. Potassium 6.3 per litre. Urea rising to a critical 305 mg/% and glucose higher than 170.

He didn't look up any more at the window.

'Skin pigmentation?'

'Incipient, Doctor.'

'Abdominal pains?'

'Miss Gardella first complained an hour ago, yes.'

'Signs of shock?'

'Not yet, sir.'

'The Senior Resident isn't in the building?'

'He's due back in at six this evening.'

Take a break, Mattox had told him, hang loose somewhere till Monday, you've good and earned it.

I'm hanging loose in Wildwood. And I shouldn't be. Not now.

You are Miss Gardella? I'm going to call you Ellen.

There was never much time to know a patient. Occasionally you'd become friends, afterwards, but you didn't have any real chance to talk with them while the crisis was on.

Don't worry, Ellen. We're just going to do this thing together. For me it's easy, and I'll make it easy for you too.

Then you were hitting the faucet with your elbow for the last time and they were just cases, living bodies not so unlike the dead ones you remembered in the dissecting rooms, except that these could change, suddenly, if you made a mistake or there were something in their make-up that refused – without having warned you – to support the demands of the knife.

With Ellen Gardella the danger had been sudden high peaks of pressure and they'd controlled it below 200/110 by accelerating the Rigotine drip. There hadn't been anything critical and though the phaeochromocytoma had been a little obstinate he'd removed it cleanly, one of his best, and good enough for an advanced-class demonstration.

It had been afterwards she'd asked him, her young skin blue-white against the pillow, her eyes overbright but trusting him: *Doctor Brett, am I going to make out?*

You never got to know them in the normal way; that was to say you didn't ask them where they'd been born or what colours they liked best or how they were doing in college; but there was an alchemy at work just the same and you didn't look at them, afterwards, as you'd looked at them when they arrived with their hair nicely brushed and their best night-robe laid out, or later when all they meant to you was that you had to go in transpleurally through the site of the eleventh rib and perform a single stage bilateral. You looked at them, afterwards, as if there'd been a minor but important chemical exchange; and in a way there had. Within them there was now a part of yourself: work that your hands had done. It was a unique relationship and he only ever thought about it when for some reason that work had been for nothing.

Yes, Ellen, you're going to make out fine. I guarantee it.

But the figures he'd just noted on the back of the telephone directory said that in Room 17 of the Hausner Clinic in White Plains, Ellen Gardella was going into adrenal failure.

'You mind if we have the air-conditioner off for a while, Floyd?'

He turned around from the mirror.

'You'll get too hot.'

'When I do,' Sue told him, 'we can put it back on.'

'Okay.' He watched her cross to the box and turn the knob. 'But you oughtn't to expose yourself to fluctuating temperatures, Sue.'

Her smile shimmered at him. 'I have my own built-in control.' She went to the windows and opened them, then opened the glass door that led on to the balcony and stood there in her flimsy pink night-robe. 'He'll be a summer child,' she said, lifting her face to the sky and shaking her glossy black hair, 'a child of the sun.' Floyd watched her uncertainly from the wall-mirror. 'Can you feel its warmth, Curly?'

Floyd turned away, wishing she wouldn't talk to someone who didn't really exist yet; it was macabre in the extreme. Also he was worried about the toga. She'd just presented it to him as a going-away gift and it looked great, an exact replica of a Roman toga; she'd seen it at Saks when she'd been buying layette and couldn't resist it. She said it was for wearing on the beach – 'You'll look just like Mark Antony striding down there, and I'll feel very proud of you.'

The thing was, he thought, as he surveyed himself in the mirror, that he might look terribly like a fag striding down there, and he could even be arrested.

'You know, Sue, I think I should use this as pyjamas.'

'But it's for the beach – the latest fashion!'

She turned and admired his brooding handsome features above the very Roman-looking toga.

'But I mean does everybody realize that?'

'Of course. You look even more masculine than Charlton Heston.'

'I think I look like a fag.'

She laughed, shaking her hair. 'Well, I'll be with you, and *I* don't look like you're a fag.'

'I guess that's right.' He had to stop thinking about the toga because the other worry was more urgent, more menacing. She looked perfectly all right except for that enormous swelling; her gossamer night-robe came out and out and then hung straight down. He wondered how she could keep from pitching right over on to her front and the idea terrified him; in fact he'd got into the habit, along the boardwalk where she could easily trip on a nail, of walking backwards in front of her so he'd be ready to catch her when it happened.

He hadn't slept too well last night. When she'd come out of the shower his eyes had been drawn again to her middle, taut and naked and terribly unnatural, looking as if it was going to burst any minute, and he wondered how it had come about that a bit more thought hadn't been given the process of human reproduction; it seemed such a desperate business, with the abdominal skin stretched to exploding-point and the embryo visibly trying to kick its way out. Of course evolution was still in progess and it could be that in another million years they *would* kick their way out and avoid all that dreadful performance of Pushing Down he'd got sick of reading about; the fact remained that during the transitional period (between Pushing Down and Kicking Out) an unnecessary degree of courage and fortitude was demanded from the potential father.

'Are we going to have our siesta, Floyd?'

'Uh-huh.' In the mirror he could see her curled on the bed, looking almost completely round. Also he thought if he pulled the knot of the sash to the hip instead of leaving it in the middle it'd look more like a toga than a pinafore.

'Floyd, is this yours?'

'Huh?'

'492-4782.'

'I made a note, yuh.' He took the sash off altogether but the whole thing fell loose and reminded him of a maternity gown, which made him put the sash back on fast.

'Whose number is it, Floyd?'

He stood away from the mirror and looked stern as if he were about to deliver a long speech to do with burying Caesar, but there was still something wrong. It could only be the tennis sneakers.

'Floyd darling.'

'M'mm-h'mm?'

'Whose telephone-number did you write down?'

He realized suddenly what she was talking about and wished he hadn't been such a damn fool as to leave that number around. There wasn't any privacy in a motel room.

'It's just a number,' he said. That didn't make things sound any better, but it was the best he could manage because the thing about the toga was on his mind.

'Oh. I'm sorry. I didn't realize I wasn't meant to find it.'

He saw her move in the mirror, putting the card back on to the telephone-table. He turned around.

'Look, honey, I didn't –'

'It's perfectly all right, Floyd. You don't have to –'

Keeping his patience he said: 'It's the number of the Beach Haven First Aid Squad.'

'The what?'

She was sitting up.

'The Rescue Squad. The place where they have the ambulances.'

'Oh I see. Don't you feel too good, Floyd?'

He felt very impatient about it. There were two distinct possibilities of crisis and it was a real strain having to handle them both at once. They were sort of merging together in his mind, becoming one huge black threatening cloud.

'I just want to be prepared, Sue, don't you understand? It's for your sake – I just want to protect you against whatever happens. I didn't want you to see that phone-number because you might think I was worried, that's all.'

'Oh, Floyd.' She was hugging her knees, or trying to, looking up at him with her head on one side and the glossy black hair hanging down. 'You'd never give me that impression. Handsome Roman senators aren't the type to worry.'

'Yuh, well – well that's another thing, Sue. This is the most wonderful going-away gift I've ever had, but I think I ought to use it for pyjamas.'

'Oh, but I want to be there, darling, when people on the beach see you wearing it. You'll look terrific!'

'Sue.' He went towards the bed. He didn't want to scare her, but she had to be told about the very real risks they'd both be running. 'That's just what I'm trying to say. Suppose we're down there on the beach and suddenly Curly starts arriving and we need an ambulance and I can't run for one because I'm being arrested for transvestism?'

Nat Renatus hit the button and climbed out and held the corner of his handkerchief in the windshield-washer jet till it was soaked, then he pinched out the excess water and got back in and tilted the mirror and started working on his eye.

'He won't show,' he said.

'He'll show.'

Rod Gould sat like a sack, watching the boats moored in the marina. There were none here big enough. There were only three or four in Cape May Harbour big enough for the trip they had to take.

'Get a plane,' Nat said on his breath, 'why don't we get a plane, the county airport?'

The piece of grit had got into his eye when they'd come off the Parkway and headed for Texas Avenue along by the Harbour. He hated anything in his eye, or a splinter, anything in his body that didn't belong to it. You could get poisoned that way. The tears ran down his face on to his pinstripe suit as he pulled down the lower lid and ran the spike of the handkerchief along it, trying to keep his fingers from shaking.

'We ain't goin' near any airport,' Rod said. 'We get a boat. Toni has one.'

'He won't show.'

'For Chris' sake.' and Rod Gould's blunt head swung to look at Nat, 'stop talkin' like that, you scared or something, for Chris' sake?'

Nat Renatus lolled his head on one side for a minute because his neck ached and the tears ran down and sent a dark blotch spreading on the new clean shirt he'd bought at the shopping centre when they'd hit the city. He'd taken a shower at a gas-station restaurant and left his old shirt there but he didn't feel any cleaner and he hated not to feel clean.

Rod watched his friend, his thin and dangerous friend whose nerve had gone because he'd done it before but never to a city cop. Nat was finished. He'd never get his style back even if he beat this rap and set up somewhere safe, because the Nolan killing had changed everything and a bit of it had spun off and got inside Nat, just like Nolan's bullet had got inside Rod himself.

'It's out,' Nat said, 'I got it out.'

No, Rod thought, you never will.

The boats heeled to the incoming swell, some tall-masted but none big enough. Something kept flashing, a tin or a mirror, and when Rod looked across the skein of mooring-ropes he saw Toni was there, smiling, Toni Lago, flashing them with a tin.

'Nat.'

'Yeh?'

'He's there.'

'Christ.'

'Take it slow. Take it slow. An' I do the spiel.'

'Okay. Okay.'

You could feel his nerves, Rod thought, feel them in the air. It was like a bomb had hit a piano, all the strings jangling.

They walked from the two-tone Chrysler, Rod moving slow and leaning to the left, the side where the slug had gone in. There hadn't been any pain for a long while; there was a numb feeling, a kind of cramp, as if that bit of his body had been shot clean away.

Toni waited for them, his violet-coloured eyes smiling for them, his little teeth white, his hands tucked into the pockets of the gold-braided yachting-jacket. As he waited he watched how Rod Gould was walking, crabwise, and wondered how many more days he was going to live if he didn't find a tame medic; and he watched how the fingers of Renatus were shaking as he lit another cigarette, and wondered how many days it would be before Renatus broke.

It looked like he could get a hundred thousand bucks' worth of sugar for next to nothing, especially when he told them about Ahmet.

'They got Ahmet,' he said as they came up.

Rod Gould stopped and looked at him, his eyes like stones under the heavy lids, his big body leaning.

A kid ran past, one of the weekenders, went skipping over the coiled ropes, a pair of red inflated water-wings flapping from her bare shoulders. The long masts sketched their tips across the sky as the swell ran.

'Ahmet?'

'Yes,' Toni Lago said, his violet eyes smiling.

Renatus said something, not quite a word, just an animal breath sucked in suddenly, a soft whimper.

'He doesn't know me,' Toni said. 'Nobody in the Istanbul-Naples chain knows me. I mean, not like they know you. Not like Ahmet knows you. They say, along the East River, if anyone squeals it's going to be Ahmet. You have a radio in that car?' He looked lazily across at the two-tone Chrysler Newport they'd left by the quayside. 'Turn on the news when you've nothing better to do. It was the Narcotics Bureau that picked him up. You know what? He was covered in sugar.'

He looked smiling into the thin squeezed face of Renatus, and saw what he needed to know. He wouldn't have to break both of them to get his price. Only one. Only Gould. He looked at Gould.

'You can sail inside of an hour.' He turned idly and they saw a mast taller than the others, Bermuda-rigged, rearing from the line of berths. 'All you need is the tickets.'

'Half the sugar,' Rod Gould said.

Renatus whimpered and Toni Lago looked at him, at the whiteness of his starved face, the bloodshot eye. So Renatus would settle for all they had, all the sugar, because he was scared and wanted to run. It looked like Gould would have to settle too because he wouldn't ever leave his friend. Everyone knew that, along the East River.

'Half,' Toni said, 'yes. Half for you, and half for your friend.'

'Half for us both,' Rod Gould said.

'She sails anyway at eleven tomorrow morning, for Haiti. I have facilities there.' He looked across to the quayside again. 'If you want to go on board, you'll have to be here before that time. You can leave the car where it is. I mean intact.'

'No,' Gould told him. 'Half.'

'The jails are getting overcrowded in the States. But they'll make room all right for you two,' Toni Lago said, 'since you'll be there for life.'

The sea was leaden, the waves hardly breaking against his thighs. He stood almost alone, his back to the crowded sands, facing the deep. Light came sometimes as the piled cumulus drifted, and reflections dappled his skin.

I'll just keep on going, Erica had told him yesterday.

His straw-bright head hung forward a little, as it did, without his knowing, when there was something he could not understand.

It was nice knowing you, Russ.

He gazed at and through the swirling water, sometimes seeing the rippled sand below, his head down a little as he tried to understand how he could ever have let her go like that. The foam burst against his thighs as a wave larger than the rest fell, but he stayed his ground, his muscles automatically compensating. A girl waded past him, laughing to someone; but he could see only Erica, and hear only one thing, they'd said, yesterday.

'What makes you want,' he had asked, 'to forget your name?'

'The yin and the yang.'

He said nothing more. He knew now she was only trying to confuse him, or trying to tell him something that had to be told in other ways, other words. He didn't mind, because if they were talking it allowed him to look at her.

When he could find the courage, he'd ask her if she had a photo, one of herself, that he could have. It would take a lot of nerve, to ask for that, because it would make him look like a moonsick collegiate, which he was.

'It's the Chinese thing,' she said, 'you know?'

He just nodded. He knew it meant female and male but he couldn't see any connection with her wanting to forget her name. He watched her slim tanned legs, the kind of rhythm they had even when they were still, her slim tanned hands, the rim of the wheel through her curled fingers; he watched the nearness of her.

'I blew them apart. Everything else went up with it, I mean all my past life.' She was looking at him suddenly and he stopped breathing because the air seemed full of red roses and their scent was too strong. 'You wouldn't know. How old are you, Russ?' He wanted to look away, so as to be able to breathe, but it was impossible, it was like drowning, and not wanting to struggle.

'Twenty-five.'

She looked at the road again and he shut his eyes and took in breath and wished he weren't seventeen and totally incapable of handling the kind of situation you got into when you were slammed in a small enclosed space with a phantasmagorically beautiful woman. All he knew was that his jeans were getting to be too tight and it was starting to hurt.

'I was lonesome,' she said.

He leaned his straw-coloured head against the padded rest, deliberately not looking at her.

'Like I'm twenty-five.' He gave an odd laugh and hoped she wouldn't hear. The whole damn thing had got completely out of hand and they were talking in a sort of Fellini script, with words not meaning what they always did.

Suddenly he was looking at her, his head almost wrenched around, and he knew why: there was soon going to be all his whole life to live through without being able to see her, so he had to drink all the roses, every one, while they were here. 'How can anyone like you be lonesome?' He didn't like her lying; he could stand her trying to confuse him and he could stand her succeeding by approximately a million per cent, but she didn't have to lie. She kept a bodyguard of hormone-reduced eunuchs and war-trained Alsatians to hold back the men swarming at her gates, so why wouldn't she admit it? He felt a terrific glow of anger and was surprised by its intensity, and his jeans were just going to have to hold out somehow. If he could only pass out. 'You could have anyone.' He'd started saying things without thinking of saying them first, so anything could happen now, a forest fire, a landslide, a nuclear war, anything.

'You only need to want one person, Russ, and not to have them, to be lonesome.'

Everything was immediately real to him and he sat up straight; all his senses were clear and he saw the hazy accelerated road sliding under them and the sign saying Wildwood Exit 44 and heard the drone of the motor and the tyres' song and the whiplash of the wind, seeing these things and hearing them and turning to look at her and for the first time recognizing her for what she was and not for what she meant to him. He knew now she hadn't been lying.

'I'm sorry,' he said.

'It happens.' She gave a kind of smile.

'I'm sorry it happened to you.'

'I'll get used to it.'

'I'm sorry I can't help.'

She turned to him and the smile was real now. 'I'd got to thinking the only thing was to lose all human contact, and I tried it for a while. Then I saw you standing there, looking as lonesome as I felt. You helped a lot.' The next sign came up and she said: 'You're heading for Wildwood, right?'

'Right.'

He couldn't ask for a photograph; he didn't want one now. That had been a long time back when he'd been just a kid, when he'd thought of asking her for a photograph. She'd turned into someone real and he didn't need her picture to help him remember her.

'D'you have friends there?'

'Where?'

'In Wildwood.'

'Yes. Yes, I do.'

'Will you be sailing?'

'Surfing. A little. If the water's right.' She was slowing and moving over to the right-hand lane and everything had gone, exploded, not sailing, a little surfing if the water's right, but how in the sweet name of Jesus could he say anything else? When there was so much? 'Will you?'

'Will I what, Russ?'

'Tell me your name.'

In a while she said: 'Erica.'

'Erica.'

'Yes.'

'I don't have to go to Wildwood.' They were going very slow and she ran on to the shoulder and pulled up, her lithe blue-moccasined feet changing their position, her slender hand curling round the gear-shift and pulling it back. 'My friends aren't expecting me, I mean.'

She turned in her seat to look at him, trying to understand what he was wanting to say. He watched her trying to understand, then he looked down and away and didn't speak again.

'How old are you really?'

Traffic passed but the only sounds he could hear were inside the car where they sat together in the late afternoon of July Third, the whisper as she smoothed the skirt of her blue print dress, the faintest creak of plastic surfaces rubbing as her body moved on the ribbed seat, the sound of his own breathing, the thumping in his chest.

'Does it matter?'

'No.'

'What'll you do, Erica?'

Her brown hand lay on her lap, the slender fingers curled, as they'd been on the rim of the wheel, and on the gear-shift. His own hand moved and swerved and touched only the crash-proofed facia ledge below the windshield as if he meant to lean his arm there, as if to show her he was capable of making a movement other than towards her, into her closeness.

'I'll just keep on going.'

He nodded.

There was no means of estimating how long the silence was. It ended when she said softly: 'It was nice knowing you, Russ.'

He stood there with the waves hardly breaking against his thighs and the sun's reflected light dappling his skin, remembering only now, as if there'd been some kind of retrogressive amnesia like you have in accidents, what it had been like to watch the powder-blue Mustang moving off from the shoulder with the dust feathering out from the tyres, a flicker of silk at the driver's window, and then other cars in the way and then nothing and now this, the sand sometimes showing through the clear water between waves as he stood with his head down a little, trying and failing to understand how he could ever have let her go like that.

CHAPTER EIGHT

Cruising northbound at 3.45 p.m. after visiting the State Police Barracks at Bass River to supervise a missing child situation, Frank Ingram came up on the small shabby delivery truck just before Milepost 77 and PA'd the driver to pull over and halt on the shoulder.

The truck had a canvas top that had been ripped and repaired in several places and carried blocks of ice covered with sacking; water dripped from its dented tailgate. By the time Frank came up from Car 73 the driver was out of the truck and waiting for him, a short bear-like Greek with tattooed arms who stood mopping himself with a big white handkerchief.

'Your muffler's blown.'

The man stopped wiping and draped the handkerchief over his bare head and poked around in his pockets and brought out a ticket and waved it at Frank.

'My muffler is blown, he says! But I already got a ticket, so what you going to do, huh? The captain tol' me my muffler is blown an' I say okay, okay, I get it fixed up nice for him, you want I should get it fixed up nice for you too? Then why not you leave me get on with delivering my ice to all these peoples who is yellin' for it, an' I get my muffler fixed tonight? He says I got to –'

'What captain?'

'Policeman captain! You not know him? One what screams siren at peoples – nearly I go off road because not expecting!' He wiped his face all over. 'Am Patras –' he bowed with European courtesy but without compromising his attitude of total indignation – 'Alexandros Patras, have been using Parkway many years, have seen yourself many times, Lieutenant, then there comes this deafenous noise of siren, why is that?'

Frank held out his hand for the ticket, and read the charge: *Operation of a commercial motor vehicle in dangerous state of repair.* The signature was *J. B. S. Darrow, Capt.* He passed it back to the Greek.

'What else was found wrong with your truck, Mr Patras?'

'Huh? My muffler!'

'But what other things?'

'None other things!'

Frank walked around the vehicle, looking at the tyres and checking the tailgate catches for operation and security and noting that the load-retention slings were in position around the heavy blocks of ice; then he climbed in and checked the steering for backlash, pumping the brake-pedal and trying the parking-brake ratchet. Starting the motor, he got out and ducked down to see what kind of breach there was in the muffler.

'Also he does all these things!' The Greek gestured with his hairy tattooed arms. 'If police stop me many times, all ice will melt, an' many peoples need badly ice in this hot times!'

Frank straightened up and turned the motor off.

'All right, Mr Patras. Where d'you aim to get your muffler fixed?'

'McTigue Service. He always keeps my truck like how it should go. With muffler –' he shrugged monumentally – 'happen always slow, so not notice till bad state.'

'You know where the police barracks are,' Frank asked him, 'at Ocean Point?'

'Oh sure, I tell you have been using Parkway for many –'

'Right. Bring your truck along there tomorrow before noon and have the duty officer check your muffler. If I get a satisfactory report on the repair you can tear up that ticket, you understand?'

Patras looked at the slip of paper as if it had just changed colour. 'Tear up?'

'Only if that repair's been done before noon tomorrow, don't make any mistake on that.'

'Not understand. Why tear up ticket, please?'

'Because people using the Garden State Parkway can expect reasonable consideration and you haven't been getting it.'

Frank walked back along the shoulder and waited for a gap in the traffic and waved the truck away and stood there for a minute while the right-hand lane flow resumed normal speed and the exhaust gas drifted past him and across the grassland.

Okay, so Patras was like most people who made a living out of a vehicle and he'd have gone on running that truck till there were actual flames coming out of the muffler because taking it off the road would cost money and taking it in for repairs would cost money, but he'd only needed telling. This was a case for a warning, a verbal injunction to the effect that if he wanted to go on running his truck on the highway he'd have to get it fixed. It wasn't a case for scaring the hell out of him with a siren and then charging him with the serious offence of operating a vehicle in a dangerous state of repair.

So he'd give Captain J. B. S. Darrow one more chance and then send in an immediate complaint to HQ objecting to the abuse of honorary privilege by his superior officer in subjecting a user of the Parkway to unreasonable enforcement procedures and additionally jeopardizing Troop E's record of effective public relationship, an inherent factor in the statewide highway safety programme.

Meantime it was going to be more peaceful for all concerned if he kept right out of Darrow's way.

Getting into 73 and starting the motor, he heard his name coming up through the background squawk and turned the volume higher, taking the mike from its clip.

Ingram . . . Lieutenant Ingram. Acknowledge, please.

Hear you, go ahead.

Calling you from Base, Lieutenant. Captain Darrow would like to know if you'd find it convenient to talk with him here inside the next fifteen minutes.

Through the windshield he watched the heat-mirage flowing across the roadway, the traffic wavering through it as if through water.

Give Captain Darrow my compliments and tell him I'm returning to Base.

When Frank reached Ocean Point he found Sergeant Gillespie manning the radio console and Captain Darrow standing at one of the telephones. No one else was in the operations room.

'I quite see the point,' Darrow said into the phone, 'but I already told Sergeant Augenblick that under the terms of Operation Homesafe any driver persisting in holding the fast lane when there's sufficient room to the right of him is to be charged with dangerous driving. Now please get that clear.'

Frank moved past him to the main desk where Sam Gillespie's great bulk presided; he'd lowered the squawk so that Darrow could hear better on the phone. Sergeant Augenblick commanded Bass River down at Interchange 52, and it seemed like somebody there had called up Ocean Point for guidance on the correct interpretation of orders.

'Anything new?' Frank asked Gillespie.

'I guess everything's kinda new, sir, this weekend.' He passed him the current reports folder.

'What exactly does that mean, Sergeant?'

Sam pulled his head back like a gigantic tortoise till the swivel-chair under him creaked. He didn't want to think how long ago it was since Frankie'd talked to him that way.

'Well, this operation, sir, I mean Homesafe. Takes a little gettin' used to.'

Frank didn't answer.

He'd found the Patras summons report in the folder and Sam watched him tear it across twice and drop the pieces into the wastebasket. Sam kept perfectly still, looking at the pieces in the basket. There were three things he'd never seen happen in the operations room at Ocean Point State Police Barracks: he'd never seen a summons report torn up and junked, and he'd never seen it done by an officer inferior in rank to the one who'd signed it, and he'd never seen it done when both of them were present; so all Sam could figure was that if ever the operations room at Ocean Point State Police Barracks was going to get its roof blown off it was going to get its roof blown off today.

'Don't hesitate,' Captain Darrow said on the phone, 'to

contact me in the event you feel undecided as to what charge should be made. As a general rule-of-thumb I'll remind you of what I said late yesterday at Bass River Barracks: you have the full power of the law in your hands and this weekend I want you to use it.'

Watching him, Frank remembered his war service and his encounters with exactly this type of officer, whose administrative status kept him apart from his colleagues of battle rank. They were usually neater men, their uniform immaculate; and their attitude expressed just that extra degree of severity that exposed their lack of practice in using real authority. To evoke obedience, they relied on their rank, not on the sense of leadership they didn't possess.

Cradling the phone, Darrow said briskly: 'I appreciate your passing by, Lieutenant.'

'I was on my way here, Captain.'

The alert eyes brightened a fraction. 'Then I didn't inconvenience you. I wanted to ask you how we can explain the fact that since I talked with your unit here the summons average has risen only nine per cent compared with the same period preceding my talk, and seven per cent compared with this period July Fourth of last year.'

'Statistical percentages are notoriously misleading.'

'Let us say, then, that there's been no general increase in enforcement cases.' Darrow was riffling through the files, and at the main desk Sam looked at the ceiling because if the Captain noticed that the Patras summons report was missing then the roof would start blowing off and the ceiling would go with it and he wanted to watch. It wasn't so often you got the opportunity of seeing things like that. 'To put it more simply still, Lieutenant, my direct orders are being disobeyed by negligence. Can you explain why?'

'Do you suggest your orders have been countermanded?'

'No. But have they?'

'No. They haven't.'

'What made the idea occur to you, Lieutenant?'

'It'd be a logical explanation of what you call disobedience, wouldn't it? But the fact is that aside from things like discipline and ethics, I don't need to countermand orders that cut right across the policy that's pushed this Parkway to third place among the nation's safest transport facilities. The men of this Troop have been trained to get co-operation from the motoring public by *explaining* why it's safer to ride the slow lane and keep a good distance from the auto ahead and check the driving mirror regularly. You've told these men to penalize drivers, instead of persuading them to see sense; and they just can't do it.'

'You mean they haven't been trained to obey orders?'

'It's not a question of orders. The men of Troop E aren't just a bunch of dumb-assed rookies at boot camp.'

Darrow's quick eyes flicked in the direction of the radio console and back, but he didn't order Sergeant Gillespie outside. It occurred to Frank that either he realized he couldn't do it, since the console had to be manned, or he wanted Gillespie to remain as a witness in case Frank spoke out of turn sufficiently to warrant a charge of insubordination.

'So I'm expected to defer to your men?'

Darrow's tone was still almost conversational, and Frank realized the danger in this. He had to watch the man's eyes to estimate his mood, because he didn't want to push Darrow too far: the only possible answer to another reprimand from HQ would be his own immediate resignation, and the Garden State Parkway was mostly what he lived for.

'You're not expected to do anything, Captain. But if you want co-operation from these troopers you'll need to appeal to their intelligence, which makes it easy for you, since it happens to be rather high. If you can persuade them that the motoring public ought to be punished instead of educated, you've got it made.'

'You oversimplify.' Darrow turned away, turned back, his bright eyes impatient. 'We've been trying to educate drivers for decades and it hasn't paid off. We devise more and more sophisticated instruction courses, we raise licensing standards, we construct highways incorporating the most exhaustively studied safety aspects, we allocate billions of dollars to safety programmes set up by States and local communities with the aid of Federal funds, we go out to reach the motoring public by way of the mass media – advising them, warning them, informing them of adverse weather and highway conditions – and we provide them with state-wide and nation-wide police and road security services to guide them wherever they travel. And they drive like idiots.'

'Sure they do. That's why we've had to give them all those facilities you've just talked about.'

'Passive acceptance isn't enough, Ingram. Philosophical toleration doesn't work. I don't accept the widespread idea that nothing else can be done. They don't *have* to drive like idiots, you know – that's just how they *prefer* to drive. But the innocent people slaughtered on the roads every single day have their preferences too: they prefer to live. Who's going to help them, if we can't? What use is the law if it isn't applied? And why shouldn't it be applied on the highway the same as anywhere else? The motoring public isn't a closed social group: once they park their automobiles they become the public at large. For their own safety they're forbidden to smoke in department stores and movie-theatres, and when they take an aeroplane they're amenable to being disciplined just by flashing instructions on a panel. So why is it that when these same people get into their automobiles, using the most dangerous form of transport by ninety-two per cent, they're allowed to pay only lip-service to the laws made for their protection? Where is the difference? Not in the type of public: it's the same one. It's in the attitude towards them – the attitude of the police.' His tone remained perfectly level as he observed Frank with his head on one side. 'The attitude expressed by officers like yourself, Lieutenant, and passed on to the men in their actual training. The attitude of live and let live, while every nine minutes someone dies on the road. Is it that you're scared of provoking the public by enforcing the law?'

Frank considered the question, moving across to the coffee machine and pulling out a cup. 'It could be,' he said easily. 'Or it could be I don't have a personal itch to dominate people.' He pressed the tap. 'This uniform gives me a whole lot of power, and the fact that I don't often choose to use it makes me feel quite okay about putting it on again every new day. Would you like some coffee? Technically I think you're my guest.'

There was an OP signal coming through on the console and Sam Gillespie had to turn up the volume.

Go ahead 78.

Can I have a lookup on KL-303215?

KL-303295. Roger.

No, one-five. Again: 303215.

One-five, hear you.

Sam put the Rush 15 through to Headquarters and waited

for the response.

Darrow hadn't moved. He stood with his feet apart and his hands behind him, the easy attitude matching his tone.

'Aren't you being rather emotional, Lieutenant? We weren't discussing the abuse of power.'

Frank sipped some coffee, watching him over the cup.

'I was.'

Darrow's eyes went very bright for an instant and Frank didn't miss it.

'Then it was irrelevant. I expected a logical counter-argument.'

'I can give you that too. Your theory's perfect, like a lot of theories are. It's because they conveniently ignore essential data, so that everything fits nice and tidy. The difference between the types of public you were talking about is real and it doesn't concern the attitude of the police. When a man climbs into his car, he changes his personality. It's like when he goes home through his front door: he feels more important, no longer an anonymous strap-hanger on his commuter train; he really means something in his own home. It's his personal territory, and man is a territorial creature. This extends to his automobile: it's part of his home, where he can be with his family, live some of his life, keep his cigarettes, listen to his favourite radio station. So when a cop pokes his big head through the window it's an invasion of privacy and that's damned important, Captain Darrow, and there's nothing we can do about it, not a thing. When you pull a driver down you've made an enemy right from the start, and your enemies don't do what they know you want them to do. The reaction's instinctive and you'd be surprised, if you ever put in any real full-time patrol work, how big a factor it is in highway danger. You'd see how resentment and a sense of outraged privacy make some drivers break the law again the minute they're out of sight, just to get even with you – the enemy. So we work on the principle of making friends.'

He waited while the response came through from Woodbridge and Sam's bullfrog tones reverberated around the room.

Car 78 – I have your Rush 15.

Go ahead.

Plate number KL-303215 owner is James Oliphant Gale – Gee Ay El Ee – of Hightower Apartments, Port Rich-

mond, Staten Island.

Okay, Sarge, that checks. Thanks and out.

Sam turned the background low.

'Point number two,' Frank said, 'is that driving is a game of skill, and drivers themselves are quick to criticize each other. Personal status is closely involved, specially when there are passengers in the car, so when a cop pulls a driver down it makes him look like a school-kid, and he'll break the law again as soon as possible just to show his family or his girl-friend he can do what the hell he likes when he's driving his own damn car.' He shrugged. 'And there's nothing you can do about that either. Even with our policy of intelligent co-operation we cause resentment, but if we used the hardline jackboot procedures you recommend we'd build up such resistance to the safety laws we'd need one trooper to every mile to police this Parkway efficiently.'

74 to Base.

Hear you, Seven-Four.

I'm tailing a Catalina through Milepost 81 southbound, speed steady at sixty-nine m.p.h. I'm not too sure about this Operatoin Homesafe pitch, Sarge – do I book him for speeding or dangerous driving?

As Sam looked up from the mike Frank knew suddenly that he didn't have to care any more whether he pushed Captain Darrow too far or not because the alternative was to stand by and let him debase Troop E's reputation and he wasn't prepared to do that.

Darrow was taking a step towards the console but Frank jerked his empty cup into the bin and got there before him.

This is Lieutenant Ingram.

Yes, sir. Trooper Levy.

Is your Catalina moving in the fast lane with a clear run?

Yes it is, sir.

Frank knew that in the fast left-hand lane the car wasn't a hazard to traffic using the Interchange 81 or the Entrance 80 ramps or the acceleration lane out of the Forked River Food and Fuel Service Area four miles farther on. He could see every mile of the Parkway as clearly as if it were on a television screen in front of him.

Levy, are there any aspects that from your experience could be called dangerous?

I guess there aren't, sir, no. Surface, visibility, weather con-

ditions are all perfectly okay, with low volume traffic. It's just that we've been told to be – well, kind of aggressive, and maybe sixty-nine m.p.h. could be dangerous if you wanted to look at things –

The charge is that of exceeding the speed limit.

Yes sir.

And in future cases rely totally on your own judgement and discretion, and you won't make any mistakes, that clear?

Okay, sir. Thank you.

When Frank turned to face Darrow he saw his eyes were narrowed in anger.

'You don't consider that as countermanding my direct orders?'

'No. I was just putting things straight along the line for that patrolman, reminding him that the deliberately aggressive nature of your campaign doesn't require conscientious troopers to trump up false charges against the public.' He waited three seconds, watching Darrow. 'Or does it?'

Tracy listened to his footsteps fading along the passage, her pony-tail flying out as she turned her head quickly to look at the phone.

She daren't move yet.

Earl was in the elevator car and it was going down to street level, the machinery whining, but she still didn't move because the building was empty and even slight sounds carried, echoing, and if he heard her at the phone he might come back and she didn't know what would happen then.

When she heard the main doors swing shut behind him she crossed to the phone, kneeling in front of it and dialling. The late afternoon sunlight leaned in bright bars across the room, broken by the slats of the blind. Her shadow lay sprawled across the floor as if someone had flung it there against the bars of light. A film of moisture covered her skin and her breathing was loud.

'Long distance please.'

Through the gaps in the blind she could see the sands and the ocean and the hundreds of people down there. They moved very little, lying in groups or wading among the shallow waves or just standing still, the burnished weight of the sky pressing them down. They looked ever so far away and nothing to do with her, because the windows were shut and no sound reached here from the beach, only from the road below, six storeys down. She could believe there wasn't a window at all beyond the slatted blind, only a screen with coloured images, so if she picked up this phone and hurled it the screen would smash and the people vanish. And Earl would be there, looking in at her.

'Your number's ringing busy.'

She expected it to be, on a Fourth of July weekend, with kids thrown out of their normal routine. *I'm on a bad acid trip and I want out.* Kids like Marie, and Jo-Jo. *I'm going to cut my wrists if you can't help me.* Hotline was better than the usual crash pad or a legal clinic or a psychiatrist who'd try to make you.

'I'll hold the line.'

There wasn't much time. He'd gone for cigarettes and there was a shop quite close and if he walked fast he'd be back inside five minutes and find her talking.

They should have stayed at the Surf Club. It wasn't isolated like here.

When they'd checked in there yesterday evening at the end of the trip down the Parkway the desk clerk had looked at them rather cagily, handing Earl some letters and a telephone message slip. She didn't mind. Earl had a lot of girls and he'd bring a lot of them here, wasn't she expected to understand that?

He read the phone message while they were cooling off in the Harbour Bar at the Club. Then he said, looking around, 'A friend of mine says we can use his apartment; he's not coming to Wildwood this weekend. It'd be less crowded than here – I didn't imagine there'd be such a slew of people.'

There didn't seem to be so many but she said:

'I'll go where you go, Earl.'

They'd come right on here. He had the keys with him. It was the top floor and there was dust everywhere.

'Nobody's been here in quite a while.'

He pulled the blind-string and the room became striped with sunlight; she noticed him watching her intently, like he sometimes did. And because of the light on one side of his face she could see the difference in his eyes: normally you wouldn't notice but sometimes you could see that one of his eyes was blue and the other flecked with green, when the light was a certain way. It made him look like two people in one.

'You mind the dust, Tracy?'

It floated along the stripes of sunshine, so it seemed only to be there, not in the stripes of shadow.

'No. It's less crowded, like you said. Isn't there anyone else in the whole building?'

'Nary a soul. It's for sale.' He tried the lights but they didn't work. 'My friend has a lien on this apartment. Guess I'll have to go buy some candles, baby.' He checked the drinks cabinet and brightened up. 'You can trust Eddie, there's just about everything.'

Watching him while he wasn't looking at her, she realized she didn't know Earl, had never known him, and would get to know him now, quickly, tonight and tomorrow, quickly and maybe too well, as of this minute. The weekend was suddenly right close up.

'I'm trying your New York number again.'

'Thank you. Please hurry.'

The people on the sands hardly moved.

She could still feel the pain, though it had gone; she felt it like a kind of memory on her skin, just at the nape of her neck. It was before they'd gone out last evening to find some place to eat; they were sitting on the sofa watching the low rollers through the slats of the blind and it had hurt suddenly, her hair pulled sharply like that. She'd been almost asleep, with his hypnotic fingers stroking her neck just where the pony-tail sprouted, then the pain had jerked her back to full consciousness.

When she looked at him his eyes were surprised, like she'd discovered him in something he hadn't meant to do, but hadn't been able to help.

'I'm sorry, baby.' He seemed anxious to be forgiven. 'My ring caught in your hair.' Anxious she should understand.

It was the only ring he wore, a scarab, on his middle finger.

You want to get eaten alive?

'Did it hurt bad?'

Her heart was still thumping.

'No.' It hadn't hurt bad; it was just unexpected. And the pain had made her remember what Judy had said.

'I'm sorry, baby.'

'It's all right, Earl.'

There was dust on the telephone, dust all over. The windows had to be kept shut, Earl said, because when there was a sea wind it blew fine sand in. The air-conditioner couldn't work without electricity and yesterday he went around to the real-estate office to see if they could switch it on just for the weekend, but the place was closed.

The strangest thing was to be here with him in a whole deserted building when everywhere was jam-packed and people couldn't find a room. Hundreds of thousands of people in the city but she was in a place where if you called out no one would hear you.

'Your number's ringing.'

'Thank you.'

She'd thought of this in the night when she'd wakened suddenly and found him watching her in the glow from the street lamps. It was then she knew she had to call Hotline.

The ringing-tone stopped.

'Hotline.'

It was always a woman's voice.

'I – I need your help.'

'We're always here.'

She'd called them a half-dozen times in the past year. A room-mate at college had told her their number one night when she'd got the feeling for the first time ever, the feeling of being totally lost. It had been scaring, a kind of mental vertigo, her whole identity sliding away and nothing to hang on to.

The second time was when she'd gone home for the weekend and found the house empty, with Daddy at the Clinic on some sort of emergency and Mother lecturing in Boston overnight, and the feeling had come in a big way and all she knew was the phone being suddenly in her hand with a woman's voice asking her what exactly was the problem.

But she didn't know, and couldn't tell them. It was just crazy that in a world so full of her friends she could get to feel lost; but it was very real, sometimes leaving her weak and shaking and in tears. Not being able to tell them what was wrong, she used to tell them other things, all true but unimportant: how she'd tried pot and got sick, how a man had called her at college and said things before she could think to hang up, how a kid on campus had stolen money from her and she knew who it was but couldn't bear to expose her, things like that. Now she said:

'I'm weekending with a man who – who's quite a lot older than me.'

'Why does that worry you?'

They never seemed to hesitate before they answered, that was what gave her so much faith in them. The only time they were silent was when she was trying to say what she wanted, and found it hard, and they made sure not to rush her. The room-mate who'd given her the number had told her a bit about them: the New York organization had been set up on the same lines as the original one in California, with help and guidance from the committee at the Children's Hospital of Los Angeles. They were all voluntary workers, people in all kinds of jobs, but with special qualifications, people who'd really got to know about life and the sort of trouble teenagers had to face. They really listened to what you said; you could tell by the way they answered; they listened to every word.

'I guess that's right. I'm not so worried about his age.'

She heard a sound and held her breath and listened and had to take the receiver away from her ear because of her blood pulsing against it, but when she heard it again she realized it was from the street below, not inside the building, the doors of a car being slammed. She took some deep breaths and they waited, not hurrying her.

'I think he wants to hurt me.'

It had been rather bitter-tasting.

They'd been out for something to eat, finding a seafood place called Abe's Lobster Pot and ordering Maryland soft-shell crabs, later watching the fireworks, leaning at the rail of the boardwalk and watching them burst like great flowers blooming and already dying, but all the time she'd been worrying about what it would be like with Earl if you trusted him all the way and were wrong.

You know what you're doing. Or do you?

By the time they got to the apartment high in the empty building her stomach was knotting up and she lay on the bed with her shoulders flattened against the cool wall. She felt weak and knew that she wouldn't be able to stop him doing whatever he wanted to her now, she didn't have the strength to scream or fight him off.

'I don't feel so good.'

He lit two cigarettes.

'Something you ate?'

He wasn't looking at her and she thought she hadn't been the first scared ignorant lost kid who'd seen in Earl Fallon a man they could trust the whole way, and then changed their mind when it came to the point. He must get pretty tired of kids like her.

'Could be,' she said. But she knew it wasn't something she'd eaten: she just wished they were at the Surf Club instead of here where no one would hear if she called out, and wished he hadn't caught his ring in her hair like that, hurting, and wishing Judy and Lorraine hadn't said things about him. 'No, Earl, I don't want a cigarette.'

'Maybe it was the crabs.'

'Maybe.'

He pressed both the cigarettes out and went over to the liquor cabinet, pouring something and coming back with two small glasses, tulip-shaped and green-stemmed. They had dark brown liquid in them, almost black. He began looking at her now.

'You need a settler, baby.'

'What is it?'

'Fernet Branca.'

She didn't know the name. From here she couldn't see the bottle he'd used.

'Is it strong, Earl?'

'No. It's made of herbs. It settles the tummy.'

'Does it?'

In the glow from the street lamps the hairs on his hand were thick, and the veins dark, the colour of the liquor in the glass he was holding to her. His eyes were translucent as a cat's eyes when headlights strike across them, the green flecks showing in the blue, and she looked from one to the other of them, seeing again how different they were, and thinking that if there could be two people in one body their eyes might be like this. One gentle and the other cruel.

The building was very quiet. There were people still on the sands, the voices of children calling to each other faintly on the far side of the window, their sound seeming to hit the window and fall away like grains of sand though she could hear them in here.

His eyes were all she could see; everything else was growing dark. She looked from one to the other of them, trying to remember why she'd been scared of him, when he was her only refuge, trying to understand why it had bothered her so much, the pain when he'd tugged, there were men who liked hair, they were fetishists, that was all.

'Why's it taste so bitter?'

Her eyelids felt heavy.

'Earl?'

The children's voices flew like sand grains at the window, so faint they couldn't get in.

'Earl, why's it so bitter?'

Watching her.

It didn't seem that long ago, all those hours of the night and nearly all of today; this was a sleeping-waking thing, the two worlds merging like a dream where you lost the sense of time.

'What makes you think he wants to hurt you?'

The receiver was slippery in her hot fingers.

'He has a kind of reputation that way.'

'Have you met anyone he's hurt?'

'Yes. No.'

They waited. They always had time for you.

'I mean girls just tell me things.'

'Are they covered in bandages?'

Tracy gave a little laugh and was surprised she could do such a thing.

They asked other things. Was she a virgin? Did she know it sometimes hurt, especially the first time? Was that maybe what the girls meant? Hotline was wide open: they could say just anything, and so could you, because there were no names ever mentioned.

'He isn't with you right now.'

'No.'

'Why don't you just leave, go home?'

'Because I need him.'

She'd said it quickly without thinking first and knew it was true.

'Do you have parents?'

'Yes of course!' You had so much faith in them that they

got you talking right off the bat, and you forgot things like there were some kids who didn't have parents. 'I guess I'm lucky.'

The whining sound had started and she jerked the receiver away and listened with her whole body but couldn't tell if it were the elevator car rising or one of those electric-powered ice-cream buggies going past the building. Her heart tripped and her breath was trying to explode but she had to listen.

'Is this man,' she heard faintly, 'anything like your father? Is he that much older than you?'

She held the receiver as far away as she could because she had to listen to the soft slow whining sound and wanted it desperately to stop but if it stopped it could mean the elevator was at the top now and he'd be coming.

'Do your parents know about him?'

The voice was so far away.

Then the soft slow whining stopped and the elevator doors thumped open and she lowered the receiver using both hands so as not to make a noise with it, then just stayed kneeling, closing her eyes and bringing her head down till her moist brow touched and rested against the base of the silent telephone, and listened to his footsteps coming.

By six o'clock this Saturday evening the hourly travel figures on the charts for the Ocean Point area of the Parkway had dipped to the anticipated 2000 vehicles per hour with an available speed of 60 m.p.h. and no delays, and though the day-long pressure of work on the men of Troop E was now easing off a little, Sergeant Gillespie brought Reserve Car 80 into the parking bay with a feeling of relief.

The heat alone was exhausting. The barometer was way down and the humidity was way up and the sky over the ocean was swollen with turgid cloud masses.

The figures on the travel charts, being statistical, didn't reveal the traffic situation in more than one aspect. Over the last few hours it had been changing progressively: with the volume lighter and the speeds higher there was now less risk of minor accidents, more risk of major ones. Most of the people who'd filled the Parkway yesterday and this morning were now at their ease along the shore; the drivers using it now were shuttling from one resort to another on both northbound and southbound roads, hunting for accommodation that didn't exist, visiting friends who'd checked in at nearby resorts, or just joy-riding.

Recently supervising Troopers Levy, Hunt, Cooper and Mill between Mileposts 60 and 100, Gillespie had found fewer incidents of hazardous passing manoeuvres and 'following too close', more frequent cases of hogging the fast lane and exceeding the speed limit. The cocktail hour was just starting and from this time until after midnight the alcohol factor alone would double the risk of major accident. Darkness, coming down inside three hours of now, would treble it.

Shutting off the radio and climbing out of Car 80, Sam heard a siren somewhere northwards, and figured he knew who was using it. From the operations room window Trooper Schultz watched him head for the entrance, walking like you'd shift a crate single-handed, tilting it first on one edge and then on the other. People said the sergeant had spent his early life on a ranch, till he'd gotten so heavy the hosses were more bow-legged than he was.

'Is that an accident?' the man under the sycamore asked. Sam hadn't noticed him in the huge tree's shade.

'Nope. It's that stu – it's Captain Darrow.' There wasn't an alert situation in progress or he'd have heard it on the squawk just now. 'Guess you'll have to be patient.' He said it with distaste. Going into the air-conditioned ops room he threw off his cap and went straight to the iced-water machine, listening to the WOR newscast that Schultz had running.

. . . Late this afternoon it was confirmed by the New York City Police Department that a Turkish national, Ahmet Sükan, arrested earlier today by an East River patrol, has volunteered information that could trigger dramatic developments in the hunt for the killers of Officer John Nolan, slain yesterday morning not far from where Ahmet Sükan was captured.

Sam filled the cup again, listening. A break like this could slip the skids right under those two bastards.

This information, the Police Department reports, has considerably narrowed the search area, and special police contingents are being deployed 'not far from New York'. On the political front today, Governor Lewis Aldermeade made it clear that his intentions toward the –

Schultz cut the newscast to handle an NCIC call from Cooper out on the Parkway at Milepost 76, investigating a

New York registered Ford Pinto. Sam dropped his empty cup in the bin and made out his report at the main desk.

71. Negative on your Pinto.

Okay, thanks.

Schultz peeled some new gum and looked at Sam.

'Did Cap'n Darrow come in today, Sarge?'

'So whaddya think that mushroom-shaped cloud was, went up around four o'clock?'

Sam felt bad about that. He didn't mind some stupid jerk from Washington busting in here with a uniform fresh off a tailor's dummy and he didn't mind having to listen to Frankie lam into him like a head of steam looking for a piston but the top brass in Trenton shouldn't have arranged it for the middle of a broiling holiday weekend when the pressure on the nerves was ten-tenths already.

Schultz took a look-up and asked Sam: 'Who's the little guy out there under the tree, Sarge?'

'A pixie.' He signed his report and filed three citation duplicates and got up and drank some more water and dumped the cup. 'What little guy? Oh him. Mr Solo.'

'Ya, I mean what's he do?'

'Picks stiffs outa wrecks.'

'How's that again?'

'He's a field-service – hold it a minute.' His hand went bulldozing through the papers on the main desk and dragged out a letter of introduction with a Boston civic seal at the top. 'He's a field-service analyst working on impact and trauma patterns in selected fatal highway accident situations for the Mobile Research Unit of the Boston Traffic Safety Bureau. You want his blood group?'

Trooper Schultz looked out the window again, his jaws working contemplatively on the spearmint.

'But what's he hangin' around for?'

'Like I just told you, to pick stiffs outa wrecks.'

Sam could see the little guy from where he stood. When Mr Solo wasn't standing under the tree he was in the ops room here leafing through the accident reports or you'd run into him along the passage or in the john or the rest-room, and when you couldn't see him you'd still know he was right here somewhere, like a bird of ill omen perched on the roof.

The orders were that in the event of a Signal 11 the first patrol car leaving base would take Mr Solo on board. *He shall be permitted immediate access to whatever wreckage there may be, and enabled to take photographs, measurements and notes, and to examine visually whatever injured or dead persons are inside the wreckage or have been thrown clear, subject essentially to the needs of police, rescue unit personnel and all others whose concern is for the injured and for the speedy protection of the scene and re-establishment of normal conditions.*

'But we don't have any stiffs in wrecks, Sarge.'

'You're smart, Schultz, you really work things out. Thing is, we gotta find him some. Like you keep a pet vulture, you gotta feed it fresh-killed rats, y'know?'

Schultz listened to the console for a minute and called up a wrecker for a burst radiator incident at Milepost 68 southbound, then looked out the window again.

'Jeeze, he's a real creepy little guy, ain't he?'

'Oh he's okay,' Sam said. 'It's just that when he looks at you it kinda reminds you to get your brakes checked.'

Schultz nodded quickly. 'Right. You know the impression I have? He's standing out there actually *willing* somebody to go smash themselves up.'

'Well, I guess it figures, don't it? He's in that line of business.' Sam stared out at the small motionless figure in the shade of the tree. 'In our line we try willin' people to drive safer. We just gotta hope he ain't any more successful than we are.'

Three miles away on Marina Drive a green Chevrolet Corvette turned through the gates of the Ingram home and backed up alongside the parked Car 73 and the Ocean Point Rescue Squad ambulance.

Frank was setting up a lawn sprinkler before going back on duty, and Debby was freeing the hosepipe where it had got snarled up below the tamarisk tree, a half-munched apple in one hand. She waved to the Chevvy with it, but it wasn't Vince after all: it was Mr McTigue climbing out, immaculate in white coveralls and baseball cap, wiping the steering-wheel before he shut the door.

'Who's that?' Frank asked, setting the tripod.

'Mr McTigue, with the Chevvy.'

'Why didn't Vince go fetch it himself?'

'Maybe he didn't know it was ready.'

McTigue had heard them talking and came through the tunnel of shade between the tamarisk and the house.

'She's all been checked over.' He never said hello or goodbye, but got right down to business. Untalkative and withdrawn, like his son Danny, he seemed to find even a brief greeting too personal a thing. 'Some new brushes for the generator, that's all she needed.' He stood in front of them awkwardly with his thin legs astride and his hands on his narrow hips, looking at the sprinkler that Frank was fixing, not at Frank himself.

Debby said: 'I bet you could use a very cold beer, Mr McTigue.'

'Guess I won't stay, Mrs Ingram. Couldn't see Vince any place so I just brought the car along.'

'He would've fetched it,' Frank said, and went over to turn the tap on. They watched the nozzles begin spinning, throwing off diamond drops in the evening light.

'Thought he might need it. Only a couple o' minutes to walk back. He ain't here, then?'

'Isn't he with Danny?'

'Could be.'

He looked at the ground, not seeming to want to stay, not seeming to want to go. A sweet musty smell came into the air, of water on parched earth. Mist clouded from the centre of the sprinkler.

'Isn't Danny at the garage?' Debby bit into her apple again, wondering what it was that Mr McTigue was trying to say.

'Guess he ain't. I closed up, a while back. Had to go along to Seaside Heights, someone wanted to talk about buyin' a new Lincoln. But they wasn't home, so I came right back.'

Frank caught a look from Debby. They hadn't ever heard McTigue say as much as this inside a few minutes, but the thing was they still didn't know what he had on his mind.

'If you need Danny for anything,' Frank said, 'we'll send him right along if he shows up here.'

'I don't need him.' Distant thunder came, and he turned to look at the dark clouds gathered above the ocean, as if he were glad of the distraction. 'He'll be okay if he's with Vince. Your boy has a real steady head, I guess.'

The three of them stood listening to the rhythmic swish of

the sprinkler. Frank said:

'Are you worried about Danny, Mr McTigue?'

The thunder came again but McTigue looked down, no longer pretending interest in it.

'I've no call to be worried. Not if he's with your boy. Last I saw of them, they were in the showroom, climbin' all over the new Venus 1000. Thing is, she ain't there now.' He looked at Frank. 'You reckon they could've gone for a ride, me bein' away for a while?'

CHAPTER NINE

Red roses cascade against the white-painted trellis, their blooms pouring from the height of the pergola almost to the level of the small grouped tables. The man is handsome, assured, his well-groomed head inclined attentively as he offers the lady a cigarette from his heavy gold case. She is in cool white tulle, the gathered bandeau that holds her hair suggesting a Grecian figure; the red rose at her shoulder complements those on the trellis, so that we can believe the man had picked it for her, his gallantry rewarded by her wearing it as his favour. For an instant she hesitates, as a woman of discrimination must, before deciding that the quality of these particular cigarettes is sufficient for her tastes; smiling, she accepts one. A waiter hovers.

Okay for the inside back page of *Marriage and Home*, Walt would have said, throw 'em a classic cliché reeking of ersatz chic.

He flicked his tooled electronic lighter for her.

Carol watched him as he lit his own, then looked away in time. He hated being watched.

He looked up at the waiter.

'Bring me a Grand Marnier. And Bourbon, straight.'

'Walt, I don't think I –'

His glance was hostile, scared. She looked down, wishing she could learn. There are quite a few lessons you'll have to master, Mrs Amberton, if you're going to handle this thing the right way. Yes, Dr Pabst.

Walt turned his head to the waiter again.

'What're you hanging around for? Didn't you hear the order?'

She closed her eyes.

'Sure,' the waiter said, and moved the pink shell ashtray nearer the lady. 'One Grand Marnier, one Bourbon straight.'

When he had gone the silence went on beyond the point where Carol felt she'd have to scream if one of them didn't speak. She now wanted it to go on forever, an endless silence in memory of all that had died between them.

It had been terrible to see how afraid he'd been, in that one glance. She wanted to help him, not scare him; but unthinkingly she'd threatened the satisfaction of his needs. If she declined to drink with him he'd have to drink alone, or worse, not at all, in an attempt to prove he too could decline if he couldn't share the occasion.

Moths flew aimlessly on the heavy air.

One of the many behavioural situations you'll learn to recognize, Mrs Amberton, concerns social drinking as a disguise for obsessive drinking. People like your husband exploit the fact that it's perfectly acceptable to drink in someone's conmpany but suspect to drink alone. If there's nobody else available they'll invite the barman to join them, turning an act of helpless dependence into a commonplace social ritual. To normal people there mightn't seem much difference, but to those like your husband the difference is very clearly defined and of tremendous importance: if they can get someone to drink with them it assuages the torment of guilt they feel. From what you say about your husband, Mrs Amberton, he's reached the phase when his own intelligence and self-awareness tell him every single time he lifts a glass that he ought not to do it, and that he must stop. But he'll do it just the same whether someone joins him or not; the only difference is that in company his agony will be less. So if you feel like a drink yourself, don't think you'll help him by refusing. You won't.

The moths flew aimlessly on the heavy air and one of them settled, gilding a rose. Later when dusk came and these candles here were lit, some of the moths would circle their flames till a wing shrivelled and the soft gilt spun, leaving a wisp of smoke. It wouldn't be seen, on the inside back page with its glossy colours, any more than the other things would be seen: the slight tremor of the hand as it held the gold cigarette-case, the hostility in the glance, the explosive quality of the silence here now the waiter had gone.

'You used to like it.'

'What?'

'Grand Marnier.'

'I still do.'

'That's great. But if you're trying to give it up you just have to tell me, then we won't need to keep the waiter hanging around while you change your mind.'

He didn't bother to blow the smoke away from the table.

There were a few things the omniscient Dr Pabst didn't warn you about, like love turning by degrees to pity and then by degrees to disgust, when you looked through the trellis and the roses and saw the stranger with the ruined face who blew smoke over you like over a waterfront whore.

You have to remember, Mrs Amberton, that it's a disease, and recognized as such by the whole of the medical profession. These people *cannot* control their obsession, any more than they could control bronchitis or cancer. Your whole attitude should be keyed to that one bedrock reality.

Understood. The lesson, Dr Pabst, is understood by this pupil of yours with the rather low IQ. It just seems a shame that people with this particular disease tend to discourage the love and comfort you could boundlessly offer them if they weren't so busy blowing smoke in your face because you don't feel like a liqueur right now. It's certainly the only disease I can think of – and recognized by the whole of the medical profession, of course – that carries the added danger of being left to kill off the patient by painful degrees because those who'd like to help have been driven to the point of saying: You're an alcoholic? Too bad. Excuse me, but I have to go now.

We grow a little weary, dear Dr Pabst, of finding yet another bottle in yet a different hiding-place, of wondering why our husband goes so frequently to the trunk of the car to sort out his camera gear, of locating the thing in the space behind the spare wheel and in sudden anger or heartbreak or mere boredom dropping it in the garbage can, only to suffer the fast tense drive and the sun's heat outside the Howard Johnson's while we wait, knowing that we mustn't ever grow too weary because if we do, if we don't do all we can to make him go into a clinic before it's too late, a wing will shrivel and there'll be a wisp of smoke.

The Grand Marnier for the lady, in a tiny cut glass with a slender stem. The Bourbon for the gentleman. She didn't touch her drink yet. He waited six seconds: she counted them. Then he drank half at one gulp and put the glass down and looked away from it as if for a while he were freed.

'What's wrong with my face?'

'Pardon me?'

'What the hell are you staring at?'

The red rose at her shoulder complements those on the trellis, but there is nothing to lead us to believe, as we would wish, that he had picked it for her.

'I don't think I was staring, Walt. Is your Bourbon as you like it?'

'Why shouldn't it be?'

'No reason.'

My Grand Marnier is delicious, thank you.

The essential preliminary, Mrs Amberton, is to get him to admit it. Once you can do that, we can propose treatment. These people *can* be cured, you know, but only if they'll co-operate.

I understand, yes. We're going away soon, for the Fourth of July, just down to Beach Haven on the New Jersey shore. I'll try to talk to him then, while we're alone together with no friends around. But it won't be easy, Dr Pabst. It won't be easy.

The light was slowly leaving the sky, and beyond the terrace the lamps of the marina were coming on. The waiter was nearing the table, bringing a match for the candles. The moths looked a deeper gold now that dusk was almost here.

It won't be easy because he loves me and I know it and it's something fundamental and doesn't relate with the way he blows smoke in my face, and he needs my respect, it's about all he has left, so when I finally drag up the courage and start talking to him it'll be a bit like placing a gun at his distinguished grey-flecked temple and pulling the trigger.

Walt, there's something I'd like to discuss. I don't mean discuss exactly, I mean just talk about.

When would it happen, the first moth, how long would it take? If the waiter didn't light the candles it wouldn't happen at all, but there was no way of stopping him, he'd say it looked better with every table lit up.

I think we know each other well enough to be able to talk something over, don't we?

For some reason they always go faster the nearer they go to the flame, spinning faster and faster till they touch; but what about self-preservation, aren't all living creatures supposed to know when they're in danger? Can't they feel the heat growing as they circle closer? Surely they do. Then why can't they stop?

Walt, now that we're alone together can we talk something over?

Everything will be just the same as it is right now, after I've started speaking. The roses and the menu card and his hand round the glass, nothing will change, the cliff and the sea look just the same a minute after you've gone over, but where do I find the courage?

Let yourself fall, just tilt forward, close your eyes.

'Walt.'

The match flared.

She was watching him in the candlelight.

'Uh?'

'Walt, I –'

A moth flew close suddenly.

She looks as young tonight as when we met, and my God that was almost twenty years ago. She always wore something in her hair, a ribbon, not a bandeau like now, she's more elegant now. How can a girl like this, a woman like this, as lovely as she was almost twenty years ago, cool in the candlelight, a rose on her dress, go on living with a human wreck?

Snap out, don't let's dramatize. Just this one and knock it off till tomorrow, take a break, I can do it. Otherwise it'll lead to the same ghastly three-ring circus and I'll say things and she'll have to get me away from people and finally help me with my clothes while I'm foul-mouthing her and punching the wall and wishing to Christ I were dead.

'Walt, I want to – to kind of make this a special weekend for us.'

'What's wrong with it so far?'

Drink up and put the glass down and call it a day. I have to start some time so why not make it tonight? And tomorrow we'll be most of the time in the ocean, so there won't be any chance of getting – no, tomorrow we're pulling out, that's right, my damned memory's shot to hell, I could've sworn I put one in the space by the spare wheel, *all right*, so your memory starts caving in and there's leg cramps and all that other stuff in the article but the whole thing's perfectly okay once you've knocked it off. And I can do it.

'I mean now we're alone together, we can talk about – oh, old times, anything. Ourselves, your career, you know?'

Their wings were gold in the flames' light. I don't like them brushing past my face like that. It's spooky.

'You want another drink?'

'No, thank you.'

'Okay.'

She's watching me again but she can't see anything just by my face. She can't *know*. She thinks I go on a jag too often, okay, who doesn't? In my job?

Frankly that's really all it is. The glass is empty and I don't want another one so I don't order another one, could anything be simpler than that? Here lies the key to a bright new future with past ghosts laid, her watchful eyes and the dust on top of the closet when I take it down, we hoped we could make it this weekend, Dad, but there's the exams, you know, the smashed glass and the vomit in the cracks of the tiles till the maid gets in and her crying alone thinking I can't hear and then the morning, oh Christ I must never do that again, never again, the shivering, the cold in the heat of the afternoon, I called them up and said you'd be in tomorrow, and the nightmare of knowing that once you begin you'll go on till it's too late to go back, the slam of a door and her empty bed, a rug on the sofa downstairs, rather be dead, why me, why me?

The glass looks so empty and the fun's over. A little willpower, Walt, if you please, a little effort of the will.

'We're not often alone together like this, and we can say things without the telephone ringing, you know what I mean?'

'Sure.'

Am I a child, then, that I can't do what the hell I want? Anyway what does she mean?

'What do you mean?'

The moths are everywhere, they ought to spray this bloody place, they think it's romantic or something?

'Waiter.'

Help me, Carol.

'Walt, shall we go now?'

'Are you bored?'

'No. I –'

'Then what's the rush?'

Get up and I'll follow you Carol but for God's sake be quick and don't just go on staring at me like I'm a kid who won't behave, I can do what the hell I want at my age and anyway aren't we blowing this whole thing up till it looks bigger than it is, how many men go through this kind of soul-searching witch-trial before they'll allow themselves a drink when they're trying to relax on a weekend out of town, isn't it time we got a little fun out of life for Christ's sake?

The waiter was here.

'What can I get you?'

Carol, please help me.

'Nothing. Look, can't you spray this damn place with insecticide or something?'

'I'm afraid there's nothing much we can –'

'Okay forget it. Bring me a Bourbon.'

'How does she feel?'

'Great.'

It was the first time Danny had spoken since they'd got on to the Parkway southbound at Interchange 81.

'No, I mean really, how does she feel?'

'Terrific, what else?'

Vince brought the speed up to around fifty, keeping to the slow lane and maintaining a safe distance behind the Pontiac coupé when they came up on it. He knew Danny wanted him to say a whole lot more about this buggy, but what more could you say the first time you drove a Venus 1000 out of the showroom and on to the Garden State Parkway?

Venus . . . created in the image of a goddess come to earth . . . lithe, compliant, trembling under your touch . . . It was printed in blue and gold right across the showroom window on a special banner. *Much more than a parade of mere beauty on the highway . . . a creature to possess . . .*

'She feels really great, I mean really.'

Danny said nothing. He sat kind of hunched, Vince could see from the tail of his eye, his pale face held forward to stare through the raked windshield over the gleaming shark-nose front end, his thin hands held tensely on his knees.

There wasn't too much traffic going southbound right now and it was tempting to overtake the coupé and notch up to the sixty m.p.h. legal limit but there was such a feeling of power under his foot that Vince was chary of using even a little of it: this was the kind of car that'd take off completely if you gave it the gun.

'How'd you persuade your Dad to let us do this, Danny?'

'He let you drive the Mustang, didn't he?'

'Sure, but this is a Venus 1000. There's quite a difference.'

'It's a question of degree,' Danny said. But he wasn't paying too much attention. His thin hand touched the rim of the wheel, caressing it. 'Go faster,' he said.

'Say, who's driving this buggy?' Vince laughed. But he was uneasy, feeling again what he'd felt when they'd been sitting in this car in the showroom – that he was disturbing some kind of secret rite, and that his friend privately wished he weren't here. Danny's pale hands still gripped his knees but he was looking down now, ranging his eyes over the facia panel, leaning towards Vince so as to see the instruments.

The Pontiac coupé was steady at around fifty and Vince thought there didn't seem much point just tailing it when there was the fast lane available for use, but this car was so different from his old Chevvy Corvette that it scared him to think what might happen if he really opened her up.

'How far did your Dad say we could go, Danny?'

'I guess we have around a half-hour. Hey listen, we're out of gas!'

Vince looked down and saw the needle drifting on the zero mark and kicked himself for not checking before they left the showroom: it was natural for Mr McTigue not to keep too much gas on board inside a building.

'There's a Citgo coming up at Milepost 76.' He eased his foot off the throttle and checked the mirror, pulling the stubby gear-shift into neutral so they could coast. His mouth had gone dry at the thought of running right out of gas and having one of Dad's patrolmen find them standing helplessly on the shoulder. *Another thing you need to realize, Vince, is that it's not only inefficient to run yourself out of gas – it can be dangerous. You just have to imagine what'd happen if you were giving your auto the full gun in a passing manoeuvre with someone right on your tail and suddenly felt the motor die on you. We've known multiple pile-ups happen that way.*

'Are we going to make it, Vince?'

'We have to.' He began sweating hard because it was okay coasting to save gas but it slowed you down and all you could do was sit and wait. He cut the motor and they listened to the soft rush of the slipstream past the louvres.

'When we've got some gas,' Danny said casually, 'will you let me take over just as far as the toll plaza?'

'Are you kidding?' Right now Vince wasn't in the mood for wild ideas. Danny was too young for a licence yet, and letting him take the Corvette twice around the block was a whole lot different from what he was asking for right now.

'Gee,' Danny said, 'you're real mean.' He gave his quiet laugh but Vince knew he meant it.

'And I aim to stay that way.'

The Food and Fuel signs were coming up but the tachometer was dipping below thirty m.p.h. and it seemed like crawling. At this speed a highway patrol would take an interest because slow driving was dangerous and discouraged to the extent that a driver would be ordered off the Parkway unless there were a good reason for doing less than 45 m.p.h. Vince checked the mirror, sweating uncomfortably. *You know who we picked up today, Lieutenant, running out of gas? Your boy Vince . . .* Dad wouldn't lam into him or anything, it was just that he'd look such an irresponsible idiot; it was at times like this he realized Dad's respect for him counted a great deal in his life.

He pressed the button and the motor didn't fire and he pressed it again and it fired and he shifted into third but there was too much snatch on the final drive and he dropped into second and kept at twenty m.p.h. and waited for the awful chug-chug. The needle was motionless over the zero on the gas gauge and he didn't look at it any more.

'We're going to make it,' Danny said.

Vince didn't answer because his mouth was too dry.

When he swung on to the Service Area entrance ramp he shifted into neutral again and coasted till the Venus was abreast of the first Citgo pump.

'Did it have you worried?' asked Danny.

'What gave you that impression?'

Danny laughed quietly.

'Two gallons,' Vince told the gas-pump jockey.

Danny put his hand on the gear-shift, flexing it against the reverse spring-gate, feeling the way it flicked back, the weight of the heavy black knob assisting the movement.

'I bet it feels terrific,' he said.

'It does.'

'Gee, but you're real mean, Vince.'

He didn't smile this time.

'Is that how you talked your Dad into it, made him out to look mean?' Vince didn't let himself feel too bothered by the kid's obsession; they'd got to a pump and the gas was going in and everything was perfectly okay. 'We'll leave here north-bound and go up as far as Ocean Point Plaza and head on home, right?'

'Right.' Danny's hand caressed the steering-wheel, his thin sensitive fingers passing across the holes in the spokes where the steel had been drilled for lightness. 'And we'll get over on that fast lane and take her up to sixty. Or is it that you're scared of her?'

Against the ivory wall of the palace the girl in green was poised like a butterfly, her hands lifting the skirt of her long dress fanwise so that it resembled wings, as if she had alighted there to rest from the day's warmth.

She had always liked green. Someone had asked her, long ago, what she'd like to be if, by waving a wand, she could be anything; she'd said a tree.

But everything had changed since then, and now she was a princess poised on a palace balcony high over the sea-born City of Atlantis, with the sun's last rays casting gold-dust along the surf.

A voice came from the room behind her but she didn't move except to turn her head.

'We think we ought to go see the Steel Pier tonight, honey, would you like that?'

'Not really, Mummy. Though I'm sure it's exciting.'

'Says here in the brochure it's the Showplace of the Nation, a hundred and one attractions for one admission.'

'Well, isn't that just wonderful? Why don't you and Daddy go along?'

Down there the lamps were coming on from one end of

the boardwalk to the other, so that night drew suddenly over the sea. Beyond the drifting lilies of the sailboats there were clouds piled along the horizon, and flashes came as the gods hurled their anger to the winds.

She had looked for him everywhere today; now it was night and she would look for him everywhere.

'But you haven't seen anything at all while we've been in Atlantic City, honey. You didn't want to go on the Million Dollar Pier or see the High Diving Horse or the Thrill Circus. Your daddy says he doesn't think you're enjoying yourself as you should be.'

This morning there'd been bicycles along the boardwalk and she had watched them go by, sitting on the balustrade so as to be easily seen, but he hadn't passed.

'If I saw all those things, Mummy, I think I'd just die with excitement. You and Daddy go see the Steel Pier showplace, and I'll –'

She saw him and flung herself into the room and cried excuse me and flew out the door and down the great staircase, upsetting the minstrels on the mezzanine and scattering the footmen in the great hall, startling the horses in the palace yard and sending the peacocks bustling in alarm as she raced with her silver slippers barely touching the path to the gates till she reached them and stopped and leaned breathless with her heart still running on, looking for the straw fedora she had seen from her balcony – there by the salt water taffy store – no, farther along, there at the end of the pier, no, not there – there where the – no, not there, no, nowhere, nowhere now.

He kept close to the line of parked cars because if Mom saw him she'd say he had to go in and play dominoes with Aunt Phyllis, holy cow.

Brand new Manta Ray with the styling way out, flared fenders to take the wider tyres, looked okay, plenty of zing, you wouldn't mind too much being seen behind a wheel like that.

The lamps were coming on. Now how in hell could you miss her every time, hanging around till you wondered if you'd gone soft in the head, she wasn't even pretty, it *was* this place, it was *this* place, he'd seen the Chevrolet Mirabelle turn in here, one of the palace hotels, the Ocean Tower.

I'm going on a bike junket, but he'd come right here. I'm going to the Wax Museum, but this was where he'd gone. Sure I like Aunt Phyllis but I kind of get spots in front of the eyes with all those dominoes, she always have to wear those fancy schoolmarm pince-nez? I'm going for a boat trip. Right here. Taking this much trouble, putting this much effort into the operation when she wasn't even the kind you'd walk under a bus for, not even pretty, hanging around here half the day like you had glue on your shoes, how in hell could you miss her?

Today's Saturday and it's almost over and they'll be heading back tomorrow sure as eggs and then there'll be nothing, absolutely nothing I can do, oh holy cow.

Police – this is an emergency.

'You mind if I ask you something?'

'Shoot, young feller.'

He didn't look young and he didn't look old, he was just a cop. You had to be careful what kind of things you asked them, they'd think you were wasting their time unless the whole darn town was burning down. Well it was.

'You think if I gave you the number of an auto plate you'd be able to kind of check on it for me, sort of tell me the name and address of the owner?'

'Somebody give you a lift?'

'Uh?'

'You leave something in somebody's car?'

'Uh, no. Yeah, that's right.'

'How's that again?'

'Boy, is it always as hot as this in Atlantic City? We going to get a storm?'

'This auto plate.'

'Yeah. I mean, you'd have records, that what you call them?'

'Why d'you want the information, son?'

'Hell, I don't want any information.'

'You're just kind of asking.'

'Right, that's exactly right.'

'Why?'

'Huh?'

'She a blonde?'

'Who?'

'The young lady in this auto.'

'How did you – well, holy cow!'

It couldn't be just experience. You heard a lot about how they got to understand human nature walking the beat but this was almost clairvoyant! They could actually *train* you to develop these exceptional powers, and stop a minute, wouldn't it be worth considering a police cadet course instead of college, just think, there wasn't the name of a girl you couldn't get simply by checking the licence-plate of the car she was in – *wow!* – and then with these exceptional powers at your command you could go right ahead and hypnotize her into positively *begging* you for a date!

Things really happened to you in Atlantic City, no kidding.

'I don't think there's anything I can do for you, son.'

'No? But all I want is her name and address.'

'Sure, but we don't have any facilities along those lines. It comes under invasion of privacy.'

'It does? How does that work out?'

'We have to assume young ladies don't necessarily wish their names and addresses known by strange young men.'

'Are you crazy? Excuse me.'

'You're welcome.'

'But gosh, I mean it's all they think about! I have a sister a bit older than me and oh boy, you should hear her on the phone. You know, you'd be doing a public service if you'd just keep a list handy so when guys like me need some information they could have it. I mean the *girls* – the young *ladies* would be grateful to you too, for –'

'We tend to feel they might complain.'

'They might *what?*'

'That's the policy we work on, son.'

'It is? Uh-huh. Well if you want my opinion it's – well, it's your policy, I guess.'

They weren't so smart.

'That's right.'

'Pardon me for taking up your time.'

College still had a lot going for it.

'Hausner Clinic.'

'I'd like Extension 9.'

'Who is it calling, please?'

'Dr Hagen.'

'Excuse me?'

'Dr Brett Hagen.'

'Oh yes, Doctor, one moment please.'

The kids in the games room next door were tearing it up and he'd have to ask the management what time they closed it so guests could sleep – that was if he decided to stay here overnight. If Ellen Gardella weren't showing any sign of improvement he'd just get in the car and head for White Plains, maybe reach the Clinic before midnight and talk the case over with Mattox or Sister Loomis.

It would mean neglecting Tracy.

Coloured light flickered on the wall near him and he looked out the window. Atlantic City, thirty miles north along the shore, was only a fuzzy glow through the humidity rolling in from the ocean; the coloured light was coming from fireworks going up somewhere nearer. Margate City or Longport, a whole shellburst staining the night sky crimson, fading and leaving rivulets. He'd entirely forgotten that today was the Fourth of July.

Had he always neglected Tracy?

It had been agreed she ought to grow up without any second-hand inhibitions passed on to her by the previous generation, left free to develop as a person in her own right, not just as the daughter of her parents. They'd never questioned the wisdom of this, and surely it was too late to question it now.

He felt for a cigarette and remembered he'd deliberately dropped the pack into the wastebasket an hour ago, tired of his own subservience to habit.

'Dr Hagen?'

'Yes?'

'This is Sister Vorhees.'

'Is Dr Mattox there?'

'He's in Intensive Care right now, Doctor. Shall I get Sister Loomis for you?'

'Please do that.'

Blue light burst against the window, colouring his reflection in the wall mirror and giving him a pallor, reminding him of Ellen Gardella's blue-white face against the pillow, *Doctor Brett, am I going to make out?*

If there were skin pigmentation or the abdominal pains hadn't decreased he'd check out of here right away and head north. His responsibility for the Gardella case had ended when she'd been wheeled out of the theatre, but technical considerations weren't necessarily paramount: Ellen trusted him – *Yes Ellen, you're going to make out fine* – and often a patient's recovery was due to the visible presence of somebody in whom there was faith. Suddenly he didn't have any doubts left: he shouldn't be here watching the meaningless patterns of a firework display more than a hundred miles from Room 17 of the Hausner Clinic where his presence could save a life.

'This is Sister Loomis.'

'Good evening.' He had to raise his voice because the din from the games room was growing worse. 'I'd like a report on Miss Gardella's condition please.'

'May I have that name again, Doctor?'

'Ellen Gardella, post-adrenalectomy, Room 17.'

'Oh yes. The adrenal failure was terminal and she died just an hour ago. Shall I give you the history, Doctor?'

He thought it was a Lincoln or maybe a Caddy. He'd never ridden in the back of a car with so much room.

'Where are you going, young man?'

'Cape May City, sir.'

'Why, that's just where we're bound for ourselves, aren't we, Eleanor?'

'That's right, Matthew.'

They could be two people in a weather-house, Russ thought, both of them small and neat, the man with a bat-wing tie and his wife with a daisy-chain hat. The car seemed too big for them.

'We don't normally give lifts,' the lady said, 'but you looked a little kind of . . . lost.'

'I guess that's right ma'am.'

She nodded and faced her front again, perhaps feeling it was none of her business.

Sitting in the middle of the back seat with the armrest stowed, Russ watched for places where he could see the northbound traffic on the other roadway. She had said, *I'll just keep on going,* which meant she'd end up in Cape May City; but there was just a chance she wouldn't actually stay there, so he watched the traffic coming the other way till the median got too wide again, in case she'd decided to make back north. He looked for the powder-blue Mustang.

She had said.

Erica had said.

Erica.

Just to know her name was incredible. If he saw her in a crowd tonight in Cape May or next year in New York or in ten years from now in any city under the sun and called her name – *Erica!* – she'd turn her head and see him and in that instant he'd have a problem breathing.

Standing there in the surf and sometimes seeing the ribbed sand below and sometimes her blue scarf floating and her eyes and all that she was, he'd finally found it impossible to understand how he could have stayed twenty-four hours in Wildwood when he'd known there was a chance she would be, Erica would be, only five miles distant in Cape May. It had been a kind of lunacy, a temporary loss of reason. As soon as he'd recognized this he'd walked out of the sea and picked up his rucksack and headed straight for the Garden State Parkway, thumbing every car.

'Last year,' the little man said, 'we visited the Bird Sanctuary at Stone Harbour, not far up the road from here. Have you ever visited it, young man?'

'No, sir, I haven't.'

'Oh, but you should!' The lady turned her head quickly, nodding with the daisy-chain hat.

'Yes, ma'am.'

'It's so very interesting,' her husband said, 'to see the herons flying in before sundown. It really is something one ought to see.'

There were trees now along the wide grass median and Russ couldn't see the northbound traffic any more, just the swift wash of leaves and the sky in the east where the storm-clouds were piled, yellow-tinted in the late sunlight.

The sea had been too slack for surfing and he'd found his friends holed-up in a crash-pad, two of them already high on speed, so he'd come away because you couldn't get any sense out of them when they were freaking, it made them dull as hell.

'Have you visited Cape May City before?'

The thing he couldn't understand was how he'd chosen to hang loose all last night and all today thinking about her, about Erica, without having the only one single possible idea hit him right between the eyes, which was to go and find her, not necessarily to talk to her but just to be there and look at her and breathe the air she breathed, listen, you take a weekend and without any warning the sky breaks open and suddenly the most phantasmagorically beautiful woman in the world touches down smack in front of you and tells you her name, Erica, and the first thing you do is say goodbye and get out of her car and the second thing you do is spend an entire night and day just thinking about her, about Erica, like you'd been turned into a bit of petrified timber, Jesus, are you clean out of thunderbolts or something, what have I done?

'Have you been to Cape May before, young man?'

'Huh? Excuse me. No, sir, no I haven't.'

'You'll find it very interesting, won't he, Eleanor?'

'He most certainly will, Matthew.'

A whole night and day just thinking, as if she was utterly unattainable, as if he didn't even know her name. Erica. Now he'd got started he'd have to catch up on all that lost time and somehow find her, find her somehow before the weekend was over and there was only one more minute left to say goodbye again. Sir, will you please go faster?

'The Victorian architecture is really something to be seen, houses like wedding-cakes, with the original façades and roof akroterians just as they were built a century ago. And you know how the streets are lighted?'

'No, sir, I don't.'

'By genuine gas lamps!'

Sir, won't you please drive very fast because she might leave before I reach there, I wasted so much time.

'And you can ride on a real horse-drawn trolley, just as grandmother did. When we get there we'll show you where the sight-seeing tour starts from.'

But that would take too long, I have the whole town to search and I've left it so late. Won't you drive so fast this whole great automobile flies off the ground, in some extrasensory way get the message I'm trying to send you, sir, with my eyes boring into the back of your head, so we can get there before she goes and the world ends? I'm not asking much.

Pushing silently, stealthily against the seat-back doesn't work, it's like you can't lift yourself up by pulling at your own shoelaces, there's a law by Newton or someone, all you can do is lean your arms along it and try not to notice how fast the daylight's fading when at dawn today it was blinding bright and you did nothing, a word as hollow as a zero.

How had she been, Erica? Smooth and honey-brown with amethyst eyes, her arms and her legs bare and her slight movements lithe as she drove the powder-blue Mustang, her moccasins matching her dress, her nearness filling a fool's head with the smell of roses till he couldn't breathe, her name in the air, Erica.

'It's very nice to find a young man your age interested in bygone things, isn't it Eleanor?'

'It's very rare, Matthew.'

Oh hurry. Please.

Hurry before she goes.

The signal came on the air at nine minutes after seven p.m. as Trooper Hunt cruised northbound on routine patrol approximately halfway between the Forked River Food and Fuel Area and Ocean Point Plaza.

75 to Base.

Go 'head 75.

There's an auto hit the trees on the median at Milepost 79 and there looks like a fire starting. I'm using the strip to go in close.

Hear you, standing by.

Hunt had noticed the tyre-marks first: the sudden crazy twisting of dark lines that led his eye immediately to the ploughed grass of the medial strip and then to the small isolated-looking wreck against the trees. There wasn't anyone around, no other cars, nobody on foot – the thing looked like it had just gone mad and died, all on its own.

The big black and yellow cruiser slewed to a halt on the parched grass and Hunt jumped out and used the fire-extinguisher, aiming the jet through the gap in the buckled hood of the wreck. Then he unclipped the mike in 75 again.

Confirm my Signal 11. And I need an ambulance.

Debby was moving the sprinkler to the far end of the lawn on Marina Drive when she heard the phone and went to answer it. The call had gone in to Ocean Point Rescue Squad from Troop E a minute ago at 7.12 p.m.

Within thirty seconds she was jogging out of the house to No. 2 Ambulance, zipping her white coveralls. A thought flashed into her mind as she passed under the tamarisk and she faltered and then ran on, climbing in and starting up.

Mr Solo was standing near the Telex booth in the operations room at Ocean Point Barracks, reading the Fatal Accident file. He was so engrossed that he failed to hear any significance in the signals now hitting the network, and didn't look up from the file.

Sergeant Gillespie didn't do anything about the neat grey-suited little man with the smoked glasses until Trooper Hunt asked for an ambulance; then he handed over the console to Schultz and lumbered to the door.

'Okay, Mr Solo.'

Driving northbound from Oyster Creek through the yellow-tinged evening light Frank heard the Signal 11 and began calling Car 75.

Lieutenant Ingram. What make of car is it that's crashed?

Hunt didn't reply. The OP network would have to wait till he was through with whatever first aid he was now giving, it being assumed he was within hearing-distance of his radio.

Frank crossed to the fast lane and went up to optimum speed for the light traffic conditions, closing on Milepost 79. The minute McTigue had told him the Venus was missing from the showroom he'd put out a signal to have it picked up just as soon as it was sighted, but there'd been no news of it since.

Ingram to 75. What make of car is it? What make of car?

CHAPTER TEN

It was quiet on the wide grass median. The heavy air, being windless, made no sound in the group of elms; and the murmur of the traffic passing north and south along the roadways on each side seemed muted by remoteness – those fast-moving vehicles had nothing to do with the one that lay against the trees, destroyed.

The huge sun, lowering above Lakeside, glowed for a few last minutes on the leaves. From the wreck of the Venus 1000 insignificant sounds came: the ticking of hot metal contracting as it cooled, the hiss of water-drops from the burst header-pipe hitting the exhaust manifold with meaningless regularity. The smell of hot oil, seeping from a buckled conduit, hung rancid on the air. The machine, in its running wild, had gouged troughs through the dry earth, wrenching the grass away; and its sharknose front end had ripped bark from a tree-bole, baring it white. It looked almost as if an insensate attack on nature had been made, and had failed.

The only movement was from the patrolman as he walked back to his black and yellow cruiser, the fire-extinguisher in his hand. Stowing it in the trunk with the rest of the emergency gear he took a camera and a surveyor's tape-measure, readying them for use. As reflected light swung across the grass he looked up and saw Reserve Car 80 turning from the southbound shoulder and heading towards him.

Sam Gillespie drew up alongside Hunt's 75 and shut off the motor, signalling his arrival by radio and climbing out.

'Perfect,' Mr Solo said, 'this is perfect.'

Sam glanced at him and away, going towards the wreck.

'No witnesses?' he asked as Hunt came up.

'I guess not, Sarge, Anyways, nobody stopped.'

Sam looked inside the Venus and turned away.

'You didn't see anything of it yourself?'

'Nope. I just saw the tyre-marks, then the wreck.'

'Okay, we take pix.'

Swerving off the northbound roadway Frank Ingram curved in towards the group of trees, slowing as he saw Gillespie and Hunt using the extended tape-measure. The only other person he could see was Mr Solo, his small body hooked across the open door of the wreck as he took an oblique close-up of the interior.

Frank had received no answer from his call to Car 75, asking for the make of the automobile that had crashed, perhaps because Trooper Hunt had been making sure there was no further risk of fire in the debris. Frank now saw for himself that it was the opalescent-bodied Venus 1000 lying buckled against the tree; and he would have left his cruiser and run toward it but for the quietness of the scene. Gillespie and Hunt were taking their time with the tape-measure, and the little civilian was using his camera with total unconcern. There was no crisis here. The crisis was over.

It's happened before. On his fourteenth birthday he took his brand-new bike and rode it right down the shore as far as Cape May without telling anyone he was going. They wouldn't have let him and he knew that. He was missing two days with the bike gone from the garage and everything, and only Debby kept me from cracking up.

It's happened today. There's a pattern to things.

But it won't ever happen again.

He brought the cruiser into line with the others, misjudging and correcting, his hands curiously nerveless on the wheel.

Put the gear into Park and shut off the motor and get out this is a Signal 11 get out and ask questions get your feet on the ground and walk and don't think it hasn't ever happened to other people and don't think it can't have happened to you because that's what they all think and they're wrong.

No eating cookies in bed.

No using someone else's razor.

No answering the phone with 'Yeah'.

No finishing the orange-juice without making more.

It had been pinned up on the closet-door in the bathroom and on Vince's last birthday when he was seventeen he'd said look I don't do any of those things any more so could we just take the darn thing down and pin up a picture of Mia Farrow instead or don't you think Dad's blood-pressure would stand it. Family joke.

Get out and walk.

Someone said something to him but he didn't know what it was they said. He walked towards the wreck of the Venus 1000, aware that walking had a very jerky motion compared with riding in an automobile, man should be born with wheels, he tripped where ruts had been cut into the earth, his feet clumsy, keep going, you have to look at your son.

No half-hour showers.

No riding to Cape May on your new bike.

But I don't see what everyone's so sore about, honest, I knew it'd be okay, gee, I can handle a bike, can't I?

We wouldn't have let you go if you'd told us.

Yeah, well I guess that's why I didn't tell you.

The ripped bark hung from the tree-bole.

I don't remember his name. Yes I do. His name is Mr Solo. Why are you taking photographs? We have photographs already in the album at home, on the shore in a sailor suit, at the annual graduation, on the boardwalk with his first girl, we don't want photographs now.

With most crashes you had to stand back while the police and medics mussed up the evidence and the wreckers dragged the thing clear of the highway but this was perfect and he took six more low-angle shots with the p.o.v. as close as he could make it to the base of the steering-column, the chief instrument of trauma.

The gyrations across the median had damped out more than half the speed of the vehicle and he estimated primary impact at near 30 m.p.h. with high magnitude deceleration by localized forces, secondary impact configurations the ignition-key, steering-column head and spokes. His ball-point was acting up so he shook it and did some doodling on the back of the record pad and got it working again. Severe crash loads, seat broken away from the runners (metal alloy, narrow lip), invasion of compartment by steering-column approximately three inches.

Mr Solo wrote fast from habit, although he knew there was no need for hurry today: the ambulance wasn't yet on the scene and the wrecker could wait until he was through, because here in the middle of the grass strip the wreckage was well clear of traffic and there was no debris hazard. He didn't have this kind of luck too often; it needed time and peace of mind to make a really adequate coverage. The police had given him wider facilities than most states offered: it wasn't always appreciated that a competent investigator, left on his own to examine wreckage and any available cadavers, could come up with data that would contribute handsomely to the research efforts directed at making the highway safer. You could do a great deal in laboratory crash-simulation using lifesize dummies and pre-mounted instrumentation – a great deal more, in certain areas, than you could do on the road, because ordinary cars didn't carry instruments ready to record the gamut of figures, rates and values involved by the forces applied; but you couldn't do it all, and there were aspects you could only examine when the crash was real, giving you an experiment *in vivo*.

He didn't record everything in his pad because some of the data would be requested from the manufacturers of the Venus 1000 and from the local hospital, but after looking at three or four hundred wrecks he'd formed the habit of making mental estimates and assumptions that would harm nobody if they were inaccurate. In this crash it was clear that certain things had necessarily occurred: a head-on primary collision with steering-column shaft and added load from the seat due to its breaking loose and hurling the driver against the wheel.

Peak deceleration of passenger compartment in the region of 30 g's with rate of onset maybe 500 g's per second; a certain degree of primary impact energy absorption by the shark-nose front end, but the fragility of the metal had allowed the steering-unit to strike the tree, lending a battering-ram effect to the column, upwards against the driver. It wasn't certain that a standard lap-diagonal configuration seat-belt would have saved this boy's life, but it was a hundred per cent certain that without such a belt he didn't have a chance. In the past seven years Mr Solo's research for the Boston unit had contributed to the statistics published by the National Safety Council: seat-belts could save up to eighty per cent of severe injuries and prevent ten thousand road-deaths annually. The problem wasn't how to make an effective restraint harness but how to make the driver wear it. Belts were now available to four out of five motorists but they were being used less than half the time, and if reputedly adult people didn't have the sense to save themselves, how could you expect a teenager in a sports car to live once he'd crashed?

Death due to ruptured aorta, severe blood loss, gross thoracic damage by broken spokes of wheel, probable air embolism, kneecap prised away by ignition-key, pelvis fractured by force transmitted by thigh-bone from knee, various whiplash injuries. There was nothing remarkable.

He took three more pictures, feeling a little let down because there were no new features that he could see. All indications composed the known classic picture: when a car hits a tree it doesn't hurt the driver; the driver gets hurt when his body starts travelling at the speed of the car and he hits the inside of it; he gets hurt much more when the manufacturer is permitted by law to furnish lethal impact points such as ignition-keys, sharp facia panel edges and resistant steering-gear; he gets hurt much less when he wears a belt that stops him hitting the inside of the car and stops the seat's momentum thrusting him forward; and until the passenger compartment of an automobile is designed as a permanent shelter from the storm conditions arising in an accident, the automobile will remain the most hazardous and the most murderous means of travelling, by a factor of ninety per cent.

Mr Solo put his camera away and stepped back from the wreckage, brushing his pants down and removing, with a leaf from the tree, a bloodspot from his left shoe. The police lieutenant had come up and was looking inside the car, standing with a strange stiffness that made it seem as if he were being held upright by invisible hands. Too, his face had a pallor, and Mr Solo wondered whether he could be one of those people who got faint at the sight of blood.

'Guess it's a routine job, Lieutenant.'

Frank walked back to his cruiser and started up and made a fast U-turn over the grass, heading for the northbound roadway because the Number 2 ambulance from Ocean Point Rescue Squad would be coming in that direction and if he could head it off before Debby saw the Venus he'd be able to tell her first. It was certain to be Debby because Number 2 was covering the Parkway this weekend and she and Ann Stefano were crewing it.

Sergeant Gillespie and Hunt were on their way back from photographing the marks on the road and he avoided them in a wide curve, making for the flat section of the median where it was level with the shoulder. He saw the big red cross on the ambulance when he was within fifty feet of the roadway, and made another fast turn so as to head it off. By the time it had left the shoulder he was out of his car and standing with his hand raised. The white Cadillac pulled up near him and Debby jumped out, looking towards the group of trees.

'Vince wasn't in the car,' he told her.

She didn't look at him; she went on staring at the wreck of the Venus and he knew she'd recognized it by its opalescent colour and what was left of its styling. Her hand was slowly going up to her face.

'Debby. He isn't there. He wasn't in the car.'

She still didn't look at him, didn't even hear him because she thought Vince must be there so it didn't matter who spoke to her or what they said, it wasn't important compared with what she believed.

'Debby.' He gripped her wrist and swung her to face him. 'Vince wasn't in the Venus, you understand?' His tone or the pain in her wrist made her aware of him and of what he was saying, and she lost her frozen stare. In a moment she said:

'Who was in it?'

'Only Danny.'

'Not Vince.'

'No. Just Danny.'

She looked back at the group of trees, their black leaves burning against the sundown.

'Is he dead?'

'Yes.'

'I don't understand.' She turned to him. 'We thought they were together.'

'It looks like they weren't.'

She nodded, and in a moment touched his hand and turned away, getting into the ambulance.

The tall masts glowed at their tips, the last of the sun's light touching them with fire. Lower, the rigging made soft lace-work across the dusk. A boy sat at the harbour's edge, fishing, and people watched his line.

'Let's go see Toni,' Nat Renatus said.

'No.'

The cigarette had gone out and Nat flicked it through the window of the Chrysler Newport and lit another; he gripped them too hard so they went out; Rod Gould had never told him and he'd never figure it for himself. His fingers shook, holding the lighter, and Rod noticed and looked away.

'Give him all the sugar,' Nat said, 'for Christ's sake do what he wants.' He'd said it a dozen times. 'We need that boat.' A dozen times.

Rod sat very still. He'd learned not to move too much; there wasn't any pain now but he had the feeling if he moved too much he'd rip something apart inside him where Nolan's bullet was.

'I'd rather they got me,' he said, 'than have a bastard wop like Toni Lago sell me out.'

Renatus twisted in his seat to face Rod Gould and spoke very fast with sometimes a kind of whimper in his voice.

'Okay so he's a bastard so we don't do what he wants so we don't get the boat, don't you see that? How long can we keep going when all we've got is an auto that can turn hot any next minute, you heard the news, there's been a squeal, we stick with this buggy an' they pick us up, we junk it an' heist another one an' it's hot before we get started, for Christ sake listen to me, Rod, we need that boat, you want to spend the rest of your life inside like Pete Wolf an' Simmermacher an' guys like them, what good's a hundred thousand bucks in sugar once we're in the pen?'

Rod Gould sat like a sack.

'I don't sell out,' he said, 'to guys like Toni Lago.'

'Will you for Christ sake listen to –'

'What do we do for cash if he cleans us out?'

'I got a thousand –'

'We're on the run. How far can we run with a grand?'

'We can lie low –'

'It can take a grand to shut one mouth, just one.'

'But we'll be in Haiti –'

'If we sell out.'

Renatus dragged smoke in and looked through the windshield, his thin starved face squeezed with nerves and his eyes flickering, the sweat running on him and disgusting him, his fleshless monkey hands feeling too long unwashed. He didn't understand Rod any more. The stuff was in the trunk and all they had to do was give it to Toni Lago and they'd board the boat, the one across the harbour there with the sun shining on the masts, and at eleven tomorrow morning they'd head out to sea. They'd be free.

'If we don't give him what he wants,' he said to Rod, 'we're finished.'

'He'll take half.'

'But he says –'

'*Christ,*' Rod cursed, and his heavy head swung to face Renatus, 'a wop bastard says he wants the skin off your back an' you want to tell him he can take it, what kinda deal is that?'

Nat snapped open the door of the two-tone Chrysler and

punched the windshield-washer button and got out and held his fingers in the jets of water, the heat of the day on his back and the fear of tomorrow like a hollow in his mind, Rod with a slug in him and a squeal on for them both. They'd never be clean, his hands would never be clean if he stood here doing this till he died.

This was where the road ran out.

In a rooming-house in Cape May with plaster seagulls on the wall and a cheap clock set in a varnished helm on the bedside table and a view of the harbour through the lace-curtained window, the whole décor unsuccessfully quaint but like it or not the new background – at least for this weekend – for the new Erica Sigrist, the self-emancipated cool-as-hell single-minded and single-handed Women's Libber, not quite the kind of background she'd have chosen for the most irretrievably lost weekend of her life but if you could find even a room like this anywhere at all along the New Jersey shore right now you were counted among the favoured of the gods.

It had been booked, the owner had told her Friday evening, by a newly-wedded couple who hadn't shown, and she was welcome. In the double bed where two young people had meant to begin what she had just ended, she'd lain awake most of the night listening to the power boats that sometimes throbbed in the harbour, watching the lights of cars fanning across the ceiling, thinking of Craig and rewriting, over and over, the note that she'd put in the mails for him to read on Monday morning . . . *I'm sorry I stayed too long, but you're young enough to start again with somebody else* . . . wishing she'd put *with Georgina or Alexis* to show she was objective enough to mention their names in an intimate farewell message . . . *At this stage we can make a nice calculated break and prove how very well-organized we are* . . . wishing she hadn't let the bitterness show in those bravely nonchalant phrases, wishing, sometimes in the darkest and most quiet hours, that it was only a nightmare of a particularly coherent kind.

Today she'd taken the Mustang from the sandy parking lot near the house and gone to mingle with the Saturday crowds in the Victorian Village, visiting the Museum and riding on the horse-drawn trolley, trying to rid herself of identity and therefore of pain by becoming one of a throng, just another footloose vacationer, till the strangeness of finding herself among the fellow-humans she'd managed nearly all her life to avoid had brought her back to the rooming-house, where this evening she climbed the stairs and closed the door and did what she'd wanted to do ever since she'd written *Goodbye Craig* and headed out of New York yesterday morning.

'Are y'okay, honey?'

There was knocking again.

But tears are a kind of frontier beyond which you've gone, and gone alone; you take refuge in them when no one in the world can help, however hard they try; so when they knock at the door you don't really hear them, because you don't want to; all you want is to be left alone with this hot salty welling-over of deliverance with no one near to deny you.

When the door opened Erica didn't look up. It was the cleaning-woman, she knew by her voice. She'd passed her sometimes on the stairs, a blowsy woman, heavy and over-blown. They called her Sadie.

'It'll come out okay.'

Gulls cried from the harbour; through the doorway came a smell of cooking.

'It always gets to come out okay.'

Erica nodded, sitting upright on the bed and blowing her nose. Sadie watched her, some laundered towels on her fat bare arm; her big square face was gathered in compassion.

'I'm all right now,' Erica said.

'Sure y'are, honey. I just didn't like to hear you goin' on that way without seein' – you know – if there was anything I could do.' She had a deep voice, a singer's.

Then Erica said what she'd never dreamed she'd say to anyone, because it was personal, and private, and sordid.

'I just left my husband.'

The woman's laugh was loud in the room, a rich ringing, and Erica looked up at her, startled.

'That all you did, honey? Sakes, I used t' leave 'em regular, did some of 'em a power o' good, others finally couldn't stand it.' The deep laughter bubbled again and she came over to the bed, moving lightly on her curiously small feet, showing Erica her left hand. 'Can you count? The three plain gold ones lasted around a couple of years each, and I kept the one with the diamond going almost a decade – I ain't no fool – before he finally ran out on me. Matter of fact I'd gone already but he didn't know an' I never told him since, because he was the kind o' klutz that always likes to be first, it was the least I could do for the poor slob. I was in vaudeville, you know?' She settled the towels on her huge red arm again and studied Erica from beneath half-inch-long stick-on eyelashes. 'You get to meet a whole slew of screwballs, not all of 'em backstage. What's yours like, honey?'

It was a minute before Erica realized that after twelve years she knew so little about Craig that she didn't have an immediate answer. Since yesterday morning when she'd dropped the letter in the mailbox she'd given almost all her thought to their marriage and what she was doing to it.

'He's – very handsome.'

'Uh-huh.'

'And very successful. He's in business management.'

Sadie observed the elegant and expensive Alex Colman print, the blue suède casuals, the diamanté wristlet watch.

'Well-heeled.'

'He's – created a substantial business in Manhattan.'

'Nothin' excitin' about him, so far. That why you lit out?' She turned away, shrugging. 'It ain't my affair, honey. I just – you know – thought maybe you were in some kinda trouble. Y'okay now?'

Erica sat on the edge of the double bed with the dark patch left by her tears, looking up red-eyed at the woman whom she could have thought of as a comic bit-player if it weren't for the fact that for the first time in her life she needed the warmth of another human being and the only one immediately to hand was Sadie.

'No.'

'Uh?'

'I'm not okay yet.'

'Guess it'll take time. How long was the term?'

'Pardon me?'

'How long did the marriage last?'

'Twelve years, this June nineteenth.'

'Gee, you got a lotta stamina. What happened?'

'You mean –'

'Why d'ya bust it, honey?'

Erica got off the bed and found some Kleenex, blowing

her nose again. In the glass next to the white china lighthouse on the dresser her face looked pinched, and her eyeblack had run.

'Craig was spending more and more of his time away from home, and finally I hardly ever saw him.'

'Other women?'

'Two or three.'

Sadie stood in the doorway eyeing the slim good-looking young woman with the blue misty eyes and the golden tan. 'What could they possibly have that you haven't?'

'Thank you. But whatever it is, Craig needs it.'

'Just novelty, I'd say. When I was your age I topped the competition for the Golden Girl shows at the Stardust in 'Frisco three years running, but my second husband still had to go right through the chorus, he was the restive type.'

'Craig wasn't quite like that.' She found her cigarette-case from the powder-blue handbag. 'Do you smoke?'

'Sure.'

'They were interesting women, one of them married and two with careers, I mean it wasn't just sex.'

'Do you have a job?'

'No.'

'Don't need one.'

Erica dropped the ashtray on to the bed where Sadie could reach it. 'It isn't that. I haven't the intelligence.'

'You mean the interest, honey.'

'Perhaps. The – the marriage was everything.'

'You got kids?'

'No. We neither of us wanted any.'

'Too busy.'

'It sounds almost irresponsible, I know.'

'It does?'

'I mean not to help perpetuate the species.'

'Is that why people have kids?'

'Craig and I didn't have any because we thought it would spoil a perfect marriage.' She looked a little defiantly at the ex-Vaudeville queen and said with emphasis: 'It was, for a time, a perfect marriage.'

'They all are, honey.' Some people were coming up the narrow Victorian staircase and she swung the door closed.

'I believe ours was special.'

'An' they're all special. Don't get me wrong, I know it can hurt.'

Erica turned away, afraid of wanting to cry again, standing with her arms folded and staring through the window to where the gulls drifted across the masts in the harbour, the sky leaden beyond them, wondering why it had to be a stranger who could tell her things her friends had never understood.

'I think it only hurts because I did everything to make it a perfect marriage – checking every day with his secretary so I'd never be away when he came home, wearing the clothes he liked to see me in, wearing my hair the way I knew it pleased him, having the cook prepare the kind of food he always chose in restaurants, till – till he stopped coming home to eat it, or to look at my hair or share the end of the day with me, just the two of us, the way it used to be. And even when I heard about the reason for the overnight business trips and the breakfast meetings I told him it was all right, he had to relax, I'd be there whenever he wanted me just the same. I – I used to leave a low light burning every night when I went to bed, so that he'd see his way, and often in the morning I didn't notice it was still on, because of the daylight, so it'd still be burning the next night, and I'd leave it for him in case he came. Then he was away four nights running, with only a call from his secretary to say he had an important meeting in Washington, and it was the fourth night when I turned the little lamp out, and the next morning I left.'

Sadie watched her, the cigarette in her bright painted lips and one eye half-closed against the smoke. She didn't say anything.

Erica turned from the window. 'What more could I have done?'

'Y' could've bashed him around a little.'

'I don't think you understand.'

'Maybe I don't, honey, but I'm just goin' on my experience an' let's face it I got a head start on you. It ain't many men who go for the idea of spending their life in a gilded cage, an' there's not too many that want their wife to be a slave-girl, whole thing gets too suffocatin' either way. These busters are world champs at self-worship an' it stands t' reason they don't want us amateurs tryin' to do it for them, also they tend to be an acquisitive bunch o' hombres an' they ain't real happy till they've gotten themselves a couple flash automobiles an' fifty neckties an' a mortgage like a millstone that guarantees they got to keep on strugglin' till it kills 'em off, an' when they want a woman it's the same thing, they like to make an effort, chase her up hill an' down dale an' fight off a few dinosaurs an' finally club the critter an' drag her all the way back to the cave an' then dust her down like she's got value for 'em. An' honey, that's the value they got, or the most of it, I don't care if they're a coupla shinin' an' ever-lovin' angels like you an' me, we're just the object of achievement. An' y' can't just leave things like that, don't y' see? They got to go on achievin' things an' it don't matter a goddam if it's somethin' new or the same darn thing all over again, they're that stupid. Thing is, you got smart finally, huh? You'll find this Craig of yours a changed man when you go back, orchids wherever you look an' Cartier's delivery truck parked right outside, give him a week for the principle of the thing but make it ten days if y' fancy more than one diamond in the setting.'

Erica shook her head.

'I'm not going back.'

'It's for real?'

'I put a note in the mails for him. It says *finis.*'

'Well that's great, as soon as he reads that he'll run back all the faster.'

'I don't want him back.'

'Y' don't?' Sadie squinted at her through the smoke. 'Then why send him a note? If you really mean to leave him then y' just quit, y' don't have to overload the US mail.'

Erica moved slowly to the bed, pressing her cigarette out, feeling weak in her whole body from the fit of sobbing. Bleakly she said:

'It wouldn't be the same, if he came back.'

'What wouldn't, honey?'

'The marriage.'

Sadie watched her steadily, her deep eyes brooding in the painted crumpled face, a tendril of smoke rising, the yellow glow from the window lighting her four wedding-bands. Someone below in the house was calling her name and she chose not to hear.

'So that's what you walked out on. The marriage.'

'Well, yes.' Erica looked puzzled.

'Not Craig.'

'On him too. I mean he – was the marriage.'

'Uh-huh.' Sadie used the ashtray, leaving a crimsoned butt. 'He thinks he's a man. You figure there could be some kind o' message tryin' to get through to us there, or are we just crowdin' Western Union?'

'Are you all right, Sue?'

'I'm dandy.'

Her smile shimmered beside him and she felt for his hand.

Floyd kept on looking around at the other people in the audience. The billboards outside the Beach Haven Summer Theatre had promised A Bumper Evening of Variety but he naturally didn't expect to pay much attention to what was happening on the stage, because Curly had been kicking much worse all afternoon and Sue had kept feeling her stomach and laughing and saying things like 'Oh-ho, ride 'em cowboy!' until he couldn't stand it any more and tried to make her take a sedative in the hope it would get through to Curly. Of course she'd refused. She just didn't seem to appreciate the seriousness of imminent childbirth, when a whole new life was in the balance.

A gentleman came to see me yesterday, the man on the stage was saying (he was billed as Doctor Delirium), *and began almost pleading with me as soon as he came into my consulting room.*

Floyd went on looking around the audience, particularly at the women, turning his eyes more than his head, so that Sue wouldn't notice. He didn't want to think about doctors, certainly not bogus ones who'd be completely useless if the crisis came. And it'd sound ridiculous if he had to stand up suddenly and shout out 'Is there a *real* doctor in the house?' This idiot on the stage was only reminding him of reality instead of trying to take his mind off things.

'Oh Doctor, Doctor,' the gentleman cried, 'you'll have to help me!' Well I calmed him down a little and asked him what was troubling him. 'It's my memory, Doctor – it's got so bad I can't remember anything even for a few seconds!' So I gave him a chair and asked him: 'How long have you been suffering from this?' And he said – 'Suffering from what?'

The laughter annoyed Floyd because it broke his concentration. He was looking for a certain type of woman in the audience and so far he hadn't seen one. Also he couldn't completely get out of his mind that awful moment this afternoon when Sue had tripped on something buried in the sands, and it was only because he'd been walking backwards in front of her that he'd saved her from going down. Even then she'd only treated it as a joke. He'd pointed out how serious it could have been, but she'd just said, 'Don't worry, darling, I'm not taking any chances – I intend Curly to have New York citizenship!' And when he'd said he frankly wasn't worried about his citizenship she'd just laughed again, for no reason.

'Floyd.'

'Yes?'

'Who are you looking for?'

'I'm not looking for anybody.'

'That's fine. Could you just stop turning around the whole time?'

'Sure, I didn't know I was doing it.'

He hated lying to her, but the situation called for extreme measures. The thing was, he didn't really know what they looked like, these women; and anyway they might look entirely different when they were sort of 'off duty' and watching a variety show – he'd never had to think about them before. There'd been one he'd seen yesterday, at the Howard Johnson's down the Parkway, and he'd wanted to speak to her alone, but with Sue there it had been impossible. He thought he'd seen one just now in the row behind him, six along, but he couldn't be sure.

If the crisis actually came, he'd bear this woman in mind, though the choice would be damnably difficult: either he could stand up and yell *'Is there a real doctor in the house?'* or he could clamber along the seats till he was facing the woman and say urgently *'Are you a midwife?'*.

She looked like the waitress in the Howard Johnson's, motherly with plump arms and her face kindly; but of course he'd only ever seen them on the movies. In reality they could be as thin as rakes with faces like vultures, and he didn't have any means of knowing. The ones on the movies were always plump and sort of secretive-looking, only half-seen behind clouds of steam, rather like well-fed witches at a cauldron. He didn't know which type he'd rather they didn't look like most.

Only last week a poor feller was run over by a Beach Haven Borough steam-roller, but when they brought him along to my consulting-room I was unfortunately out for a few minutes, so they slipped him under the door.

As people laughed a voice sounded from right behind Floyd:

'Could you please keep still in your seat?'

'I'm sorry,' he said, half-turning.

He felt Sue's movement beside him.

'Floyd.'

'Yes?'

'Who was that?'

'I don't know.'

'But you spoke to them.'

'No, they spoke to me.'

'Well what did they say?'

'I didn't hear, because people were laughing.'

Doctor Delirium was telling them about a patient of his with galloping appendicitis, and Floyd tried not to hear. Another sound came now, from outside the theatre, and some of the people glanced upwards, then at each other. It had been a thunderclap, and Floyd drew a deep breath to steady himself. Everyone at the motel had been saying there'd be a storm tonight, and he'd tried to persuade Sue to read in bed because it was well known that many people were affected by thunder and lightning. (Under 'Miscarriages' it had said that any shock, whether it be physical or emotional, could precipitate premature birth.) Plenty of women, while quite courageous when it came to washing a whole stack of dishes and things like that, would rush to the nearest man for protection during a storm. But Sue had said she didn't come to Beach Haven to read in bed, and besides she liked a good thunderstorm and hoped they'd be able to watch it from the bandstand.

When another rumble came across the roof of the theatre he began looking around for the emergency exits. It was all very fine to profess to like storms but if a thunderbolt hit this place there'd be immediate panic and a stampede.

'Floyd darling, would you please tell me what's bothering you?'

'Nothing's bothering me. I'm looking for the emergency exit, that's all.'

'Is there going to be an emergency?'

'Of course not.' It was vital not to worry her. (The husband's responsibility, it said under 'Prenatal Care', is expressed chiefly in his rôle of protector, shielding the mother-to-be from all disturbing influences.) 'I'm just – I'm just interested in theatre design.'

'Oh I see. The actual stage is an attractive feature of this one, don't you think? Would you like to study it for a while?'

The roof boomed again, though nobody paid any attention this time: it was disturbing how fast people got used to imminent danger. Floyd stared at the stage, committing to memory the fact that the woman with the plump face two rows back and three along looked very promising, and that the nearest emergency exit was on the left and around half-way up the side of the auditorium.

A lady called me up last week from the headquarters of the Beach Haven Young Mothers Association. 'Doctor Delirium,' she asked me nervously, 'we're scared at the idea of our little ones growing weak from undernourishment due to our ignorance of their needs. Just how do we tell when an infant is becoming hungry?' 'Young lady,' I said, 'when you hear what you think are fifteen full-grown lions roaring through a public-address amplifier, just get the bottle.'

Even through the laughter Floyd detected the rumbling of the storm, and braced himself in his seat. He'd been utterly wrong in letting Sue persuade him to come all this way down the New Jersey shore for the weekend. Instead of their being in the security of their apartment, where he could spend the evening fetching her cushions and cooling drinks, they were trapped here in a public place where any minute he might have to save her from being trampled underfoot by a fear-crazed mob.

Her hand tightened on his own.

'Relax, darling. Everything's dandy.'

'Look, nobody could be more relaxed than me.'

Vince had managed to get a lift from the Citgo station as far as the Ocean Point interchange, and from there he began walking to McTigue's Garage. It was almost dark, because he'd waited a half-hour at the Citgo for Danny to come back with the Venus. Then he'd started asking for a lift and it hadn't been easy.

Tramping down Marina Drive, he kept right on past his home, because Danny would have gone straight back to the garage. Vince was still angry with the kid because even for a sixteen-year-old auto-fanatic it'd been a crazy thing to do, going off that way and leaving him stranded at the Citgo station. When he'd got out of the Venus to pay for the gas he'd gone across to the rest-rooms for a drink because his mouth was still dry as hell from worrying if they'd make it to the station before the tank ran empty; and when he'd come back to the line of pumps the car wasn't there any more.

He didn't think Danny had just driven away the minute his back was turned; they were quite close friends and that would've been a lousy trick to pull. He thought maybe the gas-pump jockey had asked Danny to move the Venus along a little to make room and the temptation to keep on going had just been too much for him. And it was understandable that once he'd got started on his jag he hadn't been keen to come back to the Citgo and get bawled out.

Well, he was going to get bawled out anyhow. The two-mile trudge from the Parkway interchange to McTigue's in this heat wasn't liable to change Vince's mind about that.

Leaving the crash scene at Milepost 79, Debby had stopped the ambulance to have a word with Frank. She looked blotchy under her summer tan and her eyes were screwed up a little as though even the low light of the sundown were too bright.

'D'you want an escort?' he asked her.

'No, Frank. There's no hurry.' She looked abstractedly across to where Sam Gillespie and Hunt were completing their measurements over the grass median, their shadows long and reaching almost to the wrecked Venus 1000. Then her eyes returned to Frank. 'Who's going to tell Mr McTigue?'

'I am.'

'All right.'

The ambulance moved away and Debby didn't look back.

Fifteen minutes later Frank had left his men in charge of the accident scene and driven straight to Ocean Point, trying to work out the best way of breaking the news. Finally he thought that with a man like McTigue there was only one way. Now they were standing together under the high swan-neck lamps of the garage. Behind McTigue the showroom was empty, its glass doors still wide open.

'We picked up the Venus,' Frank said.

'Y' did?'

McTigue's long thin legs were astride, in the way he nearly always stood, as if, shy of his height, he were trying to seem shorter. He didn't look at Frank but at his thin veined hands, wiping them on a rag with ritualistic care.

'Danny must have taken it,' Frank said.

'Uh-huh. Was he speeding?'

Frank looked at the man, at his hollowed face with its eyes set deep under their brows, the gaunt angular head that he'd passed on to his son together with the reserve, the unknowability that had still kept both of them apart, here in Ocean Point, from friendship that could otherwise have been theirs. And Frank wondered, as people did around here, whether McTigue had always been this way, or only since his wife had died a few years ago.

'No, we don't think he was speeding. But he lost control of the Venus and there was an accident, McTigue. Danny didn't survive.'

The man's hands stopped moving and he stood perfectly still in an attitude of listening, as if it hadn't been Frank who'd spoken, but a voice inside, a voice that maybe was going on, telling him what to do, how to manage. Frank heard an auto slowing from Shore Avenue and coming in past the gas-pumps, stopping; but he didn't turn, and McTigue didn't look up.

Then his hands moved again and he screwed the rag into a ball, holding it on his spread palms, watching its folds opening.

'There must've been something I did, once.' His quiet voice sounded puzzled. 'Something bad. But I don't remember anything.'

Frank heard Debby coming across from the ambulance.

As he neared them Vince saw they were standing in a group under the lamps, his mother and father looking at Mr McTigue as if listening to him, though he didn't seem to be talking. The ambulance was halted at an angle between the gas-pumps and the greasing bay, as if there'd been no point leaving it correctly parked; the driver's door still hung slightly open, like his mother hadn't wanted to make a noise slamming it shut. Across in the little office the phone was ringing, but nobody went to answer it.

These signs of something wrong, and others more subtle that informed Vince quite without his knowing, began a slow terror in him. Halfway across to the showroom he saw it was still empty, and looked around for the Venus, and couldn't see it, and knew he was going to remember, all his life, these three people standing here in their private silence.

CHAPTER ELEVEN

Heading back to Ocean Point Barracks and leaving Hunt to organize the removal of the smashed Venus from the median at Milepost 79, Sam Gillespie drove with a feeling of unease.

In better than twenty years of operational police work he'd seen about all there was, and these days when he saw further evidence of what a machine could do to a human being when it ran wild he wasn't too much affected by it. It was the silence in the patrol car that was needling his nerves, and finally he decided to break it.

'You satisfied, Mr Solo?'

The little man next to him had just sat staring through the windshield ever since they'd left the crash scene, his body characteristically erect like a perched bird's, and once or twice Sam had seen his narrowed reflection in the edge of the mirror, the black brilliantined hair smoothed neatly back, the smoked glasses hiding his eyes, the black necktie reminding of mourning. If Sam had been given any choice he would have opted for a vulture as his passenger, though he thought there maybe wouldn't have been much difference. For all his two hundred and ten pounds and his bullhorn voice Sam had some imagination and it could now and again get out of hand just like anyone else's, and he could believe it was possible that if this bird of ill omen hadn't been perched on the roof of the office all afternoon there wouldn't have been a fatal accident at Milepost 79.

'It was undistinguished.'

'Pardon me?'

'There were no interesting features to that crash,' said Mr

Solo. 'There were just the expected traumata from the usual objects and forces.'

'That's a shame. An' now just a routine funeral.'

'I certainly don't think an autopsy would reveal anything worthwhile.'

Sam didn't answer.

'Of course this type of post-crash research can assist ergonomic studies in quite a few aspects. When you're trying to work out a comfortable relationship between man and machine, a satisfactory way for them to live with each other safely and fruitfully, it can help to know in detail what happens when they don't. This case has typicality: young males of fifteen to twenty-five are statistically the highest risk on the nation's roads, chiefly because at that period of their lives they need to express and assert themselves and there's nothing with more dramatic potential than an automobile. The ergonomists have to do a lot of thinking in that area alone.'

Listening to him, Sam was reminded of Captain Darrow with his hang-up for statistics. An hour ago he'd been on the line to Bass River Barracks and Sergeant Augenblick there had sounded off about him – 'You know who's just been here? That boy wonder from Washington, telling us how many shiploads of people get smashed up every month on the road, just what it has to do with ships I haven't got figured out yet. Listen, who sicked this guy on to Troop "E" in the first place?'

As Sam made a final turn and took the access ramp for Ocean Point Barracks he considered that the trouble with specialists like Darrow and Mr Solo was that instead of coming up with new aspects of the traffic accident scene that nobody'd thought of before, they just took a whole lot of obvious situations and dressed them up in fancy figures. They'd spend the entire night with a slide rule and an ice-bag and by the brave light of the new day they'd announce their sensational findings – that if a drunk drove too often he'd wind up a dead duck, that the faster a man drove the less long he'd live, that if your auto smacked into a wall you'd go through the windshield. Surprise.

The way he saw it, there was a thing made of chemistry and electricity and a stomach and a soul sitting inside a thing made of metal and levers and pistons and paintwork and this was the best they'd ever be able to do with each other – they hadn't been meant to share life anyway, it was like a lot of marriages, the people shouldn't ever have met up in the first place.

'What I really need,' Mr Solo told him as they drove into the base parking lot, 'is a high-impact case with two people in the passenger compartment and only one of them wearing a seat-belt.'

'Is that so?' Sam cut the motor and the squawk. 'Then I hope you never get it.'

Mr Solo turned his head.

'But of course I will. In my field of research there's fresh material constantly being produced.'

He didn't expect a sergeant of police to grasp the complexities of the traffic accident problem. One fine day it was going to be as safe to drive in an automobile as it was to fly in an aeroplane today, and this could be achieved only through painstaking groundwork.

'Okay, Mr Solo, to you they're just fresh material. But they're also people. That kid in the Venus was the local garage man's boy, a real auto buff. His best buddy was Lieutenant Ingram's son. It comes kinda close, sometimes, but I guess you've been lucky so far.'

In the lowering twilight the shade of the big sycamore was almost black as they passed through it towards the office with its bright windows.

'So far, yes,' said Mr Solo, 'I've been lucky.'

It wasn't worth telling the sergeant anything different. It had happened too long ago.

'Let's hope you stay that way. You're not coming in?'

'I'll watch the twilight a while.'

The usual reaction was beginning, but it didn't bother him. Visiting the crash scene, there was always the moment when he looked for the first time inside the wreck and wondered if at last he'd find what he was looking for; and later there was always this slight reaction, a sense of disappointment, frustration almost, that once again he'd missed the perfect crash that would tell him everything.

The big tree was dark above him, its massed leaves reaching so low that only a strip of sky remained between them and the horizon where the clouds were yellowed, piling on each other.

Your Ma an' Pa, the neighbour had said, *they jus' went off in their beautiful new roadster, and kinda kept on goin'.*

He didn't remember much about the neighbour after al those years, but it had been a woman with bright eyes anc warm arms who'd held him tight and kind of rocked him witl her, telling him in a shaky voice what a beautiful new roadste they'd chosen to go away in together, such a long way, anc that he must keep a watch out for it so maybe he'd see i one day riding up there in the clouds.

But there was no point remembering things like that fron way back in his childhood. It was the present he was con cerned with now. Life and death had to be thought of in thei correct perspective: the physical vulnerability of the humar frame, the gross inequality between the man who could hardl do more with his bare hands than make a scratch on the machine, and the machine that could crush him like a fly once he lost control of it.

There was only one approach: the scientific. The applica tion of reasoned thought to a situation that was otherwis nothing more than an accident. Only in this way could the problem ever be licked.

'What's new, Schultz?'

'Couple of drunk drivers, three overheats and a gas-out Sarge.' He pushed the Aid Sheet across the desk. 'How wa the smackeroo down at 79?'

'Lousy,' Sam said. 'Stinkin'.'

Schultz looked up at him quickly, opened his mouth to sa something, decided not to say it, and looked away again. Th heat was getting everybody down, even the Sergeant.

'Telex?'

'Two messages, Sarge. Right here.'

Sam looked at them.

Attention all Station Commanders. Toll Plazas will b closing down automatic lanes as of 11 p.m., repeat 11 p.m. instead of midnight, in order to bring any drinking driver under the inspection of toll collectors.

The second one was a General Alert.

NYC Police Dept informs that subsequent to new revela tions the two men suspected of slaying Officer John Nola early yesterday are now believed to be in vicinity of Cap May City. Names and descriptions follow. (1) Rod Gould, ag

45, 5 ft 11 ins, 190 lbs, brown hair, balding, brown eyes, clothing unknown. (2) Nat Renatus, age 36, 5 ft 5 ins, 98 lbs, black hair, grey eyes, slight build, clothing unknown. One of these men has bullet wound and may seek medical attention. All Troop E patrols will keep special lookout for above.

'Did you squawk this alert, Schultz?'

Measuring up at the crash scene, Sam had been out of touch with his radio.

'Went out twenty minutes ago, Sarge.'

'Okay.' Sam ran his eye over the signals board. 'Put out another one. Cancel signal to pick up the Venus 1000.'

Schultz tipped the switch.

Parking Number 2 Ambulance between the house and the tamarisk tree, Debby got out and went across to where Frank had stopped his patrol car. He'd brought Vince along with him from the garage.

They'd offered to take Mr McTigue to the hospital where Danny was, but he'd just said stiffly: 'I'll drive myself.' The lights of the house weren't on yet, and in the dusk they saw how pale Vince looked. He was walking towards the front porch when Frank said:

'Did you know Danny took the Venus?'

It was very quiet in the garden, though a murmur rolled in the east sky. Vince turned. His tone sounded numb, as if his mouth were bruised.

'I took it.'

He wasn't looking at either of them, just in their direction.

In a moment Frank said wearily: 'You took it? You were driving?'

'Yes.'

'Frank,' Debby said quietly, but he shook his head.

'We have to know what happened.' He said to Vince: 'How did he finish up alone in the car?'

Vince didn't answer for a bit. He seemed to be thinking all the time of something else, and to resent his father's interruptions. Then he drew a breath and said indifferently. 'We stopped for gas. I went for a drink. He drove away.'

'He drove away without you?'

'Didn't I just say?'

It didn't sound like his voice; it didn't look like his face.

He stood turned towards them but that was all; there wasn't any communication. They stood together by the dark house lost.

Frank said: 'What made you take the Venus?'

'I'm going up to my room.' He was looking straight at his father now. 'Is that okay?'

Pale flashes came into the sky a long way off. Somewhere crickets sang.

'Yes,' Frank said. 'Go on up.'

They watched Vince turn and go into the house. He didn't switch any lights on. In a while they heard his door close, the sound reaching them through the open window.

'Frank.'

Debby took his arm and they walked across the lawn, the smell of the mown grass still sweet, with damp rising from where the sprinklers had played. When they were far enough from his window Frank said:

'He did it before.'

'Did what?'

'Went off like that. On his new bike.'

'We have to try not to judge him.'

'But I mean he fetched the groceries and cut the grass and all the time –'

'Don't condemn him, Frank.'

With his voice rising he said, 'But listen, he took a car and a kid got killed, how d'you think McTigue feels about this how d'you think he feels about Vince? He'd be –'

'He'll hear you, Frank. He knows what he did. He doesn't need telling.'

Frank stood back, away from her, as if their breach of understanding had moved them physically apart.

'We can't just leave this thing as it is, Debby.'

She said, looking down, her hands in the pockets of her coveralls, her dark head low, 'Whatever we do, it won't bring Danny back. And whatever you want to do to Vince, remember something for me, for my sake. Only a little time ago we believed he'd been killed too. Let it affect your thinking.'

It wasn't quite dark in the room. The window cut a pale oblong out of the sky. A moth was trapped somewhere near the ceiling, maybe in one of the lamps, it wouldn't stop fluttering.

And that was all there was to it.

When we get some gas, will you let me take over just as far as the toll plaza?

That should have warned you of what was in his mind. Am I supposed to be a damn psychoanalyst or something?

All there was, a voice that wouldn't say anything again. Hands, sensitively touching the wheel-rim, a dream in their fingers. *Gee, you're real mean.* The dream of taking over and pushing the speed up and falling deeper in love, *Venus, created in the image of a goddess come to earth,* a kid dying of love for a machine. That was all there was, you couldn't have any more, Danny alive, Danny dead. And now the wreck would rust and rain would fall on the picked-over carcass with holes where the lamps had been, *much more than a parade of mere beauty on the highway, a creature to possess.* And to be possessed by, till death do us part. Hit a tree, Dad had said.

And since this is all there is, what does it matter who took the car, who drove, when, how fast, legally or illegally, hazardously, mortally? I don't think it's a very meaningful question, did I know Danny took the Venus, would he breathe if I said yes or no, what would I have to say to make him breathe again, what would I give? Don't ask me, please, what I'd give, there'll be certain questions I won't be able to take for a while, like that one. I knew him better than you.

The fluttering of the moth had stopped. A glow came from the garden, the last light of day going, light that wouldn't ever come again, the special light of this day, dying.

Crazy little idiot, *Dad says it's okay to give the Venus a run while he's along at Seaside Heights.*

That should have warned you, too, of how obsessed he was: you should've said are you sure we have his okay and why do we have to give it a run while he's away?

Leave me in peace. It's only afterwards we look back and see things in a different light, the blinding light of what they finally led to. The light of now.

They were talking down there on the lawn. Asking each other how it happened, why, when, for what reason, wanting to know all the details, so they could finally understand about Danny.

For Christ's sake, why's it so hard for them?

Put your head out the window and shout *I understand*

already, he's dead, don't you know what that means?

They must look so ordinary, Tracy thought, a man with his girl in a sports car cruising along the Wildwood shoreline on a summer weekend.

'Is this the way back to the apartment?'

'That's right.'

The neon lamps threw an eerie sheen inside the car, and Earl's hands looked unnatural on the steering-wheel, the hair on them darker, the veins almost black. They were the hands that had stroked the nape of her neck, often, under her pony-tail, calming her, making her feel less lost. She knew now that if he put them there again she'd pass out.

A man with his girl, yes, but not quite. She hadn't been born when Earl had dated his first one. Maybe it didn't matter how many there'd been in between, but it mattered what they thought of him.

You want to get eaten alive?

Lightning flashed again and she flinched and he said:

'All right, baby?'

'I think so.'

He put his hand on her knee and she had to force herself to keep still, not to draw away. There'd been a point, some time in the long afternoon, when she'd been still able to think: he pulled my hair to hurt me and gave me that stuff to drink and sat watching me while I was sleeping, but he's still Earl, who gave me a kind of refuge, somewhere to run when I get that horrible sensation of being lost. I have to go on trusting him.

Beyond that point her thoughts had done a complete landslide and she couldn't go back; it was as if Earl himself had been left behind, smaller and smaller and unable to help her while she went on through the rest of the day with this stranger who only wanted to hurt.

'We'll be okay in the apartment, baby. It has lightning conductors.'

'Yes.'

He hadn't asked her if she wanted to go back there or if she'd prefer to do a club or dance at the Starlight Ballroom; he wouldn't ask her if she wanted to make love when they reached there; this time she wouldn't have any choice. He'd been patient last night, prepared to bide his time; but tomorrow was Sunday and they'd be driving back to New York and he hadn't come all this way for a weekend with a new girl just to watch her while she slept.

The E-type Jaguar was slowing and she glanced at him quickly, her pony-tail swinging, but he was looking away from her across the shore and the ocean. Flashes came all the time from the piled clouds, and the whole night seemed to be trembling with sound.

'It's pretty impressive,' he said.

Tracy didn't answer. As he pulled the car alongside the shore wall and stopped to watch the storm she didn't object; the flashes were unnerving but she'd almost rather be out here in the open than trapped in that empty building where the only light would be from the stumps of candles. But as he switched off the motor she knew he'd reach his arm behind her as he always did; and as his fingers began caressing her neck below her hair she closed her eyes, half-expecting pain to come.

Having to think of something quickly to keep from passing out, she thought of Hotline but she could only call them when Earl wasn't with her, thought of the lighted sign 'Police Office' she'd seen a couple of blocks the other side of the empty building when they'd passed that way last night, but it was too far from here and what could she do if she went there, what could she say? His fingers thrust gently through her hair the way they always did but this time they didn't calm her, they only frightened her with their strength.

Thunder came suddenly and she could hear his voice speaking through it – 'There's something magnificently arrogant about a storm, isn't there? You can quite see why the ancients believed the gods were in a rage.'

'Is it coming closer?' She heard how natural her voice sounded, even though she really wanted to say you're scaring me, deliberately stopping here to watch the lightning, making me watch it with you, all right I'm scared, are you satisfied?

'I guess it's just about overhead right now.'

Along the ocean's horizon there was still a crack of twilight but here the massed clouds had darkened the shore and it was already night, as if they'd left the day behind before it was over.

She felt her body beginning to tremble and in the stifling

heat she sat chilled, flinching again as thunder crackled above the buildings, calling out in fear but calling something normal so as not to express it – 'Will it rain?'

'Any minute now, baby.'

He turned to her, laughing as the next flash burst, saying something she couldn't hear because the thunder came almost at once, so that she could only sit watching his face with the silent laughter on it, no longer knowing where she was, or which was the way back to where there hadn't been terror. A staccato drumming had begun, not thunder but a different sound, but she didn't turn her head to find out where it was coming from because it came from everywhere and she couldn't escape it, could only sit frozen in the heat of the drumming night until the windshield slowly became blanked out and she realized it was rain beating on the metal top of the car and splashing in at the windows against her bare arm.

Then they were moving again and Earl was hunched forward staring through the windshield as the wipers tried to knock the cascading water aside, and Tracy knew they were going to the apartment in the empty building where there were the stumps of last night's candles and dust on everything and nobody near, nobody to hear her when she cried out.

Thunder banged and the shock knocked her forward and she covered her face and began sobbing.

Driving on Beach Avenue under the neon lights Brett Hagen pulled out to pass a slowing E-type Jaguar and took a left that brought him onto Ocean Drive heading north towards his hotel.

Flashes lit the buildings and the thunder crackled almost overhead. Strange to the town, he lost his way, coming up twice on the Starlight Ballroom and the shore before he realized his mistake. Crawling with the traffic, it occurred to him that it didn't make much difference whether he found the hotel or not: there was just no place else to head for. In twelve hours he'd covered every hotel and club in Wildwood and all he knew now was that Fallon must have a cottage or an apartment where he'd taken Tracy.

When he found his hotel and ran the Buick on to the reserved parking lot the first raindrops began hitting the sidewalk, and even before he reached the entrance they were drumming on the roofs of the parked automobiles and he broke into a run.

He called New York the minute he got in.

'Has Tracy phoned?'

'Where are you, Brett?'

'Down at Wildwood.'

He didn't expect his wife to see the situation the way he did. Linda was known for her calm. But he was now so nervy that he just wanted to talk to her.

'What doing?'

'Looking for Tracy.'

'Oh, Brett . . .'

He listened to her sometimes, letting his thoughts claim his attention when she was saying the things he knew she'd say: 'But we agreed to let Tracy grow up free to make her own decisions, darling, and now you're agonizing because she's chosen to weekend with an older man. I honestly don't understand.'

He watched the street through the lobby window but people weren't recognizable any more as they ran through the rain, shielding their faces. There was the sound of a ping-pong game from the recreation room and farther away some kids were shouting but he couldn't hear any words.

'. . . Just come on home,' Linda was saying, 'and leave the younger generation in peace.' There was patience in her voice and he could picture her tolerant smile.

The noise the kids were making reminded him of the last time he'd stood here with this phone in his hand, asking about Ellen Gardella, being told she'd just died. *Doctor Brett, am I going to make out? Yes, Ellen, you're going to make out fine.* She and Tracy had been trying to pull him apart this whole weekend and now there was only Tracy.

'Linda,' he said, 'you have my number here. If Tracy calls up let me know, will you?'

'All right.'

'You promise?'

'Of course, darling. But please give yourself a break.'

When he hung up there were guests pushing their way through the swing doors, soaked from the rain, laughing and looking around them as if they couldn't believe it was dry in here. Somewhere in the building the kids were yelling, or only one of them now, and he wondered how the management allowed a din like that.

Then suddenly everything got confused because as he stood near the entrance trying to think where to look for Tracy next some more people came in and practically knocked him over and he saw two of them were uniformed policemen and at the same time someone was calling his name from the other side of the lobby and he turned to see the receptionist hurrying towards him – 'Dr Hagen, would you help us please?'

Apparently the trouble was on the floor above and he went up and ducked into his room to fetch his bag, asking people what was wrong and not getting any definite information because no one seemed to want to talk. The kid was still screaming and there were other voices and then a door was kicked open and everybody spoke at once.

'All right, this is a narcotics raid!'

'Jimmy, for God's sake get that stuff –'

'Hey, are you the doctor they sent for?'

'Stay right where you are, kid.'

'Lay off me, keep your damn hands off me!'

'Josie, don't tell them anything!'

'Listen, don't pay any attention, they're just pigs.'

'So it's a pot bust so hallelujah!'

'Oh Christ I want out I want out I want out –'

This was the boy who'd been screaming all the time and Brett found him in the corner between one of the beds and the window with some of his friends trying to help him but not knowing what they should do. The place stank of pot but there was a smashed ampoule on the floor and Brett judged this was a mixed session with almost everything going. A couple of girls were slumped on the floor singing quietly and smiling to each other and as he crouched over the boy who was having the bad trip and opened his bag somebody hit his arm and laughed. 'Okay, Doc, how's about a shoot-up!' and somebody else pulled him away.

'What's your name?'

'Jesus Christ I want to get off so help me Christ!'

'What's his name?'

'Paul. Please will you do something –'

'All right, Paul, I can get you off, just take it easy.' Sweat, tremors, pupils dilated. 'What's he on, does anybody know?'

'Instant Zen, been ridin' it days now.'

The general picture was LSD and the kid was far gone and one of them –

'Watch it, get his hands –'

Pulling at him but he hit out and began –

'Paul, you're –'

'Quick!'

Brett got his wrist and said, 'Hold him still.'

Hallucinating as bad as this, they sometimes tried to claw their own eyes out to kill the images. He found some Valium and shot 20 mg into a muscle and saw a uniformed leg near him and looked up. 'Officer, can you get these other kids out of here? And lower the lights. I want it quiet and not too bright in here, can you do something?'

'Sure, Doc. Hey Alec, call up the station, get another car, okay?'

'Paul.'

The kid went on screaming, his hands trying to jerk towards his eyes. They held him, a girl leaning across him with her long dark hair against his face, her arms locked round his own. Brett said:

'Listen, Paul, it's okay now. Open your eyes and look at this girl, look at her black hair. Look, can you see this chair? It has four legs and a straight back, and I'm leaning my elbow on it. Open your eyes, Paul, this is a hotel bedroom and your friends are here. Don't make a noise like that, there isn't anything wrong any more, you're doing fine.'

Valium wasn't a powerful tranquillizer but it'd be too dangerous to use anything else without making tests first. The policemen were hustling the other kids out and the only light in the room came from the shaded desklamp.

'Okay, come on, you want to be dragged out?'

'Leave these two, officer, just these two.' Paul would need people he could recognize; strange faces would increase his panic. The girl with dark hair was singing to him softly, not minding when he tried to jerk his arm free of her own. Sometimes she smiled up at Brett with her large pupils, a girl Tracy's age and pretty and with no thought in her mind that her long life was shrinking as she lay here singing, smiling. What kind of man was her father, that he couldn't even see what was happening to –

One question, Dr Hagen. Are you the world's best father?

'I want out I want out you're all against –'

'Quick.'

'Hold him tight, Buzz.'

'Paul, listen, you're okay now. Just give yourself a few more minutes. You see your friend Buzz here? He's going to look after you –'

'And Josie. Josie's going to look after you, m'mm?'

'That's right, Josie's here. Now look at this bag, it's black leather, look, with looped handles and a brass lock. It's on the floor, right here. It's on this red carpet, black on red. And look at that lampshade over –'

'Hey watch out he's –'

'Paul –'

Arms came free and windmilled and he kicked out hitting and kicking madman's strength *get him* the glass smashing as he hurled himself *Paul oh Christ he'll* blood springing from his wrist and then Brett got his legs crashed down the girl crying out.

'He tryin' to –'

'Hold him. Keep him still. Like that.'

15 mg Algesian intravenous.

'Wait.' There was a risk but he was going to blind himself or go out of the window otherwise. The sedative was having to fight with a central nervous system stimulated to extreme limits and if the boy's constitution were still strong it could need minutes for a knockout. It took less than twenty seconds. 'All right.' He let Paul go limp and fixed his wrist with a dry compress to stop the bleeding. 'You there, officer?'

'We take him along, Doc?'

'To a hospital.'

'Guess we need him at the station.'

'You can't take him there unless you can guarantee close medical supervision. Is that understood?'

'Okay, we'll get the police medic along.'

'I'll stay with him till then.'

The rain roared at the hole in the window and glass fragments glinted on the carpet. They got the boy upright and the officer gave him a fireman's lift across one shoulder and Brett closed his bag and went with them, a patch of blood from Paul's wound darkening on his sleeve. The girl was still singing on her way down the stairs.

Two more patrol cars had been diverted to the hotel and

Brett ducked through the deluge and got into the back of the nearest, sitting with the boy, checking his pupils and rubbing his hands.

'All set, Doc?'

'Yes. Take it slowly.'

'In this kind o' rain we won't break any records.'

The cruiser slewed away from the flooded kerbside.

At the station they took the boy into a back room and put him on one of the bunks.

'You have a couple of blankets?'

'Comin' up, Doc.'

One of the kids wandered in through the open doorway and looked at Paul's white face. 'Did he give himself a hot shot?' He meant a fatal narcotic dose.

'He'll pull through,' Brett told him. 'Are you related to him?'

'No.'

'Where does he live?'

'Philly.'

'Then call his home, talk to his parents. Tell them not to worry but to get here.'

Other kids were in the doorway and then were sent back into the main office to be charged. A man in a drenched raincoat pushed his way through and said he was the police surgeon and Brett gave him the recent history and left Paul in his care, going back into the main office where the kids were being questioned.

'Okay, what's your address?'

'Look, I don't have any regular address, can't you –'

'Sit over there with him. Hey, Alec, how'd this girl get in here?'

'She's not with the others. The Sergeant's looking after her.'

'Okay.'

'Don't *tell* these pigs anything, Josie, don't tell them a *thing.*'

'There's a general charge of constructive possession of marihuana,' one of the officers said into a phone, 'and we're getting names and addresses.'

The kids stood huddled, rainwater dripping from them. Brett was invited behind the main desk to fill in a report form indicating the treatment given to Paul.

'Listen,' a policeman was saying, 'you're being charged anyway and you won't make things any better for yourself by obstructing the law. Now I want your name and address.'

'Josie, don't *tell* them.'

A kid laughed suddenly and was told to shut up.

'Daddy,' a girl was saying.

Water had dripped from Brett's head on to the form and he started on another one. *Time called. Diagnosis. Immediate treatment. Drugs given. Drugs prescribed.*

'Daddy,' the girl said.

Case handed to. He looked up to ask someone the name of the police surgeon but the girl had come in behind the desk and was staring at him in a kind of wonder, her hair soaked and the rain still on her face.

'Tracy,' he said and she came into his arms.

It was from Ocean City that the last Fourth of July firework was sent aloft at precisely 9.37 post-meridian. It was described on the special container as a *Super-10 Sunburst with Preliminary Detonation* and its cost was a hefty nine dollars.

The town councillor responsible for the display had bravely supervised the lighting of the last dozen fireworks during the onset of heavy rain and serious competition from the storm itself. Observing from beneath his lifeboatman's sou' wester this biggest and most costly token of celebration as it streaked skywards, he entirely missed any super sunburst there might have been seen, because at that moment the next flash of lightning blazed overhead and made everybody duck.

The town councillor, being a wise and God-fearing man, gave the signal for retreat, on the grounds that since Heaven itself showed a wish to celebrate this particular anniversary of the Independence of the United States of America, neither its right nor its superior ability should be challenged by a huddle of half-drowned mortals with wet matches clutched in their hands.

As if this gesture of humility had been recognized by the Hosts above, there followed a positive spectacular of storm-light and percussion until from one end to the other of the New Jersey shore the earth, the ocean and the sky were joined in tumultuous carnival.

BOOK III

SUNDAY, JULY FIFTH

CHAPTER TWELVE

The storm had passed hours ago, before midnight.

Those it had kept awake were mostly sleeping now, not long before dawn; but in some of the shore townships there were streets still trickling with rainwater, and in places where summer winds had blown sand from the beach the rain had piled drifts of it against walls and terraces, softening the angularity of stones. Here and there cats made their way diffidently, skirting puddles.

The air was much clearer now than before the coming of the storm, and stars glittered. Sitting in his booth at Barnegat Plaza keeping the dawn watch, Mike Kehoe could see Orion burning softly above the ocean, and Diphda, southwards. Brighter than those, water-drops hung from the edge of the plaza's canopy, sometimes flashing down; and when a car halted alongside the booth it surged away again scattering diamonds.

Throughout the traffic artery of the Parkway the circulation had now reached its lowest ebb at four in the morning of July Fifth, a Sunday. Between Toms River and Bloomfield, northwards, the hourly flow in both directions was below five hundred vehicles; here at Barnegat fewer than two hundred and sixty were going through. Along the artery's nerve system the signals were sporadic, each police base passing on local material to the next. Since one a.m., when a stolen car was reported by the Holiday House at Forked River, there had been no all-commands signal; and nothing of importance had hit the Telex since last night's alert concerning the two men, Renatus and Gould, suspected of slaying Officer Nolan of New York City.

From this moment until 4.33 a.m. there wouldn't be much change recorded on the hourly travel charts, and Mike Kehoe would be able to pick out the Pleiades cluster if he left his booth and looked directly above him, in between taking quarters; but at 4.33 it would be dawn, and with the increasing light there would be increasing traffic, the vanguard of the northward march that by noon today would swell to almost two thousand vehicles per hour and by this evening double that number.

Right now it was still night, a time for owls and for this one man here keeping the dawn watch, guarding his stars and his diamonds.

Water dripped from the guttering.

Erica had listened to it for a long time now, and knew she wouldn't go to sleep again before it was daytime. Her mind was teeming, talking or listening to Craig, seeing him with Georgina or Alexis or a woman she didn't know but could only picture as a kind of shadow in Craig's arms, where she had once been. Maybe that was herself, that shadow. She'd talked a lot to Sadie too, saying again and hearing again the things they'd both said when the ex-Vaudeville queen had brought in a tray of food and a bottle of brandy and stayed to share them both with her.

'I'm off duty from here on, honey. You want to kick me out, you just do that. I have the best-upholstered ass in Cape May County so if you miss it'll mean you ain't really tryin'.'

Erica had let her stay, a little jolted by the thought that after her thirty-two years on earth there were only two people who meant anything to her at this moment: a man newly lost to her, and a woman who was a stranger.

'You must have plenty of friends, uh?' Sadie had asked.

'Do you mean men friends?'

'Is there another brand?'

Sadie's deep eyes brooded at her over the glass of liquor, their stick-on lashes throwing shadows on her crumpled painted face; her voice was low, long trained to carry even a whisper to the back of the auditorium. Sometimes when she gave her rich bubbling laugh her brass-blonde wig shifted around and she settled it back with the care of a duchess tidying her tiara.

'I have men friends,' said Erica, 'yes. But they're always pestering me.'

'Surprise.'

'I mean –' it had always worried her when people talked about her looks – 'there's more to a man than that.'

'Like marriage.'

'Yes.'

'There's a darn sight mor'n that too, uh? There's somethin' that makes the world go 'round and it ain't gasoline. Anyways, honey, any man friend of mine who don't show the good manners of chasin' me twice around the block every Saturday night regular gets dropped so fast he bounces. Lookin' from this end of the telescope, I'd say you've been kinda neglectin' yourself, not that it's any of my business. Can y' take another hamburger? Fixed these myself.'

They'd talked about Craig until Erica realized more and more she didn't even know him, and until Sadie showed she wasn't interested.

'It's you that needs straightenin' out, honey, not him.'

'Tell me what I should do.'

'Who, me?' The rich laugh bubbled up. 'Listen, I jus' said you needed it, I didn't say I could do it for you. All you want to do is save a marriage an' the only lesson I've learned in thirty-six years of genteel dalliance is that if you throw crockery hard enough you're gonna break it. This your last cigarette?'

'I've another pack in the car.'

Erica got up and shut the window, pulling the drapes across. The storm was getting nearer and the rain drummed on the roof. She didn't know if she wanted Sadie to stay or go now, because every time she asked for something constructive instead of just critical they reached another dead end.

'Your name is Sadie, isn't it?'

'Right.'

'Mine's Erica.'

'Hi.'

'I want you to do something for me.'

'Any little thing, honey.'

Erica lit their cigarettes and said: 'I want you to tell me what you think I ought to do. I know you say you can't, but I want you to try.'

'I tell you t' go jump in the lake you'd go jump in the lake?'

'I could see advantages.'

Sadie put her head on one side and studied the poor little rich girl who'd somehow arrived in Seagull Avenue, Cape May, on a Fourth of July weekend with nobody in the whole wide world to talk to except a burnt-out bird of paradise in borrowed plumage. What could anyone say to a gal like her?

'Look, honey, I ain't no head-shrinker.'

'Tell me,' Erica said. 'Don't dodge. Just tell me.'

Sadie blew out smoke and thought of something funny and laughed and let the laugh die away and looked at Miss Lonely-hearts and said:

'Okay, so you put your dime in the slot right here an' the mechanical soap-show oracle announces in slightly tinny tones that you made a gilded cage for yourself and Craig an' now you've both gotten good an' out, which ain't a bad start because at least you're not in there any more suffocating each other in the name of eternal marital bliss. So why don't you take time off an' realize there's a whole lot of other people apart from Craig, people ready to love a girl like you if you'll just stop thinkin' of yourself as some kinda fancy cut-glass goddess too good for anyone else to come anywhere close to in case you break? Let some of the sunshine in, let people love you a little, it's good for us an' the more we get of it the more we can give back on the simple principle that nobody can give what they ain't got. Sounds kinda mushy? So what? It works. And just before the dime runs out there's maybe time to say that if you'd had the good fortune to be born with a face like the ass-end of a trolley-car like I was you'd have learned the scarcity-value of other people's love and gone right out to grab what you could.'

She and Sadie had said other things but that was what she'd remembered the most, and now she lay watching the first stars coming to gleam in the sky again, more brilliant than she'd seen them for months. Through the open window she could smell how fresh the air was after the rain, and her head was so clear that she didn't feel like trying to sleep again. In the faint light she could make out the white china lighthouse on the dresser and the clock in its varnished helm nearer her on the bedside table. The pack of cigarettes wasn't where she thought she'd left it, and she remembered that Sadie had taken the last one. There was a fresh pack in the car and she put on her dressing-gown and mules, going quietly down the stairs and out the back door.

The Mustang was parked against the sea wall, and in the light of the street lamps she could see that the deluge had washed sand from the dunes on to the roadway, piling it against the tyres. Rainwater had gathered in great blobs on the hood, leaving it jewelled, and at the road's edge the gutters trickled musically in the after-storm calm. Shutting the door of the car, the new pack of Eve in her hand, she caught sight of movement beside the lobster-pots that were stacked on the sea wall, and felt a jump of fear. Somebody was sitting there, leaning against them, and it seemed that she'd wakened him, slamming the door shut.

They looked at each other in silence; she was aware of the soft running of the sea beyond the dunes, and the scent of tar and rope coming from the lobster-pots. It was a boy who sat on the low stone wall, his straw-coloured head turned to her, his hands round his knees; a boy in dark jeans and a sweat-shirt. She was moving away when he said:

'Erica.'

She swung back, frightened again because she didn't know anyone in Cape May and the world was already strange to her with Craig gone and her life to be relived.

'Who are you?'

He came slowly down from the wall, his movements stiff, and stood there uncertain of her, his hands against its edge on each side of him, his bright head tilted as he watched her.

'You wouldn't remember.'

In a while she said: 'But you know my name.'

'Yes. Erica.' He said her name slowly, as if it were a note of music. 'You gave me a lift, yesterday.'

She had to think for a while because yesterday was so long ago, in the way it is when you pass your first night somewhere strange. Then she remembered him.

'Russ.'

He nodded quickly, pleased. 'Yes.'

'How did you get here?'

There were still mysteries, part of the shifting sands the storm had left. She had put him down near the turn-off for Wildwood, where he'd said he was going.

'I looked for your car.'

Nothing seemed quite in focus, she thought. He couldn't have found her like that.

'All over Cape May?'

He nodded, and because she wasn't frightened of him any more she went closer, and saw his young face was serious and unsmiling, as if all this were important to him in some way.

'But you couldn't have,' she said. 'It would have taken all night.' And he would need a reason and she couldn't think of any.

'I guess it did, pretty well.' He still didn't smile.

The more he said, the less she understood.

'But there was a storm.'

'M'hmm.'

She realized that his clothes were dark with water, and had a sheen on them; he'd taken off his sneakers at some time and they were upside down on top of the wall. With sudden impatience, because she liked understanding things quickly, she said:

'Did you leave something behind, in my car?'

'No.'

He was looking at her with a kind of stillness, a thing she'd noticed yesterday when sometimes she'd seen him watching her from the passenger seat.

'But I don't understand. Why did you look for the car?'

'I wanted to see you again.'

She looked away. So there were no more mysteries; he was just a boy who thought she was attractive, a boy with nothing to do this weekend except get himself drenched while he searched a whole township for her. There'd been so many who'd 'wanted to see her again' and she'd always told them no, because of Craig.

Let people love you a little.

But it wasn't as easy as that, unless you were Sadie.

'I –' she began and realized there was nothing in her mind to tell him; and the word floated in the stillness, without meaning because nothing followed to turn it into anything but just a sound on the breath, to make of it I, Erica, this woman, lonely and unsure and trying to be someone I've never been, anyone in the world except the ice-cold little innocent masquerading as a goddess so that people couldn't come close. There was no reason, now, why they shouldn't; it was just so hard to let go.

'You were lucky,' she said, 'to find me.'

'Yes.'

'I mean – in a whole town.'

'Yes. But I started looking last evening.'

His eyes were quiet, watching her as people watch a stream, or a flame. She made herself not look away from him, and found even this much intimacy disturbing.

'Russ,' she said, 'you got yourself soaked with rain.'

'I guess.'

'You'll have to come into the house, and dry off.'

'The house?'

'Over there.'

He didn't look at it. He didn't look away from her.

'Is it your house?'

'No. I just have a room there.'

'Your room.'

'What did you say?'

'You want me to go to your room. That can't be true.'

She frowned, not understanding again.

'Why not?'

He didn't answer, but followed her as she turned, and walked beside her across the sandy road.

'You forgot your shoes,' she told him.

'Yes.' He didn't stop. 'Hasn't it happened to you, I mean, ever, something that can't be true?'

They reached the house and she said: 'Yes.'

Nat Renatus had not slept.

Or maybe he'd slept, some of the night, without knowing, without being able to know because through the dark hours waking had been the same as sleeping: a nightmare.

Light was coming and he watched it. It wasn't really light; it was just that he could see the thin dark streaks against the east sky, the masts of the boats making a pattern that came and went as he sat shivering in the heat, screaming in silence at Rod beside him, Rod who wouldn't let either of them go free, Rod who was maybe dying.

In the night an auto had pulled up slowly alongside and he'd started slipping the safety-catch off, his fingers moving in the dark, feeling for the death of the people whose auto drew slowly alongside and then passed on, not the police but lovers looking for someplace quiet.

Also in the night he'd talked to Rod but it hadn't been any good.

'He won't take half the sugar, you know that? Toni always keeps to his –'

'Then he can take his boat away.'

'It's our only chance, you know that?'

Rod didn't answer but just sat there doubled over the bullet in him, his eyes sometimes coming open to stare at nothing, till Nat had the fear of Christ in him.

'Rod, I'm gonna get you a medic. You –'

'I don't need a medic.'

'Listen, I can go down any street right here till I see a brass plate, then I've only got to knock at the bastard's door and grab him an' after he's fixed you up, well, Christ, there's the harbour an' no one'll know what –'

'Shaddup!'

Nat jerked his head away and shut his eyes and in a minute heard Rod saying, 'I'm not goin' to die. Get that. An' I'm not goin' to sell out to that fancy bastard wop. Get that too. So start saving your breath, y'unnerstand?'

Then in a while, maybe a whole hour later he didn't know, because the night was so long and the nightmare wouldn't ever end Nat was asking him why he was doing this thing to them both.

'I don't know why you want us to get caught, Rod, for the sake of a load of sugar,' his breath whispering out and the cigarette-smoke fluttering against the windshield, 'I don't know why you won't let me get a medic here to fix you up,' his thin face squeezed against the things it didn't want to see, didn't want to know, 'it's like you almost – almost want us to end up living all our lives in the pen till we die there, an' no one caring,' his words so quiet that maybe Rod wouldn't ever hear them, wouldn't want to hear them, 'it's like you don't have what it takes any more to keep goin', Rod, like you –'

'I c'n keep on goin' when the rest have dropped dead on their feet,' the big man said, sitting hunched over the thing that was trying to kill him, 'but if it's coming to me then I'm quittin' clean, I'm not selling out to a whoreson wop before I go.'

And once in the night Rod had slumped over and Nat had known then that he'd have to get a medic here and he'd got the door of the car open but some kind of life had come back into Rod and he'd said it was okay, don't worry, it was only because they hadn't eaten since a while back, and Nat shut the door again because he always did what Rod told him. Rod was a kind of father to him.

The sky was getting grey over the harbour and the masts were sketched like sticks against the light. The day was coming and Nat knew this had to be the day when they'd go see Toni Lago and do a deal and walk on that boat and sail away where no bastard cop could ever get them any more.

He sat thinking about it, watching the light grow stronger, telling himself over and over that Rod would see it was all they could do, if they wanted to stay free.

It was dawn when Brett Hagen took the call.

He was in the room where the kids had been: there was still a hole in one of the windows and the place reeked of hashish so he'd given Tracy his own room and moved into this one.

'Dr Hagen?'

'Speaking.'

'This is Staff-sergeant Buckman, Wildwood Police. You left the station here last night in the company of your daughter, is that right?'

'It is.'

'Is she still with you?'

'Right here in my hotel. What's –'

'We have a gentleman here says he's concerned about her, and he'd like to talk to her on the line. Is that possible?'

'What's his name, Sergeant?'

'Fallon.'

Brett took a couple of seconds to decide.

'Tell him to call back in half an hour.'

'Okay, Doctor Hagen. And I can tell him he doesn't have to feel any kind of concern about your daughter?'

'You can tell him she could hardly be in safer company than her own father's.'

'Tracy?'

'Is – is that Earl?'

'Yes. What happened, baby?'

Tracy closed her eyes for a moment, trying to get the two images of Earl Fallon to merge into one. Driving into Wildwood yesterday, he'd been her living refuge from that dread lost feeling, the only person who could pull her back. Last night he'd been a monster, laughing at her terror when the lightning had blazed like a fever in the sky, trying to stop her opening the door of the E-type and running into the downpour, trying to follow.

'I don't know,' she said.

There'd been a doorway and he'd run past, not seeing her because of the torrential rain; she'd gone on instinctively in the direction of where she'd seen the sign: Police Office. It had seemed the only place to go.

'I was looking for you,' Earl said, 'all night.'

He sounded puzzled and a little annoyed. There was nothing in his voice, though, or in what he was saying, that led her to remember him as the watchful and designing sadist she'd believed him to be last evening, a stranger with the hairs too thick on the back of his hands, with one green eye and one blue, and with the habit of hurting.

The window of the room was open and she smelt the coolness of the new day outside; the first light was in the sky and pink clouds floated there; and already it was impossible to remember Earl as anyone but the person he'd been when they'd met in New York a few weeks back: kindly, very relaxed, a source of spiritual strength. The nightmare had gone, totally, like a black rag torn from the dark and blown to the winds; and now it was morning.

'I don't know,' she said again, 'I don't know what happened.'

She remembered only that she'd been more and more repulsed by the idea of his making love to her, and that there'd been a dream, that night when she'd woken to find him watching her, a dream where her father had been, calling her 'baby' and stroking her neck, maybe because when she was with Earl she'd sometimes wondered if people who saw them together thought he was her father.

'As long as you're okay now,' he said.

'Yes. Yes, I'm perfectly okay.'

There must have been some kind of rationalization going on, making her think of false reasons why he shouldn't make love to her. She might have seized on innocent things, twisting them in her mind. *You want to get eaten alive?* It could have meant the opposite: Marie was just being sarcastic, warning her that a man Earl's age couldn't give you much of a tumble. Judy could have meant the same thing – *You know what you're doing.* And when Lorraine had said she wouldn't ever speak to her again if she spent just one night with Earl it could simply have been jealousy. But once she'd got started worrying over sadistic tendencies it had only needed his ring to catch in her hair to make her really scared.

'Earl.'

'Yes?'

'I'm sorry.'

'That's okay, baby. You just had me worried. I thought maybe there was something I'd done.'

'No. No, Earl, it was me. I got – kind of lost again. Will you forgive me?'

'There isn't any question of that.'

'There is too.' The first rays of the sun were coming through the windows, warming her bare arm. 'Earl, I'm going back home with my father.' He didn't say anything so she went on:

'He's driving back there today, so I – I said I'd go along. D'you mind?'

'I plan to stay another day anyhow.'

She couldn't tell whether he meant it, or was being nice.

'Well, that's fine.' And now she could see him perfectly clear, his faint crinkly smile with one eyebrow quizzically lifted, his strong and clever-looking hands. And she wondered what kind of madness it could have been, making her see him as a fiend. 'Earl, I think you're a wonderful person, and – and thank you for a lovely weekend.'

By seven o'clock the sun had risen above the hedgerows along Marina Drive and was slanting in at the windows of the Ingram home. Putting on his service belt in the hallway, Frank looked through the open front door at the sprinkler he'd set going last evening on the lawn, and thought how useless it had been considering the storm had later dropped so much water on to the garden. Quite a few useless things had happened yesterday; quite a few things had got lost.

The house was quiet. Debby was sleeping on for a while: there'd been a cardiac case for Number 2 Ambulance soon after three o'clock this morning. It didn't sound as though Vince was awake yet, and Frank had made up his mind to go see McTigue first and talk to Vince afterwards. Beyond this decision he didn't want to think, because the day would go badly whatever happened.

He was warming the motor of Car 73 in the driveway when Vince came out of the house and crossed the lawn towards the gates. Frank's job had long ago taught him that personal identity depended on a lot more than a face, and that often you could recognize someone a hundred yards away even though he had his back turned. This was Vince's face all right but the rest of him was almost a stranger: he held his head low and there was a robot-like jerkiness to his walk as if he were being pushed along from behind, against his will. His arms just hung from his shoulders instead of swinging easily, and his back had lost its straightness. He was hardly recognizable.

'Vince.'

The boy didn't stop and Frank ducked under the bough of the tamarisk and went after him, calling his name again as he reached the gates. Then Vince turned and stood motionless like something switched off.

'Where are you going?'

'To see Mr McTigue.'

He was up earlier than normal for a Sunday morning, and instead of sailing pants and loafers he'd put on his best suit and a dark necktie and polished black shoes; his eyes were still slightly pink from sleep and his hair still damp from the shower, and these things made him look young and a little defenceless in contrast with the set of his shoulders that drooped like an ageing man's.

'What are you going to say to him?'

'Nothing.' His tone was colourless; he spoke like he'd walked just now, like a robot.

'I haven't talked to him myself yet,' Frank said. 'I don't know what he'll ask me to do.' Vince didn't say anything, didn't seem interested. 'The technical charge is one of unlawfully taking away a vehicle and depriving the owner of its use, but Mr McTigue might decide to take you to court on a charge of indirectly causing the death of a minor.'

He didn't know McTigue and couldn't tell how he'd react when the first shock of Danny's death wore off. It was certain that he'd see Vince as responsible, and a man bereaved might want to do damage by way of revenge. Frank hoped to prevent that, but this thing wasn't really in his hands.

'Take me to court, did you say?'

'If he decides to press charges.' He wanted to hold Vince, put an arm round him as he used to do, and help soften whatever blow was coming at him; but this time there was something in his son's attitude, in the faintly cynical set of his mouth at this moment, that made sympathy seem inappropriate. 'He may not see that you're already suffering far more than you will from whatever a court can do to you. He may not press charges at all: it's just a possibility I want to guard against.'

Vince was listening now to every word but there wasn't any kind of understanding in his eyes.

'I don't see any connection.'

'With what?'

'With Danny. Pressing charges, taking me to court, what kind of talk is that? What's it mean?'

'There has to be an enquiry, Vince.'

'Into what?'

'The accident.'

'To find out exactly what?'

'How it happened.'

Frank couldn't tell whether he was being deliberately obtuse or was still too shocked to think straight.

'Oh, I see. Then everything'll be okay. Once they find out who was responsible and what time it was and how fast the car was going and which way it was facing it'll be okay and we can forget the whole thing and talk about something else, is that right?'

Frank had never heard him speak this way before, the words coming fast in anger, disillusion in them.

'There has to be an enquiry,' he told Vince patiently, 'so we can find out how to stop the same thing happening again, to somebody else.'

'How can you ever stop that kind of thing? So long as they go on turning out cars like the Venus there'll be kids like Danny who'll go all the way once they get their hands on them. Just how many kids have got killed like that already, to the nearest thousand? Just how many enquiries have there been? And what good did they do?'

He turned away, unable to say any more, unable just to walk off while his father still wanted to talk to him.

'You could've got killed yourself, Vince. Do you think I'd have let it go as just another tragedy without even asking how it happened?'

Vince turned back to face him, but looked down, digging his hands miserably into his pockets. 'I couldn't have been killed, Dad. I wouldn't have let him drive with me in that car. I wouldn't have let him drive in it alone.' Bitterly he said: 'But I was thirsty. I wanted a drink.'

'How much did he have to persuade you, Vince?'

'Persuade?'

'To take that car out of the showroom.'

'You want me to put all the blame on Danny?'

'No. I want the truth.'

'He's dead. That's the only truth that means anything.' He looked at his father for a moment, squinting against the brightening sun. 'I guess this thing's hit you too, Dad.'

'What do you think?'

Vince looked towards the house. 'And Mom.'

'Sooner or later you'll have to realize there are more people involved than just Danny.'

Vince nodded slowly, looking down. 'I'd made up my mind, in the night, not to tell anybody, because to me it doesn't make any difference. But I can see you need to know. Danny told me he had his father's okay for me to take the Venus for a run.'

Somewhere in the house a door slammed and Frank registered the sound without thinking about it. Debby was up, that was all. He heard too, without doing anything about it, the motor still running in 73, warming up more than was necessary.

'You thought you had Mr McTigue's permission?'

'I didn't question what Danny said. I should have, but –'

'This makes so much difference,' Frank said quietly.

'Is it that important?'

'It means you weren't responsible, Vince, anywhere along the line. Don't you see –'

'I didn't imagine it could be very important. Nobody thought of asking me, did they? When something bad happens the first thing people think of is who to blame, and that's why there have to be enquiries. If you need me, I'll be over at Mr McTigue's.'

An hour before noon the sands of Atlantic City were still

crowded, though one or two families were folding their sunshades and trekking slowly towards the boardwalk, winding their way between bronzed recumbent bodies.

Some children had found a spent firework floating in the surf, brought in by the night tide, and a group of them spread out in a line to look for more.

'We have to be on our way now.'

'Aw, gee! Can't we stay just another few minutes?'

People were folding their deck-chairs.

She sat not far from the water's edge, the sea-nymph of Atlantis with the long golden hair, her eyes clouded and her heart growing sad. She had looked for him everywhere and he was nowhere. More than once she had glimpsed what looked like a straw fedora but had been mistaken; on the fabled shore of this ocean city there were bound to be mirages, of course, due to the humidity; and since time was now running out it was natural that almost anything, even a flowered bathing-hat, tended to look like a straw fedora.

'Are you getting too much sun on you, honey?'

'No, Mummy, thank you.'

He wasn't here, and he wasn't there. More people were starting to leave the beach and she begged the Siren Queen of Atlantis, who could hear her every thought, to let her glimpse him just once more, even if she were never to see him again after today.

'Daddy, what time do we have to go?'

'Well, around noon, I guess. About another hour.'

'Oh.'

You couldn't go on looking for a girl this hard and not find her. It stood to reason. He'd be able to tell the fellers back in school that there was something he'd learned from long experience: if you set your mind on finding a certain girl you only had to look real hard and she was in the bag.

Well, not exactly in the bag but he could still see her down near the water, sitting between her parents. She hadn't seen him, but even if she did it wouldn't signify anything. She didn't know who he was.

He tipped his straw fedora over his eyes more, so if she looked round she wouldn't think he was staring. Also he was a little uncertain just what would happen to him if she did look round, right at him. She wasn't even pretty and there was no sign of any real development under that seaweed-design swimsuit but he had the feeling that if she suddenly turned around and looked right at him he'd flip.

It was when he'd been handing in his bike this morning on the boardwalk that he'd seen the silver-grey Chevrolet Mirabelle convertible sliding into the parking lot of the Ocean Tower Hotel, so he'd known he'd been right all along about where they were staying. It had given him a lot of encouragement and he'd hung around till they'd come down on to the beach, her mother quite a plump woman with a floppy hat and her father not too severe-looking. The thing to do now was somehow find out her name and address before it was time to go and help Aunt Phyllis with her baggage; actually it had been time to go and do it a half-hour ago but he'd say his watch had stopped and anyway the last time he helped Aunt Phyllis with her baggage there'd been a weak catch and a whole seed-pearl necklace had gone down the stairs without the string and a medicine bottle had bust and the stuff had gone oozing like ketchup over the staircarpet with some of the seed pearls drifting in it like bubbles and all she could do was yell at him that she'd *told* him to go easy with *that* one, holy cow.

Another thing was that most people in Atlantic City were getting ready to pull out, especially the ones from New York because they had to go quite a distance, and there might not be much time left for him to get her name and address and he just had to have it. After he'd drawn blank with that dumb cop yesterday he'd puttered with the idea of walking right into the Ocean Tower and saying he was an undercover agent for an industrial counter-espionage bureau working on a case for American Motors, who were looking for a silver-grey Chevrolet Mirabelle convertible with an oval section tail-pipe that seemed to be infringing one of their patents, and could he know the name and address of the owner of that model out there in the parking lot; but that kind of thing could get out of hand and he didn't want to risk upsetting relations in the automobile industry.

Now that he knew where she was, right here in front of him, he could wait till they started back to the hotel and go on ahead of them and hang around the desk till they went past, then tell the clerk he was a secret talent scout looking for candidates for the next Atlantic City Beachgirl competition and what was the name and address of that one who'd just gone past. The trouble was that people were so suspicious and it took a whole lot of nerve.

He saw a big guy in red Bermudas coming up past where she sat with her folks, and heard him calling out to her father.

'George, what time d'you figure on starting back?'

'Around noon, Dave. Beat the worst of the traffic.'

'See you in town, then. Have a nice trip.'

Around noon! In less than an hour!

Oh holy, holy *cow*.

'Will you be checking out today, Dr Hagen?'

'Yes, but I can't say exactly when. If you need my room that's quite okay but I want my daughter to keep the other one till she's through sleeping. She's had a rather exhausting experience.'

'Then we'll be sure not to have her disturbed, Doctor.'

Tracy had slept all morning. He'd gone in to her twice and the second time she'd asked if they had to leave and he'd told her there was no hurry.

He was stowing his bags in the trunk of the Buick Riviera when she came out of the hotel, shielding her eyes against the sun's glare. She said she was ready to go but he made her take some protein first by way of ham and eggs. While she was in the cafeteria he called Wildwood police station to ask how the boy was, and they said he'd been transferred to a hospital where primary withdrawal treatment was available.

Putting the phone down, he was reminded of Ellen Gardella because he'd called the Clinic from this booth to ask for the last report on her case. Sometimes during the night he had been kept awake by questions in his mind, and one of them was about Ellen. He wondered why he'd kept so closely in touch with the Clinic, when his responsibilities had in fact ended when he'd put in the final suture in the operating theatre. Before he'd found Tracy he hadn't thought to question this, but during the night he'd come to believe there'd been a connection between the two girls. There'd been nothing he could do for Tracy except search the town for her, unavailingly; but Ellen he could have helped, if he'd been close enough. How much had his need to help a stranger been really a wish to help his own child, a wish that he'd denied himself for so long?

But we decided she ought to grow up a free agent, didn't we, Brett, without any interference from our generation?

Yes, we did. And we never thought to question our decision.

In the police station, with the speed freaks still rapping and the rain hitting the roofs of the cars outside, he'd held Tracy against him and heard her saying, over and over, 'Oh God, now I'm safe, now I'm safe.' And he'd been moved to sudden anger against himself and against his wife because your child should never have to say that to you, never have to say that. Not when you've exposed her to danger because you're so busy that you've trumped up the 'progressive' idea of giving a child complete independence just so she doesn't take up your time. Because that was what had happened.

Coming out of the telephone booth he saw her waiting for him in the lobby, holding the toilette bag he'd bought for her at the all-night drugstore. She'd told him she didn't want to go pick up her valise at Earl Fallon's apartment and she'd asked him not to go there either; Earl would be sure to get it back to her in New York.

Ten minutes later as the Buick slotted into the traffic bound for the Garden State Parkway she said to him:

'I didn't ask how you got to be in Wildwood, Daddy.'

'I was looking for you.'

'But who told you I was here?'

'Somebody called me. They didn't give their name.'

She sat turned towards him, her pony-tail curled across the seat-back and her knees drawn up. She didn't remember how long ago it was since she'd ridden in his car with him, with time to talk; it seemed years.

'But why did they call you?'

'They said you might be at the Surf Club with a man named Fallon for the weekend. They implied he was a – well, just a no-good *roué*.'

'They never said who they were?'

'No.'

'Was it a girl's voice?'

'It wasn't easy to tell. They disguised it.'

She thought immediately and intuitively of Lorraine. *I won't ever speak to you again.* Lorraine had hoped Daddy would break up her weekend with Earl. It could have been she who'd left a message at the Surf Club, maybe saying she was on her way there, whether it was true or not; so he'd decided to use his friend's apartment to avoid an embarrassing scene.

'It was pretty terrific of you,' she said, 'to come all this way, when you have so much else to do.'

'No. It wasn't.'

'Well, I think –'

'How old is he, Tracy?'

'Earl? I don't really know, in years. Maybe – well I don't know – maybe fifty.'

'What did he have for you? Don't answer if you don't want.'

'I don't know that either.' She had to think back a bit to remember Earl as he really was, beyond the man in the nightmare. 'Yes, I do. He was – kind to me, and sort of understanding. Mature, you know? I felt safe with him for a while – I used to get an awful feeling sometimes of being lost, utterly and completely lost, I don't know why, and – well – he kind of pulled me out of it.'

'What made him suddenly change, and stop doing it?'

She watched the traffic bunching ahead of them towards Entrance 6 of the Parkway, the moving shapes of the automobiles making a kind of jigsaw like the pattern in her mind that she couldn't complete.

'He didn't change, Daddy. I just thought he did. But I don't know why I – there are things I just can't figure, and maybe I never will. I guess I went sort of loco for a while.'

Carefully Brett asked her: 'Will you be seeing him again?'

'If I need to.'

'If you need to?'

'Well, he filled a kind of gap. I suppose that's what he had for me – I needed him. I can't explain.'

'Don't fret about it. You may not need him again.'

'I guess that's right.'

He and Mother were always so tremendously busy at the Clinic and the Spa that she thought it was really terrific of him to have come all this way, just because he'd thought she might have got into bad company. It was really too much.

'You want this window shut?'

'I'm fine,' she said.

Brett found it hard to believe she was here right beside him: while he'd been looking for her all over Wildwood his imagination had got out of hand a little and he'd pictured some pretty nasty situations. During the night, even though she was out of any kind of danger, his thoughts had kept him awake a lot of the time; and quite a few things had been put into perspective. Driving down from New York Friday he'd questioned how an anonymous phone-call could have provoked him into spending the weekend on what looked like a wild goose chase, but he knew the answer to that one now, and he'd had to part with a great deal of his self-respect in order to find the truth. And the truth was simply this: so long as Tracy went out with boys her own age it was perfectly all right; but when she'd chosen a man of his own generation his pride had been hit, because he'd realized that the true rôle of Earl Fallon could only be the one that he himself had failed, all these years, to fill.

'Tracy.'

'Yes?'

'If you're going to lean against the door that way, just put the lock on, will you?'

'Okay, Daddy.'

There were bags all over the lobby.

'Did you help Aunt Phyllis?'

'Oh, she didn't need any help.'

'That's not like your Aunt Phyllis.'

'I was kinda surprised too. Dad, what time are we starting back?'

'About two o'clock. Your Mother's taking Aunt Phyllis to the railroad station while we go on ahead.'

'You're leaving it pretty late, you know that? I was just talking to a Triple-A man and he says there's going to be jam-ups all the way for people who don't get started from here at twelve noon.'

'Is he sure of his facts?'

'Are you kidding? He's a Triple-A man, it's his job.'

'Are you in some kind of rush?'

'Me? Gee, I'd like to stay on here the whole afternoon but I know you have a snooker match with the guys at the club tonight so I thought I'd check up on conditions, that's all.'

'And he says we ought to go around twelve?'

'Not a minute later. According to him the best route out of town is along Pacific Avenue and make a right at the Ocean Tower Hotel.'

'Uh-huh. Why there?'

'It takes you up Arkansas Avenue to the Expressway, then you get on to the Garden State Parkway at the interchange.'

'You seem to have it all worked out.'

'Look, Dad, I'm only saying what the Triple-A man told me. If we don't have to leave till two o'clock can I go along to the Wax Museum?'

'I guess you better not, if we want to miss those jam-ups. Can you get packed in twenty minutes?'

'I can try, Dad.'

'You do that, and we'll start off at midday and you can route me past the Ocean Tower, okay?'

'You're the boss.'

There were bags all over the lobby of the Rosegarden Hotel at Beach Haven, just as there were bags all over the lobby of every hotel along the New Jersey shore. From now until six in the evening the populations of the coast resorts were going to be reduced on the average by one quarter.

'Have you seen my husband, please?'

'No, ma'am, I haven't. Charlie, have you seen Mr Amberton around?'

'I think he's in the bar, shall I go look?'

'Sure. No wait – he's right there, Mrs Amberton, just coming out.'

'Thank you.'

'You're welcome.'

Carol turned away but didn't go towards Walt. He didn't like being watched and he didn't like being followed around, because sometimes when she got smart he had to look for a new hiding-place and it would be embarrassing if she found him putting strange things in the space behind the row of encyclopaedias or on the ledge above the towel-racks in the bathroom closet, strange things like for instance a bottle of Bourbon.

He also turned and the moment he saw her she spoke, not to make it seem she'd just been standing there watching him.

'Are we ready, Walt?'

'You mean I've been keeping you waiting?'

'Of course not.'

She noticed the desk clerk glance up and quickly down again and she felt surprised she'd noticed it because her life was full of little embarrassments like that and you'd think you'd finally become immune, it would be merciful.

'Did they take the baggage out?'

'Yes.'

He went out to the courtyard and she followed.

'Have a nice trip home, Mrs Amberton.'

'Thank you.'

The baggage was being stowed in the trunk of the Lincoln-Mercury and they both avoided looking in that direction because the spare wheel was there and neither of them was meant to know about the space behind it, yes Dr Pabst you were so absolutely right when you said we'd find ourselves playing childish games with each other.

'Thank you, sir. Have a good trip.'

The pearl-finish Lincoln-Mercury Cougar leaves the forecourt of the plush little rose-covered hotel, the initialled pigskin bags in back and the husband's gold wrist-watch catching the sun's rays and for an instant flashing on the lean tanned wrist as he turns the wheel and heads for the Parkway and New York.

The Amberton image, long established on Mad Ave, was so earnestly perpetuated by its original that Carol could never be in Walt's company without seeing herself as part of an ad for any one of those little things that make life less primitive for people of note: a Cougar, a Rolex, a few Lanvin scarves.

Last night there hadn't been anything smashed.

He'd just ordered a couple more doubles and gone to bed morose, and she'd been relieved and failed to appreciate that it would have been better if he'd gone all the way and lost control and smashed the place up and passed out, so that today he would have been exhausted and contrite and eager to please, and for a few hours totally sober. That would have been safer.

The sleek automobile makes a left on to State Highway 72 and the driver speeds up again in a positive surge of acceleration, confident in his machine and in himself and ignoring the availability of a seat-belt. Beside him his wife sits languidly, pleased with the masculine assertiveness of her escort, her own seat-belt adjusted to – cynically she let the image slip out of focus – to the correct tension in the hope that when the two or three Bourbons he took in the bar just now hit his central nervous system and his reactions slow and his hands move the wheel less surely as the two-tone automobile weaves among the high-speed traffic there'll be a chance of getting out alive or only just smashed up a little when he finally loses control.

Meanwhile she can only sit here feeling the refined brand of fear that is experienced by the trapped animal.

In Cape May Harbour the surface was dappled as boats came in from the sea, their owners giving themselves time to stow canvas and coil ropes before they had to be on their way home by road. The blue heat-haze across the water made a mirage beyond the mole, where small boats seemed to be afloat on the air.

'It's almost eleven.'

Across the harbour the tallest of the masts had not moved, though a half-hour ago a motor had started up and was still throbbing. Sometimes men shouted over there.

'Rod.'

Seagulls planed in the sun's great heat, drifting on the bronze air, their cries plaintive, recalling to mind the saying that they were the souls of dead mariners.

'Rod,' said Renatus.

He watched from the driver's window of the two-tone Chrysler Newport, his face squeezed with nerves and his eyes narrowed to slits against the glare. He watched the tallest of the masts. When they moved there'd be no more hope.

'He's bluffing,' Rod Gould said.

Toni Lago was every kind of a stupid jerk but he wouldn't let half this sugar go just to save his face. The cost of shipping them both to Haiti was maybe a thousand bucks including keeping people's mouths shut and the price of half the sugar was fifty grand.

'The boat sails at eleven,' Nat said. 'It's almost eleven now.' His cigarette had gone out because he always gripped them too hard and he lit another one and pulled the smoke in deep, his hand trembling. 'We gotta get on that boat, Rod.'

'He'll send somebody along. They'll say he'll settle for half. Then we go.'

Rod sat humped, his barrel-body tilted to the left because when it was like that the numbness was bearable. In a way the numbness was worse than the pain had been because pain is a live thing to feel and this was just deadness; but if they went to a medic they'd have to turn him off after he'd done the job, and the cops would figure things. Sometimes when the sweats came and he had to fight not to pass out he thought of the deadness spreading from Nolan's bullet till it reached his brain and killed him.

He tried the radio again. They listened every hour.

When Nat heard the strange voice so close he jerked around – *'Christ!* – and almost slumped for a minute with his eyes screwed shut. Rod didn't like that. Nat had always lived near the edge but now his nerves were shot and it could give them away if they got into a jam.

. . . are reminded that all major highways are going to carry a heavy traffic volume this afternoon and especially from the shore resorts to the northern metropolitan area and New York City.

Nat Renatus opened his eyes and sat up straight and talked above the voice of the newscaster. 'I'm goin' over there, Rod. I'm goin' to tell Toni it's a deal, the whole of the sugar.'

'You can't do that.'

'Try an' stop me.'

He snapped the door open.

'You can't do it,' Rod Gould said. His blunt head had swung to watch Renatus and his eyes were like stones.

'It's for both of us, Rod. It's Haiti or the Cage. I'm doin' this for both of us.'

'You can't.'

Nat sat with the door half-open, his head going slowly down and his thin skeletonic hand covering his eyes.

Rod looked away.

. . . but according to the Los Angeles Justice Department there can be no question of a trial until the Fall of this year. On this same subject, the news from New York concerning the slaying of Patrolman John Nolan early on Friday is that information indicating that the two suspects, Gould and Renatus, may be in Cape May New Jersey is right now activating local police units. In particular the Cape May-Lewes

Ferry sailings are being given close attention. Commenting yesterday on the increasing hazards of routine police patrol work, Deputy Governor Charles L. Harriman called for a wider public understanding of the risks undertaken by policemen when performing their –

Rod cut the sound.

He expected Nat to say something because his nerves acted up worse when they turned on the radio. He wasn't saying anything and Rod swung his heavy head to look at him and saw he was just sitting like he'd been before, except that he'd looked up a little and was watching the harbour. Rod looked there too and saw the tall masts had begun moving.

'Rod. That's the boat.'

'He was a bastard. He was a bastard wop.'

Nat didn't have the strength any more to turn around on the seat. He had to talk over his shoulder. His voice sounded strange, like he was talking out of the past.

'We coulda got that boat. You thought Toni didn't mean it but he meant it. We coulda taken his word an' we didn't.'

'He was a sonofabitch bastard wop an' we didn't sell out,' Rod Gould said, watching the masts riding slow across the harbour. 'So we keep all the sugar. A hundred grand.'

'Rod,' Nat said, 'tell me what we do now.' His voice went suddenly thin and what he was saying was squeezed out in a kind of whispering scream. 'Tell me what we do now because they're lookin' for us in Cape May an' that's here an' the boat's gone an' they're gonna get me for that cop, they're gonna –'

'Christ sake get a grip on yourself!' Rod saw the thin shoulders jerk as if he'd put a slug in them but he couldn't care because this wasn't Nat any more, this stringy ruin of a man scared in his soul. 'We go back, that's what we do. We go back to N' York.'

Slowly Renatus turned around and stared with his white pinched face.

'We couldn't ever make it.'

'We have to.'

'All that way.'

'We can make it by tonight.'

'I can't do it, Rod. There'll be police –'

'We'll be there by tonight.' The sweat was coming again, the fever, and he leaned over his bullet, Nolan's bullet, and began fighting the dark that was trying to get in his head. 'Then we c'n get Doc Regan, fix me up.'

'Okay.' Nat didn't want him to die. Rod was a kind of father and if he died there'd be no place to go. 'Okay.'

He pulled the driver's door shut and started the motor, checking the gas and making a U-turn across the harbour road.

At fifteen minutes after eleven the two-tone Chrysler Newport hit the Garden State Parkway and a minute later was whipping up speed past Milepost 1, northbound to New York.

CHAPTER THIRTEEN

By noon this Sunday the graph line on the travel chart for the southern leg of the Parkway was climbing into the two thousand five hundred vehicles-per-hour sector as the combined exodus of traffic hit the northbound road from Cape May, Wildwood, Atlantic City, Long Beach Island and intermediate resorts.

As the sun reached its zenith the temperatures recorded at the toll plazas along the Ocean Point patrolling zone were rising through ninety-seven degrees and comparative humidity was keeping pace through the eighties. The electric storm had cleared the air during last night but the torrential rainfall had soaked the countryside and now the sun's heat was drawing the moisture out again and producing what one of the Troop E highway patrols called 'steambath conditions'.

The average flow in this area was fifty m.p.h. with only minor delays of ten minutes or so, but as the traffic kept on hitting the northbound access ramps the speed was falling progressively.

The radio and telephone networks were now carrying peak loads as signals volleyed between the police units at Avalon, Bass River and Ocean Point with information relayed from patrols reporting to base.

Car 75 – I have an overheat, Milepost 32 southbound. Do you have a tow available? Chevvy Impala.

71 to Base, hear me?

Hear you, Cooper.
There's a compact flipped over at MP 62.5 and I'm taking a look. It's clear of the roadway so I won't need a wrecker unless there's somebody underneath.
I'll stand by.

Barnegat Plaza to State Police Ocean Point.
Go ahead, Barnegat.
I think I have a drinking driver for you. Pearl-finish Lincoln-Mercury Cougar, New York registered, just pulling away northbound.
We'll get on to it.

Since eight o'clock this morning the Hughes 300 helicopter from the Ronson fleet had been flying almost continuous police duty under Code No. 66 and had so far made sixteen landings to investigate stranded automobiles, snarl-ups and accident situations. 'This isn't a flying-machine,' the pilot was heard to say at one time over his radio, 'it's a jumping-bean.'

The legal speed limit on the Parkway changes at Milepost 80, and driving northbound drivers must reduce speed from 65 to 60 m.p.h. at this point, since here the two-lane roadway becomes three-lane and the traffic conditions are heavier.

As it overran Milepost 80 the pearl-grey Lincoln-Mercury Cougar didn't reduce speed.

Walt, could you please slow a little?

She never said it aloud because he wouldn't listen. It was always just a silent prayer, always unanswered. Someone had said to her once, but Carol why don't you *make* him slow down, threaten to jump out or take the ignition key or something? Or something. Because you can plan things like that sitting safely at your friend's coffee table but when you're in an automobile doing more than sixty miles per hour with Walt driving you don't think about jumping out and if you turn off the motor and take the key the power steering will go and that'll throw him. No. You can only sit there and pray.

Coming through the toll plaza just now the front tyre had glanced off the concrete bullnose and the collector had given Walt a long close look. Walt knew that kind of look and it always angered him and he'd been driving aggressively since then, one time going too close to another car and having to swerve.

'Walt, will you slow down?'

She couldn't remember having said it out loud before. For the first time she was more than just scared of dying or being maimed: she felt intuitively that the conditions were right and that it was today that it was going to happen.

'Walt. I'm asking you to slow down, you hear me?'

His handsome ruined face was blank as he turned to look at her.

'What'n the hell's got into you?'

'The limit's only sixty here and you're doing over sixty-five, d'you want a ticket?'

She was angry herself now. Yes Dr Pabst, alcoholism is a disease and they can't help it and we have to show patience and fortitude and compassion and sit there while they blow smoke in our face and humiliate us a dozen times a day in front of waiters and friends and even our own children but we have a life to live too and their unfortunate affliction doesn't give them a right to smash us up just because they're in a tantrum, does that sound too dismayingly heretical?

'This has turned out one hell of a weekend!'

'Yes, Walt, it has.'

'Watching me the whole damn time, asking the hotel staff where I've gone, and now telling me I don't know how to drive a –'

'Slow down, Walt. Or so help me God I'll make you.'

Someone was blaring with his horns: they'd clipped a car close again and Walt had to look away from her while he got some kind of control back. She closed her eyes and hoped for unlikely chances: that they'd run out of gas or come up on a traffic jam or attract the attention of a police patrol, anything that could save their lives.

'You think I can't read a goddam speed limit sign?'

She didn't open her eyes. She didn't want to look at the reeling roadway and the other cars moving so close. By the sound of the motor and the slipstream they weren't slowing.

'You think I can't damn well drive?'

Acting-out behaviour. That was the fancy label Dr Pabst had used for it. The wind rushing past sounded louder than normal and the tyres were roaring over the pavement. Dear God make him slow down.

Then there was hooting again and she opened her eyes when the bump came, the slight ricochet carrying the Cougar to the left before it veered back and hit again and lurched wider, the tyres whimpering as the suspension flexed and the long sustained zig-zag motion began, and she saw trees tilting as the scene began breaking up, the other car with a face at the window, frightened-looking, the grass of the medial strip and the roadway pitching, rising and falling away, the wind's sound roaring, then she held her breath and made herself keep silent because a scream wouldn't mean anything, wouldn't save her.

'Are you okay, Floyd?'

'I'm fine.'

'You're kind of quiet.'

'Well what d'you expect?'

Sue brushed back a wing of black silky hair and looked at him. He was brooding more magnificently than ever she'd seen him, so she fell in love with him for the third time today.

'I expect you to be filled with slowly-mounting joy at the thought you're soon to become the proud father of our very own customized Curly. But you don't look a bit that way.'

'Don't worry about me, Sue. As long as you're all right it's all that matters. And please can you stop feeling your stomach like that?'

'But he's kicking again, darling. He gives me a big kick.' Her smile shimmered amid the silky black hair.

Floyd frowned, watching the speedometer and keeping to a steady fifty. The thing was that Sue didn't understand – thank heavens – that it was a pretty important thing, bringing a new life into the world. It was typically intelligent of Nature to protect the mother-to-be from any thought of alarm or crisis by automatically tranquillizing her as part of the bodily processes, but it put an extra burden on the husband, who had not only to deal with his own anxieties but to keep his true fears hidden for her sake.

'Oh Floyd, isn't that really cute?'

All he could do was try getting back home to New York before the final crisis could overtake them. Sue had suffered pains early this morning, and of course she'd just laughed and said it was indigestion, since she was in an autotranquillized condition. It was clear enough there wasn't much time left now. To humour her he asked:

'Isn't what really cute?'

'You remember the man at the toll plaza gave us a little book? Well it's a guide to the Parkway, and just listen to this bit: *The New Jersey Highway Authority has formed a unique group called the Garden State Parkway Stork Club. One of the world's most exclusive clubs, it admits only those who have been born somewhere along the Parkway. So far the stork has overtaken more than thirty mothers who –*'

'Sue, I wish you wouldn't make a joke of such a –'

'But I'm not, darling, it's right here in the guide. Do listen to what it says! *From time to time Parkway officials throw a bumper birthday party with Stork Club members as their guests. As the enrolment figures show, they regard these happy but impromptu events as just part of normal operations.* Now don't you think that's cute?'

'Oh my God.'

'What's the matter?'

'Do you really expect me to think it's "cute" that any next minute we could provide them with a new member for their darned Stork Club?'

'Well, why not, darling? Wouldn't that make it all the more fun?'

'All the more *what?*'

'After all, if it's going to happen there isn't a single thing we can do to stop it, so why not –'

'Oh my God!'

Since it had come on to the Parkway at Cape May the two-tone Chrysler Newport had been snarled up in two minor-delay traffic jams and Renatus had been driving beyond the limit trying to make up lost time, riding the fast lane and clearing a gangway with the horns.

'Take it slower,' Rod Gould told him sometimes. 'You get a ticket an' it'll be for the Cage.'

'Okay. Okay.' But Nat couldn't let up speed.

'Take it easy,' Rod kept saying. 'We ain't in no hurry now.'

'Sure. Sure.' But Renatus drove fast, the only way he could go, his eyes flickering with nerves and the half-smoked cigarettes going out of the window every few miles.

Sometimes he said: 'You okay, Rod? You feel okay?'

'I feel okay.'

But Rod sat leaning to the left, curving his body over where the bullet was. Nolan's bullet.

'Rod, you got a quarter?'

They were slowing towards Barnegat Plaza and Rod Gould dug in his pants pocket, trying not to move around too much. He found a quarter and gave it to Nat but he dropped it and had to scrabble his thin fingers over the floor, cursing.

'Get the damn thing,' Rod said low. Sweat was running on him and he began pulling his Smith and Wesson in case Nat couldn't find the quarter and they had to pay a collector. Sometimes there were police patrols hanging around the toll plazas. 'You got it?'

'Ya. Okay.'

'Chris' sake don't miss the scoop.'

Nat slowed and threw the quarter and heard it bounce around the rim of the scoop. There weren't any police here. He accelerated and swung out to pass a silver-grey Chevvy convertible.

'Not too fast,' Rod said.

'Okay. Okay.'

Something hit the front end of the auto a mile after the toll plaza, something hard but not metal, by its sound.

'What was that?'

'I dunno,' Nat said. 'Nothin'. It wasn't anythin'.'

He kept to the fast lane but stayed below sixty-five. The strange noise had scared him and the sweat was getting into his eyes and stinging. The red light began showing on the facia panel at Milepost 69 but he didn't notice it. He noticed the steam a mile farther on. It was coming out of the hood, where the join was.

'Nat.'

'Ya.'

Renatus looked down and saw the red light on the facia.

'Christ,' he said, 'oh Christ.'

'It was the fan-belt,' Rod said, 'the noise.'

Steam whirled past the windshield and Nat took his foot off the gas, hitting the stick into neutral, coasting.

'Whadda we do, Rod? Whadda we do?'

'We need another auto.' He straightened his body and felt red heat and ignored it. The Smith and Wesson was resting on his lap. 'Can you get as far as the picnic area?'

Nat shifted back into drive and gave her the gas again and pulled over into the right-hand lane and saw the sign come up and hit neutral and coasted, wanting to say something but not wanting Rod to know how scared he was.

'The first auto, that one there,' Rod told him.

Nat slowed to a halt alongside the parked sedan. Nobody was in it. There were quite a few other autos in the picnic area, most of them empty. Rod was climbing out, moving like a great soft crab, his big body leaning. Nat got the jacking-lever and used it on the trunk of the sedan, swinging the top open and jerking a look around him and seeing nobody close. They began putting the one-kilo reinforced linen bags of morphine base into the trunk of the Pontiac sedan, Rod holding his gun in his left hand now, keeping it pressed against his side, looking around every few seconds with his stony eyes and telling Nat to hurry.

Nat saw the black-and-yellow highway patrol cruiser coming up northbound and he just stopped moving. He tried to tell Rod but couldn't make his mouth work. He stood with a kilo bag in his hand. Rod saw he'd stopped moving and looked at his face and then saw the police car and turned his back and slung another bag into the trunk of the sedan.

'C'mon for Chris' sake!'

Nat moved and dropped a bag and the linen caught the trunk catch and the brown powder streamed out and Rod cursed him. The police cruiser didn't stop.

'We're okay,' Rod said. The light was thumping against his eyes like it was a bright hammer. He heard Nat say something but didn't pay any attention. Two people were coming away from the main picnic area and when they were inside of a dozen yards Rod showed them the gun and they just stopped and stood there, a man and a woman. When the last of the kilo bags was slung into the trunk Nat pulled the top down and went round to the driver's door, watching Rod and the way he moved like a heavy crab, shuffling over the ground holding his side.

'Get goin',' he told Nat, and dragged open the passenger door and slumped inside, *'Chris' sake get going!'*

Her headscarf stirred to the slipstream of the powder-blue

Mustang. Slowing for the toll plaza, she moved her lithe honey-brown legs and snicked the gear-shift into low, her slim fingers curled around the knob. He watched all this.

He watched her lithe movements and the play of the light on her honey-brown skin and the glow of her amethyst eyes as she turned her head and looked at him and smiled in the way that made him feel he'd swallowed roses. He watched all of Erica.

'Where do you live?'

She said: 'New York.'

'I know. But where?'

'Manhattan.'

'I live in Queens.'

She slowed to a crawl behind the Buick Riviera and threw a quarter into the metal basket, turning again to look at Russ. He sat low in the passenger seat with his bright straw-yellow head against the squab and his thumbs hooked at the pockets of his jeans. He blinked slowly as she looked at him, as if the light were suddenly too bright.

'We shan't see each other again,' she said.

The Buick ahead was speeding up and she shifted into fourth and he caught her hand before she could put it back on the wheel.

'Why not?'

His hand was gentle; it had caught hers as if a sudden gust of wind had come and he'd been afraid she'd blow away.

'I'm going back to Craig.'

She'd talked to him about Craig when they'd sat drinking their coffee at a place near Cape May Harbour, before they'd left. Russ had asked her about him.

'You just left him,' he said.

'It was only for a while.'

'You thought it was forever.'

'Yes.'

'We'll be in the same city,' he said. He looked away from her, learning to lose her by small degrees. 'Don't think I'm not dying a lot. It's only because I've lived such a lot this weekend that makes it possible. I mean not to die altogether.' He let go of her hand.

'You've met other girls.'

'Have I? I don't remember.'

He remembered only her shyness of him once they were

naked, the single ray of sunlight coming through the gap in the drapes in that small high room where she had unbelievably taken him, the smoky colour of her skin in the warm low light, the way she'd cried and not said why, and later the way she'd laughed about something he'd said, something forgotten.

Look, you stand thumbing at a Citgo station and out of the sky drops the most phantasmagorically beautiful girl in the whole universe and you know that if you touch her hand you'll blow like a fuse that was never built to handle ninety million volts and then she makes love with you, so how d'you expect to feel now?

'Erica.'

'Yes?'

'I don't have any energy.'

She laughed again.

And listened to its sound, not being able to remember how long ago it was that she'd laughed like this. Craig must have missed it. All she'd offered him was her quivering anxiety to please, and her watchful custody of a marriage so precious that you could almost say it was deliberately designed to be smashed. It made her want to drive faster when she realized that if she didn't reach New York in time he'd receive a letter of farewell from an embittered little dullard and try to feel appropriately desolate.

Let people love you a little. And let yourself love them back.

Somebody was hooting and she pulled over to the right-hand lane and a two-tone Chrysler went by very fast.

'Russ.'

'M'mm?'

'I loved you.'

He looked at her for a long time.

'You don't mean that.'

Quickly she said, 'I loved you. With a "d".'

'With a "d".' He nodded. 'Past tense.'

'Yes.'

'One hell of a "d". "D" for difference. Oh boy.' He watched her profile, remembering how he'd watched it before as she'd lain with her eyes closed, the amethyst light of them hidden, lain in the small high unbelievable room, loving him, being loved.

'You don't care how tough you make it for people.'

'Dearest Russ, you're young. You'll heal.'

'Sure.'

'Don't feel –'

'I'm not. Look, we don't see each other again, right?'

'It wouldn't do any –'

'Right.' He sat for a time, silent. 'If things don't work out with you and –' he shook his head and started over – 'I mean if ever you feel kind of –' he said goddam under his breath and gave up because he knew it wasn't any good. 'I hope you never do. I hope they will. Work out, I mean.'

'Thank you.'

'Please don't mention it.' He gave a sudden lopsided grin. 'But do something for me, Erica.'

'If I can.'

'It's easy. When you receive roses every Fourth of July, don't think they're from anyone else. Do that for me.'

Captain Darrow was sitting at the main desk of the operations room when Frank got back there after a snatched meal at home. He gave Darrow the required salute and they both left it at that, realizing that if they wanted to settle their differences they'd have to do it some other time when traffic conditions weren't approaching saturation level.

Sergeant Gillespie passed Frank the current report sheets and got back to his chair behind the radio console. The minute Sam had seen the Lieutenant come into the room he'd tucked his massive head back into a stack of chins and stayed that way. With these two people in close proximity you could only hope nobody'd strike a match.

Mr Solo was perched neatly on a stool in the corner near the Telex, absorbed in the Fatal Accident files, sometimes swivelling his head when it sounded like a Signal 11 coming over the radio. With Captain Darrow, Lieutenant Ingram and Mr Solo in the same room as he was, Sam found himself considering early retirement.

'What happened to the compact that flipped over?' Frank asked him.

'Property damage, sir. Nobody got hurt.'

Frank leafed through the reports for a minute.

'Did anybody pick up the drinking driver signalled by

Barnegat Plaza fifteen minutes back?'

'Not so far, Lieutenant. I diverted Mills from southbound to northbound below Oyster Creek as soon as we got the alert, so it oughter be a matter of time.'

A canvas-topped delivery truck slid past the window and its driver came into the office, mopping the sweat off his round doughy face with a big white handkerchief.

'I am Patras!' he said. 'Alexandros Patras!'

Sam looked at him.

'What can I do for you?'

'Please, is necessary for someone look at my new muffler. Is fixed nice now.'

Frank looked up from the report sheets.

'I asked you to be here before noon, Mr Patras. What went wrong?'

'Oh yes, is you, Lieutenant!' He gave a huge Greek shrug. 'Mr McTigue of service station all closed up, so I have to go all way to Toms River. Take time, an' everybody asking me for ice, these hot weathers!'

'Sergeant,' Frank said, 'will you just check the muffler?'

Sam went outside with Mr Patras.

Car 76 to Base.

Frank went over to the console.

Go ahead, 76.

Signal 11. Milepost 77.6 northbound. A Lincoln Cougar just went off the road at high speed. I need –

Is that Mills?

Yes, sir.

You were going after a suspected drinking driver. Is this the car?

It fits the description from Barnegat, sir.

Okay, what d'you need?

Rescue Squad, sir. The car's on the median and there's no obstruction at the scene. Seems it struck another one, and I'm taking a statement from the other driver.

Frank reached for the telephone and dialled as he went on talking. Mr Solo was standing near him, trying to get his attention. Darrow watched from the main desk.

Wrecker needed?

Not right away, sir. The car finished right side up and I got the passenger clear: she was using her seat-belt and she's okay except for shock, but the driver hit a lot of things when they looped.

What shape is the other car in?

There's only a dented fender – the driver kept control and pulled up on the median. I'm checking on –

Hold it a minute, Mills.

The line to Marina Drive had opened.

'Debby, this is Frank. We need an ambulance at Milepost 77.6 – seven seven point six – northbound soonest.'

'I'll be there right away.'

'And Debby, we'll want a blood sample from the driver.'

'Alcohol?'

'Could be.'

'I'll tell them at the hospital – 'bye, Frank.'

He hung up.

Mills?

Hear you, sir.

There's an ambulance on its way. D'you need support?

I don't have any problem, sir, just the injured driver.

Fair enough, report progress. Base out.

Mr Solo was still at his side.

'You'll have to take your own car,' Frank told him. 'We don't have one available right now.'

The little man ran into Gillespie and the Greek as they came back into the office.

'The muffler's okay, sir. They did a seam-weld.'

'Mr Patras, did you keep that ticket?'

'You think I throw away, Lieutenant? Look, fifteen dollar for welding job an' five dollar for overtime because garage man says he –'

'Just give me the ticket.'

Frank took the slip, tore it across twice and dropped it into the waste-paper basket. Watching him do it, Sam Gillespie drew his head back a final notch and concentrated hard on the radio.

'So!' beamed Alexandros Patras. 'No fine!'

'No fine,' Frank told him. 'But watch that muffler and when it starts blowing again just get it fixed before we have to tell you, okay?'

'Okay!'

Mr Patras stretched out his bearlike arms in a blessing of all persons here present and went back to his delivery truck.

In the silence there was only the murmur of the air-conditioning unit. At the main desk Captain Darrow put aside the papers he was examining, got up and went over to the filing cabinets, getting out the enforcement reports of the previous day. Sam stole a quick look at Lieutenant Ingram, whose face lacked any expression as he went on checking the records. Sam looked down again, strongly tempted to put his fingers in his ears.

The sound came of papers being shuffled.

'Lieutenant.'

'Captain?'

'I'd like you to confirm something for me.'

'Certainly.'

Darrow was replacing the files, talking over his shoulder. 'Yesterday I checked that man Patras for a violation of the laws of the State of New Jersey and handed him a citation.' He pushed the cabinet drawer closed with a slight bang and turned around and looked directly at Frank Ingram, hands behind him. In a conversational tone he said: 'Was that the citation you just destroyed?'

Frank put his papers on to the corner of the main desk and faced Captain Darrow with his arms folded.

'It was.'

'You of course knew that it carried my signature.'

'I did.'

'The enforcement report filed yesterday appears to be missing. Can you throw any light on that fact?'

'I destroyed that too.'

'Why?'

'For reasons of consistency. There's no point filing the report and tearing up the ticket.'

Captain Darrow put his head on one side, his expression characteristically one of polite interest. 'Did you check this driver for the same violation as I did myself?'

'Yes.'

'And he told you, I assume, that I'd already given him a citation. What did you say to him, Lieutenant?'

'I told him to bring his truck here today with the muffler repaired, and that if I were satisfied I'd tear up the ticket.'

Darrow nodded, his youthful-executive's face attentive.

'And that is what has just occurred.'

'Correct.'

He watched Darrow take a turn around the space behind

the main desk. A signal was coming over the radio and Gillespie lowered the volume, leaning close to the loudspeaker.

'Lieutenant Ingram, before I acquaint your headquarters of these facts and your admissions, do you wish to say anything in your defence?'

'No.'

'There could be a perfectly good reason why you chose to override my authority.'

'There is.'

'I'd be interested to hear it.'

'You charged this man with operating a motor vehicle in a dangerous state of repair, which exposed him to a heavy fine. In fact it was a clear case for a verbal warning and an injunction to get his muffler fixed, nothing more than just that. So I set the record straight.'

Captain Darrow waited five seconds. His expression hadn't changed but his eyes were brightening and Frank noticed it.

'Your action, Lieutenant, constitutes a flagrant breach of discipline, calculated insubordination and wilful interference in the duties of a superior officer. Do you realize that?'

Frank didn't reply immediately. Last night he'd slept only a few hours, getting home late from extended duty and talking with Debby about the Venus crash and Vince's apparent responsibility for Danny's death, till all they both knew was that they were face to face with a nightmare. Meanwhile he had to help shepherd a half million vehicles along the Parkway in heatwave conditions over a three-day period, hour by hour and mile by mile and in all possible safety. And he just didn't have time to cope with Darrow as well.

'Captain,' he said a little wearily, 'I quite appreciate how you feel, because you think this is West Point. In fact we have a tough job to do here and there isn't any time for playing at toy soldiers, apart from which I don't intend seeing users of my Parkway being treated as petty criminals without doing something about it. If this doesn't happen to –'

'You have a nerve!'

At the sound of the Captain's voice Sam Gillespie swung round from the console and stared at him. Darrow's face had reddened and his eyes were feverish. Watching him, Frank saw what had happened: rage had been building up inside the man all the time he'd been trying to show perfect control, and the pressure had got too high.

Darrow was already at one of the telephones and dialling. As he waited for the connection he told Frank softly: 'If you value your career, Lieutenant, I'm sorry for you.'

Frank turned away impatiently.

'Sergeant Gillespie, I want that radio run at normal volume.'

'Yessir.'

A call was coming through as Sam turned the dial.

75 to Base.

Go ahead 75.

I have a steamer, Sarge, MP 84 northbound. Fan-belt gone, which makes my total for today a round dozen. Do I get a cigar?

Brusquely Sam said:

You get a wrecker.

He called up 250, the code for Dunes Garage.

Frank checked the last three reports in the folder and dropped them back in the tray, listening to Darrow talking to Woodbridge HQ, repeating what he'd said about 'breach of discipline' and 'calculated insubordination'. As Frank went over to the Telex board to make his routine check Darrow spoke to him sharply –

'Lieutenant! Captain Westover wants you on the line.'

Frank turned and picked up an extension.

'Lieutenant Ingram here.'

'Have you heard these accusations, Ingram?'

'I have, sir.'

'I'd be glad to know what you have to say.' Westover sounded nettled. It was a busy day up at Woodbridge HQ, just like here at Ocean Point.

Frank looked up at Darrow as he spoke into the phone.

'I have to say this, Captain. If Mr Darrow isn't relieved of his duties on the Garden State Parkway before midnight you'll receive my resignation in writing.'

In the silence the telephone at the console started ringing. Sam took it.

'State Police, Ocean Point Barracks.'

Frank waited. He knew he'd handed his commanding officer a situation that could cause repercussions throughout the hierarchy of the New Jersey State Police, but if the top brass in Trenton wanted to try out fancy innovations when Troop E was under heavy pressure and if Westover chose to go along with them, they'd have to expect trouble.

'Lieutenant, your attitude doesn't help me to weigh up this situation. You'd better report here first thing tomorrow morning.'

Frank heard Sam telling his caller to hang on a minute and that could only mean he needed advice.

'The situation's very simple, Captain. Either Mr Darrow or I will be leaving by midnight this date, and in either case there won't be anything to discuss in the morning. I'm passing you back to him now.'

He dropped the receiver and turned to look at Sam.

'You have a problem, Gillespie?'

Sam took a second to answer. He'd just heard his station commander throw down his career like a dice in a crap game and it rocked him.

'Could be, sir.' He picked up the console extension and held it out to Frank. 'Will you cut in on this call? There's been an auto theft at Oyster Creek picnic area but I think there's a little more to it than just that.'

Frank took the extension.

Sam said into the phone: 'Will you repeat that, please?'

It was a woman's voice on the line.

'Surely. We've just had our car stolen by two men, and they went off towards New York. They left their own car right here, with steam coming out of it, and one of them pointed a gun at us when we called out for them to leave our car alone. They put something into the trunk, and –'

'What did it look like?' Frank cut in.

The woman hesitated, maybe puzzled at hearing a different voice. 'It was a lot of small sacks, the kind you buy flour in at a country –'

'Small white linen bags?'

'Why, that's absolutely right! How did –'

'Will you please describe the two men?'

'I'll try, but they didn't let us get a close look. One was a big heavy man with a strange kind of walk – he sort of clutched at his side all the time, like he had stitch. The other man was very thin and kind of jumpy – in fact he dropped one of the sacks when he –'

'Just a minute.' He looked at Sam. 'Break an all-stations priority alert and repeat.' Into the phone he said: 'Will you please give details of the stolen car?'

Sam went on the air.

Ocean Point to all stations, all stations priority alert, stand by. As the woman on the telephone gave the description he repeated the essentials on the radio. *Pontiac sedan – colour dark green – New York registered – number TYA-353623.*

Frank dropped the extension receiver and took over the radio mike while Sam looked after the caller.

Ocean Point to all stations: this car was just stolen from Oyster Creek picnic area at Milepost 71 and is now heading north carrying two men who resemble Rod Gould and Nat Renatus, suspects in the slaying of a New York policeman. Local patrol crews stand by for orders.

'Over to you,' he told Gillespie. 'You know the drill – block every exit. I'm taking Reserve Car 80.' He broke for the door.

CHAPTER FOURTEEN

The telephone message from Oyster Creek had come in at 12.31 p.m. and it took Sam Gillespie six minutes to complete all necessary signals by phone and radio, talking direct to Troop E patrols and calling on Central New Jersey's Troop C commands to deploy all available forces in the immediate area. As he sat alone at the console his bullfrog voice intoned the details of the operation with precision and without hurry.

Points for immediate manning are Exit 69, Entrance 74, Entrance 80, and Interchanges 81, 82 and 83. Additionally the toll plazas of Ocean Point and Barnegat should seal off all traffic and we require coverage of Forked River Service Area in the interests of public safety. I repeat: these men are armed.

If the Pontiac sedan feared a trap ahead and made a prohibited U-turn across the median and drove south again it would be blocked at Entrance 69 and Barnegat Plaza. If it tried to leave the northbound road by breaking into the access ramps at Entrances 74 and 80 it would find barriers there. The normal exits at Interchanges 81 to 83 were likewise to be sealed off, together with the toll plaza at Ocean Point.

What Sam Gillespie had done was to truncate a sixteen-mile section of the Parkway and turn it into a trap with the quarry still running inside.

Final instructions for Ocean Point patrols: this is Sergeant Gillespie calling you from Base. Lieutenant Ingram is using Car 80, which therefore becomes the mobile radio headquarters for this operation.

Making a fast U-turn south of Oyster Creek Car 80 merged with the northbound traffic and slotted in behind a grey Chevrolet Mirabelle convertible, moving it over with the PA loudspeaker and passing it in the fast lane to peel off at the picnic area where Frank could already see a group of people gathered around a two-tone Chrysler with its trunk-top still raised.

Leaving 80 with the motor still running and the driver's door open he checked the Chrysler, finding dried bloodspots on the front passenger seat and a split linen bag dangling from the trunk lock with some brown powder still left in it.

A scared-looking man and his wife were keeping close to him and he asked them if they were the owners of the stolen Pontiac.

'That's right,' the woman said. 'Our name is Campbell, and it was I who called your office when –'

'Okay,' Frank said, 'you'll get your car back, Mrs Campbell.'

He was turning away as the man said: 'They won't get too far, Officer, without they'll need to take on some gas. I was running pretty low.'

He said something else but Frank didn't hear it because he was climbing into the black and yellow cruiser, unclipping the mike as he dragged the door shut and hit the siren to clear a freeway on to the road.

Car 80 to all commands: I am now satisfied that the two men in the stolen Pontiac are in fact Gould and Renatus, wanted for murder. They have to be taken.

Five miles north of Oyster Creek the Pontiac sedan was holding the fast lane and coming up on the Forked River Food and Fuel Area at Milepost 76.

Nat Renatus flicked another half-smoked cigarette out the window and drew in a long slow breath. Rod Gould sat like a crumpled sack, bent over to the left. He knew he'd torn something getting out of the other car and throwing the sugar in the trunk of this one. He didn't know if he was bleeding again and he didn't want to look.

'How low is it?'

'Near empty.'

Renatus checked the gas gauge again in case the needle was stuck and had moved up, but it was still in the same place.

'Okay,' Rod said. 'We use the Citgo station.'

'But Christ, we –'

'Look, they're not on to us yet. We can fill her up, take it nice an' slow. Once they get on to us we'll need a tank full of gas. So start slowing an' take the pump at the far end if it's free.'

'Okay. Okay.'

Rod Gould watched him with his stony eyes. Nat had steadied up a little: he was still jumpy but he seemed to know this was for real now and he'd need all the nerve he could find if they meant to get through.

'We'll make it,' Rod told him.

'Sure. Sure we'll make it. You feel okay?'

'I'm okay.' He kept his Smith and Wesson on his lap, covered by the corner of his jacket. 'Just say to fill 'er up and tell him to keep the change.'

The Pontiac swerved on to the access road and headed between the restaurant and the line of parked autos, the sun flashing off their chrome into Nat's eyes. A half-dozen cars were at the pumps but there was room on the right flank and he pulled in. A few people were walking around to stretch their legs while the gas-pump jockeys worked, and Rod looked everywhere for a uniform. He didn't see one.

'We'll make it,' he told Nat.

'Sure.' Renatus lit another cigarette, the sweat on his fingers darkening the paper. He hated the smell of it, the smell of himself.

When the man came he said to fill her up and got out and leaned through the window and couldn't find the windscreen-washer button because this wasn't the Chrysler, then he found it and pressed it and held his fingers in the thin hot jets and wiped the dirt away, his eyes narrowed against the reflected glare off the hood. Turning back to press the button again he saw the police cruiser curving in towards the line of pumps past the grey Chevvy convertible and pulling up, the driver's door coming open even before the wheels stopped rolling.

Renatus dragged his gun out, his wet fingers clumsy.

None of the people standing around seemed to have noticed anything was wrong. It wasn't unusual to see a police car come in to a gas station. The pump jockeys went on working. The sun was hot and colours were bright; the smell of the gasoline was heavy on the air.

The patrolman was coming across to the Pontiac and Renatus saw him go for his holster.

He heard Rod calling to him from inside the auto.

'Nat! Grab that girl!'

Renatus took a couple of seconds to react because he saw the cop coming and knew he'd have to kill him but he was too scared because killing Nolan had left his nerves shot to hell and for these two seconds he couldn't move.

'That girl in green!'

Rod was clambering out of the car because Nat wouldn't do what he said and he'd have to do it for him or they'd never make it, never get through.

Then Renatus saw what he meant and grabbed the girl in the green jumpsuit and hustled her into the Pontiac as Rod slumped back and slammed the door shut.

'All right.' Rod Gould leaned with his gun-arm hooked over the seat squab. He was looking at the girl but speaking to the cop. 'You know the set-up. No tricks.' The girl didn't move; she sat staring down the muzzle of the Smith and Wesson. 'Nat,' Rod Gould said. 'We go.'

Renatus got behind the wheel.

The gas-pump jockey had taken the pipe away but hadn't shut the filler cap. He stood not knowing what to do.

Renatus snatched a look at Gould and started the motor. The patrolman was standing halfway between his car and the Pontiac, his hand coming slowly away from his holster. Gould called out to him.

'Listen, copper! You try stopping us an' the girl gets it. No tricks, you unnerstand?'

He told Nat:

'Get going.'

Frank Ingram was moving northbound at Milepost 75 when

the signal came on the air.

Car 77 to Car 80. Seven-Seven to Eight-Oh.

Go ahead 77.

This is Trooper Schultz, sir. I just made contact with the wanted men at the Forked River Citgo station. They took a young girl on board the Pontiac as a hostage and I held my fire.

Where are you now?

Coming up on Milepost 76.5 and tailing the Pontiac at a distance of about one hundred yards.

Stay like that and don't lose touch.

Yes, sir.

Frank took his speed up into the region of eighty miles per hour and used the warbler to keep the fast lane clear.

80 to all patrols. The Pontiac has a hostage on board and you are ordered to hold your fire if at any time you move into close quarters. Do not threaten these men at any time but be ready to act immediately if ordered.

In front of him was a Buick Riviera and he had to touch the brakes before its driver heard the warbler and pulled over to let him by. Moving up into the eighties again, he tried to weigh up how much chance there was of parleying with the two men if their run could be stopped, but in all hostage situations there was the deadly unknown factor in play: no one could guess how far the captors could be provoked before they decided to kill out of hand. If they were intelligent they'd never kill at all, realizing that once the hostage was dead their own last chance was gone; but these situations were literally hair-trigger and a life could be lost just by the breaking of somebody's nerve.

All he could do was to close up on the quarry and keep it in sight till a chance came to take positive action without risk to the hostage.

Car 80 to 66. Calling Six-Six.

He had to repeat because of static.

Can hear you, Lieutenant.

What's your position?

We're just now overflying Toms River southwards at three hundred feet altitude, sir.

You know your target for observation?

Dark green Pontiac sedan northbound.

Okay. It should be one hundred yards ahead of Patrol Car

77. Keep in contact with 77 for ground guidance. 80 out.

Within two minutes of his signal he sighted the Hughes 300 helicopter making a sharp turn and heading northwards at low altitude, keeping pace with the fast-lane traffic flow. Thirty seconds later he came up on Car 77 and brought his speed down to around seventy-five m.p.h., unclipping the PA mike.

Schultz, pull over. I'm going past you.

As 77 took a slot in the right-hand lane Frank could see the dark green Pontiac ahead of him, immediately below the helicopter. Another car was baulking it in the fast lane and the Pontiac was using its horns in a series of short blasts to make it move over. It refused, and already Frank was having to bring his speed down to avoid closing right in on them both. It was a situation familiar to every highway patrolman: a motorist keeping precisely to the legal speed limit in the left-hand lane and refusing to move over on the grounds that anyone overtaking would be breaking the law.

For another half minute the situation was static. The right-hand lane traffic flow was moving at a steady fifty-five m.p.h. with constant gaps. The Ford Galaxie blocking the Pontiac's way was keeping to a steady sixty-five and taking no notice of the blaring horns. Then a fifty-yard gap appeared in the slow lane and Frank saw the Pontiac take it, swerving to the off-side and accelerating to overhaul the Ford and cut into the fast lane again in front of it.

It was a dangerous manoeuvre and somebody else was now using the horns as the Pontiac swerved back into the left-hand lane across the bows of the Ford, squeezing through the fast-closing gap between the two files of traffic.

Then a fender made contact and two of the cars drifted apart and drifted back as one driver overcorrected and they hit again and Frank was already standing on his brakes as the whole scene began running wild.

80 to Base.

Go ahead, sir.

We have a nine-car pile-up at Milepost 82 northbound with probable severe injury cases. All patrols to converge.

Frank didn't need to say more than that because Sergeant Gillespie would automatically send in rescue vehicles, ambulances, fire-tenders and wrecking trucks from Ocean Point,

Toms River and Lakewood.

A station wagon was still lurching with a burst tyre at the edge of the main collision area when Frank took his cruiser on to the medial strip to follow the dark green Pontiac as it swerved clear of the roadway and bounced across the undulating grass before it struck a hummock and slewed sideways, losing momentum. Car 80 slid to a halt alongside five seconds later and Frank hit the door open and got out and stood looking through the window of the sedan at the face of Rod Gould.

'Stay just there, copper.'

Frank looked past him to the girl in the back. He said:

'Don't be afraid, young lady. We won't let them hurt you.'

She nodded, looking back at him with wide eyes, not altogether hearing or understanding what he said, not altogether believing what was happening to her.

'She'll get hurt,' Gould said, 'if you make a wrong move.'

'I understand that.'

Above the roadway the rotor of the Hughes 300 chopped rhythmically at the air. Frank could hear Trooper Schultz using his PA system to control the scene as people began climbing out of their cars and gathering at the crash area.

'You're a smart cop.' Gould said. 'You're smarter than that stupid –' then he gave a sudden grunt and his head fell forward and he jerked it back and steadied the gun against the seat squab, his teeth bared in pain.

'*Rod,*' the thin man said. 'Rod, what's –'

'Shaddup.'

Frank saw Renatus jerk his own gun, aiming at the girl.

'He needs a medic!' The eyes in the thin squeezed face were flickering. 'Get him a medic!'

'For Christ –' said Gould, and fell against the seat squab with his back arching and his hands groping for his stomach.

Frank saw the gun fall and looked at Renatus and knew the danger was there in the bright feverish eyes and the thin nicotine-stained finger flexed inside the trigger-guard. The girl's life would end when this man's nerve broke and he killed wild.

'I'll do what I can,' he told Renatus.

'You better get one fast!'

Frank turned and climbed into the cruiser, starting up and swinging it round to face the crash area where Schultz was working. Then he unclipped the PA microphone.

Car 77. Car 77.

His voice boomed across the helicopter's chopping as it lowered to the grass to pick up injured.

Trooper Schultz turned and looked towards Car 80.

I need a doctor here. Use your PA system. That clear?

Schultz waved acknowledgement and went over to his car.

Frank shut off his motor and got out. 77 was closer to the file of automobiles stacked up behind the crash area, and he remembered seeing an MD's sign on a windshield as he'd warbled for gangway a few minutes ago.

Between here and the roadway the Hughes 300 settled, whirling dust aloft, the rotor slowing.

Frank said:

'Renatus. Let that kid go free and you'll get a lighter sentence.'

'I killed a cop.' His voice was shrill with nerves.

'He was out to get you. This kid's done nothing. I'll make a deal with you.'

There wasn't any deal he could make with a killer and he knew it. They both knew it.

'Get that medic, damn your eyes.'

'We're trying.'

He looked at the heavier man, Gould. He was still conscious but the pain seemed too bad for him to talk or make any movement. He looked at Renatus, judging the distance to the man's gun-hand, weighing the chances. There weren't any. The instant he tried to move for the gun the tobacco-stained finger would tighten by reflex and the girl would be dead.

'Let her go, Renatus. I'll speak up for you at the trial.'

'Damn your eyes.'

They could hear the magnified voice of Schultz over the loudspeaker system, asking for a doctor. The churning of the helicopter's rotor died away as the pilot and patrolman left their machine and began running for the crash area. As quietness followed, Frank heard the squawk of signals on Car 80's radio as Gillespie's alert took effect.

No. 2 Ambulance now heading north from Interchange 81.

Ocean Point to 251. You better ride the shoulder and make a U-turn as soon as you can.

This is Barnegat. Do you need our help?

Could be. I'll clear you.

OP Rescue Squad. Can I take Access 80?

Yes, but there's a police trap so use your siren.

Wrecker 250 heading south at MP 83 and crossing the strip.

Reflected sunlight flashed against the side of the sedan as a Buick Riviera turned from the northbound roadway and came pitching across the uneven terrain to halt near the two vehicles. A compact man in a tan seersucker suit got out and reached inside, bringing a bag. A teenage girl came with him.

'Is somebody hurt?'

'This man here,' Frank said.

Brett Hagen took another pace and stopped, seeing the thin man inside the Pontiac sedan, and the gun he was holding. He saw the girl in the back.

Frank said evenly: 'Okay, Doc. Just see to this one. I'll look after everything else.'

Brett looked at the State Trooper. There'd been something on the radio this morning, about a hunt for two men wanted for murder.

'Tracy. Go back to the road and help people.'

Staring at the gun, she said: 'I'll stay here with you, Daddy.'

'Please do as I say. I'll be all right.'

In a moment she turned away.

Brett looked at the heavy man crouched on the front passenger seat. 'What kind of injury is it?' He opened his bag.

Frank said: 'He has a bullet in him.'

Gould's face was waxy and sweat dripped from his stubbled chin. He didn't move, didn't speak.

'Are you in pain?'

'Sure,' Renatus said quickly, 'do something Doc, fix him up.' His breath came fast, as if he'd been running. He took brief glances away from the girl, wanting to see how Rod looked, how bad he was. 'Rod,' he said, 'he's a medic. He'll fix you up.'

Brett Hagen said: 'There's nothing I can do right here.'

'Get the slug out.'

'But I can't do that.' He looked at the thin man, not sure how much his nerves would let him reason.

'Get that goddam slug out!'

Frank tensed as he saw the gun jerk.

'All I can do,' Brett said, 'is to stop the pain and then try and stop the bleeding. We'll have to get him to a hospital before I can –'

'You got your stuff here, haven't you, for Chrissake? You jus' better do somethin' fast.'

Brett filled a hypodermic, preparing a swab.

'If I try to operate here I'll kill him. Try to understand that. I just don't carry the means of preventing septicemia – bacterial invasion of the wound.' He lifted Gould's sleeve and swabbed the skin.

'Doc,' Gould said. He spoke through his teeth. 'Gimme a local. Unnerstand? I don't wanna pass out. You gimme a knockout an' the girl don't live any more, you get that?'

Brett glanced up at the police lieutenant, hoping for guidance; but he was watching the thin man, his eyes alert.

'I'll work on the pain. You won't lose consciousness.'

A siren sounded from the southbound road and a wrecking-truck went bouncing across the grass towards the crash area. On the far side of the line of cars on the northbound section an ambulance was riding the shoulder, its white paintwork flickering among the other colours.

Rod Gould watched the medic, his eyes narrowed in pain.

'For this job we need a hospital?'

'Of course. I'll only do more damage if I try to work here.'

'Okay.' He swung his head up and looked at the lieutenant. 'We want that helicopter. Fix it up.'

Over a period of ten minutes the wail of sirens made a continuous background of sound on the hot summer air as the scattered fleet of police cruisers and emergency vehicles from Lakewood, Ocean Point, Toms River and Barnegat converged on Milepost 82, the first arrivals already pressing their way alongside the file of halted traffic and breaking across the grass median to bypass the obstruction.

OP Rescue Squad to State Police. No. 2 Ambulance is now at the crash scene.

Debby eased the white Cadillac through the gap in the traffic that Trooper Schultz had established, checking her watch and noting mentally that accident victims had been in trauma for thirteen minutes, the time she had taken to reach here; it was a routine factor that always affected the condition and therefore the emergency treatment of the injured, especially bleeding cases.

Her paramedic assistant was already hitting her seat-belt release and swinging the door open as the wheels stopped rolling. A patrol car slowing along the shoulder nearby was using its PA loudspeaker system.

Please stand clear and leave room for the emergency crews to work in. You will delay the rescue of the injured if you obstruct the scene.

A siren died to silence. On the fringe of the area a wrecking crew were using oxyacetylene equipment to flame-cut a smashed body-panel clear of a trapped driver. A fire-tender was nosing its way between two of the wrecks to an overturned Catalina whose crushed gas-tank was spilling fuel on to the roadway. The crew of a Lakewood ambulance were sliding a metal-frame litter from the tailgate of their vehicle, hampered by the press of people who had left their cars and walked down the roadway to stand here rubbernecking.

'Will you please make room so we can do our job? Won't somebody go and comfort that child over there? Please try and co-operate.'

As a highway patrol moved in to control the scene the assistant paramedic gave a morphine injection.

'Debby, will you check this one?'

'Okay. Get some more blankets and the resuscitator. Did you bring any spinal frames?'

'They're right here.'

Debby moved the driver's head back to free the airway and made a routine check: pale blue 'shock colour' skin, no visible bleeding or limb deformity, poor reflex response of pupils to light, carotid pulse slow on inspiration, no marked reaction to mild pain stimulus. She felt the bones.

Towards the forward edge of the wreckage zone a black Cadillac sedan was halted on the shoulder. It had reached here with the first patrol car and for these few minutes its driver was alone with the two people in the telescoped estate wagon.

There wasn't any kind of post-crash phase configuration that Mr Solo hadn't already seen a dozen times, and the scene ran through his mind like a film of the events that had occurred thirteen minutes ago: the Plymouth in front had struck the compact, spinning full-circle and presenting a high-impact obstacle front-on to the estate-wagon as its locked wheels had dragged their tyres over the pavement in a desperate effort to slow. Medium-severe deceleration forces, zero-degree impact angle, marked whiplash effect. Neither the driver nor his wife had worn safety-harness.

They sat together looking almost as if nothing had happened. There was no arterial blood loss and there were no flesh lacerations, but the secondary impact had exposed them to intolerable g-loads and the whiplashing had been severe, so that most of the damage was to the skeletonic structure with localization about the spinal cervix.

Mr Solo stood looking at them, his short figure erect as always, his black necktie circumspectly knotted, his polished black shoes and brilliantined hair gleaming in the sun, the image of the two people reflected in his dark glasses. His camera was slung from one shoulder but he didn't feel there was any need to use it: the accident was unexceptional in all its aspects, save perhaps for the lifelike attitude of the persons involved. This should perhaps be recorded on film, to demonstrate that intolerable trauma could sometimes be suffered with little apparent evidence; but just the same he felt reluctant to take pictures.

Pictures were for others to see, and he felt there was something rather private about this scene that he would prefer to respect. It was rare for him to be alone with an accident victim, because the police and rescue squads were normally on the spot even sooner than he was; in this case they had so much to deal with that this couple, the man and his wife, were having to wait their turn. He was aware of a certain sense of intimacy: to wait here with them, sharing their patience, was a subtle privilege that he enjoyed without fully understanding.

Under the fierce heat of the sun and in the half-silence that had followed the wail of sirens he stood without moving, not wishing to disturb this special relationship that he felt. Perhaps he'd take photographs later, but not now.

The tiny crucifix the woman wore reminded him of the one he'd played with when he'd been small, swinging it on the delicate gold chain that had hung from his mother's neck, until the hot summer day had come when the neighbour had rocked him in her arms, talking to him in that strange half-singing voice with her wet face pressed against his own. *Your Ma an' Pa, they jus' went off in their beautiful new roadster, an' kinda kept on goin'*. He'd asked why he couldn't have gone with them but she'd said he mustn't ever wish for no such thing. He must be content to keep watch for them, so maybe one fine day he'd see them riding up there in the clouds.

But that was a long time ago.

Metal screamed as a tow-truck dragged a wreck clear of the roadway, and Mr Solo looked around him. A half-dozen ambulances were here now, and the police had the crowd under control. Traffic must be piling up for miles behind the obstruction but the police and the wreckers had to wait till the injured had been taken out of their cars, sometimes with infinite care. He could see two Boy Scouts helping to clear the debris from the pavement, and a priest was crouched beside a litter where a woman lay, while a nurse made splints for her leg.

Mr Solo went across to them.

'He's in fair shape,' the priest was telling the woman. 'As a matter of fact he'll be up and around again a few days before you are.'

'Do you really mean that?'

'But of course.'

He was a young man with steady eyes, his skin olive-brown and his accent Spanish.

'Father,' Mr Solo said, 'can I ask a few minutes of your time?'

'Am I needed?'

'Yes.'

They went together to the estate wagon.

'Is there any hope?' he asked Mr Solo.

'Nobody can say, till a doctor gets here. There's always a danger in moving them.'

The priest nodded, his shoe grating on broken glass as he turned, taking a flask of oil from his pocket and unscrewing the cap.

'Do you keep that in your car?' Mr Solo asked.

'Always.'

He moistened his right thumb with the oil and made the sign of the cross on the driver's forehead. '*Si vivis, per istam sanctum Unctionem indulgeat tibi Dominus quidquid deliquisti. Amen.*' He ministered likewise to the woman.

Replacing the cap on the flask he looked at Mr Solo.

'They are not relatives of yours?'

'No.' Mr Solo turned away. 'They're nothing to do with me.'

Frank unclipped his PA microphone.

Will the pilot of the helicopter report immediately to his machine and start up ready for take-off.

As he went back to the Pontiac sedan he saw Gould getting to his feet. The doctor was watching him critically.

'All I've dealt with is the pain. You need a stretcher.'

'I'll go on my own two feet.'

Renatus jerked a glance at him away from the girl.

'Rod! You oughter do what the medic –'

'Shaddup. Let's get movin'.'

Renatus climbed out of the sedan, keeping his aim on the girl. 'C'mon, liven up. Walk in front of me an' don't turn around.'

Brett Hagen put his things back into the bag.

'Do you need me any more, Officer?'

'I guess not, Doc. You'd better get on over there to the roadway.'

'Hey, copper!' Renatus said. 'Walk in front where I c'n see you.' He moved forward as if his feet were on a tight-rope, nervy as a cat. The girl walked one pace ahead of him and the gun was trained on her spine.

Frank went forward, walking between Renatus and Gould.

'You don't have to worry, kid,' he told the girl quietly. 'I'll just do everything they say and they won't hurt you.'

Gears whined and the rotor of the Hughes 300 began turning.

Rod Gould walked crabwise, bent over his bullet. He knew he could last out if Nat could. They had to make it to the hospital and they had to take the girl along, but he didn't know how fast the medics could get this goddam slug out and set him up again on his feet. Nat would have to stick with the girl, use pep-ups to keep awake, till he could take over. They'd had to leave the sugar behind but that was better than handing it over to that bastard son of a whore Toni Lago. They hadn't sold out to Lago.

'Rod.'

'Yah?'

'Y'okay?'

'Sure.'

Nat Renatus felt the sweat running on him and was disgusted. His hand was sticky on the gun. The heat pressed down on him like a weight across his shoulders and he longed for shade. Once as he tripped on the grass he felt the spring flex under his finger, and started worrying that he might drill the girl without any need. But everything would be okay so long as Rod got well. Rod mustn't die. He was like a father.

'Rod. Take it easy. Take it slow.'

'Sure. I'm okay.'

Brett walked alongside, holding his bag. They needed him in the crash area but he didn't feel he could leave this group until the young girl was out of danger from that gun. He couldn't think of anything he could usefully do: it seemed that the police lieutenant himself was powerless; but he couldn't just walk out on them either. He watched the big man, feeling he should warn him again; he was only aggravating the damage, walking like this.

They felt the wind from the idling rotor. The pilot came to meet them, halting when he saw the gun, glancing at the lieutenant.

'You'll be taking this man to Ocean Point Hospital,' Frank told him, his face dead-pan. He was going to play it by the rule-book till a chance came: the risk was too high for pulling tricks. That thin stained finger hadn't left the inside of the trigger-guard for an instant, and the man's nerves alone could spark off a tragedy.

'Tell him, copper,' Renatus said.

'This child is a hostage,' Frank said to the pilot. 'Use your radio in flight and call up one of the rescue squad headquarters and tell them to telephone the situation to the hospital before you touch down. There must be no interference and no attempt to free the hostage until the police have had a chance of parleying – and that goes for you too. Is that clear?'

The pilot shifted his wad of gum from one side of his mouth to the other.

'Loud and clear, Lieutenant.'

'Get back in the plane,' Renatus told him.

They started off again with the pilot leading them, the grass at their feet shivering to the rotor's draught as they neared the machine. When Rod Gould fell they didn't stop because he made no sound and they were looking ahead of them. He fell sideways, his left leg buckling, and lay with his face to the ground and his arms flung out in front of him. Later it was inevitably reported in the tabloids that a bullet fired by a New York police officer on the morning of Friday July Third had killed a man on the Garden State Parkway in New Jersey on the afternoon of Sunday July Fifth, and that John Nolan had settled an account from beyond the grave.

Renatus spoke without taking his eyes from the girl, raising his voice above the churning of the rotor.

'Rod, get on board first, okay? Then I bring the kid.'

It was Brett Hagen who looked back a fraction before the others, perhaps because he knew more than they did about Gould's condition. He turned and bent over him.

'Rod,' said Renatus, and looked round.

Frank watched him. Renatus stood with his face open in shock, looking down at Gould. The gun was still aimed at the girl. Frank watched the gun.

Renatus saw the way Rod had gone down, with his face hitting the ground and his hands stretched out like he'd tried to break the fall and couldn't. He'd never seen Rod look beat before, defeated. He'd always been big, always made the decisions. He'd been like his own father.

'*Rod,*' he said.

As the tension went out of him his gun-hand fell slowly away from the aim and Frank moved in fast but Renatus had nerves like a cat and his gun came up and exploded as Frank spun him half-round and hooked at his legs and pitched him down as the gun banged again and the slug ripped at Frank's shoulder. Renatus was half his weight and didn't have any science but frenzy alone drove him to fight back with the speed of a crazed animal and the third shot seared flesh as Frank rolled with him and kept his lock on the man's gun-wrist with his fingers slipping on sweat but holding, forcing the aim lower an inch at a time while above them the blades of the rotor windmilled against the blinding glare of the sky till they rolled again together and the fourth slug bit turf away in a dark clot and the stink of the cordite fumes came to the air as they lay choking for breath. Twice Renatus twisted away and tried to bring the gun where it could kill, but Frank was ready and hooked for a new hold and got it and forced the gun-hand down with the fingers opening, quivering, clawing for the gun and losing it, at last losing it.

A foot kicked it away.

Frank chopped at the thin forearm to paralyse it but Renatus was done.

'Nobody got hit?'

'We're all okay,' someone said.

CHAPTER FIFTEEN

'Oh excuse me, are you Mrs Walt Amberton please?'

'That's right.'

'We have your New York number on the line.'

'Thank you.'

Carol followed the young candy-striper across the lobby but couldn't keep up; her legs were still shaky and she realized it was early evening and she'd eaten nothing since breakfast at Beach Haven.

'Number One booth, this end.'

The air pressed against her ears as she pushed the door shut. 'Dr Pabst?'

'Who is that?'

'Mrs Amberton. I'm calling from Ocean Point Hospital, New Jersey. We were in a road crash.'

'You and your husband?'

'Yes. He recovered consciousness a while ago and I've been allowed to talk to him.'

'Has he any serious injuries?'

'It depends,' she said, 'how good a cosmetic surgeon we can find.'

'What was the diagnosis?'

'Multiple lacerations of the face and head, concussion of brain with possible skull fracture. He –'

'Facial surgery doesn't have too many problems left these days, providing the nerves are restorable. Has he recovered his speech and motor activity?'

'He's perfectly lucid, and he realizes what happened.'

I might have killed you, Carol. The first thing he'd said. The last thing she'd imagined he'd think of.

'You came out all right yourself, Mrs Amberton?'

'I was just shocked. I had my seat-belt on. Dr Pabst, I'm

calling you because –'

'He's admitted he's an alcoholic.'

'How did you know?'

'I have many patients like your husband and many of them finish up in a road smash, though some aren't so lucky. He says he wants to be treated?'

'Yes.'

'That's all we need. He's already under medical care and supervision so we can start treatment without the usual psychological barrier present when these people go into hospital specifically for a cure. I'll talk to the Resident MD and we'll work out a programme.'

'I just can't believe you can do it.'

'That's understandable. And in fact we can't do it unless you believe, and until you've got your husband to believe. If you can do that, we'll do the rest. Is it a deal?'

Car 74 to Base.

Go ahead, 74.

I got a gas-out at Milepost 62 southbound, Sarge.

Don't go 'way.

Sam Gillespie called up a wrecker and took a new Aid Sheet from the box, stamping the date on it.

'What day is it, Trooper Cooper?'

'Sunday, I guess.'

'That figures. Thirty-five gas-outs, twenty-three flats, nineteen overheats, seven drinking drivers, eleven toll violations, three stolen cars, five children lost and found an' a grand-slam nine-vehicle pile-up. That's Sunday.' He got up from behind the radio console and lumbered across to the coffee machine, hitting a cup out. 'An' you know what? The Stork Club gets a brand new member today – delivered the kid myself just an hour back, Milepost 91 northbound, three weeks premature, name of Curly.'

Cooper leaned his chair back, laughing in disbelief.

'You wanna kid me, Sarge?'

'Who's kiddin'? Ain't it part o' the job?' He trained the jet of coffee into the cup. 'Fourth time I've done it, it's easier than shellin' peas. The mother was no trouble but the father fainted right off so we put him in the ambulance too. An' you know what? They want me to be the godfather, can you beat that?'

Debby was throwing some white coveralls over the washline when Reserve Car 80 backed up the driveway and parked under the tamarisk. Frank climbed out and threw his cap on the seat, his movements weary.

'High time,' said Debby.

'Hello, lady.'

'You left the squawk on.'

'So I did.'

He went back and cut the radio.

'Have you finished?' she asked him.

He came and stood on the edge of the lawn, feeling how soft the grass was underfoot after last night's rain.

'Officially.'

'Which means you'll be going back.'

'Just till midnight. There's still a lot of traffic.'

He turned for the house as they heard the telephone but she was quicker. 'I'll take it.'

He loosened his necktie and ran his handkerchief over his face; it came away black with traffic-film. His shoulder had started to throb, as Debby had told him it would; she'd dressed the bullet-graze herself at the crash site. When she came out of the house he was still standing there watching the line of vehicles strung along the horizon. Some already had their riding lights on. Beyond them the western sky was hazed with ochre as the last of the long day's heat burned low.

'Did you want to talk to HQ?'

'Not unless I have to, Debby.'

'That's what I thought. I told them you weren't here.'

'What did they want?'

'It was a message from Captain Westover. He'd like you to know that Captain J. B. S. Darrow was recalled to Washington a half-hour ago. Are we too bushed to holler out three little cheers?'

He went on watching the skyline. In a while he said:

'I don't need people like him on my Parkway.'

More of them were putting on their lights and now they began making a continuous glowing chain through the dusk.

'That's how you really think of it, isn't it, Frank?'

'How I think of it?'

'As "your" Parkway.'

'Did I say that?' He didn't look away from the distant chain of lights. 'I guess that's how we all think of it. It's the only way you can run anything.'

Fifty miles to the north the linked lights were closer and moved more slowly. Traffic along the New Jersey Turnpike had begun piling up to a bumper-to-bumper crawl past Newark Airport, and near the access ramp to the Lincoln Tunnel the inbound lanes were at a standstill for minutes on end.

In the heat of the summer evening people sat in their cars with the windows down, hoping to catch a breeze from the river; but the air was still. The glow of the city filled half the sky, growing brighter minute by minute.

At the approach to the ramp a black Cadillac sedan moved up a space, the driver touching the brakes to leave some room if the car ahead had to back up a little: there were always breakdowns when the traffic was thick. The radio aerial flexed softly as the car's movement stopped.

It's much the same picture, folks, at the George Washington Bridge and the Lincoln and Holland Tunnels, with stop-and-go conditions all the way into the city. There's just nothing you can do except leave it to the police, and they're doing all they can.

Motors throbbed everywhere. Against the background of their sound, people talked quietly.

Not far from the Tunnel a Buick Riviera with two people in it, was halted between a station-wagon and a muscle-car.

'Will Mother be home?'

'Sure. I called her this morning, while you were still sleeping.'

'I bet she was surprised you'd found me.'

'You can imagine.'

'I still think it was a kind of – you know – miracle.'

'Let's just say it's been a good weekend.'

The traffic began shunting again as the red lights came on above the roadway. Somewhere deep in the Tunnel there was another breakdown, and Big Yellow was going to work to get things cleared. In the distance a boat's siren sounded from the dockside, and farther still a jetliner was lowering above Kennedy Airport, its red lights winking through the dusk.

At the interchange a powder-blue Mustang slowed behind a truck and came to a halt. A scarf lay on the rear seat, the same blue as the paintwork.

'You'll soon meet someone.'

'I have.'

'Somebody new, and younger than me.'

'Someone who won't mind when I send you roses every Fourth of July?'

The truck ahead jogged into life again.

Eastbound travellers into Manhattan should have it a little easier now because the breakdown in the Lincoln Tunnel has been dealt with and all lanes are on the move again. Along Riverside Drive there's still a two-mile snarl-up and you'll just have to be patient. And if you feel like making a face at the man in front, remember it isn't his fault.

Coming out of the Tunnel the mustard-yellow sports car gunned up in low gear just to make it sound as if it was doing more than a frustrating five miles per hour. The boy in the passenger seat tipped his straw fedora back on his head the way Frank Sinatra sometimes did.

'It's on the hour, Dad. Can I try the news again?'

'Just how many times will that make?'

'There could be a new report, with more details.'

'So long as it keeps you happy.'

'Okay.'

. . . while the Traffic Department estimates that most of the three and one half million New York citizens who left town for the past three days will have returned by midnight. A spokesman for the Department has described this Fourth of July weekend as 'hot, humid and hectic'. Meanwhile the WOR Newsroom has received very little more from the New Jersey State Police about the two armed men arrested early this afternoon on the Garden State Parkway. One of them, Rod Gould, died from a bullet wound, while the other, Nat Renatus, is being held under close guard. During the hunt for these two men they seized a teenage girl, Holly Dillon, daughter of the manager of a Bronx movie-theatre, as hostage; but prompt action by a highway patrol officer saved her from

any harm. No official statement has yet been made as to whether –

'That's exactly five times we heard it already.'

'Okay, Dad. But there were more details, just like I said.'

'I didn't notice anything new.'

'Sure, there was the name of the girl hostage.'

'Big deal.'

'Uh-huh. Dad?'

'What?'

'How many movie-theatres are there in the Bronx?'

The clock had chimed quite a while ago but the boy sitting on the bridge watching the licence-plates had told himself, just ten more, and then, just another ten more numbers before I go. Now he came to the end of the page in his exercise-book, and squeezed the last number between the bottom line and the edge of the paper, writing it carefully; then he closed the book and got down from the parapet, trudging home alongside the lines of traffic and leaving behind him seven apple-cores and a paper bag.

The last of the daylight had left the sky by now, and the lamps alone were shining on the procession of coloured automobiles as they crossed the bridge where the boy had been, and other bridges and roadways, appearing from the softly-roaring tunnels below the river and bringing their lights to burn among those of the streets, the sound of their motors rising hour by hour until the whole city was astir with home-coming.